Dedication

To my late father A.S.A.,

You gave me purity of heart, taught me to be strong

and stay the course.

First edition August 2022

To request permission contact: akblock2022@gmail.com

Book design by Izii_Designer: Fiverr.com

ISBN 978-1-64153-443-7 (Paperback)
ISBN 978-1-64153-442-0 (E-book)

Acknowledgments

My cousins Dennis, Marya, Claire and Late Horace.

Who made the time to read it, gave me their insights and support, only out of love.

Dennis, you literally walked me across the finish line.

Thank you.

TABLE OF CONTENTS

LIST OF PRIMARY CHARACTERS

AS PER THE GENERAL STORY FLOW

NAME	CHARACTER
Montero Calderone	Pointe Trois rainforest militia leader, also Rebecca's brother, fighting to protect their families and homeland from attacks by the army.
Rebecca Calderone	New York based lawyer working against a 7 day deadline to save her homeland from being sold by a military based government.
Marc	Personal Assistant to Rebecca.
Chief Denabala Denzanga	Tribal Chief of the Burajon tribe of Pointe Trois rainforest.
Council of Elders	Council responsible the security and welfare of the inhabitants of Pointe Troise and coordinating with the rainforest militia to fight on their behalf.
Elder Butawan	Responsible for military operations.
Elder Dhaka	Responsible for supplies.
Elder Katan	Responsible for intelligence and communications.
Elder Parsien	Responsible for external communication (diaspora).
Elder Punakata	Responsible for social welfare.
Father Peter Raines	Headmaster and Priest of the missionary boarding school - Pointe Trois rainforest.
Richard Simmons	Chief Executive Officer - G. Tech. headquartered in Paris.
Michael Drier	Board Member military focal point - G. Tech.
William Baynes	Chairman - G. Tech.
Philippe Lannier	Caramondo black market agent and dealer in precious minerals out of the Pointe Trois rainforest.
Ambassador Daniel Holstein	United States representative – United Nations. Former Chair of the Security Council.
Senator Gregory Hill	U.S. Senator and Chairman of the Defense Sub-Committee.
Dr. Elizabeth Sheldon	Chair, Roundtable of Global Donors.
President Salvatore Gebajara	President, Republic of Caramondo.
General Bazilio Bugazon	Clique member of army officers trying to sell the rainforest.
General Piquant	Clique member of army officers trying to sell the rainforest.
General Pitua	Clique member of army officers trying to sell the rainforest.
Brigadier Kazolo	Clique member of army officers trying to sell the rainforest.
Major Calizar	Clique member of army officers trying to sell the rainforest.
Sergei Bladovich	Private investigator of Richard Simmons.
Franco Frapacha	Transporter of supplies to Pointe Trois rainforest.
Edward DesChampes	Human rights lawyer & activist, Caramondo.
Chenchon	Paralegal to Edward DesChampes.
Kamara	Personal Assistant to Father Peter Raines.
Christian Didier	Owner and head-chef to Avalon's most chic restaurant.
Dr. Nigel Fruthers	Senior software systems developer – G. Tech.
Dr. Lao Pei Qing	Lab Director - G. Tech., Hong Kong. - research wing.
Julia Dames	Public relations expert, Dames Communication.
Etienne Frechan	Director, Fund Management, Continental Funding Organization.

Ian Thorton	Human rights lawyer. Coordinator – Rainforest consortium.
Emily	Right-hand to Ian coordinating information flow between Caramondo and New York.
Reginald Carthwaite	Lawyer - G. Tech.
Boris Kreshnakov.	Military field operator - G. Tech.
Theodore Piquant	Son to General Piquant.
Simone Piquant	Wife to Theodore Piquant and Rebecca's childhood friend.
Speaker Benjamin LaFonte	Speaker of Parliament, Caramondo.
Hon. Maxwell Fisher	Chief Whip of Parliament, Caramondo.
Lawrence Carrion	Business tycoon, Caramondo.
Edgar Pratt	Senior Manager, Institutional & Corporate Accounts, Central Bank, Caramondo.
Avi Goldman	Diamond dealer Antwerp, Belgium.
Grondike	Minerals specialist – G. Tech.
Speewell	Software analyst – G. Tech.
Dr. Penelope Billington	Secretary of State, U.S. Government.
Roman Sandbourne	U.S. point man at U.N. Human Rights Commission, Geneva.
Richard Pican	Legal Officer - State House, Caramondo and friend to Rebecca.
James Prescott	Team leader - G. Tech. Operations – Caramondo.
Belinda Ruiz	Principal Private Secretary to the President Gebajara – Caramondo.
Hon. Mesach Manywar	Member of Parliament representing part of Pointe Trois rainforest.
General Dijan Duegaro	Head of the Army and Military High Council, Caramondo.
Michael Anderson	Deputy Minister of Defense, Caramondo.
Hon. Victor Mekash	Head of the Defense Sub-Committee, Caramondo Parliament.
Henri Riseau	Chief Financial Controller, Continental Funding Organization.
Alexander Bijoubela	Director, Global Investment Banking Services and from one of the wealthiest families in Caramondo.
Raphael Pachara	Elder Pachara's son, from the family of one of the largest land owners on both sides of sovereign borders shared by Pointe Trois rainforest Seremanta is the neighboring country.
Brigadier Arman Velasquez	Army Field Commander of Pointe Trois Operations.
Fisch	Second in command - Pointe Trois militia.
Frederick Chiles	Chairman of the Environmental Activists Association, NY.
Tristan Coldwell	Board Secretary, G. Tech. and high powered lawyer Washington D.C.

CHAPTER 1

THE TURNING POINT

POINTE TROIS RAINFOREST
REPUBLIC OF CARAMONDO
DAY 1 - 15:00HRS

Being ambushed on this narrow treacherous mountain path with sheets of rain battering down, they could hardly see a few feet in front of them.

"No one could have known we were here, no one." Montero the battle hardened militia leader whispered to Francesco responsible for that sector.

He was charged with leading this squad from the attack point against army forces that were now less than an hour behind them to the rendezvous point with a number of other squads. Costing them time was cutting through kilometers of rainforest that had consumed even the most experienced hunters from their villages. Their trackers informed Montero that the army was fast gaining upon them. The army battalion commander was among the most ruthless in military maneuver and macabre malice towards the militia of Pointe Trois. He had lost his son during the young man's first command in the rainforest and every killing of a militia fighter was an act of revenge that could never be quenched.

"Only the Elder Council members and Chief knew of our movements. How could the army have known?" replied Francesco right behind him.

The unrelenting rain, dark clouds and foliage reduced the gun fire coming from the next mountain face to sharp sparks and bursts of noise less than half a kilometer away.

About 20 feet behind Ponterno yelled, "Man down! Man down!"

Montero squinted, wiping his face trying to zero in on the rapid bullet fire. He turned to see young Jorge lying in Ponterno's arms. In violent convulsions, pupils dilated, gurgles of thick blood spurting from his mouth. Ponterno kept Jorge's intestines from falling out with one hand and his M-16 pointed towards the rain of bullets with the other. Descent of the government forces from the mountain side was imminent. Time was not on their side. The militia running straight back on this narrow mountain path was easy target practice for the army. Montero knew they were trapped under that ledge. They had been set-up. The army had been waiting for them. It was a 500 foot straight drop from the other side of the mountain path. He looked around feverishly.

"Francesco cover me!"

Montero slipped his rifle over his shoulder and struggled up chips of the slippery rock face onto the top of the ledge. The rivers of mud from the rain did not give him the traction he needed to steady his position, lock and fire.

He spotted two large boulders about 50 feet ahead behind some trees. Crawling on his elbows and knees, he removed his SD 550 from his shoulder and sprayed bullets in parallel wide arcs across the mountain face in the direction of the gun fire. The almost instantaneous response was random fire from a figure that tumbled down into the valley. Cordero then fired an RPG in the range of the gun fire. 2 small but heavy explosions went off on the mountain face. Montero saw a body thrown and roll down the mountain. He heard a whistle blow from a distance. Montero signaled to the others below not to move. He remained behind the boulder for another 10 minutes closely monitoring movements. The movement slowly started retreating further back up the hill. He slid back down to the top of the ledge and jumped down onto the path.

"Armando, Panto, Tio run ahead and see what weapons and ammo. you can collect from their dead." He moved back to Ponterno's position to see him looking physically, mentally and emotionally shattered as Jorge lay dead in his arms. "When will this end? Do we have an end?" Montero asked himself.

Nobody heard it, nobody saw it. Only if it was a miss, you heard it spin through the leaves. It was your split moment access to a second chance at life. He didn't know what had hit him and probably felt no pain even though the gray flesh of his brain was unevenly splattered across the large emerald leaves immediately around them. His dark red blood flowed like a small stream drank by the soil as if in final Holy Communion with Mother Earth. In an instant Montero's body lay lifeless on the soil. The 6 around him instantly knew there was not much that they could do for their leader.

Rapidly scanning their surroundings Fisch the second in command calculated, "We're surrounded by snipers."

In the same moment Armando, Panto and Tio came back panting from different directions in short sequence without any weapons. Without talking they signaled to Fisch that their squad had been sighted by 2 snipers to the north, 2 to the east and 1 to the west. Fisch realized it was a well laid trap. Distract them with an ambush and reel them in. Instructions were not required. Montero and Jorge's bodies were thrashing through the leaves deeper into the jungle on the shoulders that fought through into deeper cover.

PARKER RUTHERFORD & SHALES
NEW YORK CITY
DAY 1 – 09:00HRS

Rebecca was alone in her office. "Not again. I can't control this!" she winced as the flashback gushed through her like a steaming pressure cooker that needed to release itself.

I can't run faster. My heart can't beat faster. It's so dark, so cold, so wet. The leaves slap my face and arms. My flimsy night dress soaked from sweat and drizzle covers whatever it can. The dead branches and stones cut my feet but I can't feel the pain. I want to cry but I can't cry.

Footsteps behind us, men following us. I can still hear their heavy breathing like a pack of animals chasing us down. I look behind and see our village go up in flames. So fast, too fast, everything. I last remember my brother and I falling asleep in my mother's arms and then awoken by the loud explosions all around us. Our door was kicked down by army men.

"Militia sympathizers we'll teach you a lesson!" were the words I remember from one of the soldiers.

My father shot out from the bedroom, "What have we done to you? What do you want? We mean you no harm. Leave us alone."

I remember seeing balls of explosions going on outside. My mother chases Monte and I outside into the balls of fire.

"Get out now! Run!" were the last words I ever heard from her.

"Come Rebecca!" Montero grabs my hand we start running through the village gardens into the forest. In a second we hear shots come from the house.

"Nooo! Mama, Papa!" I run back. Montero grabs my wrist dragging me towards the forest. I turn my head again in pure fright. I want to go back. I see 2 soldiers coming from the compound. They've spotted us and are running in our direction. My feet take flight. Monte didn't have to ask again. Somehow we're on the path to the stream where all we kids play hide and seek around the caves. We keep

running. Our feet slide in the mixture of mud and leaves as Monte treads carefully trying to create safe footsteps for me to the mouth of one of the deeper caves. We reach and see three other friends enter the cave. We all stand at the mouth too panicked, too shocked to speak. Then we see another small group coming to the same place. Monte looks at me, knowing I can't figure out how we we're all coming here.

"Don't worry, the fathers showed all the sons and some daughters what to do if we were attacked." He says.

He runs a few feet deeper into the cave and comes back with a bundled ragged cloth. He unties it as we all keep a look out. In the cloth are 5 home-made knives. We help the other kids climb down into the entrance and remain silent for several minutes expecting more of our friends. Like a crash to the gripping silence, the 2 soldiers jumped from the top of the cave and stood there blocking its mouth. To this day I can still remember their foul stench and dirt covered uniforms. I couldn't understand why they looked excited in my worst moment of terror, until one violently grabbed Chandria the oldest among us about 15 years old and Anna about 12 years old. They are kicking and screaming as we helplessly watch the terror in their eyes while the soldiers dragged them up out of the entrance. We look at them unbutton their belts as they disappear back into the forest with our friends. The screams turned into muzzled cries. I don't know for how long, then we hear two gun shots. Some of us start to cry. We didn't know what else to do.

Monte shook me. "Take this!" He shoves one of the knives into my hand.

He and 3 of the other boys direct the smaller kids to keep moving further into the cave and tell them to stay there until they come for them. The rest of us watch the soldiers running back to us like they want to hurry and get on with something.

"Not me!" I charge back in terror, backed into a corner.

I'll never know where that strength came from. I just felt the knife tighten in my little fist. I didn't even notice that the boys had taken hiding positions in the cave. The darkness was their cover.

"You little whore where are the others?" grunted one of them. I vehemently shake my head. The other, bellies out a merciless laugh. "Then we shall both use her." Like an animal to slaughter he grabs my hair. My hand behind my back, I shove the knife straight into his thigh as hard as I can. Blood spurts out running down his huge leg.

In a throaty gasp of pain he cried out, "You animal you'll pay!

He slaps me so hard I spin and crash to the ground. The thud, my head. I can't see straight. The rain of blows. He keeps punching me. I can't see through the blood that runs through my eyes. Just a green blur of a monster on top of me. I feel so weak. Trying to fight, but I can't".

"Ok here. Now. You like it!"

The other soldier laughed as he looks on at this fight between a soldier and a girl about to be raped. I roll over to reach for my knife. Longer and stronger than me, even with his thigh bleeding he gets the knife. He drags me on my stomach like a slab of meat as he kneels and pins me down at my waist with his loins.

"This is my trademark before I work on you, to remind you that you are rejected."

Relishing his terror unleashed, not in a rush, he rips my night dress open with the knife blade. The pain of the blade searing through my flesh bleeding out an X across my front from my shoulders to my hips as the blood spills; I knew I was dying. Despite the agony of my head crushed by one hand against the cave floor I could tell he was unfastening his belt with his other hand. I see the other soldier close by while he laughs on in tense excitement.

"Hurry I get my turn too." He grunts, licking his lips.

Just then the boys run out from their hiding place. One of them gets on his hands and knees. Monte leap-frogs onto the laughing soldier and stabs him right through his neck. His jugular continues to pump out his blood as he falls over.

The four of them, mustering all the strength they can, lunge onto the soldier kneeling on top of me from different directions. One knifes him in his private parts, one in the heart, one in the stomach and Monte went straight for his eyes. The boys kept stabbing and stabbing at the soldier fighting back with one arm. The grip on my head releases. I hear this gurgled cry as this huge monster with stab wounds all over dripping in blood falls on top of me. Fighting his weight and gasping for breath, the boys push him off me. Monte pulls me up. I am still paralyzed in shock. Crying, I'm staring at my whole body covered in blood. His blood or mine, I don't know.

I remember Montero keeps saying, "Come on Rebecca. It's over." As he wipes my bleeding wounds with the ragged cloth that kept the knives, "I'll find some leaves to stop the bleeding as we run to the next village to get some help. I'm here with you. You'll be okay. The smaller kids hesitantly come out, too scared to cry. We all start running, powered by fear.

Almost 30 years later, Rebecca's willowy frame and pin-straight jet black hair, full lips and deep brown eyes would have passed for any model. The small scars above her right cheek and just below her chin were a daily reminder of the blows from the soldier in the cave. The ripping of her flesh from her shoulders to her hips had long healed, barely visible. But the scar in her mind continued to knife through her reality whenever it suited itself. The flashbacks had intensified horribly over the last 2 days. Last night a cold shiver would not leave her wrapping her like a blanket of fear that kept her awake. Throughout her morning routine it stalked her, hunted her down. At her desk she was exhausted even before the day began. This eerie dark feeling she could not shake drowned her. It dragged her mind her heart, suffocating on what she could not see. Throughout the years the nightmares of the sound of boots thrashing through the rainforest coming for them, never stopped. The image, the stench of the soldier on top of her punished her with awkward flinches, cold sweats and the shakes every time a stranger crossed into her personal space whether on the subway with a new client or at a restaurant and all without warning.

Some of those flinches were not only from the trauma she received. They were also from the trauma she gave. During the school holidays she and Montero went to stay with Elder Butawan as many orphans took turns doing so. She was among a group of 5 responsible for planting Improvised Explosive Devices at specific locations as instructed by Butawan's bomb expert. There were intel. mistakes made and subsequent collateral damage incurred. On one occasion a Lt. Col. was expected to take a particular route from the army HQ to the Ministry of Defense. Abruptly he changed route to take a meeting at Parliament before reaching the Ministry. The IED instead exploded on a school bus of Burajon children in a communication mix-up between the planners and the Burajon youth expected to detonate the IED. On another occasion an IED failed to explode on the intended target who was an army officer known to be circulating photos of maimed girls and women of Pointe Trois. It instead killed 2 of the 5 undercover militia who had gone to investigate why the gadget had failed. Rebecca then switched to a unit of girls who dressed as delicate beautiful creatures batting their eyelashes looking to supplement their families' income. They befriended army officers at local drinking joints, spiked their drinks and lured them to the forest where the militia extrapolated whatever information they could break out of them and then kill them. The army soon issued standing orders on personal engagement with the local population. She rationalized it as the price of war. Over the decades Rebecca had become a master at locking down that monster of fear and anger coated in guilt. No one would ever know. No therapist, no best friend, no priest, except the monster had started to break out of its cage. She couldn't figure out, why now?

Caramondo was 6 hours ahead of New York but within the same time frame of western continental Europe. Pointe Trois was such an expanse of the rainforest it sat between 2 time zones depending on which side of the forest you were. It could either be 5 or 6 hours. Her home that seemed so far away was the center of her existence. Her thick lashes sheltered her eyes lost in a shapeless worry as they spanned out the panoramic view of her 39th floor office. Parker, Rutherford and Shales, the blue chip corporate law firm in New York whose services spanned from tax law to high-end white collar crime had a newly created department of environmental law due to some lucrative cases being filed within and outside of the U.S.

Rebecca Calderone, a 37 year old established lawyer, was raised at the missionary school in Pointe Trois jungle with her brother Montero as orphans. Father Peter Raines, the school headmaster, chaplain and physics teacher, became their parent throughout their primary and secondary education. Both excelled at school and graduated from Ivy League Universities. She from Yale and he from

U. Penn. She remained at Yale and went on to law school and he, with his degree in mechanical engineering, broke into the mercenary industry by taking on several assignments with private military companies that executed contracts for governments and conglomerates carrying out sensitive operations throughout the world. Montero had built his own exclusive network of high ranking government contacts and powerful corporate executives that required discretion and security in execution of their large-scale projects. With 2 decades of enviable experience under his belt, the increasingly brutal war compelled him to return to Pointe Trois to build a militia movement with 21st Century capacities and competence. He could not suppress the call to repel the army forces that were giving cover to corrupt government officials raping their families and land since the time they fled their home in the rainforest.

UNDISCLOSED LOCATION
POINTE TROIS RAINFOREST
DAY 1 – 15:30HRS

It was an ugly run. It was not fear that moved them. Death was an honor. The disfigured bodies of Montero and Jorge flailed as they thrashed a path through the rainforest. The trail of blood, discharge of urine and feces from their dead, did not require bloodhounds as they charged to the boundary of their next closest squad 3 kilometers away. They had to protect what they had; their people, their homeland. 2 carried the bodies and the other 4 carried a large assortment of assault and sniper rifles, rocket propelled grenades and radio communication equipment.

While the rest barreled through, Fisch intermittently stopped to communicate to the squad of their advancement as well as warn them to avoid running into the same ambush that may have nearby support. Fisch had witnessed his teenage daughter, his only child, gang raped and shot in the face by a particularly vicious field commander and his men. His wife hung herself in their home. She felt responsible for not hiding her fast enough. For many, there was nothing to lose but everything to save in this battle.

He quickly rattled off, "Squad Raven, emergency communication. This is Eagle's Claw. We have been attacked. Changing direction towards you. Beware, we're coming in. Dragon Head down. I repeat, Dragon Head down. Activity Within, Hotel Papa or better yet Romeo Sierra."

The response was immediate, "This is Squad Raven. Communication received. When we spot you we shall pull you in."

The communication was clear. Activity Within meant they were trapped, encircled. But how far, the receiver could not tell. Hotel Papa meant Holding Pattern. Do not advance without further clearance. Romeo Sierra meant Reverse Steps. Quietly dissect yourself out of the area if you can. Tio kept a look out to the rear to make sure that the army in pursuit to finish them off didn't get too close.

PARKER RUTHERFORD & SHALES, NYC
DAY 1 – 09:30HRS

"Marc, where are those background files on the defendants? Court is tomorrow. I'm under fire here." "With you in a flash boss." as he hurriedly arranged some files on his desk.

Even on the quietest days Marc could feel her pulse. The signature of a fighter bursting through. He had seen too many an opponent look too long at her tenderness softly shaped in her fragile smile while her tenacity systematically undid their arguments. He reasoned it to being afflicted with the gene of justice, whether from the most pristine rainforest or privileged boarding school.

Rebecca, who had travelled extensively in her own work of environmental law, was always taking on the case of the under-dog being dissolved by the corporate giant. She ensured justice and a sizeable cheque were delivered to her clients. During this time she had also developed a considerable network of human rights and environmental law activists from neighborhood entities to international organizations. Parker, Rutherford & Shales saw the genius of snatching up this talent from an environmental NGO battling to solve the issues of its clients. The law firm needed a human face to its blue chip, high-brow persona and desperately needed to win -or at least quietly negotiate- a few high profile environmental cases for its most felonious clients.

But Rebecca never really took her eye off the ball that was her moral compass and mourning of her parents wrapped up in every case she undertook. The freedom and justice for her people was all she could ever think about. A throb that walked with her in her every action, spat out between the lines of her every word. In the past 2 years she had painstakingly spearheaded, and would conclude in the next 3 months, an umbrella of environmental, conservationist, human rights and scientific research organizations that would take out a 98 year lease on the Pointe Trois rainforest to preserve and protect the people, their way of life, plant life, wildlife and other natural resources.

Two indigenous tribes were in that region, the Burajon and Pekweh that had co-existed harmoniously and were never really included in the country's development. Most of the Pekweh migrated cross-border back to their ancestral homeland. But much of the land in the Pointe Trois region was still owned by clans from both tribes and the rainforest spread across a number of borders. It was also the spectrum of mixture of genetics from the indigenous population and the missionaries.

The region was named Pointe Trois because the colonialists saw the immense richness of this region and divided it –as equally as possible- among the 3 Protectorates that would later become independent sovereign nations. One nation had a natural boundary of an impressive mountain range, the other 2 countries were divided by a river, spreading half a kilometer across in some places and reduced to a stream in others. Caramondo suffered the blessing of largesse with its natural resources. A country poor in industrialization that was unable to astutely trade its vast unmeasured deposits of precious minerals and other natural resources for a path of long term development.

The potential was untapped and some government officials ensured it remained that way to allow them to continue to ravage this region under the impunity of their regime and in particular, army license plates. The rampage had been going on for over 30 years through different regimes at different levels, but the past 15 years had the obfuscation of government at the highest levels. The sale of gold, cobalt, timber and especially coltan had come in particularly handy during the last re-election campaign 4 years ago. The only problem was that it was now very difficult for the Head of State to cut the taps on the line of unlimited, undocumented money by corrupt officials after the election. And the man wasn't about to cut the taps off on his own people, lest they go complain to the wrong people.

Pointe Trois itself was almost 800 kilometers from Avalon, the capital city. Separated by thick unchartered jungle, crater lakes and mountain ridges, the Pointe Trois region was neglected in infrastructure, health and education development by the government. The Republic of Caramondo with a population of 12 million had an estimated 400,000 dwellers in Pointe Trois rainforest scattered over a vast extremely difficult landscape approximately 17,000 square kilometers within the Caramondo border. The government reasoned what the missionaries were doing was more than enough. They had built a central boarding school from primary to secondary level that excelled in comparison to schools in the nation's capital. There were well stocked clinics in each village community and a small central hospital at the Pointe Trois town center, Amour Dieu.

Pointe Trois airstrip was, interestingly, meticulously maintained by government. The frequent traffic of military and unmarked cargo planes ensured of this. The Town Mayor wrote a letter of concern to State House about the unlimited movement of traffic; empty in and full out, without declaration of cargo or payment of airport taxes to Pointe Trois airport authorities. He was invited to State House to present his problem. President said he received the letter, but never invited the man. The night he landed back to Pointe Trois he was shot in the head on the runway. Nobody could trace the man he met with at State House. Nobody saw where the bullet came from and government investigations or the family lawsuit never really took off.

UNDISCLOSED LOCATION
POINTE TROIS RAINFOREST
DAY 1 – 16:00HRS

Nobody knew how long they'd been running. Their knowledge of the rainforest was unmatched. It was their home, their backyard. Fisch heard the eagle call. They modified direction slightly and ran towards the call. It was not more than ten minutes later four large militia in camouflage gently stepped through. No one was startled. In a swift exchange of eye contact 2 men took on the bodies, equipment was split among them all to make the run as fast as possible. It was a hard climb for another 2 kilometers. They reached the squad who saluted Fisch and his group. 3 of them quickly set about preparing the bodies for travel to bury at the next village they would reach. They could never allow the army to locate and dig up their leader's body. Fisch set up a scrambled frequency as fast as he could to communicate.

"Elder Katan, Dragon Head down. Hit by sniper fire. Activity Within. By how far we cannot tell. Please scan, assess and revert. We shall re-strategize upon your communication."

"Communication received. This is tragic. We shall revert on the expanse of activity."

Elder Katan, responsible for military intelligence and communication, had moved to a corner of the study with a notebook imagining it was just another call of coordination and updates. The Council of Elders was comprised of 5 driven men that had seen much over the years. They were responsible for over 300 large villages scattered throughout the rainforest. This afternoon they had congregated at the Chief's residence in his large oak study. The others of the Council engrossed in their meeting saw Katan lean against the wall to steady himself. His notebook slipped out of his hand.

"What is it Katan?" one of the group enquired.

"Montero was shot and killed by a sniper at Negras Ledge. They were surrounded. I must make some calls first." He distractedly replied as he picked up his notebook and rushed out to a more secure room.

In their swathes of rich somber material that covered their large frames, the room was silent. Hands sank in faces, wrists banged against the wall, pacing up and down in worry. Butawan the overall head of military operations calmly removed his palms that buried his face.

"Elders, we need to stay focused. This news could easily spark off a blood bath. Word will certainly get out quickly with the army congratulating itself. But the first person that must know as soon as possible is Rebecca, his next of kin."

After 15 minutes of debate, it was finally agreed that the person who knew them both since they were children and by good chance happened to be physically there to hold her when breaking the news, was Father Raines. Truth be told, no one could stand the level of grief to be on the phone when she was so far away and words could not suffice for what both of them had done for the movement. Katan returned to the room after making his radio calls and reverting to Fisch with surrounding squads' feedback and rendezvous coordinates. Butawan updated him as he started to dial Kamara, the assistant to Father Raines, to get his number in New York. Kamara read the number on the phone while sobbing and hung up. Butawan dialed. On the second ring Father Raines picked up. The greeting was minimal.

"Yes Butawan, we just landed 3 hours ago. But from the sound of your voice this is not a social call."

"Father Raines, I need to convey some tragic news to you and to break this news to Rebecca in the best way you know how." Butawan went on to explain the trap. Raines who was dozing off after a long flight immediately got up and now sat on the edge of his bed as he listened in shock. "Father, are you there?"

"Yes I'm here. I will go to Rebecca's office at the soonest. I'll be there as long as she needs me." Raines asked himself how he was going to find the words.

PARKER RUTHERFORD & SHALES
NEW YORK
DAY 1 – 10:30HRS

The gentle chime of her phone brought her back to her office. From: Richard Pican – a State House Legal Officer. A former university mate of Rebecca's, they had completely different backgrounds but the exact same lens on principles. Never mind the crush he had on her while at University. Her stunning beauty and purity of character had always attracted the best of the boys. But in her own turbulence she never opened up to any of them. Using his personal e-mail address: '*Becky, you've got a problem. Global Technologies conglomerate is coming to sign the sales agreement of Pointe Trois rainforest in 7 days. President Gebajara and the Board Chairman of G. Tech.., William Baynes, spoke last night. Seems the President doesn't want to lose this convenient discreet client. Rumors are the conglomerate was looking elsewhere. So in 4 days they will come and do a preliminary visit and discuss the draft agreement to ensure it conforms to earlier negotiations. The army has been given its instructions and is trying to kill off anything that moves in Pointe Trois.'*

Rebecca swirled back around in her chair to her window. Unknowingly her fists clenching, heart beat accelerating, throat tightening, subconsciously wrestling a fear that infiltrated her every thought. The fleeting peace found in the Manhattan sky line quickly altered itself into a panic of thoughts to stave off a sure death of her homeland. Everything needed to happen in an instant. In the reflection of the window, her plasma TV screened an ambulance parked at the junction of 57th and Lexington. A woman's severely bruised forehead, bloodied torn hair, bleeding through her bandages with the rest of her face covered by an oxygen mask was being wheeled into the ambulace on a stretcher as the sirens blared on at the junction. On the corner of the screen was past footage of her addressing a press conference. Rebecca swirled back to watch the clip directly.

"What the heck? That's Catherine. What's she doing..? Hey Marc, get in here!" Marc's elegant figure shot through the door his eyes immediately focusing on hers and quickly turning to the screen.

"Oh yes, thrown out of an unmarked van that sped off witnesses say. She was only able to mutter the words that she was grabbed uptown almost beaten to death and repeatedly sexually assaulted as they drove around what cops estimate to be about an hour. It was her cel. phone ringing that saved her. She managed to hit the answer button and scream for help. Seems they were forced to throw her out of the van with the phone. Probably in case they could track her. I don't know what to make of it right now. Maybe a really hot case she's working on?" as he looked at the screen with concern.

Catherine was Rebecca's right hand Counsel, meticulously documenting all the human rights violations in Pointe Trois while Rebecca focused on the environmental and conservation issues of the region. Catherine's work in her own career had developed a name for herself bringing to light arrests, tortures and mass graves of vulnerable populations in different parts of the world sitting on immense valuable reserves that were being quietly 'handled' by spotless façade blue chip companies.

"Find out which hospital, at least send the biggest bouquet that can be put together for now." She murmured to Marc.

Rebecca's eyes anxiously shifted around her desk like she was already moving parts of agendas and programs of institutions that moved slowly. Seven days and counting, the Board of the World Fund on Wildlife was meeting in two months to sign their resolution that they would be co-signatories to the lease on the forest. The Science Research for Medicine was carrying out their site visit in six weeks to scope the type of plantalia and implications on medicinal research. The Global Association of Human Rights

Organizations was planning their site visit in one month and wanted to make their statement of condemnation after the trip. Cathy the chief liaison was in an ambulance on her way to hospital. And the Global Roundtable Donor Conference was taking place in a few days. Only the collective, coordinated communication of this Roundtable of Donors could put financial pressure on the Caramondo government into respecting the rights of its indigenous people. And after all those Agreements are signed, findings declared and statements made; it would take another 2 – 3 weeks minimum for the Caramondo government to come around due to the internal negotiations among themselves. The main issue being the road blocks put up by a corrupted legislature after the general obfuscation by State House.

"I need another plan to match 7 days and I need it now." she said to herself. "Marc, I need Ambassador Holstein on the phone pronto."

CHAPTER 2

THE MEETING

The meticulous spacing of the hardwood furniture and finely polished floor did not leave any doubt to the precision and strength of the holder of this office. The larger than life portraits of the fallen army heroes since independence greeted you on the facing wall of the doorway. On the east wall was a clear view of the army training grounds with a visual to the main gates on the extreme west. Behind his desk was the singular portrait of the Head of State who was also the Commander-in-Chief of the Army, known as CiC, President Salvatore Gebajara. He had led the coup d'etat 20 years ago from a civilian government because he did not agree with election results and saw some severe cutbacks, in every sense, for the army. In the last election he handily won with a 99% approval rating. The international press alluded to evidence of false opposition candidates, intimidation of the real opposition and general citizenry along with use of plain clothes police encouraging citizens to vote 'wisely'. General Bazilio Bugazon had left strict instructions with his aide not to be interrupted unless it was a call from State House.

The *Pointe Trois Project* was strictly under the final authority of President Gebajara and General Bugazon. In the corner of this office huddled at the conference table were 3 Generals, 1 Brigadier and 1 Major. General Piquant was not a willing member. He had been identified from a long way off. A photo of a well laid trap of him with a prostitute in a night club in Milan was the sword that hung over his neck. Bugazon chose him for his reputation of integrity and transparency to 'officially administer' the necessary movements of resources as and when required. General Pitua knew why he had joined the army. He'd decided he wasn't going to retire broke and had been actively skimming the system all along. Bugazon appreciated this slice of ambition in the man. However, Pitua was clever. He brought on Brigadier Kazolo to do all the dirty work and Kazolo was known since time immemorial not to have a straight bone in his body even before he caught the eye of Pitua. Major Calizar had been mentored by General Piquant since the early days of his career, having been identified as a brilliant operations analyst. He felt obliged to protect his boss in any way he could when Piquant opened up to him in confidence. More senior Generals in charge of the institution saw the damage this operation did to their reputation near and far.

"General Pitua, well done. You finally managed to nab him this time. Montero was killed by one of our snipers. Now time to get the rest, but we must move fast. The Commander-in-Chief called me to State House at 01:00hrs to inform me in seven days we are selling off this region without one single pocket of resistance in it. No more militia attacks. The forced migrations and complete neutralization of this militia must take place in the next five days and the remaining two days to clean up any signs of evidence of debris or strife. Don't want to sell a land with unhappy looking people on it. Makes it look like we had a hand in something?"

A sarcastic low laugh came from his creased long face that had slits of cold narrow brown eyes casting a deep unforgiving look at every set of eyes around that table.

"We need to clean house on these people looking like product ready for market."

Gen. Bugazon's body leaned forward to General Pitua across the table in a stiff combination of disbelief and salivation. The astounding wealth he had already amassed from the procurement deals with arms companies, sales of old artillery to broke governments looking for cheap arms and the ongoing rampage of the Pointe Trois rainforest; had never been quantified. And with this wealth brought power to ensure he was an untouchable. Bugazon's name would never show up in the media or litigations by aggrieved parties or investigations by the legislature. His one failing was his insatiable appetite for more. It was never enough. And carefully crafted immunity gave him free reign, blank cheque on his own country. Gen. Pitua talked about the new large gold mine that had been discovered.

"Is it close to the others? Can it be quietly drilled while G. Tech.. gets their bearings on the forest?" inquired Bugazon.

"It depends on the location of the mine." replied Pitua.

"After all, we'll be the ones to show them around. Can it be isolated and the geologists keep it off the map?" He immediately let go like an animal unexplainably distracted from its prey. The General turned his head without moving anything below his shoulders. "Brigadier Kazolo I assume you have everything under control ensuring the locals are cooperative with their employment services. What others indelicately call slave labor, such an insensitive term. Reposition them to work in the most lucrative areas. Gentlemen, we're going to max-out that Pointe Trois, finish off that miserable militia and present a happy pacified population."

Everybody gave a tense nod or guarded affirmation.

"I'll keep State House up to speed and I sure as hell do not want any screw-ups. Failure is not an option."

PARKER RUTHERFORD & SHALES
NEW YORK
DAY 1 – 11:30HRS

The past 2 hours flashed by as Rebecca politely threatened 3 clients to make good on the environmental spills of their factories and contamination of their workers due to insufficient gear, training and quality control measures. The last tested her patience.

"Mr. Winthrop while you may have a family dynasty as a wall of financial protection, it will not protect you from the law. 2 workers have died, 3 are in ICU and another 10 are displaying the same symptoms of the others who died. The negotiated amount on the table is $12million or a three year jail sentence. Pay the money or your family won't have a legacy in history to stand on. The world talks back now days. Give you two days to think about it."

The client and his CFO scowled, politely bade goodbye and walked out of her office with barely a smile to Marc. As they walked out, Father Raines walked in with a box that he quietly placed on Marc's table. Raines had called Marc in advance to confirm they were both at the office and told him to clear her schedule for the next 3 hours but would not explain why.

Marc was raised by a single mother from the hills of Montana who worked three jobs to give her son the best education possible. A dignified proud woman, she swore her son would have the same skills and confidence as the other kids from a more privileged background. He was saving up for his third year at law school while working at PR&S. When Rebecca joined PR&S he learned about her and briefly met her, he asked to work for her specifically because he knew that loneliness and fire that he saw in his mother's eyes every day. He wasn't sure whether it was his protective instinct or a way of giving back to the woman who worked tirelessly to make a way for him.

Raines requested that she not be told that her schedule had been cleared to avoid setting off any alarm bells. But his were already ringing. Marc spotting Raines somber expression immediately rushed up from around his desk. This was not a time for pleasantries. With worry inscribed all over his face he inquired, "Father Raines, what is it?" Raines eyes met Marc's in sadness and silence.

"Is Rebecca in her office?"

"Yes, of course. I did as you asked and put out word to her colleagues that she's in a meeting and doesn't want to be interrupted." The worry became even more deeply etched over Marc's face.

"Come, let us go in together." said Father Raines.

Marc fretted to himself. He really didn't like the sound of this. Rebecca was at her desk working away on legal briefs. The plush furnishings and soft lighting would have passed for any luxurious hotel suite. Rebecca lifted her head up from her paperwork with a huge smile towards her surprise.

"Hey! What a wonderful surprise!" as she threw her pen down on her notepad. Her smile immediately dissolved into worry and fear seeing the pained expression on Father Raines face. He could not fight back the tears that had already started to well up in his eyes.

"Come, my child. Let me hold you." Rebecca quickly moved into the arms of Father Raines like a daughter rushing to her father's arms for protection. Protection from all the harm she didn't know if she could prevent that she feared for her people. Raines held her for a long moment. It was a soft but highly protective embrace. Marc struggled to maintain his composure. He didn't know what this was about, but he knew it would do some serious harm to Rebecca hence the careful selection of the messenger. This much he could tell.

"Let us sit." His embrace continued as his arm remained around her shoulders guiding her to the couch. Marc quietly followed to an arm chair. They sat.

"Father, what is it? You're scaring me." Raines continued to hold her with one arm, taking her hand with his other hand.

"Rebecca I don't know how to say this. This afternoon Montero and his immediate squad were being pursued by the army in the Rainforest. They were surrounded and he was shot and killed by a sniper. His men are now certain it was a trap laid just for him. Rebecca I am so deeply sorry my child. Come." as he moved to embrace her.

Everything shattered. Rebecca was hurled far deeper into her world of pain. She felt every cell in her body splinter apart. Their fight, their family and now him; were all gone. She wished she could feel numb but the blade-sharp anguish would not stop cutting through her body. It would not go away. A cold sweat seared through her in shock. She balled her fists and clenched her jaws fighting to suppress it but the sobs of pain punched through. Rebecca shot up from the couch her eyes tortured in tears of grief. Angrily she looked down at Raines who remained seated.

Understanding that she needed to ventilate for a moment, caringly he watched.

"No! No! No Father! How can you come to me with such lies? My big brother! Who will protect me? Montero is all I've got." She was sobbing so hard, she lost her balance.

Marc, in his own ball of tears, sprung up to catch her and gently brought her back down to the couch right next to Raines. He continued to stroke her arm holding her tightly as she laid her head on his shoulders and wept. Rebecca wept. They were taking her home away from her. Now they had taken the only person nearest and dearest to her. What more could they take? She could not control her rage that her last anchor in life that had kept her breathing over the years when she didn't know where to turn; had now been shot down. Rebecca sat up for a moment. "I want to know who gave the order on that ambush. Find out for me Father."

Concerned by her cold revenge, Father Raines tried to dissuade her. "Rebecca, I can't imagine the pain you're going through now but let us focus our precious moments and energy on securing the agreement or his ultimate sacrifice would have been in vain." Raines saw a dissatisfied look shoot past him as her eyes scanned around the room.

"But I shall find out and convey the name to you." "Good." she replied without a hint of emotion.

Raines tried to lighten the air a bit during the silence in between sobs. In a tender whisper and a pained laugh, his voice wandered; "You know what Rebecca, it has hit me quite clearly during this annual visit. I don't know how or why now, more especially at this moment. But I've decided that I'm retiring from life at the Missionary. I'll just relocate myself. I don't know where to. I also want to have a family. I've seen so many children grow up. It's not too late to build something and leave something to pass on to my own when it's my time. You shouldn't neglect this part of your life too my dear."

Slightly raising her head from his shoulder Rebecca interrupted with a small burst of laughter. "Well I do observe you have a new 'do' again?"

Between snivels leaning on his shoulder, she popped her head up again and a trace of a smile crept through. He shyly looked away trying to avoid the joke.

"Oh yes well, my never ending mid-life crisis that's graduating into a late-life crisis. Have to keep it busy."

She chuckled, "I don't mean to be rude but don't make me cry in laughter. I thought you raised so many kids and knew the little terrors they could be, the last thing you'd want would be a bunch of rascals of your own. Peace and quiet in your home was all you could want."

Raines was glad the news had proved a distraction, no matter how brief. He also knew he had been thinking of leaving the school for some years. The basic conveniences and comforts of life were only memories after these annual visits. He knew his genes lay in cosmopolitan conversation and more close company.

"Well, believe it my dear. This simple aging Priest, who is only 15 years older than you by the way, desires the same thing as others in life."

Marc smiled as he looked on. He could see Rebecca slowly regaining her composure. They had spent some time on the couch. Marc excused himself but brought the box back into the office and left. Rebecca insisted Raines get back to the students who were just as excited as she was when part of the group 20 years ago.

"The workload is my mission, my distraction, the medicine that I need Father." He gave her a long hug and looked deeply in her eyes before leaving.

Rebecca returned to the couch. She curled her knees up to her chest and held herself tightly for 15 minutes in a self-protective embrace against the world thinking of her brother, her mother, her father. A certain silence and loneliness echoed through her. It cracked her consciousness permanently. Something had separated in her, the essence of her forever changed. She could not feel further broken yet more strengthened, more resolute. She got up and slowly walked to her desk.

Rebecca took her time opening the box. The pain had now settled into her skin, calmed down into a manageable pierce through her heart. She could breathe. She could function. Every year the school took a group of ten girls and ten boys, courtesy of the Coriamese government to the U.S. Sixteen of the students were there to attend the final interviews for the Ivy League universities they had applied to. The other four having excelled academically in their second to last year were now being incentivized to set their sights to attend an elite university and have a more global perspective of their potential. An envelope in the box described the group's program for the coming ten days they were in the U.S. and would afterwards fly to the U.K. for another five days for interviews at Oxford and Cambridge. Father Raines accompanied the students every year. The rest of the box was the critical up to date evidence that she had been waiting for.

The students sometimes heard the female teachers giggle about how such a commanding well-polished look should not have been wasted on a Priest. It was known his wicked charming smile and assuring presence, camouflaged in his demeanor of innocence and humility caused more confusion rather than clarity among some of the staff. Father Raines joked back it was the fruit of the forest. Raines had been with the missionary school before the time Rebecca and Montero were orphaned. The interesting thing about him was that every year he travelled abroad for three weeks. He said to find further learning among the best minds at various educational institutions, ensure money for the school's needs were in place and get some rest. Some of the male teachers jealously joked that it was his time to get away from the missionary lifestyle and enjoy more primal temptations in complete anonymity. One of the older teachers before the time of Raines teased his younger counter parts that there were layers to this man, more than they could ever have. Much of the school's viability was due to these trips. It never lacked for what it needed despite its far flung location and charitable school fees structure. The banter religiously resumed when these trips occurred.

Father Raines was a surrogate father to Rebecca, Montero and all of the orphaned other kids. Rebecca fondly remembers how he taught all of them in such a personalized way about strength and tenderness of heart in the same breath. How to excel and believe in yourself when everyone and everything you loved was gone before your eyes and that he was always there for you no matter what. It seems his work was his life and this approach greatly influenced Rebecca. Raines who had a talented interest in geology, introduced her to her first love for the environment as a profession. But her covered wound of the injustice of her family and her tribe drove her to become a lawyer to defend the innocent, the wounded.

Rebecca was banking on Raines package of hard core evidence she'd just received to include photos of exploitation of the mines, slave labor camps, acres of felled forest, medical samples of critically ill patients and burned villages with assaulted civilians. She was not disappointed. In a note attached to some photographs of identified black market mineral agents, Father Raines pointed out that some of the largest U.S. tel. comm., IT and military technology companies had been buying huge quantities of coltan and other minerals through agents. At the bottom of the box was an envelope. Rebecca recognized the handwriting.

'*Dearest Sis*' was inscribed on the envelope. She opened it. A brief note. '*Sis, I have always kept this over the years, but I think it's your turn now to keep it to know that no matter how far I may be, I am always looking out for you. I will always be your big brother. Sis, we are so proud of you. Keep up the good fight out there for all of us.*' In the envelope was a small blood and dirt stained cloth. It was the cloth in which the knives were wrapped when they had to defend themselves in the caves.

Rebecca buried the cloth in her face. She could not fight back the storm of tears. She took a deep breath and forced herself to get a grip.

"For you Montero, for you. For our people, I will finish this fight. *This*, I swear to you." She said to herself.

Rebecca carefully folded the ragged, stained piece of cloth and placed it in her pocket. She would carry it with her every day until this fight was over.

PARKER RUTHERFORD & SHALES
NEW YORK
DAY 1 – 12:00HRS

Marc did not want Rebecca to spend too much time alone in thought. Rebecca picked up her landline. Ambassador Holstein came on.

"My dear, I am so sorry about the news. My deepest condolences are woefully inadequate." "Thank you

Daniel." Rebecca tried to stay on point. The other option was a complete breakdown.

"Ambassador Holstein, the government of Caramondo seems to have no hesitation and in fact is quite keen to conclude signing away Pointe Trois rainforest." reported the restrained urgency in her voice.

Amb. Daniel Holstein had seen too many cheap governments violently suppress or even cream off pockets of their populations while pontificating democracy and the rule of law at all the international conferences they attended and international conventions they signed to. He was sick of it. Too many lives lost at the hands of greedy individuals who had no interest in national development. As the Permanent Representative of a world superpower at the U.N., Ambassador Holstein was the previous Chair and now a member of the Security Council.

He started out his career at a think tank established by unseen entities and individuals that shaped U.S. domestic and foreign policy. His 40 years that followed at the U.S. State Department was a career of navigating government's interests through some very muddy environments. With his leisurely pace of voice, diplomatic colleagues in the day had seen Holstein undo the most vicious rulers that found themselves mired in duplicity and treachery from within, leading to their implosions. He had now left those activities to a younger crowd while he danced a more subtle game on this world body ensuring no one got any grand ideas without his shadow of authority.

Amb. Holstein was known to be very close to Senator Gregory Hill, the Chair of the Defense sub-committee of the U.S. Congress and Dr. Elizabeth Sheldon, the current sitting chair of the Roundtable of Global Donors. These 3 were known to be quite the trio during their university days at Yale Law School. This being one of the reasons Holstein took quite an interest in Rebecca's work.

In his late 70s, his paternal tone responded, "Yes, m'dear. I'm aware of the new constraint. I'm trying to organize a meeting with Gregory and Elizabeth in 3 days or so, or at least a conference call. Lizzy is held up at the ASEAN meeting in Hong Kong for the next 5 days. What you can do in the interim is send me a preliminary report within 24 hours that'll have the key facts and arguments of the case as it stands now and then send me an up to the minute report 72 hours from now. I'll use the draft to set up the right support. With some urgency you will also need to create a groundswell of opposition to this sale. Public outrage and media-focus need to make these Global Tech. fellows look bad and a certain government look even worse. Whether you are ready or not to take the case to the public, you have to let public opinion weigh in on the matter. Always makes our work much easier when we have the social conscience appearing to give us the instructions. You need to get that case report sewn up as one nice consolidated picture that will become the global hymn sheet on this matter very soon."

Focused on his words, Rebecca knew she needed a lot of facts at her fingertips and needed them now.

"Understood Ambassador. An interesting thing to note is that U.S. tel. comm., IT and defense companies have been procuring large amounts of coltan and other precious minerals through agents. So there may be economic implications at stake as well." She responded.

"Call me when you have a binder that'll make me cry. And there isn't much that'll make me cry nowadays. But what you've just pointed out gets my attention."

"You will have that binder in 24 hours Ambassador and you will cry. Talk soon."

Upon the click, Rebecca exhaled a deep breath. It wasn't a question of ability. The question was whether it was humanly possible to collect this information and coordinate these organizations into a particular agreed position in 3 days.

"Whatever it takes to get it done, whatever it takes. At least all the attaching evidence will be in that binder, from the illegality of the transaction to the poisoning of the population." She murmured to herself.

"Marc!" she yelled out, "I hope you have a spare change of clothes in your car. You're not going home tonight."

Rebecca ran her fingers on her phone sending a message to Pointe Trois. She needed up to the minute information on the abuse in Pointe Trois at the soonest.

HOLSTEIN DIALED.

"I'm listening." greeted the caller on the other line with concern and regard. Holstein's voice was croaky, but merry, in a gentle aged way.

"Securing of a rainforest is about to be a done-deal to a company that isn't American and our companies are buying large amounts of coltan and certain other precious minerals from this forest through agents. There aren't too many other tidy parcels of land like that anymore on the planet, maybe 2 or 3 at most. As the Defense Sub-Committee Chairman I thought you should know, but more importantly also as the Priority Alpha Network. This could pose a threat to our national security interests. We may need to make sure we don't find ourselves on the back end of any deals being done."

Senator Hill grunted every few seconds as he listened, "I'll make my calls in the network and get a picture on things."

CHAPTER 3

THE SECRET

In his plush office of tasteful Roman décor with tones of cool cream and beige, Richard Simmons had just finished a meeting with the CEO of Infrastructure Construction. He was in the process of negotiating the first phase of a national highway system with a government known for loopholes in selling anything that could fetch a price.

Richard Simmons was the CEO of Global Technologies, known as G.Tech, one of the largest corporate conglomerates comprised of medium to large scale entities involved in everything from building national infrastructure such as bridges, dams, highways and railways systems to large commercial investments such as mining and electronics. As a major line of revenue, the conglomerate also became highly respected in the niche of national defense software systems. While huge in projects and revenue, none of its directors or staff worldwide were socialites. Only strategic corporate social responsibility investments were taken on. A journalist for a global finance magazine who had once done an exposé piece on corporate conglomerates that transformed themselves to stay relevant and competitive was able to reveal the most information on the company to date.

G. Tech. was founded in the mid '60s by a Sheikh who was an oil baron from an extremely wealthy, politically connected family. He had a vision not only for his own multiplying profit but also his country's development and global positioning. He could foresee that both his and the country's wealth based on oil alone were too vulnerable. So he expanded into what he envisioned as the economic platform of tomorrow's growth; the digital age for developed countries and infrastructure for developing countries. The Sheikh went on an acquisition spree during the mid to late 80s, but part of the problem was his sons' involvement in the day to day operations of the business. When the IT bubble burst in 2000 they found a huge hole in their balance sheet. The profits from the conglomerate's divisions of infrastructure and electronics kept the cash flow from going into cash shock. When the sons saw the value of their personal wealth plummet, despite the pleas of their father they sold their shares to another Middle Eastern company; a company that had happened to have fundamentalist leanings. The sons' shares constituted 60% of the company. They said it was too rich an offer for them to refuse. The new shareholders always willingly pumped in the necessary cash to invest strategically. As part of their long-term turnaround they invested in cutting edge software development while they continued to be exceptionally profitable in infrastructure development in difficult territories. The journalist noted that the new owners were seen only through their bank representatives and no one knew anything beyond the name of the holding company called *SaHraa Saif*, loosely translated as the *Desert Sword*. But everyone understood that they were the majority shareholder. The Sheikh gave 20% of his 40% to his 2 daughters and now is barely seen by his own extended family. Some say battling depression as a result of this new shareholding mix.

G. Tech.'s veneer of a conservative socially responsible conglomerate that moved with the precision of a stealth missile worked well for the entity. It was able to carry out its work in the most controversial environs in an unusually calm manner. Somehow there were no protestors, violated populations or mediating groups. Work was always carried out on schedule and on budget. The journalist surmised the conglomerate to be a very neat global empire, perhaps a bit too neat for the types of lines of work they were in. A huge amount of money invested in keeping the right people happy and the conglomerate keeping its nose clean.

Simmons had nothing typical about a CEO background. His thick wavy black hair, penetrating black eyes and handsome refined features complemented his 6'2" muscular graceful build. His speed and charisma of movement commanded respect among his staff. His disregard for his looks drew even more attention to them. There was the long scar on the back of his right hand everyone talked about, but he never discussed. It was the collection of his experience, periodic gaps in his CV and unknown personal life that brought great discomfort to a government five years ago that carried out security checks on key personnel of companies tendering for the largest dam and other key infrastructure in their country. Simmons bio-data lay only in the files of the U.S. intelligence services. He was orphaned at 8 years old through a bomb planted by American intelligence targeted to hit his neighbors that were pursued terrorists in an elite neighborhood in Riyadh. The terrorists had already left the house but booby-trapped the place with explosives. The impact of both detonations took out the houses on both sides. Simmons entire family was killed. The only reason he survived is that he had to take an entrance exam at a school for gifted children during that public holiday.

Upon this discovery by one of the senior U.S. intelligence officers at this Saudi branch, he adopted him and gave him a first rate education and secure family life in the U.S. Richard Simmons, formerly Sadiq Farah Mohammed, was a loyal and dutiful son. He was given his adopted mother's maiden name for security reasons. Upon graduation from college he made his own way into the world. He served a 4 year stint of stellar performance in the Armed Forces then paid for his MBA and Masters in Software Engineering. His adopted parents were particularly proud of their son's patriotism, but were disappointed he didn't pursue a career further in the Forces. It was clear he had the potential to go far. Simmons was a Silicon Valley techie with a nose for business and power. He was on permanent over-drive. His father could see there was something unresolved about him, but was afraid to probe further. Too afraid to open up on his own unresolved guilt, on which he had thought he had neatly made good. All of his previous employers recognized him as one of their best employees, delivering results and breaking new ground.

When his employer, a leading software developer, was acquired by G-Tech. its human resources were pruned and Simmons took to his new employer like a fish to water, demonstrating particular diligence in ensuring G-Tech. was the leader in its U.S. and European markets. The Directors were pleased with this new acquisition. However nothing was known about his private life. Where he took his holidays, always showing up with a different beautiful face at every function was the envied chinwag. He joked with his colleagues and superiors that he was a wondering spirit unable to settle into the routine of family life. They admired and adored him for his business ruthlessness and boyish restlessness.

Simmons concluded the meeting as he gently rose from his glass top desk and smoothly ushered his guest through his double arched doors into his private lobby and into the larger lobby suite where the private elevator of G.Tech executive offices awaited him.

With the quiet confidence of a company that had just won its next tender even before it was announced, "Mr. Del Gado, it was only my complete delight. Both copies of the tenders shall be forwarded to your government as agreed. And our other arrangement shall be swiftly executed upon signing of the contract with your good government." The Minister of Energy of the Republic of Kechata could barely conceal his squeal of delight as he stepped into the elevator.

As soon as the doors shut, Simmons spun on his heel and called out, "Andrei! My office please."

Within 2 seconds a gawky curly sandy brown haired analyst with rosy cheeks was following behind Simmons with the focus of a techie listening to his mentor reveal software clearance codes.

"This is the file – *Pekata Dam – The Republic of Kechata*. Prepare the tender documents as per the spec.s in the file. His SBA details are in the file with the agreed amount and terms. I want those documents couriered out by close of business tomorrow. Understood?"

"Understood sir." Countered Andrei, excited by the laborious detail he would have to go through to ensure the tender application was prepared with meticulous detail and differences in both versions that even the trained technocrat would not notice until it was too late.

Global Technologies knew why they hired who they hired and they were handsomely paid for it. Not to mention their unorthodox recruitment approach. It also had the unique record that no one had quit the company to work in a similar industry and these were many industries. G-Tech.s retirement packages were known to be legendary. The same journalist surmised that this employer picked the best cherries from the tree, -both the holy and unholy.

As Andrei closed the door behind him, Simmons reflected on the breakfast meeting he had earlier in the morning with one of the Directors in the private dining room of the San Tropé Country Club 2 blocks from his office. He didn't want to forget a single detail of this meeting.

Michael Drier updated him that the R&D department had made a combination of hardware and software breakthroughs that could possibly change world order. What started as a routine operation to secure large deposits of coltan in order to avoid being at the mercy of agents, had now become one of the most sensitive and sought after projects of G. Tech in its 64 year history. Drier explained that while the department was running through a battery of tests for certain unique mineral variations found in Point Trois; the mineral composites were found to be able to slowly disable the software circuit boards of satellites. Combined with the right software programming you could then have a brief window to breakdown all the security codes of the satellite to enable you to download any data that you wish from its source until the satellite circuit boards were burnt out. The level of software programming you applied determined how much information you could download at source before the circuit boards were fried. In other words you could penetrate any computer, server or network that required a satellite connection. The 2 minerals that are the key ingredients that melt into this undocumented variation are found in Pointe Trois rainforest specifically. The issue was how long this would remain a secret within G.-Tech. Simmons knew the gravity of this information.

"Baynes called President Gebajara last night and told him G.Tech would be interested in a negotiated price for Pointe Trois rainforest knowing that you can actually get chunks of land pretty cheap in a rainforest. In order to keep the man interested Baynes told him the price was a mere detail that would be well worth his while but they were exploring other options just in case. The company just wants to move into a clean house. That meant both militia and population. Simmons, your job is to ensure the agreement is executed in 7 days, without fail." said a straight shot look of a tall athletic built man.

"Got it." replied Simmons.

Drier had built an outstanding career in the Army Special Forces-Field Ops., then spent his final government years at the Headquarters – Department of Defense as a special adviser - field operations worldwide. In his mid-50s he now wanted to retire to a life in the private sector and enjoy his work without certain inconveniences in the form of Congress investigations or international diplomacy. But he never really retired. He only officially retired. Drier's skill set and network were unique to U.S. defense interests. In the private sector, he'd build the plan and ensure its execution to a T without one phone call of accountability for lives or costs. Global Technologies signed him on quietly even before he left the Defense Department. The Board of Directors was unanimous. He was well worth the $1.5M they paid him every year.

Simmons strategized in his mind this new finding was priceless. This was power and control that would make the world's superpowers bow down to the highest bidder. Whoever had the software program and hardware mineral composite held the key to being the world superpower on both economic and military levels. This was not a question about money; it was about power; raw, unfettered control in its most pure form that could not be measured. He recalled that there had been some human resource changes at G. Tech particularly in the software development department between the Paris, New York and Hong Kong offices due to the acquisition of a Silicon Valley company, Quantum Software Development, three months ago. Like a thunder bolt, it flashed back to him that the company was doing cutting edge research in the area of software development and satellite communications. But they simply ran out of cash. G. Tech said they would let them continue with their work as long as they shared their knowledge with other company projects and research. Acquiring and moving talent around to maximize the most out of people's skills was a forté of G. Tech. It was clear to Simmons that the discovery was made shortly after the acquisition of Quantum because G. Tech had been all along collecting materials from Pointe Trois for over 3 years without significant discovery.

Buying this rainforest would be obliterating the security codes of sovereign nations ranging from nuclear missile clearance codes to central bank and interbank money transfer codes. World security and stability lay not in the hands of the U.N. or the global donor community, but instead in the mines well nestled in the deepest jungle of Caramondo. And whoever bought, leased or simply had access to that land was the one who had the key to world peace, co-existence and instant superpower status. The only difference was that the tree-huggers worldwide, corrupt government officials of Caramondo or G. Tech's competition didn't know this. And no way could they ever find out. Simmons felt a visceral rush of adrenaline surge through him. The matter had to be handled with surgical calm and precision.

His mind set things in motion. He knew he would immediately have to carry out investigations on all staff in the R&D and software development departments respectively. This was critical to reveal any underlying weaknesses that could give away vital company information. Particularly because the new faces from the acquisition could affect the career aspirations and team spirit of staff when the discovery so obviously came from the recent acquisition. Plotting and planning as fast as he could, Simmons concluded it would be best to carry out these thorough investigations from the outside, not through the usual investigative channel of the HR department in case it raised the wrong flags of folks sniffing around that there was something valuable to hide. This was one secret without margin for error. The job had to go to his private handler that no one at G. Tech knew about. Over the years colleagues may have wondered how he got certain impossible tasks done or intransigent positions turned around. Simmons started dialing.

"You know I'm always glad to hear from my most near and dear friends." Was a well-honed British accent with strong Russian undertones greeting him. "Before you were calling me every hour, now I am hearing from you only on the odd occasion."

Simmons cut him off speaking in a hushed tone trying to cover his sense of urgency. "Sergei, I need you to be on standby. I will be in touch soon."

"I missed you too darling. I'll wait for your call."

Simmons was mildly irritated at the things people could say on the phone when others were around. Sergei Bladovich, was an investigator, spy, assassin, IT expert all wrapped up in one. When the cold war went into melt down, most governments had not bothered to follow up on the next generation of secret service agents the Russian government was training at the tender age range of 7 to 17 years old from a private school tucked away in the middle of a snow desert of Siberia. He and a number of his former schoolmates went into business for themselves selling their unique set of skills to corporations and governments that required particularly talented hands for intricate tasks, normally of a dark nature. Sergei and his former classmates could seamlessly move in and out of government offices, the private sector and most importantly intelligence offices throughout the world. Retrieving information that would take weeks to assemble was normally done in hours or minutes. The fast turnaround of information was their niche and why they were so highly paid. This was a clandestine network of remarkable expertise that, if needed, could change the course of events in any region of the world they temporarily inhabited.

Simmons ballerina figure Assistant in her early 40s walked in to remind him, "Don't forget the 1:00pm luncheon with St. Anne's Children's Hospital." Simmons despised these cocktails, lunches, dinners and soirees. He couldn't send his Deputy to all of them. It was beginning to look rude and G. Tech. never made an investment without an expected return striving to be known as a powerful player with a human face, a trusted partner for life. An indiscreet employee once titled it as foreplay.

TRIBAL CHIEF RESIDENCE
ARMOUR DIEU, POINTE TROIS
DAY 1 – 17:00HRS

Army officials knew how easily one sentence of disapproval from the village chief would immediately make their operations very complicated by calling an all-out war on these imposters drilling on their land without consulting them. While the people of Pointe Trois would be massacred, it is that very massacre that would draw a global spotlight to their operations with investigations of every stripe at the mouths of the mines they were drilling. These officials fully aware of this sensitive factor in their operations proceeded to build the Chief of Burajon a lavish bungalow under the government's guise of support for cultural institutions and the positive role they play in communities. When the Chief enquired and was looking forward to the building of the University, a few additional schools and several youth projects throughout the region, his requests were always met with some bureaucratic delay that resulted in postponement into the next financial year. Finally wise to the message and already well settled in the sprawling bungalow, it was always a tense relationship of mutual disdain for one another. He had witnessed his people degenerate over the years and was virtually helpless to do much about it.

Plates of the most intricate design of the purest gold-diamond necklace and an arm brace ordained only to the

Chief were understated yet powerful. At 6'4" his body had changed from a lean warrior protector of his people to a pained leader in never ending wars at different levels with the government. The light in his eyes had changed into a somber expression of frustration, anger and loss. In his mid-60s now a large man with a clean shaven head, he was still taut and strong leading the Council in war strategy and managing the crisis of his people.

With a quick and purposeful walk, Chief Denabala Denzanga rejoined the Council of Elders in the study after being briefly called away to give his moral support and blessing to the last group of trackers making a run to drop supplies to hard hit squads within a 30 kilometer radius. Pointe Trois was one hour in time behind the capital city but because of the dense foliage around, darkness always seemed to arrive earlier than its appointed time. Butawan updated the Chief on the phone call to Father Raines. He was silent for a moment.

"I will call Rebecca. Ok people, we are fast running out of time. This is even more reason that we must fight to protect our homeland to our last breath or die while trying in solidarity with Montero. I have received word from our contacts in the army that this so-called agreement will be signed in 7 days. They now plan to destroy our homeland without delay? Where do such wretched people come from?" The Chief snorted in indignation, struggling to control his disgust.

All eyes fixed on him, he continued in his solemn tone. "Our young men and women are being slaughtered as we speak. We are slaves on our own land. Grown men and women are sickly and our children are stunted. We watch people cut away at our forests and drill huge mines and we see not even one dollar from this. We must act now and act decisively. Let us receive our updates to strategize how we must now settle this battle that has been in their favor for far too many years. My brothers it is now or never. I don't know that we will even survive this never-ending onslaught another month."

Chief Denabala could see over the years that a once a big, proud and fearless people now looked worn down and exhausted but still carried the fire in their hearts. The pain of too many burials, too many complicated illnesses and children born out of rape was palpable in the room. Nobody cared to talk unless it directly related to getting these murderers out of their land. The Chief gestured to Elder Butawan in charge of military operations to give his update to the group. Butawan formerly headed the Pointe Trois Militia until a grenade scraped off the majority of his left leg about 5 years ago. By good fortune, this was a few months after Montero had joined the group and brought with him a wealth of knowledge and valuable contacts that were experts in sourcing high tech arms at basement prices as well as moving those arms without so much as a blip on anybody's radar. The wealthy Burajon in the city and diaspora had been a solid supply network of funds. Their ingenuity and loyalty towards the fight had become an inspiration to the militia itself.

Butawan updated, "The army has stepped up its game. They have now introduced airpower in the form of bombing raids on sections of the forest where they suspect we're passing. They have had a 50% accuracy rate so far and most importantly for us to be aware of, are the several helicopter drops where they parachute in large squads as well as using those birds to throw down their supplies at strategic coordinates. Their supply birds are accompanied by some seriously armed copters. Their movement has become much faster much deadlier than 2 months ago. Our trackers perched at various observation points throughout the forest are piecing together that they are forming some kind of a net to close in around us. The danger is that these nets could choke us in a month at the speed with which they're dropping these boots on the ground. We need to turn this around now. As far as I can tell this operation does not have the support of the army as an institution. We have to make it bloody enough for their own to start asking questions and pull the plug. That is the essence of this approach."

Elder Dhaka responsible for supplies added. "Our boys are strong, but the food rations are down to one good meal every 2 days. Otherwise it is a diet of raw plants. We don't have the basic penicillin drugs to treat bullet wounds and these infections could have an impact on our agility pretty soon. The group that you just blessed are the last to go into the rainforest for a while, hence the importance of their trip." His wiry figure looked like he could run a marathon without breaking a sweat, covered with his warm laser stare telling you that you could put your life in his hands.

Elder Katan sharing the intelligence and communications update chipped in, "Their brutality is becoming their signature. If they catch a supply or militia tracker they will torture him to find out his exact village of origin. They will drag him back there, get his whole family identified then dismember him right in front of them like a courtyard execution and leave him in a heap. They call these *Execution Exercises*. Or they simply leave their bodies hanging from trees nearby the village knowing that the villagers will run into them."

There was a brief silence in the room. Everyone knew this vicious brutal behavior was not far from one of their own. The militia had witnessed their internal executions. Betrayal was not a weakness Montero tolerated. Each knew the sacrifice they were making for their homes. "Are you willing to sacrifice yourself to the death?" was the first question he asked any person that presented themselves to the militia and the last question before they waged into any battle. When the militia intel. had verified an information leak from one of its own, Montero did not wait for the Council of Elders to pass judgment. He had a high court of his most trusted and tried men read the list of charges and the results of the betrayal. The judgment was the same. An act of betrayal deserved treason. The sentence was consistent. Sliced and knifed to death by members of your own squad. Left to bleed to death from your wounds. Montero called betrayal 'an act of ugliness' that had to be revisited on the betrayer. To some militia who had participated in butchering the flesh of their own; the torture from within was more devastating than the torture from the enemy.

Katan continued. "It is true that some of the senior army officials not part of the coup d'état clique and are complaining among themselves about the damage to their reputation throughout the Continent."

"Good. Then we'll use that at the right time to make them fold from that end as well." The Chief replied. He nodded to Elder Punakata, the head of social welfare, "What is the condition of our people?"

"I agree Chief. We must act decisively now. The welfare of our people has deteriorated to a point that I cannot guarantee the survivability of our tribe. The slave labor camps are generally eating away at our people. Many people are getting black lung and heart disease as a result of working in the mines with no protective gear. They work 20 hours a day with only 1 poor meal. More than half have developed wound infections due to lack of proper treatment for the bad cuts they get on their hands and feet. While the fighting spirit still exists when I talk to them, their physical health is in very bad condition. Some of these are also complex illnesses such as blood poisoning and renal complications. The health issue of venereal diseases never before in our communities can at least be treated or contained. To our horror babies die soon after birth due to preventable complications. But Chief, you must make a pronouncement on the matter of rape babies, not to reject or blame their wives for being victims of war. Women are regularly raped with their men forced to watch."

"You are right. I will include this in one of my weekly radio pronouncements. We cannot let the sins of others tear us apart. Please keep their fighting spirit alive. There is a fair chance that they will have to defend themselves at some point."

The Chief turned to Elder Parsien responsible for external communication whose primary responsibility was to drum up as much support from the diaspora, but equally important the international community that could apply enough pressure to force government troops into a withdrawal. Parsien a human rights lawyer, spoke in a direct tone as if presenting a bad scenario to his client that must be tackled in a direct manner. "It is in regard of the 7 day deadline Rebecca has asked us to urgently compile an up to the minute picture on the present situation. Some of you are already working on this, but we have only a couple of days or so because she needs to fit it into a larger dossier for the international organizations that are strategizing among themselves in efforts to force a decision from government. This is the only window of opportunity we have. The only bullet left."

The other Council Elders nodded in agreement with focused brows expressing a task that must be executed immediately.

The Chief concluded, "These are the main exchanges we need to have as a group. Please continue with the necessary coordination required of each other." He pulled Katan aside. "I want you to find out who leaked the intel. on the location of Montero's squad. It had to have been from within this room. That's why I need you to do it quietly."

Katan grabbed the Chiefs hand firmly, "Whoever the leak was, you'll get to know it Chief." He replied.

G. TECH. HQ, PARIS
DAY 1 - 18:00HRS

Towards the end of everyday Simmons dutifully checked his communiqués to get the situation reports on prospective and ongoing projects around the world. His cel. phone rang.

'Meet me at the corner of *Sonnier & LaBouche* in 5 minutes. I have a message for you from Lannier.' instructed a French nasal accent.

Philippe Lannier, trader, smuggler of all items with substantive value was also Simmons key intel. point in Pointe Trois. Through his network, it was his job to make sure that the Globe Tech. team did not run into interference or mysterious difficulties from invisible quarters when going about their work or receiving their particular menu of minerals through their agents. Lannier had proven very helpful over the past year when certain government officials were trying to cut off the coltan mines on behalf of another competitor. It was also his task to provide the necessary updates on political earthquakes brewing threatening the government's existence, thereby threatening their cozy relationship with the sitting Head of State. Simmons surmised trading a few trinkets of Lannier's among his own well placed contacts throughout the world was not a difficult favor in exchange. As long as he squeezed him to remind him who was in charge, all went smoothly.

Despite his method of a nervous wet street rat, Lannier had developed a powerful network of contacts in political, business and military circles. You could never tell who was his friend and who was his enemy. But sharp as a blade when working a deal, you just had to be sharper and make sure he knew it. His network could erase you without his fingerprint. A few notorious international black market traders trying to intimidate local agents were no longer around to attest to this. Shifty and nervous, you had to manage the man.

Simmons grabbed his jacket and was at the intersection within 6 minutes. Calmly looking around for any anomalies in his scenery, within 30 seconds just another face walking towards him was an average looking gentleman in his mid-40s wearing nerdish glasses with a camera in his hand looking like a tourist enamored with his surroundings. The man didn't make eye contact as he passed Simmons but authoritatively said, "Room 1712, Hotel Carlisle in 5 minutes."

The Carlisle was just across the street. The door was slightly ajar when he got there. "Bien. Let me be quick." said a well-dressed woman whose voice he recognized from their phone conversation. "Lannier asked me to inform you of an especially precious find that he thinks may be of interest to you. A diamond mine has produced the most stunning collection of stones he has put aside just for you."

"My, the man is generous to a fault." Simmons retorted wryly. His slightly intrigued expression betrayed him.

Scanning as she talked, the courier carefully glanced through the see-through curtains at the intersection where he'd been waiting. A slight frown registered on her face and interrupted her thought process, "Are you being followed?" she inquired. As she stared at a yuppie looking gentleman who looked to be too focused, too rigid to be yet another happy tourist in the middle of Paris in his cream slacks and navy blue sweater shouldered over his grey polo shirt. Simmons peered over. He simply found it a rude thought that G. Tech. would have dared to have him followed and warily dismissed the character.

"Have a look for yourself. Don't be shy." She teasingly gestured to a velvet black sachet on the side table.

Simmons opened the sachet, rolled out the contents onto the table and was startled to find about 30 high grade diamonds spread out. Simmons heartbeat picked up a pace or two. Trying to feign muted appreciation, "Mmmm…not bad."

Her voice brought him back to the present moment. "This is just a sample. With a few discreet inquiries, these alone in front of you have fetched $7-8million. Lannier says your cut would be 5%." She leaned in to him as if to share something off the record. "Let's be clear, the only reason he has to flog them through you is because you can make it happen and you know how to make the paper trail –or any other trail for that matter- disappear."

She could see Simmons trying to figure out the catch as he studied as her boxy jacket and shapeless slacks, knowing she surely carried a Walther P99 or something of equally good taste to contain any situation that may unexpectedly go awry. But she was still stunningly elegant.

Lannier was known for his unusual transactions and his real intentions always remained a mystery even to his couriers such as the attractive lady standing in front of him. He only had to take special care to ensure that Lannier was handed over to the military authorities in Caramondo in the event anything went wrong. Not the Police or some global law enforcement institutions, only to people who would take his thievery personally. Other thieves who would not tolerate another thief stealing from them. Simmons had made this abundantly clear to Lannier during his third transaction with him when he found himself semi-conscious and drugged in an Army safe house after he'd tried to withhold some of the gold during the last delivery of a transaction. Only upon release of the full consignment and through some frantic instructions to his people did he awaken in an alleyway in one of the seedier neighborhoods of Avalon. Lannier knew Simmons network had more bite than his.

"Tell him I'll get back to him."

He kept a sharp eye on her while he guardedly took the sachet from the table and walked out. The good timing of this transaction would provide him with the supplementary cash as and when he needed it. This rainforest held power and, he, a once traumatized child staring at the charred ruins of his home and smelling the burnt flesh of his family, now held this power in its making.

Out of the sharp sun, Simmons walked into the cool air conditioning and soft lighting of his building. Walking through and making a right hand turn to G. Tech.'s private elevator bank Simmons pondered to himself as he entered the lift. Even before the doors completed opening, "Graciella, please ask Timmell to attend the luncheon. He has a certain manner that can tolerate those well-coiffed bored ladies much better than I can." Timothy Timmell, G-Tech.'s Director of Operations had a ruggish handsomeness that seemed to captivate the ladies of leisure. If only they knew of his military, engineering and IT capabilities. He was a consummate operator when the deadlines had to be met. Letting the soft velvet pouch roll in between his fingers in his pocket, his cel. phone rang as he opened the door to his office. On the other end was a high pitched slightly lyrical voice of a man. Caller ID was a private number.

"I trust you received the package?" The voice asked.

"Why now?" Simmons responded.

"Let's just say it would be more difficult or rather intricate for me to have access to a runway a little while from now so I've decided to dispose of all my trinkets and trivia accumulated in my basement and possibly retire out of the business before I lose certain privileges and clearances I've enjoyed for some time." replied Lannier in a rather congenial tone.

Simmons knew Lannier had bribed the right army officials in Armour Dieu, Pointe Trois as well as customs officials at the national airport in Avalon to ensure his items found their way onto both the army cargo and civilian passenger aircraft whether accompanied with a courier or not. But this access would become certain impossibility once the army cleared out and G. Tech. officials took control over movement of goods and personnel in and out of the region. Their own small little country if you like.

Simmons with slight irritation in his voice responded, "If I understand it correctly, you need to get these diamonds out of Pointe Trois and sold very quickly before the rainforest changes hands or else their origins will raise all sorts of questions on the market with the concern of blood diamonds raised by every government pretending to do good. Worse yet, you don't want to sell to people you don't know when you're time bad. You know they'll smell your desperation a mile away and outright fleece you of your little stars."

Lannier interrupted. "Now, now old friend, you take such a severe view of things."

Simmons replied. "25% is my cut and you don't get to see one cent of your cut until the full consignment has been sold."

"Simmons, is this the harsh manner in which you treat your old friends? I'm devastated. Mortified. 15%."

Simmons found it difficult to hide his irritation, "Fine. You will be sorry if you cross me on this deal. I'll be in touch in a couple of days. Start making arrangements to have the full envelope reach me within that time."

Lannier didn't like the tone of that conversation much less Simmons reminding him who was in control of his diamonds. And now he had to arrange to move an additional $10 million worth of valuables without any assurance he was ever going to see one cent of these stones that sat right in front of him in his room. He had a sick knot in his stomach.

CHAPTER 4

SAVING THE SOIL

Bugazon demanded intel. updates almost every 2 hours in his own state of angst and Kazolo had ran out of new information to give him. He could only avoid his calls for so long before he would be storming through his door raising his voice in his office. He needed facts and needed them now. The timing of Franco Frapacha's arrest was nothing short of an unqualified miracle.

Kazolo smiled to himself while he punched the numbers on his cel. phone. "Officer McGuire has our little task been completed?" Officer McGuire knew full well the calm but threatening voice on the other end of the line was that of Brigadier Edward Kazolo. Despite McGuire's hate for Kazolo and his clique, he casually responded.

"Kazolo dear friend our little program was handled 2 days ago and is in full gear." "That's good." retorted Kazolo in a patronizing impatient voice.

With the recent death of Montero and the 7 day deadline, the mission was now to capture as many of them as possible and simply torture as much information out of them as they could in the time available about the campsites, ammunitions hideouts and planned movements. The purpose of which was to break the back of the population, force them to surrender and get their militia to lay down their weapons for an amnesty deal. This was a window to cripple them and kill them off from the inside out. McGuire quickly walked down the hallway of his police station then down some stairs and continued to the extreme end. He took a right turn and then another short series of steep steps to a cold grey stoned corridor row of cells each with its own steel door. Very few knew of the existence of these cells. Those who did, did not speak of them for fear of a return trip to an address of extreme torture. From the last cell on the left came screams of a man who sounded to be at the end of this tolerance for the torture dispensed upon him. McGuire banged on the door 3 times. A slit opened for confirmation and closed. The door opened. He walked into a cell stinking of bodily fluids of every type.

"Anything yet?" McGuire looked with concern at a man without the strength to raise his head.

Bruises, blood and saliva covered the swellings on his face, complimented by his badly busted lip and what looked like a couple of broken teeth. The concern was not about his condition but instead how quickly he would talk and reveal the date and location of the next supply point, movement or any information. McGuire wanted that information as quickly as it could be beaten out of him. He disliked the patronizing pressure he got from those army boys and their mistaken superiority complex and swagger to accompany. It was an open secret that it was only General Piquant and Maj. Calizar that had received a formal military education and had been known for their professionalism and discipline despite the particular group they were seen with. McGuire gave the signal to the interrogator to tighten the screws a bit on Franco Frapacha and to let him know when he had something. He gave Frapacha a look of sorrowful pity to a man he knew was experiencing a terrible injustice. Quickly he unbolted the doors and started back down the hallway with a heavier dose of tension working on his ulcers than when he arrived.

Franco Frapacha, a wholesaler based in Avalon, came into some big money by being the exclusive wholesale supplier to the Pointe Trois region. He had taken on a couple of high risk missions for the army in Pointe Trois because his local couriers within the region knew some shortcuts when trying to move product from the mines to the airport.

Intelligently he reinvested this money from wholesale supply into transportation, expanding into other parts of the country. What the army didn't know until very recently by accident is that he was also running clandestine lines to the PT militia by making deliveries to the residences of PT sympathizers. A Sergeant one day was walking into the Frapacha central depot at Pointe Trois. The 3 wheel motorbike of a Frapacha courier had just finished loading and set off down the road. Despite the canvass tied over its carriage, a box of penicillin slipped and fell out. The courier did not notice and rode off. The curious Sergeant picked up the box in his path and finds it odd Frapacha was also dealing in medical supplies when none of his products displayed anywhere ever suggested so.

He doubles back to his vehicle and has his driver covertly follow the 3 wheeler. And there began the harsh logistical challenges of being able to receive steady supplies for the Pointe Trois militia.

"Ok Frachapa, we've been polite and patient with you. You leave me no choice but to go and visit your wife and those beautiful 4 year old twin daughters of yours. I must extend my personal comfort, if you know what I mean, to her in the presence of your girls. To have her husband away for so long and not even knowing whether he'll come back deserves a whole lot of special attention. Very special attention as I can already feel my hand up her thighs. I'm almost hoping that you won't give us this information pronto that will compel me to go and make this special visit. Frapacha you either speak now or I rape your wife in front of your baby girls. Yours is not the first and it surely won't be the last. So don't act like this is some big deal."

Frapacha spat out a semi-solid combination of fluids and flesh from the continuous blows and bashing of the last several hours. Breathing heavily, he started to cough and spoke softly. He couldn't stop sobbing because he knew his trackers were going to die by giving out this information but he knew he had to protect his wife and children. He was sobbing at the injustice of it all. How could he be made to choose between his own family and the boys he had raised as his family? An intense sharp kick to his knee cap jolted him back to reality.

"C'mon Frapacha, we haven't got all night. You wanna get back home in time for supper with mummy and the kids don't you?"

He struggled to control his sobs. "There are two trackers that have just set off with large loads passing through the hunters den and shallow ravine. You'll be able to catch them on the main route if you send your goons now." He sobbed, even though he had given out the details of only two of the twelve trackers that had just set off. His two best that would be hardest to catch, especially given the path they would be on. But they had the most valuable loads.

"Ok, let's get you out of these unpleasant surroundings. Process your paperwork and out of the building within the hour."

With that news, despite his hand and ankle shackles, Frapacha mustered the strength to raise himself from the chair. As he started to walk towards the door, his interrogator circled behind him and pulled out his Beretta 92 tucked at the back of his belt. He had already taken the time to attach the silencer to it, as loud gun shots may tend to attract all sorts of questions from his superiors. The majority of whom were not supporters of brazen disregard for rule of law and impunity that hampered proper investigations and the inconclusive findings of which had affected the reputation of the Police. Just as his interrogator pointed the pistol to the back of Frapacha's head, the loud banging of someone's fist on the steel door fought through. Frapacha couldn't believe new orders were coming through to electrocute more information out of him. He couldn't believe his misfortune.

The effort of rushing his long thick legs a couple of blocks from the parking lot to the Police Station wearing his only suit and tie his ex-wife spitefully left him, that was now a very wrinkled dark blue linen and a strip of gray material around his neck, produced a feisty film of sweat that had started to moisten his cream yellowish shirt and darken his strawberry blonde hair around his forehead. It had been a long day in court, but this matter usurped his attention.

"This is the lawyer for Mr. Franco Frapacha. Open this door immediately or your whole Police Station will be under charges for detaining citizens without trial and you, in there, will be up on charges of assaulting an unarmed citizen, torturing and extracting information under duress without access to Counsel. And I give you my personal guarantee your case will continue into perpetuity."

His interrogator stunned into confusion for a split second, quickly tucked his pistol back into his belt and even bothered to slip on his jacket to give an air of calmness. Frapacha standing hunched due to his state and shackles, slowly turned around and in a voice of complete exhaustion blurted out, "You heard the man, what the hell are you waiting for? Open the damn door."

His interrogator was un-amused by the sudden impertinence of a man who was begging for his life less than 3 minutes ago. He stepped forward, pulled back the locks and opened the door to be met with the glare of a lawyer looking for a target to litigate into powder if he could. Frapacha's lawyer stepped forward forcing the chunky cop to step aside. He looked at Frapacha and then looked at the hefty man who carried an expression of shameless thuggery.

"You will pay for this and you will pay hard."

Edward DesChampes turned to his client, put his arm over his shoulder and escorted him through the dimly lit corridors.

With his worn out diaphragm he murmured, "We've got to get word to the two key trackers to abort the drop-off. Frapacha gave the details. But I don't think the message can get through in time to set up a different location."

"Don't worry Frapacha, I'll handle it. They've probably tagged each and every one of your people from your biggest courier to your housemaid's children."

While aiding Frapacha up the stairs DesChampes called his paralegal, Chenchon, and told him to be at the Police Station within the next five minutes to process Franco out, personally deliver him to his home and arrange local security for his home. Local security was code name for the powerfully built Pointe Trois men that worked at the market abattoir and could wrestle down a huge panicked cow with such grace and efficiency, it was almost an art form. DesChampes assisted Frapacha a few feet past the registration desk to the Police Captain's office and entered without knocking. The Captain already had with a miserable expression of exhaustion chin cupped in hand as he listened to another attorney belabor his point. Frapacha now also ensured his expression of pain was made known to the Captain.

"This, I can assure you, will cost you your next term." As DesChampes gestured to Frapacha, "My client will be your next poster child vividly describing the achievements of your Police Force." With mouth ajar, frowned forehead he leaned further forward, his hands now gesticulating in the air in disbelief revealing his hairy forearms under his rolled back sleeves, "What....?'

DesChampes interrupted, "Courtesy of the hospitality of your Detective Solz Sueca. Let him explain it all to you. Expect our law suit on your desk tomorrow morning. I won't bother to tie a ribbon around it. C'mon Frapacha, let's leave these thugs to their cage management. We'll see who'll be captive in their own cage."

The attorney who had previously hijacked the Captain's attention with his matter was speechless with an expression of cynical disdain at the Captain, because he knew the sheer volume of sewage the man would have to come up with to explain yet another case of police brutality. The Captain yelled out to the front desk officer.

"Patkins, get me Sueca now! Not in one minute. Now!" He turned to the attorney who barely could contain his glee. "You're the lucky one with one minute to wrap up your point."

Chenchon sprang up the stairs into the busy reception area. His low maintenance long strings of black hair and alert black eyes were attached to a thin body that tried to fill his white shirt and black cotton polyester trousers. A brilliant legal mind that ignored the offers of guaranteed success in corporate law, his heart and talent fed on the elimination of human rights violations in Pointe Trois rainforest. "Got it boss, I'll take it from here."

DesChampes handed him over and whispered to Frapacha, "I'll call you in the morning. Let me try to get the message out in time."

Just as he turned to dash down the corridor to the main lobby, Frapacha grabbed his arm, "Thank you for coming in at the right time. You probably saved my life. Many have not made it out of those cells before."

DesChampes clasped his hand for a brief moment and said, "Don't thank me. Your angel is the little old lady in the back there." He nodded to an elderly lady quietly humming to herself as she carefully mopped the floor one line across to another. "She said she recognized your face from a photo you took with her son, who is one of your local couriers in Pointe Trois. Young fella couldn't stop talking about how you'd changed his life, changed their lives." The elderly woman continued to mop like she knew they were there but would not make eye contact. She wanted to remain unknown, unseen; precisely because of what she had seen.

"Talk soon." And in a second, DesChampes was rushing through the door into the fast approaching night back to his car. In the privacy of his beat up station wagon he had to make a quick phone call to Christian Didier, owner and Head-Chef of one of the most popular restaurants of Avalon's well-heeled class. Settling his growing pot belly underneath his steering wheel, he shuffled for his cel. phone in his lower right jacket pocket.

"Chef Didier, I am so sorry I did not inform you earlier but the family is forced to postpone 2 of grandmamma's favorite dishes in her upcoming thanksgiving dinner. It seems the root ingredients of those dishes are giving her some health complications that crop up from time to time. You know her tender condition these days."

The tattooed arm held the cel. phone of the bald head man who listened in silence as his chiseled body marched up and down his high tech. kitchen directing orders to his sous-chefs busily preparing and arranging dishes. "Of course, I remember my days with grandmamma so fondly. Not to worry, we shall remove those dishes from the party menu. My affection to her."

"Thank you Chef. We shall be in touch." Chef Didier moved to one of the side counters where he proceeded to write down a grocery list of items and quantities which he then gave to one of his cleaner boys to take to the largest produce wholesaler at the city's central open market. As the boy scurried out the back door, he yelled out after him, "Tell him I need those items fresh in the morning." Never mind that Didier had placed an order earlier in the morning and the wholesaler would immediately recognize what the list was the minute he saw its format. The message was delivered to Elder Dhaka within 20 minutes of its dispatch and it was his job to get to the two trackers of the group that had just set off after their blessing from the Chief to change the routing, timing and location of the supply drop off.

AVALON INTERNATIONAL AIRPORT CARAMONDO
DAY 1 – 17:30HRS

5 double carriage long haulers were positioned to the side of the parking bay area as 2 huge Hercules cargo aircraft taxied off the runway into their respective parking bays. The Civil Aviation Authority was not given much negotiating room when the army decided it would put in place a system to section off almost half of the airport for their own supposed classified activity. When the head of the Civil Aviation Authority complained about the inconvenience caused to commercial aircraft and violation of key international civil aviation protocols, President Gebajara promptly asked for his resignation citing his simplistic disregard for State security operations. Never mind that he was one of the foremost civil aviation experts on the continent with respected international experience. A mid-level technocrat was appointed with a job description of one word: *compliance*. To avoid too many questions being asked about the rapid increase in activity after the last elections, the army went ahead and built their own airport wing of several multi-purposed hangars. But they still had to integrate their flight plan paperwork with the Civil Aviation Authority.

Put in place was a Lt. Col. who treated civilian operations at the airport as a mere inconvenience to be tolerated. What the Lt. Col. had dismissively overlooked was that most of the casual labor and junior aviation officers at the airport were of the Burajon tribe from Pointe Trois. Technical aviation and planning staff also had close friends who were put under house arrest during last elections. The customs staff did not appreciate the pressure their Commissioner General faced to increase the country's tax revenue base while a few corrupt military folk, government and private sector conspirators laundered a section of the country that would have almost tripled the nation's tax base within a space of 6 months. As long as he had his spies placed in civilian garb in every department the Lt. Col. was satisfied these 'general employees', as he liked to refer to them, would be kept in check. Again he completely did not take into account that these general employees saw his spies bright as day and even had a code system for identifying them and their duties.

A frequent visitor of the Lt.Col. was General Bugazon. He had no interest in the serving officer or his administrative paperwork as the Lt. Col. ambitiously thought. The General never missed an appointment to collect the diamonds that would be subsequently tucked away in his wife's handbag on their way to the European or Asian continents. He was intoxicated by the sight of the planes landing with natural resources that he'd decided he owned. Keeping his and the President's bank accounts well serviced were the primary objective. The Lt. Col.

rushed to Bugazon's car door to salute him before he stepped onto the tarmac.

"Lt. Col., everything in order here?"

With the most rigid of salute, "Everything in perfect order General."

Everybody stood up and saluted as the General walked by and the Lt. Col. proudly walked next to him. In his office, the General never sat. The standard protocol was to immediately hand over the envelope of diamonds. The Lt. Col. had been too afraid to ask around of its contents, but he could guess. Then Bugazon would walk to the window and satisfactorily scan the runway.

"I can see you are doing well here. You seem to be managing the civilians just fine."

"Yes, they don't give us any problems. They do as we ask." As part of the routine, the Lt. Colonel would hand over a summary sheet of flight movements with particular attention to their contents from Pointe Trois since his last visit.

Bugazon was just in time to watch the orchestra of maneuvers. Today's landing took place earlier than usual due to inclement weather. Normally it took place at night when nobody could see most of the activity in the cargo section, and most personnel -they thought- would have gone off for the day with a skeleton staff remaining. As soon as the cargo doors of the aircraft were opened, the massive cargo haulers in skilled precision quietly rolled up and reversed up leaving a gap of 30 feet from these doors off loading. From the hangar came out 2 jumbo cranes that placed themselves in between haulers and the aircraft. With the sloping ramp of the aircraft door opened; the process of off-loading the largest tree trunks anyone would have ever seen in their urban imagination began. A conservationist would have fainted and a logger would have gone mad at the sheer immensity of each trunk.

"I shall leave you now." The Lt. Col. had stood next to him in silence as Bugazon admired the riches for him and his chosen few.

"Of course General." It was a minute's walk to the car. The Lt. Col. saluted as he closed the car door for him. His career aspirations more energized after every visit.

REBECCA'S APARTMENT
UPPER EAST SIDE, NYC
DAY 1 – 23:30HRS

Starting to doze at her study desk, she picked up her phone. "Rebecca, my child, you must know and carry the spear in your heart that you are one of the fiercest warriors at the forefront leading the battle. You do not stand alone my child, no matter where you may be. We stand in front of you, beside you, behind you. We move together. Montero may no longer be physically here but, you know more than I, his Spirit lives in our strength, just as your fighting Spirit forges through in our bones. Your pain is our pain. We shall go through together. For the generations coming, never give up, never give up; my fellow Burajon warrior."

"Thank you Chief. We shall fight on. We shall fight on." Rebecca closed her eyes to re-center herself, her strength flowing back to her.

CHAPTER 5

THE MECHANICS

DAY 2

SIMMONS PENTHOUSE, PARIS
06:30HRS

Sitting at his immaculately laid out dining room table, Simmons received an interrupting prompt from his phone as he sat for breakfast. *"Expect the stars today accompanied by a courier. It'll be hand to hand. –Your old friend."* He arose from the table walked to his bedroom and straight to his walk-in closet that was discreetly sectioned off next to the marble bathroom. Once in the closet area, at the top of the shoe bay on the rear left corner was a small control panel of buttons that no one could ever notice unless they walked completely into the cubicle of this bay area and closely scanned the woodwork. He punched in a 7 digit code and the back wall of his closet slid open from left to right without making a sound. The way it was constructed, a person would not have had the slightest idea that someone had just opened a secret study that carried the most formidable weaponry and communications equipment. Simmons called this his place of peace. His space of meditation where he had an inner calm among a display of modern automatic assault rifles, bazookas, rocket launch missiles, grenades, among other artillery. This was his family replaced. It was only in this space that he allowed himself to remember each of their faces. Pure, unharmed and killed in innocence. Some wounds never healed. They just quietly festered. The healing process had been long abandoned. *Duty*, was the only word that drove him. In the second drawer of a study desk against the wall Simmons picked out a small black book, logged into a laptop that was stationed at that desk and set about sending his message to Sergei.

"Run a thorough background check on the attached list of G. Tech employees. I want their full bios and will need this turned around within 48 hours. Look forward to your report at the soonest."

Sergei knew a bio meant the most detailed research into the weaknesses, dirt and soft spots or anything that could act as an opening for a leak on any information valuable to G. Tech. There were 12 employees. Simmons remembered he had already requested a background check on 7 of them about a year ago. But he knew habits change. People run into new problems and create more problems when trying to solve them.

He then sent out a coded message to 3 diamond dealers, 1 in Paris, 1 in Amsterdam and 1 in Antwerp. Trusted wholesalers in the business who were powerful and invisible. *"Priceless stars available. Rare find. Substantial margin guaranteed."* He logged off. Simmons gave one last look around and inhaled a whiff of the place as if he wanted to take a part of it with him to his outer world. He walked to the door, punched in the code and it started to slide back presenting a seamless walk-in closet carrying exquisite tailoring.

Very shortly after Simmons was placing some files into his briefcase that lay open on his study table, which was positioned in a mini-lounge adjacent to his living room. This intimate section was most appropriate when G. Tech did not want to be seen to be engaging certain clientele due to their reputations, a certain category who were happy to pay handsomely for the quality work of the conglomerate world. In minutes he was entering his chauffeured sedan to the office that was a 10 minute ride away. Given the signing of the agreement in 5 days in the Republic of Caramondo, a briefing report on the current position in the country had to be prepared. There were a few points that had to be highlighted in its political, economic and social mix.

Because of its vastness and variety of natural resources, governments that were the big donors to Caramondo were quite happy to cut a cheque in the form of a grant or long term loan to ensure internal stability while also containing the interference or influence of other world powers in Caramondo's affairs. This, in essence, kept the government and population at large, indolent and unambitious.

It also meant a poor tax base, educational institutions of barely survivable standards -except the missionary ones-, which resulted in a labor force that was not employable beyond its borders. The point Simmons was conveying in his report was that Pointe Trois rainforest in

Caramondo was ripe for the taking. A sleepy government crawling with corrupt officials at every level, an army command up for sale to the highest bidder and a judiciary system cowered into compliance and complacency to the ways of the chosen few. Now was the time to secure the access and rights to the Pointe Trois region, before anyone got a thought to look at their Constitution and make a mess of things.

Despite all the legalese there were 5 main driving points in this sales agreement that had to be fully consented to by the Caramondo government. They were: i) upon the date of signing, inhabitants were required to have left the rainforest no later than 6 months and no visitors of any category shall be allowed to the rainforest, ii) The Government would be fully responsible for eliminating any elements opposing the presence of G. Tech in the forest, the liquidation of which would take place within 1 month of the signing of the agreement. iii) G. Tech would be able to mine and/or extract any resource from this land as they wish upon signing the agreement. iv) G. Tech. would not be subject to any environmental or other technical audits pertaining to the rainforest. And v) Procurement of the rainforest would be an upfront payment, there would be no shared revenue arrangement arising from materials extracted out of the forest.

So far State House had not raised any objection to these major clauses in the agreement through previous negotiations. It was understood that the company would pay the Caramondo government $900 million. G. Tech. would have been willing to pay much more.

G. TECH HQ, PARIS
DAY 2 – 11:00HRS

Simmons returned from a series of meetings with his Deputy and some new clientele. They agreed between themselves that Simmons would be available for only key strategic decisions over the next 10 days. His phone chimed in his hand. It was Sergei. '*We should meet. At our usual place. Come as soon as you can.*' Simmons could not have been more pleased with himself. He hurriedly made a few calls to clear his desk for the next 3 hours and in 10 minutes was in a taxi on his way to the 15th Arrondisement that was recognized and respected as one of the most violent neighborhoods in the city. He had deliberately selected a taxi that was a bit bashed up to ensure he blended into the environment despite the signals his $3,000= Bond Street suit screamed out.

"Where to exactly sir?" Simmons murmured out the address.

The driver gave an anxious frown through his rear view mirror. Barely making eye contact, Simmons leaned forward and handed over a hefty amount that would suffice for a return trip along with a generous tip. They finally reached the Arondissement and weaved their way through a maze of rundown high-rise apartment buildings. A ghost town in some places, pockets of life in others, Simmons seemed to know his way around the works of graffiti and litter in this maze and directed the driver to the building of his awaited appointment.

As he got out of the cab Simmons muttered, "I shan't be long."

Reaching for the broken heavy door of the building, he heard the wheels of the cabs screech off. Simmons gave an unperturbed glance over his shoulder. The cab driver had noticed the expensive coat that Simmons had purposefully left behind knowing the headache it would cost the driver to disappear off with such a piece of property in his back seat.

Walking up the 8 flights of stairs, Simmons walked down a dimly lit long corridor of 10 doors on each side, most with their own internal cacophony of loud music, TV or spirited conversation. He walked to the 10th door on the left and knocked on the door hard three times.

"Who is it?" A coarse voice that was probably in his early 40s interrogated through. "The insurance agent. Policy renewal sir."' Simmons replied.

He could hear the chains being pulled back from their latches and doubles bolts being unlocked and the door handle turned. Simmons background had trained his mind to expect the unexpected. With his hands casually at his side, the man that opened the door was sculpted with walnut brown hair and long thin side burns. To any outsider it was obvious that the man and the apartment did not match. A hiding cell, local branch office, if you like. An address where matters of sensitive detail could be discussed where the rest of the world did not rush to visit. His butter yellow sleeveless Polo turtle neck and light grey tailored slacks were even more of a mismatch for his setting. Simmons walked in. The man quickly shut the door returning the locks to their original position then turned around to Simmons.

"No news is good news for my clients. It means all is well and you do not need my help to sort out your quandary. Let me come to the point. 10 of your staff in these departments seem to have respectable lives save for the odd drunk-driving offense or high credit card debt. However there are two that do come to my attention.

Namely a Dr. Nigel Fruthers your senior software systems developer, part of the recent acquisition from Quantum Software Developers and a Dr. Lao Pei Qing, your Lab Director in Hong Kong who runs his department like a little military outfit. That unit is among the most disciplined of your 2,531 staff of several companies performance figures show. Nigel Fruthers, aged 39 an only child of Michael and Gail Fruthers is a genius but also a man of a few weaknesses, or should I say vulnerabilities. He hails from the English countryside recognized as a math genius since his early days of primary school in one of these rural counties. Scoring among the top in the country in his A-level, he received a full scholarship to Cambridge. After Cambridge, he did his PhD at MIT in molecular structures in minerals on loans. By the time he'd completed his education he was in debt to the tune of $350,000=. A good chunk of that was interest growing. He would occasionally commiserate among his few friends that he had no idea how he was going to clear this debt.

According to a close friend of Nigel, his problems really got bad when he failed to kick a certain habit that started during their graduation night celebrations of their PhDs. This was about 12 years ago. The group of friends had never spotted him with a girl in the 5 years they'd been with him in Massachusetts, but he would often ogle at them. Sort of like his boyish countryside innocence dogged him. He never became more cosmopolitan with his new environs. So his friends decided to give him an initiation of sorts and took him to a brothel where they had a special party arranged for him. They went their separate ways after graduation but one of his friends a few years later told another, that the brothel owner said Nigel was one of their best customers when he was in town. Whether making up for lost time in that department or as a stress reliever, he would rack up quite a bill which he would clear periodically. My contact at the Boston Police Department said his name came up in a case 4 years ago when a 19 year old known to work from that brothel overdosed in his living room. He called an ambulance; she was dead on arrival at the County General Hospital. The girl's parents, who looked to be in an equally difficult position as their daughter, wanted to sue him for murder and it is an open secret that the Chief Investigator is taking a monthly bribe from him, as he does on so many other cases, so that this investigation never quite comes together. Quantum Software Development was impressed with his PhD and signed him on to a salary Fruthers simply could not turn down even though he was more interested in research than commercial applications. He managed his education debts but never his weakness. He developed a name for himself with his cutting edge work through papers he presented at global forums. The acquisition of Quantum Software by G. Tech made him and his colleagues very wealthy. The only detail being, that if something happened to that Chief Investigator he could go straight to jail. Not to mention the publicity of the lawsuit from the girl's family would end his career."

Simmons was annoyed at Nigel's indelicate position. He knew if Sergei's associates worked for the competition they could have the same file whipped up in the same 5 minutes he did. There needs to be some action on Dr. Fruthers he figured. As Simmons tossed around ideas in his mind, Sergei started to talk about the next employee that posed a threat to those who would have G. Tech.'s control over world security.

"Dr. Lei Xiao Ping is the Director of the Research Laboratory in Hong Kong. He is also at the top of his field and known for his regimented approach to the Lab. The competition has constantly tried to poach him but G. Tech. keeps increasing his salary or providing some perk or another to keep him on their team. It was only through a recent argument that caused a major shake-up of staff within a competitor company of Research Labs that we found out. The competition was expecting some breakthrough formula from Dr. Ping that he'd promised to sell to them but never came through and their Directors were none too pleased with their unrealized product launch. Dr. Ping, unbeknownst to all of us, has been a very active man. If this company had been a satisfied customer we would never have found out about his roaring business. The good Doctor has been keeping company secrets under wraps alright. But once G. Tech. launches the product that uses the research breakthrough, instead of the competition waiting for the patent to come out, Dr. Ping sells the patent application with a slight variation or modification in Hong Kong and mainland Coriames, so it doesn't look like direct theft. Nobody is sure if he is a serving member of the communist party, but it is known that his father is a big wig in the Party. I have my people working on it. The man doesn't dream big though. He sells these secrets for a poultry $100,000=, $200,000= a piece, probably because the research is no longer a comparative advantage or he doesn't want to attract any attention. But your problem is that the man does move information on the streets. And we need to be clear whether he is a quiet member of the Communist Party. Because then it becomes a question of loyalty, duty and honor; not bank account. The selling part could be diversionary or just a bad habit he's developed."

"I get your point." Simmons responded with a perturbed frown.

He didn't like the feel of this one. Experience had taught him that dealing with people who were carrying out their duty for the honor and not the economic gain of it were a real pain to deal with because they were willing to outbid, outperform or outwait you all in the name of honor and this could prove extremely uneconomical to you in time or money when gunning for the same prize. The fact that another world superpower was involved was even less appealing a factor. This could score him either major loyalty points or even a promotion if he was a cadre in the communist party. Not to mention if he got a brain wave he could decide to sell his information before it was applied by G. Tech. and get a healthy sum for it.

"My dear friend," Sergei interrupted, "you seem a bit perturbed by this second individual. I would suppose for obvious reasons. I will confirm to you whether he has political links and revert."

"Very well." Simmons said with a sigh.

"Anyone else that comes to mind that might be a problem waiting to undo itself all over us?" As I mentioned, just some traffic offenses, gambling debt or credit card bills; a reasonably boring lot I must say. If anything new crops up, will let you know."

Simmons started to arise, still quietly mulling over the information just received. He scanned the room as he reached into the right inner breast pocket of his jacket and pulled out an envelope that contained $30,000=. He remembers behind the door of the next room was actually a 10ft by 12ft space of the most hi-tech. equipment probably available in Paris that was able to intercept, access and download data from several mainframes that ran the most mundane –but revealing- of data. Essentially tapping into mainframes of different entities across the globe ranging from bank details, hospitals records, government files, police reports to private companies of any type. Sergei's IT capabilities could match up to the best at G. Tech. The Russians had invested heavily in training their next generation. Sergei invested heavily in keeping his skills current. Removing the locks, he gave Simmons a quick nod back as his client swiftly made a turn back out into the hallway. In a few minutes he was standing back on the pavement.

The cab driver looked mildly frantic with a perspired forehead. He had already turned the vehicle around positioned for a hasty exit in case any human being walked in his direction. In 20 minutes Simmons was back at his office walking past Graciella with a questioning look on her face. He looked at her with a distraught expression. "That take-away last night, just didn't agree with me."

Graciella had never known her boss to be sick in the 9 years she'd worked for him. But she wasn't paid to tag his movements. Her job was to make sure her office of double contracts and discreet clients ran like a dream machine. Her focus was being a magician not a matron.

PR&S, NEW YORK
DAY 2 - 07:30HRS

Overnight information kept streaming in from other lawyers that had been in the process of compiling their dossiers of research. On Rebecca's conference table were some of the bodies of work received in hard copy, besides her own set of compiled evidence in the form of affidavits, case precedents, photographs, environmental technical assessments, analysis of human rights violations among other documentation. It was a sea of information that was shaping into a clear convincing story. She and Marc had spent the night constructing a comprehensive case. He was feeling fresh and smelling fragranced after taking a shower at the building's health club facility. His change into his smart casual clothes and a strong cup of coffee had him rearing to go as he fine-tuned his thoughts on the body of work they had woven together thus far. Rebecca on the other hand was operating on a mixture of caffeine and pain, embittered with anger.

She could feel her blood thicken. If this case presented to Ambassador Holstein and his colleagues was not convincing to the certain powerful governments that were part of the U.N. Security Council, then her own tribe was going to die out quietly and quickly. And she knew that she would die along with them because she couldn't live with the thought of having let down her own people when it was only a signature on an agreement that determined their extinction or survival. And it was very clear to Rebecca that if it was signed, she would never see her home again since the conglomerate would deny her entry due to once being identified as hostile to the agreement.

Rebecca thought out loud, "Marc, do you realize this agreement between the government and G-Tech. cannot be signed. The Rainforest Consortium has to get the lease on Pointe Trois because if it isn't G-Tech, it will be their competition or another company sent by G-Tech with a much smarter strategy?"

"Yes, I do." He replied while re-organizing pages of reports.

Rebecca fought off sleep like a sedative slowly working on her. She guzzled her coffee, straightened up her spine, patted her cheeks hard with her palms, bolted open her eyes then focused her gaze on Marc whose eyes perused files as he sipped his coffee.

"Ok, hit me. What d'ya got? Convince me to never allow a private entity to purchase our spot on our planet." said Rebecca.

Marc flashed out an excited grin as if invited to a draw. "Well, no matter what may be in that agreement, the case is based on 3 simple but fundamental premises:

The first is a straightforward legal issue. The government cannot lease out or sell land on which it does not have the authority to transact. Most of that land is owned by clans and families and final approval from the Chief is required if a family or individual decided to dispose of it. There is a major debate in Parliament going on about this right now. So, as of today, G. Tech. and the government are treading on legal quick sand.

The second is that the inhabitants of Pointe Trois rainforest require protection from government forces of which there is sufficient evidence of human rights violations. Essentially, a people who once existed peacefully among themselves and in harmony with nature are now enduring constant attacks from government and are reduced to sickly slave labor. Today they defend themselves from those that are supposed to defend them. Tomorrow they will defend themselves from the greed of a private entity with unlimited resources where no one will be able to hear their call for help because there will be no access to this spot on the globe. Innocent populations must be defended by a global social conscience and international organizations with the responsibility and authority to prevent the continued abuse of human rights especially in the most remote regions of the world. If the global community does not act now, it would have sanctioned the extinction of a people at the mercy of a conglomerate that believes shareholder value of the very few is justifiable to the extinction of anyone or anything standing in their way.

The third is conservation of the most pristine parts of the world that still has untapped contribution to science, technology and medicine. It is in these most remote regions that the wildlife, plant life and minerals have been documented as extra-ordinarily unique or even not yet documented at all. The obnoxious idea of this agreement is to serve as global prohibition to companies with an itch to drill, mine or cut through the few remaining pristine spots on this planet, especially in light of the current greenhouse emissions that must be reduced. To preserve the forest in its current condition and prevent the uprooting or ruin of everything in it, remains a global responsibility."

"I'm still with you." She egged on.

"A major concern is the lack of institutional independence and integrity in every area of government and the public sector at large, the Judiciary has not been immune. The Supreme Court and High Court Judges are not appointed only because of political affiliation with the Head of State, but because they are there to do the specific bidding of the person that appointed them. The consequences of following the Law and one's conscience are not only early retirement or outright removal under sudden 'medical' or 'personal' reasons; but clear persecution of one's legal career. Rebecca, nobody needs to tell you that these fellows are not taking any prisoners on this deal. Even with a global stink about it, they'll still go scrambling for the mega-bucks air freshener public relations machine and squeeze this transaction through like an elephant through a key hole."

Rebecca sounded neither perturbed nor discouraged. "Please schedule a meeting with Ian Thornton who I think is taking over from Catherine, Julia Dames for some PR clout and Etienne Frechan who fund a fair chunk of Caramondo's national budget with his organization. These three will be strategic for us over the coming days. Time to kick up a storm that G-Tech or the government of Caramondo will find very difficult to quietly manage away."

"Done." He replied walking out.

Julia Dames was known in New York City and Washington DC as the no-nonsense PR powerhouse that had bloodied the noses of a few established organizations trying to defame her clients and Etienne Frechan was an aristocratic, unassuming Director of Fund Management at the Continental Funding Organization known for his rigidity of his principles.

Marc walked back in a couple of moments later. "Strangest thing a young man, I don't know from where, says I should walk in immediately and hand this over to you. He says it's from Father Raines."

Rebecca felt the tension of revenge spike through her for a brief moment. She suspected the content examining the plain white unaddressed envelope as she opened it. Father Raines was careful not to identify the sender or the beneficiary. Marc had decided he was not going to move as he closely studied her face. What more could there possibly be to tell her? Her head tilted slightly as she read the plain sheet of paper: *General Paint brand did the damage to the building*. There was a coding for each high ranking member of the army. General Paint referred to General Pitua. She knew his greed and ruthlessness were his trademark. Rebecca instantly reminded herself to gloss over the steely glaze that had surfaced in her eyes.

"Great, thanks. Travel agent versatility."

"Uh huh." was his slightly suspicious stare, as Marc turned walking out. Rebecca waited a couple of seconds with her cel. phone in her hand just to be sure he wouldn't turn back in surprise checking to be sure she was ok when he knew she was not. He had the habit of doing so irregularly.

Quickly she dialed an anonymous number in the capital city Avalon. There was only tapping on the other side. Rebecca spoke in a matter of fact tone. "General Paint needs to be scratched off. It has been the cause of the damaged to the building. Please be thorough." The end of her sentence was met with a thud. This was the acknowledgement the conversation was understood. Rebecca hung up. She exhaled a deep breath. She thought she had walked away from that life. Those killings would always haunt her. "But this one, I have to finish." She said to herself. The conflict mounted. Was she a lawyer or a killer? Her mind cross-examined her.

G.TECH HQ, PARIS
DAY 2 – 12:00HRS

Simmons worked through some of the files his analysts had piled up on his desk for the 2 hours he was out visiting the basic architecture of the Arondissement. Drier slowly but authoritatively walked through the door without knocking as a way to be politely impolite. He was the only one unannounced by Graciella. And Drier never stamped his authority on anyone. It was just understood. He gave orders that were never questioned or delayed.

"I'm sure you're aware that the 2 specialists from New York are en-route to you and should be landing about 5:00pm. They've asked for an hour to freshen up then we'll have a meeting at the hangar with Baynes at 6:00pm and then head out to Caramondo in 2 separate jets. Reason being that some of us will head straight to Hong Kong to follow-up on the test results based on samples of the mineral mix from the soil collected and some will come back to Paris."

Simmons was furiously calculating in his mind how between 12noon and 6:00pm how he was going to handle his personal agenda of the diamonds. Not to mention the files that he still had to handle on his desk. He had to figure out a way to get Drier out of his office at the soonest without rousing his finely tuned suspicion.

"Ok, that sounds good. I'll organize my crew from this end in the coming hours and we'll be at the hangar at 6:00pm." said Simmons, knowing full well he would not be able to do his needful within the confines of his office. To his relief Drier had not even bothered to sit down. Instead he casually walked about Simmons office very slowly admiring his artifacts large and small as if he was looking for something out of place. Simmons quietly eyed this slow perusal and didn't appreciate feeling as if he was getting a once-over with smooth precision.

"The report you sent out highlighted the basic facts succinctly enough. My main concerns are to ensure that the Head of State and his cronies trip up on their own greed and would be happy to sign with their own blood. After killing its leader, their main task is to snuff out that militia. You know the corporate policy, we don't get involved in other people's wrangles. It all needs to be neatly tied up before we dispatch any of our personnel or drilling equipment. This operation has to go through without a hitch and that's why we pay you the big bucks.

See you at the hangar at 6:00pm." He said as he walked out without closing the door behind him.

Simmons didn't appreciate the smug remark. He knew the $700,000=per year plus bonuses was entry level salary compared to what Drier was receiving. He would take his legal and military experts with him. He summoned for Reginald Carthwaite and Boris Kreshnakov.

Simmons hands flicked through the updated Caramondo intelligence file. He couldn't stop staring at photos of all the key players, analyzing and re-analyzing their profiles, looking for that crack in their background that would be a convenient blackmailing point when push came to shove. There she was. The one he couldn't bribe or blackmail to his agenda. He stared at her photo. While he found Rebecca to be the problem that needed to be purged, he admired and respected her patriotism to defend her homeland to her last breath as her brother had just done. He knew that was the only family she had remaining. He stared at her long black hair and vulnerable smile. He felt a connection with her. He knew her loneliness. That particular type of pain that now motivated her mission. He reached out and touched her face. Graciella opened the door. He snapped the file shut. Dare he fraternize with the source of the biggest complication on his desk, he chided himself. The two gentlemen walked in.

Reginald was his sharpest and most ruthless legal mind. *'Fearless and furious'* was his nickname among his colleagues. Simmons wanted him on task in case the Head of State much less government counsel decided to tamper with his key clauses or if the environmentalists wanted to question the legality of the transaction. Reginald could have a cup of tea with anyone and had the talent to interrogate them in the form of a casual interview or shock an informant into involuntarily providing information in record time. He left no stone unturned and moved fast. His mixed heritage combined with his very average height and looks made it difficult for people to place him and subsequently grossly underestimated the character in their midst.

Kreshnakov was the quiet operator. Mostly in the field, by chance he happened to be in Paris receiving a briefing for his next assignment deep in the rainforest on another continent. But that would have to wait now. His specialty was tracking and neutralizing of hostile threats to G.Tech. operations in rainforest type territory.

Simmons wanted him there to assess the capacity of the militia and see if the Caramondo Army really knew what it was doing with its unending operations to eliminate the Pointe Trois militia. But he was well aware it was also the government's cover to loot as much as possible for as long as possible in the rainforest. Boris was hand- picked by Drier out of a specific Russian Special Forces Unit. Among other Special Forces Units they were the elite of the elite and their Unit Commander received orders only from or answered directly to the Russian President. His tall muscular build, pale skin, platinum blond hair and blue eyes were typical Siberian off-shoot. To the contrary of his physical appearance, his training and experience had made him most at home in 100% humidity, mosquito infested tropical rainforest. Simmons briefed them for 10 minutes highlighting salient points he wanted each of them to cover in their respective areas of expertise. He subsequently gave instructions to Graciella to have detailed files prepared for each of them and for the other analysts to be available to them to provide whatever additional information they required.

"See you at the hangar at 6:00pm then gentlemen," concluded Simmons. "Yes sir." They replied in unison.

As they left his office, Simmons spoke into his intercom and informed Graciella that he had some key potential client meetings that would be handled from his penthouse. Some very lucrative accounts had come this way. Graciella did not question.

He threw the pack of Caramondo files into his briefcase. In 3 minutes he was in the elevator as he closed his eyes in a moment's reflection while it whizzed him down to the lobby. He walked out of the building into the sunlight and undisturbed concrete he would not know for a few days. From previous secret visits to Pointe Trois he knew you could work up a sweat from just fanning yourself to cool down. His driver gently swayed through the traffic lights as he observed tourists and residents with their precisely cut bags from courtier stores in their own fish bowls of shopping experiences. The thousand twinkles of the chandelier in his building foyer felt like little sparks of ideas in his mind gathering together to put his plan into seamless execution.

But Simmons did not miss the nodding signal the front desk attendant gave to the slender, elegant gentleman in a pin-stripe suit seated at the back corner of the foyer. He couldn't have been more than his early 50s but also looked a little too agile for a corporate executive. With the distant indirect eye Simmons kept on him, he knew he was the subject of the man's mission. An instant pang of regret hit him that he had stopped carrying his FN-P45. The path to the private elevator for the penthouse suites would not be to his advantage. In the event this was a skilled operator he could do some damage without making a fuss. There were no unfortunate witnesses or objects to alter the trajectory of a bullet. To slow down his pace would alert the man and surprise was his only weapon. Simmons made a sharp right to the elevator hoping it would open immediately. He breathed a sigh of shallow relief as he stepped in turned around, inserted his key card and pushed the close-door button as fast as he could. As he leaned back watching the doors, a hand firmly intercepted the infrared beam automatically programming the doors to slide back.

"Mr. Simmons, do I detect a rush? That would be so unlike you."

Simmons mind rolodexed with lightning speed to all the people he thought would send a British assassin to neutralize him and this one didn't look like he came cheap. He glanced at the man beckoning him to continue with his point.

"Alrighty then, if you wish.'

The elevator doors opened into Simmons's vestibule, as far as he was concerned he was now on his territory and this man would be returning back down in a body bag to the basement into the boot of his Jaguar X5 Cougar and a drive straight to the dog fighting camp where the animals there were driven by behavior that would traumatize their domesticated counter parts. Simmons had given some lucrative contracts to the owner's brother in Algeria some years back. As the man walked straight to Simmons dining room, he reached into his inner breast pocket he pulled out a black velvet pouch and delicately untied it on the dining room table. Simmons watched in disbelief and slight confusion since he knew that these were not the movements of an assassin. One of them would have been long dead by now. From the black pouch he pulled out a black velvet cloth the size of a handkerchief then sprawled out its contents. Simmons was pleasantly surprised by the quality of the stones that lay before him. They were consistent with the initial sampling at the hotel room.

"There we go chappy. Come closer, take a good look. Why don't you go and find your telescope?" Simmons couldn't believe he was now taking instructions from a man he was about to kill five seconds ago.

He walked to some cabinets in the mini-lounge next to the living room and pulled the telescope out of a cabinet and was back at the dining room table.

"Courtesy of Lannier, he was rather particular that you should roughly grade each stone and acknowledge receipt."

From his shirt pocket the man pulled out a pen and paper and patted them onto the table. Simmons was now asking himself how he was going to flog these diamonds before heading out to Caramondo. The man noticed his slightly distanced gaze.

"Say old boy, are you okay there? Let's get on with it shall we?" he said looking at Simmons a bit warily wondering what had overcome a man he knew to be in precise control of his faculties.

"Yes of course." said Simmons looking slightly jolted back into reality.

As he scanned the stones, Simmons appreciated that their quality was not bad at all. Pending the level of supply in the market the total consignment could fetch up to $17-18 million if he didn't let on that he needed to sell fairly quickly. He would never share his appreciation of these stones with Lannier before he got any ideas about decreasing his cut or even developed a tone of confidence that he was giving Simmons a good deal. After 15 minutes of roughly scanning Simmons was through. He unfolded the sheet of paper laid next to the diamonds and signed against the one sentence acknowledgement, slid it back to the man who in one deft move confirmed the signature, put the pen and paper back into his breast pocket.

"There now, that wasn't too hard was it? For a moment there you looked a bit edgy. Like you thought I's some kind of assassin, dear me." He walked toward the entrance of the dining room, opened his jacket but opened it just wide enough to make sure Simmons would see the HS2000 with a suppressor attached. He pulled out a cigar, put it on the table and cheerily said, "On the house. You know, there are good transactions and there are bad transactions. Glad we were a good one."

In a few footsteps he was standing at the elevator doors. Lannier's courier stepped in, turned around and gave a tight smile as the doors closed. Simmons could feel his body temperature rise and fall. He did not appreciate transactions riding up on him like that, asserting themselves in his penthouse. He made a mental note to have the front desk attendant beaten within an inch of his life in 2 weeks and then fired. Doing it immediately would be too obvious a connection.

He walked to his secret study to check his messages. Had any of the diamond dealers responded? This was the only window of opportunity to see them. *"How brightly do your stars shine in the night? Let us look through the telescope. Come around."*

"Very good." Simmons declared to himself.

A dealer in Antwerp had responded. He had only a few hours to get there and back to Paris by 17:00hrs. *"I shall come around soon."* He replied and logged off walking further into the study to pick some equipment that he thought might be of use to him while in Caramondo. From the rack he removed his SIG P250, Glock 17 as useful handguns and decided to bring down the FAMAS G2 what he thought to be a very handy assault rifle. Boxes of cartridges, his custom design Swiss army knife and global satellite phone that could fire off 3 lethal darts at close range were thrown in the bag. Because there would be no baggage scanning he was more intent on protecting himself, his mission objective and his team should the need arise.

PR&S, NEW YORK

DAY 2 – 10:30HRS

The pain choked her. Rebecca's eyes froze. The cold sweat on her forehead and the warm sweat in her palms were now presenting themselves to the world. This regular visitor of the unknown that gripped and sucked her into her deepest fears without notice was a nightmare forcing its imprint on her. Being raped in her mind over and over, it was too much. She grabbed her glass of water, lunged for the tissue box at the end of her desk and hurriedly patted her forehead, lips and palms.

Marc was on the intercom. "I'm coming in with the group."

Rebecca grabbed a last gulp of water. In a moment he opened the door. Ian, Julia and Etienne walked into Rebecca's office. Marc quickly looked her over to see how she was holding up. He shot her a look saying "I'm here for you". He had informed the group earlier. They had each called her and spent a few minutes with her on the phone. It was a somber mood. Each gave her a warm hug before they sat down at the conference table. Ian spoke with firmness and deep affection.

"Rebecca on behalf of all of us, we are with you all the way. We will get through this together. Together, we shall."

The strain was evident on her face. "Thank you Ian. Thank you all for your kind words and love that you have shown me. Interestingly, focusing on the task at hand is the best medicine for me or I will go into total meltdown losing the brief window of opportunity that we have." Rebecca jumped straight into the matter at hand. "Obviously you're aware of the pushed up signing. I'm even told they'll make it as low key as possible to avoid attracting any unwanted attention, particularly any bad PR towards G. Tech. I've just received a package with the most alarming evidence to date. In it are photos and film footage of the rampage of the land and its people.

Ambassador Holstein at the UN says its needs to be a case of global social conscience or it becomes a tough sell purely because we're talking about a few hundred thousand people versus the millions that have been massacred by other militant leaning governments and the U.N. hasn't yet effectively applied any real pressure on those folks. What we need is to do is shine the spotlight of world social outrage and strategic institutional pressure on them in order to maintain the heat just hot and long enough to melt down their deal. And bear in mind it's not the first time for G. Tech. to operate in a sensitive location and continue to maintain a spotless record. The President needs to know his decision to go ahead with this deal will be directly linked to his external budget support. Keep in mind that many of the conservation organizations that have agreed to be signatories to this Rainforest Consortium are yet to meet in a month. Realistically the whole process could take up to 3 months and we have only 5 days." As her eyes drifted out to the window, Rebecca began to doubt whether the rainforest consortium could manage to come together even if they wanted to; given the procedures and protocols these international organizations had to comply with.

Julia's calming voice brought Rebecca back to the meeting. "Ok, that's the bright side. It could be worse. I like that. Let's start disseminating the facts of the case to a few hundred million people in real time. We need to put some attention to their activities in Pointe Trois. People need to see what they are actually doing right now, this minute. Need to get live footage from Pointe Trois like yesterday. 5 days is a fast closing window of opportunity to do some real damage." Rebecca looked at Ian, who looked like any pragmatic comfortable law student from a wealthy upbringing, but was an encyclopedia of information of laws on how to nail governments violating their populations' rights, structuring and networking local legal groups to be effective in their daily struggles of intimidation, harassment and advocacy.

Ian chimed in, "Rebecca, you mentioned to me on the phone earlier you'd sent a message to Pointe Trois requesting the updates. I'll coordinate with the human rights activists in Avalon. They normally make sure we get whatever we need."

Julia continued, "We'd like the coverage to be on CNN, BBC, Sky and Al-Jazeera within 72 hours because that's only 3-4 days remaining. I realize that gives them only 48 hours or so to get the coverage given the nature of the territory they'll be moving around."

Rebecca was re-energized by Julia's target-lock approach.

"Along with the TV stories, I'll line up the New York Times, Washington Post, USA Today, the Herald, Sun, Guardian, Observer and Le Figaro newspapers for starters. The point, however, is to create an emotional wave of outrage as soon as the facts come out, otherwise the media won't stick with it and we only have 48-72 hours max of publicity. The purpose of the media blitz is to kill the pristine image G. Tech. has worked so hard to protect. So charities, corporate partners and consumers back away from them and they start to look shady, shifty and simply unattractive. The conglomerate would have to decide if that's the price they're willing to pay. Have to get to G. Tech. through their customer base and other entities that matter to them. A couple of quick surveys with a few key questions that all mean the same thing, 'Do you think Gen. Tech. should pull out? Do you think what G. Tech. is doing is right? Would you buy your products from a company like this?' Survey done to 1000 people on the East coast, 1000 on the west coast, 1000 in London. The objective is to make G. Tech feel like they are in the process of serious irreversible damage. It is possible for a conglomerate to lose mega-bucks in sales or through their share price drop and shareholders don't stick around for that kind of loss. It is possible to make a global corporation, even if powerful and spotless, to become so unpopular all of a sudden they look ripe for a hostile take-over. The point being that this may look insurmountable but it is doable. We just have to manage our timing very tightly with the remaining days left." Julia was clear, powerful and charged without blinking her large hazel eyes not even softened by her freckles and large ginger curls. She stiffly nodded her head as if to say the war had been declared, time to launch the missiles.

"One more thing Rebecca, what public sentiment needs to understand is that the rainforest consortium is not a bunch of green-extremists. Everyone is aware our cel. phones and laptops rely on certain minerals found largely in the rainforests. But the simple point is that there must be a transparent, responsible way to preserve these unique eco-systems while also utilizing and continuing to explore the resources they hold. Social opinion should be clear that agreements signed, resources extracted and profits earned must resemble some levels of sustainability and free-trade. Their lawyers and lobbyists must also stop acting like mercenaries for hire on behalf of their clients. We'll shape the discussion with the media."

Etienne looked a bit worried with his bushy boyish hair and sky blue polo office shirt, expensive khaki slacks and loafers to boot.

With his deep French accent he started, "Mes amis, Caramondo has always been a difficult client for us. Just between you and me, for the grants and development financing we have put into this country in the last 15 years which is about 22% of their budget, we have very little to show for it, beyond a section of the country that happens to be related to the President. So if there's an opportunity to squeeze a pint of compliance from the government or simply knock them off our budget, then that opening would be most welcome. We get too much grief from our own funders about this particular country and its performance on our books. Please alert your people in advance we are willing to participate, provided it will be a strategically coordinated pressure. We don't want to cut their line and then they simply go to another funding organization which would leave us politically exposed for all our ongoing jointly funded projects."

Rebecca's voice now picked up in hope. "That is precisely why we have Dr. Elizabeth Sheldon, current Chair of the Roundtable of Global Donors as part of a larger more strategic group that would be the comprehensive approach to ensure that they wouldn't be able to look left or right for alternative funding on a bi-lateral or multi-lateral basis. The room to bargain, shift and maneuver around wouldn't be there. And that is the aim of this thrust, to ensure it is all or nothing and they find themselves dead broke within 3 months. The weak link in all of this is the Coriamese government that is funding about 45% of their budget support in grants and very soft loans, not to mention the value of the road infrastructure. The Caramondo government could easily decide to request that a certain amount of the road fund be redirected to emergency cash for public service operations and they'll keep hobbling along until the global social outrage moves on to the next hot topic. Trust me, they'll be banking on that. These guys are in for the long haul and they'll lay low stagger along until it's good for them to resurface with re-negotiations."

Rebecca turned her body towards Ian as she continued to speak while still making eye contact with Etienne.

"The decisive factor that will work here is the collective threat on the budget cuts. If it's only 1 or 2 they'll make up the difference with the others." She shot a glance at Ian, who cut in.

"The local human rights and environmental bodies will need a lot of support. We'll put them on a salary for 3 months so they can focus exclusively on the task at hand getting the feeds, working with the Members of Parliament and making sure the donor representatives are up to date beyond the government spin. I'll get my right hand person, Emily, to coordinate full-time on it. She's our angel with a sword. She will also ensure the live feeds are sourced from the rainforest within the next 48 hours. While it is the next 3-4 days that are the most relevant particularly with the debate in Parliament about the legality of this sale agreement, it is also the laws that need to be put in place thereafter so any attempts down the road by corrupt officials and investors to bend the legal environment to their favor legally or illegally are met by a steel wall of laws and commercial regulations. We don't know where the Parliament vote will land, but we have to be ready to install a legal foundation in the country that will undo any votes or private group consensus anywhere to transact on the natural resources of the country. And you can be sure G. Tech will not take this lying down. That's why it is essential to have a world of witnesses to see in plain view what their version of commercial justice is all about through the media coverage."

Rebecca pondered for a moment.

"Let's reconvene day after tomorrow and see what holes are left to fill in plans rolling out. They bade goodbyes and Rebecca walked back to her desk with a pensive gaze, palms clasped together in a brief prayer.

"God it is not for me. It is for my people for my homeland. Let not Montero have died in vain." Her eye caught a delicate lace envelope peeking out from in between her files in her in-tray that would not have survived any courier system. As she opened it and read the wedding invitation, she couldn't imagine a more inopportune timing of her best friend's marital vows. Thankfully it was one of those weekday evening weddings. Both she and Simone came from Pointe Trois together in the first scholarship group and were star performers throughout their education. After Harvard she had gone onto John Hopkins Medical School where she met General Piquant's son who was also studying medicine about 7 years ago. Simone had just received her Pediatric license and her fiancé was about to complete his residency as a Cardiologist. It was a shining moment for the Caramondo community in New York.

Rebecca decided that she would offer her most profound apologies for missing the Church service and be at the reception for only 2 hours in order to maximize every hour she had. As a couple they had both been hugely supportive of her efforts so far to stop the transaction on the rainforest. The groom had seen for himself, through his father's colleagues, how brutal and ruthless this closed group could be. She knew Father Raines would also be attending the wedding.

Marc walked in with a sense of urgency. "I've dispatched the package of material to Ambassador Holstein. He'll have it by end of today. But get this, an engineer buddy of mine who works at the company that maintains corporate jets has G. Tech. as one of their clients. He knows we're working on the case. Says a small team of theirs just took off for Paris with 2 jets where they'll join other colleagues and both jets are set off to fly to Caramondo tomorrow night. He overheard one of them on the phone talk about an agreement."

CHAPTER 6

SOFT HANDS

As Speaker Benjamin LaFonte took his chair, you would have thought that the 3 gentlemen awaiting him respectfully looked at him as he took his throne. When he had expressed an urgency in meeting them and told them to come prepared to handle business, they each knew that meant they better be prepared to put some blood on the counter, park some manure and move some mammoths into place without the slightest ruffle of a feather. They had been selected because of their skill of making the improbable and downright illegal look like business as usual.

With solemn and pensive expressions in front of the Speaker sat Lawrence Carrion a business tycoon in the country that had earned the initial bulk of his fortune through overpricing government when building the army and police barracks followed by most of the Ministerial and state-enterprise buildings. He soon decided to globalize his investments to give him more of a legitimate façade and bought into prime real estate in major capitals of the world. The bulk of his local fortune still came from his mysterious knack of winning over 80% of contracts at the Ministry of Housing for government housing and other key infrastructure all under different company names.

Next to him was the man voted by Caramondo's populace as the country's most shrewd politician for almost 2 decades. Maxwell Fisher had been Chief Whip of Parliament for the past 20 years and developed a power base not only within the ruling party but also among opposition members. A calculating negotiator, he had navigated the most controversial Bills into Law such as the removal of term limits, impunity for members of the armed forces found guilty of gross human rights abuses in Pointe Trois and a law that allows you to build your mansion or commercial building in environmental wetlands. Not to mention that it was an open secret that he owned the most well-resourced and effective investigative agency in town. He had enough dirt on the majority of prominent figures in the country. Hon. Fisher had made powerful people do things they had no plans of doing, including his colleagues in Parliament. The most recent of which was a powerful politician of the opposition stepping down a year before his term ended to allow a weak corruptible entrant to replace him in order to ensure some Bills would pass through in view of the close numbers. His aristocratic features that complimented his slender muscles carried an odd dry smile and unexpected delicate gait about him. Maxwell was respected purely out of fear. It was too dangerous to like him.

Next to him was a diminutive younger man wearing thick spectacles that covered half his face with a nerdish youthful haircut. Edgar Pratt, a genius with numbers, wore an expression of a pit-bull ready on the go for the discussion outcomes of the gentlemen in this building. These were individual power centers he had met before on separate occasions. Edgar was the senior manager of Institutional and Corporate accounts of five hundred thousand dollars and above at the Central Bank. He supervised a staff of twelve to ensure the reconciled position of accounts between the Central Bank and financial institutions. These were Real Time Gross Transfers that had to be precise and efficient due to the cost of even minor delays. The Speaker did not waste a minute.

"Gentlemen, I gather you are all aware that the G. Tech. group is already on their way here to admire the bride before the marriage, if you will, and we 3 need to ensure that this transaction doesn't cause so much as a blip on anyone's radar screen in this country. While it may be getting all sorts of attention among certain groups in New York we know, and they know we know, that there isn't a blesséd thing that they can do about it unless we invite them to intervene."

As he sarcastically rolled his eyeballs, LaFonte fixed his gaze on Maxwell first. "I've heard the debates on the floor and frankly it sounds like it could go either way. Now the Bill as it stands, it is to simply ratify it into Law that the government has the right to sell or lease any portion of land in the country where it deems fit to any party, whether foreign or local. It does not require consent of the owners. Obviously the opposition is up in arms and swears over their dead bodies that this will never happen because they know specifically which parcel of land we're referring to." The Speaker briefed.

Maxwell responded, "Not to worry. I know who the ringleaders are. They really are waving their principles all over everyone's face with interesting comments about patriotism and protecting the land for the people, defending the most innocent. It can become exasperating sometimes. I'll put my people onto it and I'm sure we can arrive at some negotiated position." He flashed a wicked smile. "In 2 days we'll sign the Bill into Law without a hint of disagreement."

The Speaker returned a brief iron smile. "Glad to hear it. We can't afford any vote numbers changing the tide of events."

"Not to worry Benjamin. It's taken care of."

The Speaker switched his eyes to Lawrence, "What I understand from State House, G. Tech. will wire the money to one of your external accounts which you will subsequently wire to one of your local accounts?"

Lawrence in his elegant brilliant white Cuban shirt, expensive black slacks and Italian shoes, also with ease and calm responded, "I'm waiting to hear of the timing and amounts we're talking about from State House. Are we talking installments, if so how many or a lump sum?

Because I need to prepare the paperwork surrounding each transaction in advance so my people know how to handle it as part of business flow in case anyone comes sniffing around. A day's notice is always nice. I'll also need to forward that paperwork to Edgar."

Edgar straightened up in his chair and cleared his throat. His deep authoritative voice was not compatible with his small frame.

"Yes, it's extremely important that I have the paperwork before the money is wired so it seamlessly fits into our checks and approvals process without attracting any attention. When an error needs to be rectified I have to go through a consultative process and get the Deputy Governor's approval. He dislikes such irregular procedures so he sits on the money a bit to discourage second time offenders. Not to mention that his friends are in the opposition. It can all become a bit sticky if we don't stick to our Bank's protocols." Edgar's eyes flipped between the Speaker and Lawrence.

"Ok Edgar. This needs to work like clockwork. You can be sure the tree-huggers have put their feelers out on the Central Bank among other government institutions to find out how this transaction is being completed." said the Speaker.

"We'll do our part and get the information to you on time and you do your part to make it look like any other transaction sailing through your pearly gates." responded Lawrence.

Edgar rigorously nodded. 'Yes I will. You can count on me. In the event of anything, I'll call you."

"In the event of nothing! There is no margin for error on this. We have the U.N. and other governments sniffing us up like we're a government of street thugs. Of course you can call me. But only to tell me everything has been expeditiously executed." replied the Speaker.

He broadened his gaze to look at everyone, "We only communicate on our secured lines. I don't need the Courts subpoenaing the tel. comm. companies for our phone records." The Speaker then proceeded to stand up as if closing a session of the House. The others followed suit from their chairs. "Gentlemen, it is always a pleasure doing business with you. We'll reconvene in 2 – 3 days upon execution of our tasks."

SHOP #32
DIAMOND MARKET, ANTWERP
DAY 2 – 15:00HRS

Simmons sported on a smart casual outfit to try and blend in with the environment. He was relieved with the time management so far. Chartering a helicopter to and fro had been the only possible solution. The bell chimed as he opened the door.

"Aaaah, Mr. Eckbert Schweitzer, my client with a very Jewish name who looks nothing Jewish." The crouched elderly man laughed that caused a cough.

"I was adopted." Simmons mumbled unmoved by the humor as his eyes nervously moved around the counter top.

The shop owner with his long graying beard shuffled his feet with his cane up to the counter directly opposite to where Simmons stood; surrounded by old trinkets, antiques and aged precious minerals behind the scratched glass counter. People came to his shop to hock whatever they could when they needed money to materialize out of thin air. What the average eye could not see and many in the diamond business did not know was that Mr. Avi Goldman was one of the largest wholesale diamond traders in Antwerp. His portfolio of clientele was the most exclusive in the industry. One of his areas of expertise, given his established network spanning from law enforcement to black market, was his capacity to absorb precious stones from illegal sources into a legitimate system.

"Yes my dear man. I received your message. I am surprised to see you at such short notice. What is it you so anxiously wanted to show me?" Simmons resented this aura of desperation he had presented to the only buyer he was going to see before his flight out this evening. His sense of urgency had probably cost him $500,000= at least. The old man smiled showing a set of incredibly strong teeth. Knowing he had the upper hand, Simmons just waited to see how far he was going to play it.

"I wanted to show you some stars that dropped from the heavens quite recently."

"Well step into my office then?" His toned hand of unusually soft skin beckoned Simmons to come round the counter and through the curtain of beads.

Only a trained eye such as Simmons was able to see that this shop had a security system that could rival any bank. On previous visits he had marveled how the old man kept such an unassuming almost disheveled façade of an outlet for the type of business he was really doing. They walked past a small open space with an old wooden table that had 2 rickety chairs on either end of it. This open space then led to a long poorly lit corridor of faded gray paint that had 2 doors on the end at the end. Goldman punched in a code to open the one on the left. It was an ultra-sleek room filled with small steel drawers. A room of safe deposit boxes similar to what you'd see in any bank. On the right corner of the back wall as you faced the room was a 4 foot silver grey door of an ultra-modern safe. Right in the middle of the room was a baroque antique desk with 3 small drawers on its left and 1 long mini-cabinet on the right. Goldman gestured Simmons towards the table.

"Please." Simmons knew the protocol well, being a known client –as known as you wanted to be. "Let us see what you have."

They both sat at the same time while Goldman got out his high-powered telescope. Simmons was fully aware in the second drawer was his Marc 23 Heckler and Koch and in the third drawer what seemed to be a sleek looking laptop. A few visits ago some young thugs naively misread their target of a dingy shop door.

One went away with a bullet in the foot, another took one in his arm and a third limped away with a complimentary in his buttock. It was a humorous sight watching them wailing and running with their baseball bats. Something nagged Simmons about this wiry elderly Israeli gentleman. But this was hardly his concern now. He was reliable and the only buyer in this time frame. That was all that concerned him.

Both fully focused on the moment at hand. Simmons reached into his left inner breast pocket and slowly brought out the black velvet sachet holding the diamonds. He carefully removed the velvet handkerchief from the sachet that carried the stones. Simmons eyes were fully focused on the stones. One of them missing could easily mean up to six hundred thousand dollars permanently misplaced. Goldman rarely cracked a smile at the sight of product. Today appeared to be an exception.

"Beautiful indeed, they are." he grinned. "Which heavens did you say they dropped from my dear man?"

Simmons tried to take advantage of the moment, "The one that may no longer forgive sinners. With the purity of these stones, their quality and cut my good friend, we know that they are not worth less than $18 million or so."

"Haa,..too rich for my blood dear friend. You'll have to rob someone else's bank account." "$17 million." Simmons looked at him with a cold unthreatening gaze.

"Still too high. From what I can see you have a time constraint should we say, and I don't know of anyone else that can pick these stones up so quickly. It would appear I'm your point man Mr. Schweitzer." He raised his left eyebrow with a crooked grin. Simmons could see Goldman was slightly amused to have cornered his client, like a friendly chess game. He decided to amuse himself even further. "Ok, let me take a closer look."

Looking through his telescope he methodically started to work his way through analyzing this pile of stones one by one. Simmons decided to while away the time by closely analyzing this so-called diamond dealer whose hands at his advanced age exhibited remarkable strength and calm. His arms were always fully covered under his full length black coat and tunic shirt underneath. His face while showing a few lines from his nasal bridge to his mouth had intense dark brown eyes. It would have been difficult to have traced his origins without his clothing. In 20 minutes the analysis was over. "Alright Mr. Schweitzer, the cut and purity of some of these stones is not as sharp as the others. The best I can do for you is $16million."

Simmons was relieved to hear this. He was hoping not to go below $15 million. "$16.5 million Mr. Goldman. You and I both know that you're not going to sell these diamonds off for less than $18 million and stones of this quality move very fast on the market."

Goldman smiled at Simmons desperation cracking through. Because Goldman knew he would have been willing to have paid $18 million knowing how to break up the consignment and get not less than $20 million for them. "Then $16.75 million it is." Simmons gently declared. Goldman nodded. The 2 men shook hands.

"If I may escort you to the grand foyer." Simmons very well understood that Goldman preferred the customer not stay in the room while he executed his bank wire transaction. In 15 minutes Goldman called Simmons back into the room to receive the verification code of the transaction. It would go through the banking system within 2 days.

"Here you are my dear man, your very own reference tracking code." "Mr. Goldman." Simmons said.

"Mr. Schweitzer." Goldman responded.

Simmons briskly stepped out to the closest intersection looking for a cab that would carry him to the heli-port.

GLOBAL ENVIRONMENTAL NETWORK
NEW YORK BRANCH OFFICE
DAY 2 – 13:00HRS

"Hi Rebecca, it's Ian. Emily is coordinating with everyone in both the capital city and the forest to get the feeds directly from sites however possible. I've spoken with each of the 15 organizations here. We'll have to grind this out for the next days coming. Just wanted to give you the update."

"Thanks Ian." She breathed a small sigh of relief. She reminded herself she had to celebrate the small steps of progress too.

CHAPTER 7

TAKE OFF

It was a tight group, no extra baggage here. Everyone selected for their area of specialization and the fact that they were the very best at it from the G. Tech group. A mineral specialist, a software analyst, the lawyer, the military expert, Drier and Simmons; 6 men, 2 top of the line corporate jets. The Chairman of G-Tech. was present in a casual smart outfit trying to look matter-of-fact and calm about this meeting. The mere fact that he was attending at this odd hour at this peculiar location did not intonate anything matter of fact or calm about this meeting. At 6'2" his crew cut trimmed look complemented his silver cashmere sweater and navy slacks. William Baynes, Chairman of Global Technologies LLC, was a blue blood raised in the old boys' network. He grew up in a world measured by the elite private boarding school and Ivy League university you went to, which country club you were a member of, the family name you married and the network that opened doors for you. It was a ruthless world with tall fences.

Baynes chairmanship was a result of tenures as CEO at 2 electronic companies that he turned around through brutal competitive management techniques. His ground rule was to hire people much smarter than him. Baynes would literally poach from the competition if he saw fit. In Baynes business form he swooped in when the final decision was to be made and the credit was to be taken. Despite his ingrained insensitivity he was known to be highly strung and given to panic if an explosion appeared to be heading his way. But right now he was closing in on the deal of the century and wanted to be right front and center to take credit.

"Gentlemen, this is a preliminary visit to confirm that everything is in order before we sign. If it is, we sign in 3 days, not 5. Drier will be giving me daily updates and will inform me immediately in the event of any unexpected problems. Any questions?"

Everyone knew taking the invitation to questions was interpreted as showing your lack of preparedness and confidence to execute the task. Questions resulted in delayed promotions and unenviable assignments. Baynes made eye contact with Drier. Drier stood up, legs slightly straddled as if carrying out a final platoon briefing.

"Gentlemen, there are 3 key markers to completing this visit." What Drier was saying, without saying it, is that there were no excuses and surely no failure on any element of this trip. "They are, i) they agree to the key clauses and payment terms in the agreement and that the consequences of trying to tamper with this content are made very clear to them. ii) we are moving into an undisturbed location from our assessment on the ground and iii) to determine the volume and composite of the minerals in Pointe Trois by running the tests in Hong Kong. I will fly with these fellows", as he cocked his head toward the mineral specialist and software analyst, "who will give me the detailed position on the last point. Let's get on with the mission."

Simmons was the first to stand up and head towards the glass doors that put him on the tarmac where the jets were lined up. He hated those pre-flight pep talks. Everyone knew the mission and everyone knew very well that they couldn't fail. In 20 minutes the jets were taxing on to the runway with passengers that could hear their hearts beating and adrenaline pumping even before take-off from the airport.

DINING/HOSTING WING
U.S. SECRETARY OF STATE
WASHINGTON D.C., DAY 2 – 18:00HRS

The shuttle flight and limousine to and from the airports made his very regular jaunts between New York and Washington D.C. effortless and were very necessary when lobbying and coordinating disparate positions between various countries, and the U.N. Some salient and sensitive matters required face to face contact whether the art of ancient old bargaining for critical votes in different organs of the U.N. or requesting clumps of co-partner support for several programs. Meeting with the Secretary of State almost became a weekly event when escalations in different regions of the world took center stage ranging from weapons inspections to troop deployments or dictator despoliations.

The Secretary of State was hosting an early dinner for a delegation from a block of Middle East countries that was suffering from a fast growing fundamentalist movement recruiting poor unemployed youth, funding them well and setting up local cells that were presently engaged in vicious crimes targeting modern western upwardly mobile Arabs. The Movement decided that these traitors, they called the Middle Eastern yuppies, were poisoning their young with the ways of the infidels and their main aim was to destroy the country of infidels at all costs. The killing of their leader by the country of infidels, they said, was the sign that the infidel must be destroyed at the soonest before it destroys them all. The U.S. came to know about them through a routine check of a University student going to attend a talk by an invited American foreign policy adviser at a main campus auditorium. His backpack was found to be loaded with Sentex wired to his cel. phone. He had already left a suicide note neatly on his study desk at his apartment off campus. During a long interrogation process the boy revealed details about their network. A joint Middle East-U.S. intelligence operation discovered a massive network, but the funders were yet still to be discovered. In the interim the U.S. wanted to dismantle this network by ensuring these boys would be supported in gainful employment, have an income without the stress of violent crimes, terrorist acts and suicide missions, not to mention the political re-education. The delegation was reporting that this was working very well in different countries, until their funders found out what was going on and started to kill the boys off one by one. So the negotiating point was how to put them in the Witness Protection Program in the U.S., the very country they were meant to kill. During the course of the dinner, the Secretary of State stepped out of the dining room to meet with Ambassador Holstein.

The Ambassador was known for his elegant 3 piece Tweed outfits, suede loafers, fedora hat and walking stick. He was shown into the private study cum meeting room adjacent to the dining room. As he browsed the 17th Century art work, Secretary Billington walked in. Holstein turned around and was met with open arms and a broad smile.

After a chuckle during their brief hug, "Madame Secretary of State, the pleasure is always mine."

"Oh Your Excellency, the title makes me blush. It feels like only yesterday I was your novice intern and you were the Department Head revered by all at the Center for Global Studies."

Penelope Billington in her late-50s had a petite figure and a bouffant from the 1960s that increased her height by a couple of inches. She had a meteoric rise through the State Department due to a combination of being a workaholic with brilliant insights, managing her relationships very strategically creamed by the background of the family she came from with significant connections in both political and business worlds.

"Tell me Daniel, I know you're not one for late night meetings. Who's on your radar for the wrong reasons?" Both seated on the couch chatting like old friends.

Holstein filled her in. "We have a rather interesting situation. The government of Caramondo is about to sell off the Pointe Trois rainforest."

"Oh, I didn't know they could do that? I've heard rumblings about that in some corridors." She sounded curiously surprised.

"Therein lies the problem. They are about to pass a Bill into Law in the next 48 hours. That's one side of the pickle. The other is that they're severely guilty of human rights violations, environmental destruction and continue to dig up any inch of forest floor that looks like it can be uprooted for their own benefit."

With focus and finesse she interjected, "Daniel, you know my heart bleeds for the human rights violations and there are major environmental and maybe climate factors once they mow down the forest, however it does still remain a domestic matter. We may not agree with their policies or practices, but in principle there isn't a law or legal instrument to throw at them. Now days we need to choose our battles carefully." She said looking a bit worried knowing she wouldn't be able to take up her friend's case based on its merits.

"Oh and I should mention, a recent discovery was made."

The Secretary raised her eyebrows revealing she always loved a new twist in the story. "Oh, do tell?" She probed.

"It turns out some of our largest tel. comm., IT and defense type companies are buying large chunks of minerals, particularly coltan, from the Pointe Trois rainforest as part of the key raw materials for the products. But they've been buying through agents so no one really picked up on it. If the sale goes through to this G. Tech. that is also in several industries similar to our companies it becomes private land. And I doubt they'll continue to allow their competition to access even just a glass of water from that region directly or indirectly once they've secured the forest."

"Well, let's just revisit this for a moment shall we?" came a very protective tone from Penelope as if spoiling for a fight. "You mean our companies could lose a key raw material source in industries that are fundamental for world economic power or military positioning?" she said in disbelief. "Well as I said Daniel, we do need to choose our battles carefully."

"We do indeed." He zeroed in on the focused stare in her eye. "What was your plan?"

Daniel lunged in, "I'll get Roman Sandbourne, our point man at the Human Rights Commission in Geneva to kick up a stink about these ongoing human rights violations. Such offenders normally tend to draw his ire. He'll recommend that there be some statement of condemnation from the U.N. at large with the threat of targeted sanctions on the country from the Security Council. I will then meet with my colleagues to brief them of the violations from the view point that it is also in their own interests that access to the rainforest doesn't become restricted. Penelope, what would be a helpful edge is a phone call to the Chair of the Security Council to express your gratitude and future reciprocity for agreeing to have an extra-ordinary meeting of the Council called in the next 24 hours to discuss this matter. This will also buy enough time for my colleagues to consult with their countries. The main pitch that they will give to their governments is that we are thwarting off a potential security threat. One company having access to such a rich region is not good for all of us."

"I'll make the call first thing in the morning. We'll see how to protect the indigenous population of Pointe Trois and to protect our companies to continue to get whatever they need out of that place, directly or indirectly."

"I'll bring Roman into the loop and hold court with my colleagues in the morning. Madame Secretary, I'll let you get back to your dinner." As he carefully raised himself from the couch and she quickly followed suit.

"Your Excellency let me do the needful on my end." They walked out through their respective doorways.

As Holstein was driven back in his sedan, he typed away on his phone. *"Roman, please find attached file for your honorable indignation. Have just discussed it with Secretary Billington."* He then sent out an e-mail to his most trusted colleagues on the Security Council requesting an urgent meeting. Holstein strategized in his mind how he would convince his colleagues on the Council to agree to a statement of condemnation along with the threat of sanctions when some of them had signed defense contracts with certain developing countries that had not even put together their health budgets. Despite his career history of machinations in the interests of his country, Holstein had never revealed to anyone that the cynicism of it all still bothered him. Noble intentions and moral countries had to be clothed in sovereign interests in order to get the action they required.

REBECCA'S APARTMENT
UPPER EAST SIDE, NYC
DAY 2 – 23:00HRS

Even though time was not on their side, Rebecca could feel the case coming together. The legal brief, the essence of the argument, had been drafted. A compelling body of the most precise and current evidence along with a global social opinion of outrage must be delivered on the table of Ambassador in the next 36 hours. The draft earlier sent was a detailed enough start. She knew Holstein was only the first strike at cracking the foundation of this poisonous partnership between G. Tech. and the Caramondo government. They had both tasted the benefits of this mutually agreeable arrangement and neither party would be willing to walk away so easily. Both parties were used to mud being slung at them from different directions. One party had a whole department to neatly neutralize potentially inconvenient scenarios. The other party simply didn't care whether people died while they achieved their objectives. Rebecca knew. It was quite obvious actually. This was not a fight about the best ammunition to win this case. It was a fight about willpower. The will power, sheer grit and determination required to beat these two giants at their own game. That same willpower she used to fight off the soldier trying to rape her, she felt rise up in her gut. The willpower she felt in Montero leading his troops all these years. She saw what had to be done in the next 36 hours with clarity and precision. A big task, but a doable task. And she was ready for it.

CHAPTER 8

PRESENTATION IS EVERYTHING

DAY 3

AVALON INTERNATIONAL AIRPORT CARAMONDO
00:00HRS

The midnight stars populated the sky like citizens of the heavens shining so largely, so brightly in their peace. The two jets pierced through descending in preparation for their landing at Avalon International Airport. It had been a largely uneventful trip. In the second jet the mineral specialist and software analyst had given Drier a detailed briefing of how the programming worked on satellites. The test results had proven promising so far, but a key vulnerable element was balancing the composition of the two minerals to ensure consistency in the mix. Where could the best mix be found in the forest based on the locations they would be visiting. G. Tech.'s policy was not to publicize and take credit for this technological and IT breakthrough, but to quietly own every chain in the process that resulted in this security golden key. From owning the land that produced these unique raw materials to the software codes that could cause havoc on any satellite. During this trip it was essential to visit at least two sample sites where the composite had been found to ascertain the volume and subsequent viability of what they had.

On the first jet Simmons had been awake for the past 3 hours turning the same problem around in his mind, examining every angle of it like a surgery he was about to execute, except his subordinates had no idea of his objective of the operation at hand. While Reginald was typing away on this laptop completing legal opinions that had followed him from the office; Kreshnakov was surveying the few city lights against the darkness of the surrounding undeveloped land as closely as he could. During his conversation with the pilots he learned that the airspace of Pointe Trois had been declared a high risk zone and only essential flights were recommended in the past 3 days. One of the army's utility choppers had been shot down 2 weeks ago by a surface to air missile but the government claimed it was a technical fault that caused the unfortunate accident killing all 15 soldiers on board. The pilot was also saying that the government had increased its intelligence operations in Avalon to root out any supporters of the militia, hence the unexpected night raids that might occur throughout town be it a residence or cheaper hotel, but that should not cause any scare.

The jets touched down onto the runway, one shortly behind the other. It would have been far from wrong to have mistaken Avalon Airport for a military airbase. The jets parked on the civilian side as directed by the runway staff right outside one of three civilian hangars. The passengers noticed an individual waiting for them on the runway as they alighted the aircraft.

"Gentlemen! You're most welcome." Exclaimed Jean Puidot, Head of Protocol, State House as he reached out to greet Drier with a two-hand handshake who was at the head of the line and continued with the others. Puidot did not waste any time as if he wanted to complete the receiving of these guests as quickly as possible. "I imagine you have had a long flight. Please, come with me to the lounge."

Waiting for them in the lounge huddled among themselves were Jules Sneider, assistant to Mr. Puidot, Richard Pican-State House legal officer, Major Calizar-military representative from the army and James Prescott-team leader-G. Tech. Operations-Caramondo. Hearing their footsteps, their worried grim expressions altered into pleasant, courteous smiles. Formal handshakes were done. There was a pat on the arm between Prescott, Kreshnakov and the mineral specialist.

In an exchange of laughter, Prescott asked Kreshnakov, "Did you bring my whisky and cigars?" Kreshnakov who rarely smiled chuckled back, "Only from the best source."

Little did the others know Kreshnakov was tasked to bring the most modern, lethal small firearms and personal defense equipment for Prescott, now that his staff would be based deep in the jungle instead of short outings.

Sneider interrupted, "Gentlemen would you please provide your passports for quick processing?"

Each of the team obliged. It was a luxuriously decorated lounge, unexpected of the settings within the airport hangar adjacent to the simple terminal buildings in a country struggling to hold together its national budget.

Simmons knew that this was separate from the official VIP Lounge that he had used before on previous visits, it was not as extravagant as this. Probably reserved for unofficial, clandestine so-called investors that they themselves happened to be during this excursion. Two attendants took orders and served them drinks.

Puidot kept the conversation busy. "Tomorrow is a long day. Brace yourselves. At 08:00hrs you shall fly out to the Pointe Trois region to survey some of the sites ensuring everything is in order and returning to Avalon by 15:00hrs. The legal and military meetings have been scheduled for 15:30hrs and 16:30hrs respectively. A working dinner with the Head of State has been scheduled for 18:30hrs to discuss your findings of the trip, iron out and confirm any details so that the signing can take place a few days after. By 20:30hrs you shall be at the airport ready for takeoff. Would that sound agreeable to you gentlemen?"

Drier gave a quick look to Simmons to ensure that there weren't any major omissions. Simmons gave the slightest nod.

Drier nodded, "Yes that sounds good. Thank you for putting together such an efficient schedule." However Drier in his mind was cursing at this prudent, erudite looking man, wondering why they could not have landed directly in Pointe Trois and had all the ancillary meetings take place at Pointe Trois and then only fly to Avalon to have the 30 minutes wrap up with the Head of State. Both Carthwaite and Kreshnakov studied Puidot closely as he spoke and they could see the rush in him. The man did not want anyone to depart from his tightly managed script.

Kreshnakov decided to tease him a bit. "Mr. Puidot, could you at least give us an initial briefing on the general security in Pointe Trois, mainly because we've heard of a rapid increase in military exchanges in the last few days? And we're very interested to know your indications on the matter."

Major Calizar from the army clique had no intention of finding himself in a corner and immediately responded. "The military team in Pointe Trois is preparing a complete briefing for you which you will have as soon as we reach Pointe Trois in the morning." The tight smile he conveyed to Kreshnakov was to be understood as a friendly warning to discourage further questions on the subject.

Carthwaite sat at the end of the couch wearing a disarming relaxed smile, pretending to appear slightly distracted and worn down by the fatigue. Little did the government officials know he was studying every inch of their body language to assess their confidence and competence of the situation they found themselves in just a few of days before the handover. In Carthwaite's assessment, the army official seemed too rigid and almost scared like they were in the battle of their lives. The legal officer looked like something was terribly wrong but he'd be the last person to tell you. And Prescott the short, stocky well-mannered technical officer looked like a field hustler managing a multitude of people and things who was happy to see his colleagues but seemed to be searching their faces trying to figure out why the sudden urgency?

Just then the Protocol Officer's assistant returned with people's passports. The young man avoided eye contact with the G.Tech. team at every turn covering up his nervousness with concentration of his task at hand. He updated his boss that the aircraft paperwork was just about completed, the pilots and crew would be ready to leave within a few minutes. He bowed out as if exiting a stage to complete his task. Puidot nodded impatiently as if wishing his speedy return. Determined to dispel the uneasy silence that had consumed the lounge, the man offered small talk. "Were you aware that Pointe Trois was recognized as one of the richest rainforests in the world?"

Asking himself where this was going, Simmons chipped in with a dry smile; "Yes, yes with all the wildlife, flora and fauna, we look forward to their multiplication." His dead gaze to Puidot made it clear that he had no interest in pursuing chitty chat small talk.

Puidot's assistant returned and nodded to this boss.

"Gentlemen, shall we?" Puidot stood up and motioned to the doorway of the lounge.

In a moment they were all in the vehicles provided and on their way. No one said a word. It was standard operating procedure as a G. Tech. employee not to say a word in the client vehicle. It was well known that any half-functioning government would have listening devices and seasoned spies operating as drivers and aides to pick up every scintilla of information possible from the time they picked you up at the airport until they waved you off on the runway again. When reaching the hotel Kreshnakov would have the laborious task of ensuring that all the rooms were debugged and one room, normally his, was used as the regular meeting room.

STATE HOUSE, CARAMONDO
DAY 3 – 09:00HRS

Despite the titles, wealth or sweeping powers you may carry within or outside Caramondo, the Principle Private Secretary to the President, Belinda Ruiz, was not a woman to bulldoze, bamboozle or badger. It was almost a rehearsal in respect before you met the President. The right contact put you through to the PPS and then you waited for Madame to call you. Dare you make attempts to follow-up on your appointment there would be no meeting because of your wrong attitude. She now peered her head through the door of the President to see how he was doing on his phone conversation on the line 1. He was rotating his index finger in circular motion as he looked at her with a sarcastic pained expression. The caller just would not seem to wrap up. She walked up and placed a little note on his desk. It read '*William Baynes, Chairman, G. Tech.*' and pointed to the third light flashing on his console.

He nodded in acknowledgement. "Yes Mr. President. I assure you it is not a problem. We will not spill into your borders. You know these miscreants we've been dealing with for years making outrageous claims that we've been violating their rights for decades. Yet we've invested significant military resources towards their development. Really, it is just shocking. Well their leader met his unfortunate demise in a skirmish. But I assure you again the problem will not spill over the border. My dear brother, we've known each other for years and trust me when I say you shouldn't believe everything your clan elders tell you. They still see things, well...a certain way."

The voice on the other end didn't sound too convinced. "Your Excellency, I think you can understand your increased airpower and so many of the Pekweh tribe fleeing cross border to their relatives signals a real military offensive. This is beginning to cause stress on our local resources at the border and from reports of my Defense Minister, we're not sure if the full population of the Pointe Trois region would be on our side of the border any day now."

"Don't worry we shall have handled this decisively for once and for all."

The voice on the other end sounded like it didn't want to take any chances at all. "We trust you to do the right thing my dear brother. But just as a precautionary measure we shall deploy some of our troops along the border to ensure there isn't any stress or military exchange coming too close to our people along the borderline."

"As you wish." replied the President sounding annoyed and disappointed at the idea.

The other voice could pick up on this change in tone and didn't want the conversation to end this way with such an unwieldy character. He tried to pepper his closing with some false confidence. "Of course we trust you to do the right thing."

"Of course Mr. President, we shall be in touch real soon. All shall be solved. You shall see." He put down the handset and rolled his eyeballs as if he'd been trying to placate a hyper-sensitive individual.

President Sebastian Gebajara's size and bulldozing manner were intimidating to most. Only because he settled scores underneath the table using the army like his personal group of bandits which was a poisonous atmosphere for the professional soldiers trying to build a career. Power and control were his aphrodisiacs from the first days of his enrollment. His father, known as one of the old guard most professional, disciplined soldiers retired at the rank of Major General. Gebajara learned about the system and, in his own mind, calculated how to manipulate the game from dinner table stories. The honors, accolades and respect bestowed upon his father during his retirement ceremony, Gebajara interpreted as his opening to a path of power that he would take and not earn. He now found himself in politics as an inconvenient, but necessary, tool to remain in power. The man felt and looked uncomfortable compressing his grand size and mannerisms into suits. His rich black voluminous hair, thicker eye brows, deep black pools for eyes set in his flawless olive skin only accentuated his 120 kilo solid, but not muscular, frame. He was a presence to contend with.

He pushed on line 3 flashing without missing a beat. 'William Baynes!' he exclaimed with a garrulous laugh in his voice. "It has been a while since we last spoke. I expect all is moving well. I must say I am struck at your sudden interest -or rather, urgency- in concluding this arrangement. The soldier in me asks is there something that you're not telling me here?"

Baynes hated being spoken to in such a patronizing manner. And these Heads of State were the only ones who could get away with it given the scale of benefit he knew he would derive from these relationships. Baynes feigned a polite laugh. "Now Mr. President, would I keep a thing from you? This arrangement stands to be beneficial to both sides, wouldn't you say?" Baynes retorted as if being pulled into a dual that he did not want to waste time with.

"Yes it has indeed." The President recalled his mansions and lifestyle that far exceeded that of any Head of State in the region. This was indeed one arrangement he wanted to see continue in the form of a significant wire transfer to his personal account.

"My staff informs me that your group arrived last night. My legal people are still examining the document. We need to be sure that this arrangement leaves both of us smiling. That is G. Tech. and the people of Caramondo."

"Yes of course Mr. President. It shall be extremely beneficial to all who put pen to paper." replied Baynes. The chill in his voice becoming even more frozen.

"I'm glad we understand each other. Of course I'd like to be sure that the wiring details are in order, all sorted out before your people leave my people?"

"Absolutely, that is one of the main items on the agenda my team will sort out with your team when on the ground. All is well on our end. We look forward to a smooth visit with yourselves." said Baynes.

He knew if the President responded he would be lying through his teeth and putting himself in a precarious situation. Baynes looked for every opportunity to push him to the edge and see what extras he could get out of the man willing to sell his own.

"Trust me. Everything is absolutely in order. In fact, I think we're giving you a bargain for this territory. I'm even tempted to re-negotiate the numbers."

Baynes interrupted doing everything possible to sound humorous at a casual remark which was anything but that. "I assure you that won't be necessary. The investment costs we have put in, we wouldn't recoup for a number of years."

"We are ready for you. And if all goes well, we shall perhaps even take the next step of signing the agreement." "That would be the idea Mr. President."

"Alright, my people shall meet with your team. I shall meet with them at the end of their visit. My secretary must already have their details. I am glad, we both look forward to a smooth visit."

"Yes we do Mr. President. We shall stay in touch."

Riding on the triumph of Montero's death and urgency of the deadline, Bugazon took advantage to run amok on the army's budget getting the CIC to sign off directly on approvals for millions of dollars for deployments and supply procurements. He accounted to no one, just his fixated desire to wipe out the militia and enrich himself.

Department Heads complained, Bugazon threatened back. This draining of the army budget was expertly hidden under other routine approvals of much smaller amounts for his department and unit transfers into Pointe Trois. This afternoon was no exception.

Belinda flicked her eyes at her phone console. She motioned her arm, without lifting her head up from her paperwork, to the President's door for Bugazon to enter. She had known too many of these meetings. The corridors had whispered to her what he was getting away with during these one on ones. Even she had her limits on correctness and protocols. Bugazon sprung up from his chair, marched in and saluted.

"Aaaah, psychic abilities must be among your many talents. Just the person I wanted to see." declared Gebajara.

Bugazon was swift. He had to walk out with his paperwork signed. "CiC, I just brought in some formalities for your quick signature." as he opened his file and handed over the papers.

"How are you wrapping up? We're now down to the wire." Gebajara spoke while he signed.

Bugazon was relieved the President was not paying attention to what he was signing. The President knew exactly what he was signing away. He had just decided to look the other way a long time ago. Presidential immunity was such a handy tool. The wire transfer of this transaction was what he was signing for. Bugazon narrated the minimum to avoid a cross examination. "With these increased deployments we're flying in, we're putting in place more security rings. These nets will cut off their supply roots and outmaneuver their battle movements. The capturing, torturing and threatening of the population also seem to be yielding some results."

The President cut in, "Look, fair enough. Get it done. That's a two-headed monster. You got the boy, now get the bloody girl too. Just how difficult is that? She's the one getting all these opposition folk fired up with…impractical hope. Talking to those people abroad setting off this chain of pressure. Now threaten her or knock her off altogether. Just handle it for goodness sake." as he handed the paperwork back to him.

"In process, we've already disabled one of the key people helping her in NY out of the picture."

"Great. Now these G. Tech. characters flew in last night. You better have a very specific route to show them only where the plumbing works."

"It is being hashed out as we speak."

"Very well." Was his blank, unmoved smile.

Bugazon saluted and marched out avoiding any more questions by all means. It was a quick drive back to his office. He unlocked his side drawer and picked up his scrambled cel. phone.

"This is your international cleaning service. How can we help you lead a cleaner life today?" was the professional mundane voice on the other line.

"I need you to clean the girl. As you well know, the boy has been handled from here."

"At your service, I thought you'd never ask. We'd dusted off one of her friends we thought she'd pick up on the hint, but it seems she didn't. We were actually working on something to spruce up the girl. May we go ahead with that initiative?"

"I'd be just as happy if you did something in the next 30 minutes.

"Your wish is my command. Wishing you a clean, germ-free day."

Gebajara and Bugazon maintained an invisible international network of 'cleaners' that was called upon to wipe out 'difficult' people standing in their way of military matters, politics or high-stakes business. Handling difficulties outside the country was a much neater way of doing things.

PARLIAMENT

CARAMONDO

DAY 3 – 10:00HRS

The ethnic tensions reflected in the citizens did not escape the members of the august legislature. The budget allocations, lack of accountability, obvious development in some areas and undeniable poverty in others had MPs sitting in a Chambers of tension. When Benjamin LaFonte had first presided over a House of healthy debate that could tackle corruption and social degeneration, he felt respect and pride for himself and for his colleagues. Ten years later, he felt deep disdain for members of his party and disappointment in himself for frustrating laws and programs that would enable equitable development throughout the country. All at the behest of a Head of State and a few cronies who felt it best to protect their interests and multiply their fortunes at the expense of the most vulnerable of their citizens. LaFonte wanted to retire quietly without offending His Excellency. The guilt of his sins had eaten into him and reproduced itself in the form of an aggressive prostate cancer. The Speaker shot a look to the Chief Whip as if to say, you better be ready. The MPs were still arguing among themselves about their committee allowances. LaFonte gently hit his hammer on its gavel.

"Order to the House. The second point of debate in the House this morning is the Bill tabled by Hon. Ezra Panchu that will give government the right to sell or lease out tracts of land where it deems fit in the interests of security or significant economic development. Government reserves the right to clear off all inhabitants of the land or transact on it in a state as is. This is the Bill brought to the floor. Hon. Members I do not need to remind you that this Bill has been presented for voting twice before and the last time we got into a fist fight which resulted in the suspension of the offenders from this House and I can assure you, any fracas will result in expulsion of the offenders with no opportunity for appeal."

The Speaker gave a prolonged grave stare to the House. The briefing Hon. Pachu received from the Chief Whip was very thorough. The House was 49% pro-government and 42% opposition, with the balance being voted in on an independent ticket. Hon. Panchu did not miss a beat as he thoughtfully stood up from his seat. He took the microphone and cleared this throat.

"Hon. Members, on prior occasions we have exhaustively discussed the benefits and maybe some of the disadvantages of this Bill. But I continue to reiterate to you the urgency to accelerate the development of our country and ensure the continued economic security of our nation in these rapidly changing global times."

A few of the MPs rolled their eyeballs and smiled at each other in sarcastic amazement. Each legislator in the House knew Caramondo had always enjoyed stable relations with all of its neighbors. Pointe Trois region had 2 of those neighbors with barely a skirmish in past generations. Border disputes had always been settled by tribes along the borders with a few government officials from either side to confirm lines of sovereignty. This is the way it had always been. Hon. Panchu continued.

"Infrastructure development such as roads, dams, water systems, mineral and botanical research that would have fundamental impact on national development cannot take place because land lays idle in the hands of tribes that have no intention of developing such a fundamental resource but letting it remain idle like some prize on a mantel piece. Honorable colleagues, we have parts of the country that remain backward and isolated because there is no infrastructure that can bring service delivery to them or create a foundation for economic development. We have agricultural, tourism and mining potential. All of these are key steps to graduating our economy from the trade of our raw material at giveaway prices to manufacturing. How could we take advantage of a digital age if we can't get our basics right?"

About 15 members of the pro-government party banged on their benches in support of this argument. "Here! Here!" they roared. Fisher looked on without expression. Hon. Pachu charged on with confidence.

"Honorable colleagues, the strategic jewels of the few are holding back the right to access basic welfare services and economic development of the many. I beg you, in the interests of the growth of our country; let us vote to sign this Bill into Law that government can take control of identified tracts of land in the interests of national security and economic development."

Fisher thought his script had said the needful. Hon. Thomas Galona then stood up. "I second the motion to pass this Bill."

"Do I hear any nays?" asked the Speaker, praying the usual suspects were suddenly taken with selective hearing.

Hon. Maxwell Fisher was willing to bury whoever interfered with the performances of this sitting. His finely covered ruthlessness was now in full command of events of this proceeding. Gentle negotiation was not par for the course anymore. Hon. Meshach Manywar raised his hand. The Speaker motioned him to the microphone. LaFonte felt his body temperature rise. His resilience to stress was not nearly the same as a few years ago. Manywar walked up without taking his eye off the Speaker.

His portly energetic figure was at the microphone in a minute. His receding hair line, kind dark brown eyes and pronounced hunch presented a man who had not known a life of luxury, but instead had seen struggle that he overcame with humility and strength. His faded gray Safari shirt, now teasing his figure, had been worn in his more slender days. He took a moment in silence then looked up to the ceiling that displayed intricate paintings of the different coat of the arms of the respective tribes of Caramondo. He cast his eyes across the floor and then behind him. The silence added a note of sobriety to the House.

"Fellow members of this House, we have travelled a long road together in the many years we have been here as one. It is like a marriage, should I say. We know each other's games and tricks. We know who tells the truth, who lies, who lies well. We know what is actually on the ground against the budget allocations actually made. Dear colleagues and friends, this is not a time to lie to each other. Why would any of us stand in the way of security or the economic development of our country? How would we benefit as a nation? How would we move forward as individuals? This is not a decision or a time in our history to reduce this vote to political posturing and pontificating. Forcefully taking away land from people is illegally taking away their future economic development as a clan or family. Where infrastructure development requires procurement of land for large scale projects, negotiations and compensation arrangements can always be done with the specific owners of the land for those particular projects. It does not require a whole draconian law putting a particular population at serious risk from losing their land due to shady business deals arrived at under the umbrella of this dubious would-be law. Dear colleagues, we all know what this law is about. It's about the long-standing, insatiable, unabated appetite of government to sell the Pointe Trois region."

Jeering came from the same group of pro-government politicians. Other moderate politicians siding with the opposition cheered him on.

"The matter is plain and simple. You know it and I know it. Caramondo is in no way an exception concerning the need for land for development by government. All our neighbors are doing it. We have debated each case at length, even visited 2 of our neighbors."

Hon. Manywar raised the file for all to see then slammed it back down on the table next to the podium and continued. "In neighboring countries, whether they use the lease or procurement option, those arrangements are working just fine without a hitch and everybody benefits. Discussion of government bringing in such appalling Laws never even arose in each of these scenarios. This is why we, in the opposition, cannot assent to this Bill because it is simply not necessary. We are even bigger proponents of security and economic development. You all know the region of the country we hail from is more destitute than any other. But we cannot do it at the expense of the most fundamental asset and in many cases the only asset that the people have. In this Bill there is not one mention anywhere about fair compensation or relocation programs. We, as a Parliament, would be signing off on the long term poverty on the most destitute of our nation. My brothers and sisters, I am sorry. But we cannot be so irresponsible, so callous and reckless with the lives of those we are supposed to represent in this august House."

He took a moment of silence to make eye contact with each member seated across. The Speaker threw a look of warning and annoyance to the Chief Whip. The pro-government politicians, especially the hired cheerleaders, were a little more silent and somber. It was becoming clear that it was difficult to dispute the logic and practical concerns presented in his argument. Hon. Manywar looked up at the ceiling again and started to speak with a tone of reflection. There was a distinct grief and sadness that he was trying to cover, short of tears welling up in his eyes. Then there was a faint quiver in his lip. Members listening to him focused their attention, trying to psychically give him the energy to move on.

"I've received reports from my Province in Pointe Trois that there have been increased attacks on innocent villages by government forces, torture and maiming of women and children. Why, how, could a government do this to its own people? We have evidence to this effect and have never gotten a clear response from the army or the Ministry of Defense. One time they even had the nerve to tell us that they were targeting only people who were interfering with government research work. But we, as Parliament, after several requests never received a clear report or even a mere statement on the nature of this research work. But I do have a thick file of human rights abuse and environmental degradation all in the name of research work that I cannot explain to anyone, much less my constituents of Pointe Trois. Fellow members of this House let us be crystal clear, we in the opposition and in particular those of us from Pointe Trois would be the first ones to support the growth and development of our country on the basis that it benefits both the land owners and beneficiaries of government programs. It would be completely un-necessary to vote this Bill into Law and probably trigger pockets of war due to land grabbing and forced re-settlements. Let us make the right decision for our children and grandchildren. Do not be tempted or convinced by a few Parliamentarians with hidden agendas that will benefit only a handful in this country, but shall surely be disastrous for all of us in the long-run. It may start with Pointe Trois. What will you do when it gets to your Province or Region? Please, I beg you not to vote in favor of this Bill becoming Law. Thank you.' He picked up his file and walked back to his bench.

Fisher's eyes slowly looked around the Chambers, especially at his pro-government party colleagues. He got nervous. A few of them looked back and shot uneasy glances at him hinting they were not so sure about their position anymore. Fisher's problem was that this vote was done by secret ballot. Hence he would never find out which way Parliamentarians voted. No one had to fear what Fisher would do to them afterwards if they voted against the Bill. Hon. Manywar sat back down at his bench. He did not feel victorious, just sad. But Fisher could sense that the wind was not blowing in his direction. The body language and piercing look from the Speaker made this abundantly clear. A sudden change in plan was required. Fisher waited for the Speaker to look in his general direction again. He looked at him wrap-up a conversation with the Clerk, as the Clerk was pointing to some tables in the corner from where the materials would be brought out and the exercise would take place. The Speaker pulled away from the Clerk as he scanned the House. The MPs were busily chatting among themselves waiting for the Speaker to direct them to the voting booths when ready.

There! The Chief Whip gave a subtle hand signal to the Speaker and he replied with an even more subtle nod of acknowledgement.

Maxwell remembered the words of another member who attended the previous evening's briefing. "People no longer feel they are getting their fair share of mining out of Pointe Trois and neither did they expect the army to go so far with the vicious attacks on the villages. They're not as hungry to vote for this Bill. Besides there are a sizeable chunk of MPs that are hot about the unchecked corruption and feel this is just another big ticket item in the whole game. This is dicey."

Maxwell signaled to the Speaker. There was still work to be done, a different work to close the matter. Quickly, the Speaker motioned to the Clerk to return and said a few words. The Clerk looked surprised and frowned for a second but nodded his head and exited through the back door.

Hon. Manywar seated with 3 others of his colleagues representing each Quadrant of Pointe Trois said to them, "They are up to something." He said to the group without taking his eyes off the Speaker. "I can feel it. They just never give up. Look at him." was the scowl on the Parliamentarian's face.

Benjamin was studying the schedule of the House for a brief second. He immediately grabbed his microphone. "Hon. Members we have a change in program. There has been a mix up with the delivery of ballot papers. We were waiting for them up until the last minute but the courier company is still trying to ascertain where they are."

Hon. Manywar could not contain his fury. "That's a lie!" as he stood up. The three others started banging on their benches chanting. "Lie! Lie! Lie!" In a moment almost half the opposition was chanting in unison and banging away on the benches.

LaFonte angrily hit his hammer on its gavel.

"Order! Immediately! I will not tolerate any such nonsense in this House. One more word and you will be expelled." LaFonte was extremely relieved that he could use the outburst to now dictate the agenda without question. Looking angry and intolerant he barked, "Members as soon as the ballot papers arrive in the next day or two we shall immediately take the vote without any debate on the matter. For now the next item on the agenda is deliberating the increase in the Agriculture budget."

LaFonte shot a look at Fisher an expression of relief of dodging a bullet. Fisher raised his eyebrows ever so slightly and returned to the papers in his hand he pretended to study.

"Colleagues you have just witnessed that eye contact between those two. I swear to you something sinister is going on here." Manywar said.

"Not to worry brother, we will continue to work very hard with our colleagues in and out of the House to make sure that this Bill does not pass. It cannot pass and it will not pass. This is our commitment to our people." replied one of other three.

Fisher still studying the papers pulled out his phone, fired off a text message and returned it to his pocket. He thought to himself, this Bill not passing was simply not an option.

CHAPTER 9

TYING THE KNOTS

In the privacy of his office, General Bugazon schemed how he could extrapolate as much as possible from the cobalt mines while they completed the wipe out of the militia in the remaining days. Genine dashed in.

"Marjorie of General Duegaro's office called. Says he wants to see you immediately. It's urgent."

Genine's look conveyed to Bugazon that he should not disregard this summons. She had never known Marjorie to hang up, ever. Bugazon charged out of his office not impressed with the interruption and walked to the hallway of 3 offices two floors above him. The hallway was nicknamed throughout the institution as "the corridor of absolute power". A respected professional and a staunch Christian, Gen. Dijan Duegaro had not participated in the coup d'état. He had steadily risen through the ranks and President Gebajara thought that he was the most strategic choice to make that would keep the army happy as well as looking and operating like a professional institution. This did not sit well with Bugazon who thought being appointed Head of the Army and Military High Council would be his reward for being one of the key masterminds and the largest risk taker of the coup d'état. What no one knew was that Duegaro's maternal grandmother was from one of the most powerful clans of the Burajon tribe in Pointe Trois but migrated to Avalon for her University studies and married a Muchanta while she was there. But she had taught Duegaro everything she knew about Burajon traditions until her death. Nobody knew how much Duegaro actually knew about the degeneration of Pointe Trois and the role the Caramondo army continued to play in it. Marjorie had made it her business to know the friends and enemies of Duegaro. Bugazon was way in a league of his own.

Where Bugazon's office engulfed you with an energy of precision and strength, Duegaro's office was a space of power, dispensed in an unspoken and mysteriously elegant manner. The sort of power that was the aura of the man, his office only expounded on his personal stature. His large frame and angular features sat squarely on the tall black leather chair as he gently moved between the files on his desk.

"Aaah General, we seem to have a bit of a situation. One that I've never had in the 20 years I've sat in this Chair. Head of Finance and Administration came to me ready to burst a gut. Tells me he can't make most of the salaries and some key procurements next month because most of the money has gone out to procure some rather expensive airpower and ammunitions we don't need, on procurement terms not suitable to any wealthy government. Which we are not, in case you haven't noticed." He concluded moving between his files. "I ask him how all of these approvals invisibly flew past his radar? He says officers in his own department were threatened by you personally, something about career derailment and an abundance of poverty outside of the army." Duegaro's steely stare did not mince words.

"Further yet I'm getting heated questions from the Legislature demanding I go and give an explanation to the Defense Sub-Committee. The Ministry of Defense has the clear position that they have nothing at all to do with this, questions should be directly for the army. I have my counterparts from 2 of our borders telling me they are extremely uneasy about the situation and will make some significant deployments just as a precautionary measure. Activists are having a field day with this giving us lots of undesirable public relations. Members of the High Council are asking me to explain in substantive detail what exactly is our role in Pointe Trois when there was no official approval to this. Before you know it I'll have the neighbor's cat meowing at me, this is derailing her breeding cycle. Is there anything more I can share with you to express the gravity of this situation Gen. Bugazon?"

"General with my deepest respect, I am sure the Commander-in-Chief has updated you on the accelerated time frame of the signing of the agreement." Bugazon had taken special note to refer to the President as the CiC in order to remind Duegaro that he was not the final authority that he was answerable to.

Duegaro interrupted, "That would be an excuse to find yourselves in a shoot-out in an area -excuse me, region of

17,000 square kilometers- where you can't even transparently explain why you're there in the first place?" Duegaro gave a look of simmering impatient disbelief.

Duegaro asked with a tone of finality, "So Bugazon, but just what exactly have we been doing in Pointe Trois all this time? I'm seeing significant resources going in, but I'm not seeing anything coming out?" It was a silence where the unspoken feelings about each other were at peak in conversation now. Duegaro's intercom rang.

"Yes Marjorie." He picked up the line without taking his eyes off Bugazon, "Oh yes. Tell him I'll be with him shortly. And please tell Hon. Mekash I'll call him back as soon as I'm finished with Anderson."

Bugazon tried to look disinterested or unperturbed that Michael Anderson, the Deputy Minister of Defense had come by to have a chat with Duegaro. Hon. Victor Mekash, a former soldier, was the Head of the Defense Sub-Committee at Parliament. "Bugazon I want a complete detailed report on the purpose of our presence in Pointe Trois, status of the army's apparent engagements, our resources committed to date and casualties incurred."

"Of course sir I shall ensure all the details have CiC's approval." Duegaro gave only the slightest salute as the indication that this conversation was over.

Bugazon smiled to Marjorie and saluted to Anderson who was on his cel. phone. Anderson smiled back.

PR&S, NEW YORK
DAY 3 - 07:00HRS

Rebecca popped by the office first to again go through some of the photos sent in the box from Father Raines before heading out to serve as a technical opinion on a case at a Judge's Chambers. A few of the faces among the mining operations looked vaguely familiar but she just could not place specifically from where. And these looked like well-trained technical personnel. She heard Marc come in and settle himself in his work area.

"Morning." He energetically announced.

"Morning." Mumbled Rebecca with pen in mouth as she frowned at a full size photo in her hand; 6 men, 3 women, each one of them were holstered with pistols on their waists but fully engrossed like they were searching for something on the ground or a sign of some kind of environmental development.

Marc had walked in following the perplexed gaze of his boss. "I'm rushing down to pick up an envelope at the intersection. The driver of a courier service said his van was just hit in a fender bender nothing serious but would like me to come down and pick the envelope if possible because he can't leave the scene. I'll be back in a jiff." He said with a reassuring smile.

"Great, whatever." Rebecca replied without raising her head.

Rebecca, Ian and Emily had compiled a detailed record of the systematic degeneration of the people and the forest. Time was running. She had to get across town in 30 minutes during this morning rush hour. She heard traffic of other staff come in and out. As she was moving between her desk and conference table putting files in her bag she heard Marc declare that he was back.

"Is this the wedding gift for Theodore and Simone?" he asked as he walked through the door with an elegant embroidered silver box that could fit in any small office printer. "Just found it on my desk."

Rebecca looked surprised but still preoccupied with closing her satchel. She looked at the box as she put her bag over her shoulder. "No, haven't even figured a gift for them." She replied in a hurry, her hair waving with her body movements.

"Or do you have a secret admirer? Come clean now?' He teasingly scrutinized her eyes.

"I can assure you that is not the case." replied Rebecca with a gentle stare. "I'll open it when I get back. Am running late already."

"And leave me in all this suspense? I don't think so Madam. C'mon, here are the scissors." Marc snatched the scissors from the crystal jar on her desk.

"The things I do for you..." she rolled her eyeballs taking the scissors from his hand. Rebecca wondered to herself who the sender was. She had been too busy, too pre-occupied to notice a possible prolonged stare or any other hint of affection. After carefully untying the light silver grey ribbon, she took the lid off the box. Rebecca screamed.

She remained frozen transfixed at the sight in the box, paralyzed in fear. No longer aware of her luxurious surroundings, Rebecca was viciously transported to being the little girl in the cave, half naked, shivering in terror. Marc grabbed and held her.

"It's ok. It's ok. I'm here. You're fine. It's only a box from some disgusting people whom you're going after. They want you afraid." Marc pushed the box aside as he sheltered her with his embrace. Facing the table, he methodically surveyed the box and its contents looking for any clues and what the content of the box actually meant.

An Associate came rushing through the door. "Everything ok here?" he asked looking ready to pounce while surveying the office.

"Oh yes. Don't worry Paul we've got it covered, just some fan mail. Thanks." Marc quickly responded motioning with his hand for Paul to remain at the door. He didn't want this incident becoming office gossip, giving it attention it didn't deserve.

"Okay let us know if you need anything."

"Thanks, will do." Rebecca's hands were still shaking while she stared at the contents of the box from a distance. As if something struck her, she quickly composed herself.

"These bastards! We'll get them for this. To my last breath, I will make sure that their agreement is torn to shreds and no one will ever touch Pointe Trois again."

They were staring at 2 items in the box each in its own tray, elegantly lined with blood red paper maché. One item was a pair of beautifully manicured female hands that still looked very fresh. Next to it, still showing signs of moisture but not dripping, was a human heart. You could still pick up the odor of formaldehyde. Both their eyes kept searching the box for any other clues. He stretched over to pick up the lid. Taped under the lid was a silver envelope which was also tied with a slender black ribbon. Marc carefully removed the envelope from the lid and untied its knot. Rebecca took it from him. Neatly inscribed with a fountain pen, it read *"Dearest Rebecca, now what good would you be to your profession and your people without your beautiful hands. And well...is this Montero's heart? Drop this nonsense or else..."* Rebecca felt a piercing migraine shoot through her head as all the stress of the past few days concentrated itself in her skull at this one moment.

"Rebecca are you okay?" He motioned to her to sit down and poured a glass of water for her from the side consul. She fumbled through her purse for some aspirin, swallowed it and gulped the whole glass of water down. Rebecca slammed the glass on the table closed her eyes, inhaled a long deep breadth then exhaled to try and expel all her stress.

"Oh no! I've got to give this technical opinion at the Judge's chambers. Please call her and tell her I'm on the way. Please handle all of this." as her hand waved towards the conference table where the box of dead body parts lay.

"Tell the cops I'll come by and make a statement at the Station when I'm finished with the Judge."

"Sure, don't worry about a thing. But we probably will have more information than them."

"But we do need to have this on file officially.'

AMBASSADOR HOLSTEIN'S OFFICE UNITED NATIONS – NEW YORK
DAY 3 – 09:00HRS

As per normal procedure, Holstein needed 9 votes to have a majority position on a resolution being passed at the U.N. Security Council and not every one of them was friendly. Hardly the first time he had to maneuver through varied responses that required cajoling and corralling. Given that Council members had to consult with their home capitals, the challenge was the timing. Holstein had reserved the majority of the day to address this issue definitively. 4 of the 5 permanent members and other strategic partner countries met informally on occasion. This morning they were in his office at 9:30am. The understanding was, being like-minded nations, they needed to be sensitive to each other's interests to protect their positioning in the current world order. They knew each other well, no formal sales pitch here. In the afternoon, he would meet one on one with 6 of the 10 non-permanent members to dole out his sweeteners and call in favors.

Holstein comfortable in his arm chair among them, removed his reading glasses as he rubbed his eyes, "Dear colleagues, am afraid we have a delicate situation brewing on our hands. It is more of a long-term security threat arising from an irresponsible decision about to be made by corrupt government officials more interested in lining their pockets rather than developing the inhabitants of this rainforest or protecting its delicate eco-system."

"Forgive me Daniel. Yes, we got the file." interrupted Harry. "Don't get me wrong. They should be hanged if it were up to me. But what's so different about this government of thugs being bumped up the list from other despots around the world? What's the long term security threat to us in this room?" Harry Stiles, the British diplomat, believed in the glory and restoration of the British Empire. This was the understood objective of the older generation from the Foreign Service Office. The cousins across the pond were the front line soldiers in the cost of things militarily and political popularity. And the sovereign mother empire would be placed as the behind the scenes power broker at the right time.

"Well Harry." Daniel tipped his head towards his colleague. "I will share with you that we have a few of our largest companies in the IT and tel. comm. sectors buying massive amounts of certain minerals that they need from Pointe Trois through agents; something about the use of these materials for their circuit boards. Now I don't think it's only our companies. I would urge you to cross check in a few phone calls whether your companies are, and I don't think any of us wants a scenario where this supply point of key raw materials for sectors critical in our 21st Century becomes closed off to one company in a matter of days?"

The diplomat from a European company historically known for its precision based engineering asked, "Daniel, when I read the file the name was familiar. It caused a bit of a scandal in our private sector a little over a year ago. One of those things where everybody is doing it, but if you get caught you will be crucified for the sins of the many. The company Helleschkapft Engineering manufactures various components of high altitude equipment and innovative materials for fighter jets, space shuttles, missiles, satellites and the like. Some human rights group had been watching them for some time because of the defense contracts they'd been signing with various governments. Anyway, the activists trying to get as much information out of a disgruntled ex-employee were informed about their procurement of certain minerals that they required in their manufacturing process that were coming from Pointe Trois however only through agents as well, never direct procurement. Apparently the agent they were using ran into some problems and a large consignment was delayed. This ex-employee was tasked to quickly find another agent to avoid ruining their manufacturing schedule. The new agent they hired was sloppy with the paperwork. A customs agent traced Helleschkapft as one of its clients for materials sourced from Pointe Trois. The employee was fired and the company disassociated itself from anything to do with the agent. It was all very messy. The case was mediated out of court and the company paid a hefty fine for undocumented illegal raw material and tax evasion among other charges. But yes, to answer your question we do have some of our companies buying from the Pointe Trois region. And these are not mercantile traders looking for the best quality textile related crops. These are very sophisticated software companies, who I will confess to you, play an instrumental role in our security and defense sectors. We cannot allow what would ordinarily be an open market - legal or illegal- to now be closed to one company."

Stephan DuPlessey, the French diplomat, had reached the pinnacle of his diplomatic career and had political aspirations. He was aiming to be the Minister of Foreign Affairs as an entrée to other bigger offices. Stephan decided that aggravating one of the largest foreign investors of Western Europe who was domiciled in France would not be allowed to be even a faint stain on his CV that had been carefully nurtured and cultivated over the years. But he would surely let his colleagues know his was one of the team.

Stephan started with a long sigh. "G. Tech. as you all know is headquartered in our country. They are known to be super conscious of their image and I am told very low key. It would be difficult for me to make a ruling against a company that contributes so much to our tax payer revenue and maintains a squeaky clean image. Mes amis, I think you understand, non? Before you know it they'd be complaining to the Ministry of Foreign Affairs and threatening to relocate their headquarters accusing the government of betraying foreign companies and frustrating private sector innovation. That would put me in an awkward position, non? Vraiment. It would be difficult for me to vote against them on this one." Stephan looked very concerned that he was going against the collective interest of his colleagues on this matter that appeared urgent to Holstein.

"Stephan, pas de problem. We understand." Holstein responded trying to sound practical and non-chalant.

Then with sudden optimism Stephan returned. "However what I can do for you is to place some pressure on two of the non-permanent members that are expecting significant funding from our government to support some infrastructural projects. I can assure you, you would not have any problems there mes amis."

Holstein felt extremely relieved because they were two members beyond the ones he planned on meeting.

Another diplomat, a retired Lt. General sent into diplomacy as punishment, gruff and known to be abrasive, was short in words. "Comrades, veee cannot have this nonsense of one company owning that little forest or vaaatever over there. Veee must stop this. Maybe my government sends fighter jets to talk to their three second-hand fighter jets we sold to them six months ago? They forget we send our mechanics to do the maintenance. We know where all the lose screws are. Intelligence tells me they were about to fly out four Ka52 Alligator helicopters they had bought *weeeezz* cash. I tell them to hold that order indefinitely? *Vvvvhhy veee* even spend time discussing such?"

"Thank you for your support Ambassador Vladinakov. That would not be necessary. Although you could you hold on to those copters until this matter is settled." Holstein smiled.

The diplomat waved his hand with an impatient smirk, communicating the matter was closed. It would be done.

The most quiet but most astute of the diplomats in the room, offered his position. "Our concern is the fifth permanent member of the security council that is already very active in Caramondo and well-placed with the people of Pointe Trois rainforest, the Coriamese government. We would not wish for them to have a bigger advantage in the securities industry when everybody else loses access to this forest. My analyst says our companies are very tight lipped about whether they are actually accessing any minerals of any sort from this location and became a bit agitated with the inquiry, which means that they definitely are. You have my government's support. I know how I will present it to them." He concluded with a nod and smile.

"We are grateful Ambassador Okinada, my thanks to you and your government." Holstein returned with a nod of respect while he thought of how he was going to bring the Republic of Coriames around on this vote.

Ambassador Sharma gave a similar explanation without detail why it would be in her country's interest to affirm this vote. Any delicate re-balance of geopolitics could easily put them at a disadvantage if their enemy neighboring countries were to be able to get through to G. Tech. and access the material when they couldn't - whether in the short or long term.

Holstein concluded, "Lady and gentlemen, grateful you could send me your confirmations by end of today. I am sure we will be able to reciprocate in future." He also knew what highly sensitive matter could bring his colleague of Coriames around in a brief undocumented meeting.

They collectively stood up from their intimate setting of sofas and armchairs and filed out with brief handshakes.

CONTINENTAL FUNDING ORGANIZATION HQ
BRUSSELS, BELGIUM
DAY 3 – 12:00HRS

5 men, 3 women. Among them included the Program Director, Head of Fund Management, Head of Risk Management and Deputy Secretary General who were seated around the conference table on the 42nd floor of their glass building. Minimalist furnishings in cool shades of grey represented the austere tone of the organization's philosophy and its approach towards its clients. Money was not to be lavished. It was to be invested wisely. The Deputy Secretary General wanted to handle this portion of

the meeting efficiently; country performance against targets. They had just completed the update on 3 countries on another continent that were performing well above target on service delivery, tax revenue expansion and debt reduction.

"Before we move from this area," the DSG quickly turned to Etienne. "There is a particular update you'd like to bring to our attention? It has been long since I've received any encouraging news from Caramondo."

"Well Gregoire, it is an interesting development. Some activists in New York are doing everything possible to prevent the signing of the agreement of Pointe Trois you are all aware about. They are trying to mount as much international pressure on the Caramondo government to signal to them that the consequences would far outweigh the benefits of selling this region of the country knowing the that the population and the environment of Pointe Trois will be destroyed and the citizens of the country at large will see very little of these proceeds. The agreement will be signed in 4 days."

There were brief gasps around the table.

"They have asked us to threaten the government that aid will be either cut or removed if they go ahead with the agreement given that we alone support 22% of their budget. Their national budget is a total of 64% donor funded. Because of the obvious human rights and environmental violations and the opportunity to squeeze a few pints of compliance out of them, I advised them that we would participate provided it would be a coordinated operation with other global donors so they would not be able to borrow from Paul because Pierre had turned off the taps. They are coordinating with the Global Council of Donors to ensure that they are cut off with other development aid. It is good that Henri, our Chief Financial Controller is at the GCD meeting in Hong Kong right now. I have already been in communication with him."

"Oui. I couldn't agree more. Etienne until the government changes, am afraid we'll see little value for our money we put in Caramondo. If there is an opportunity to bleed compliance out of them, well and good. You know how to work that angle in communication with Henri. If there is an excuse to withdraw our money and put it in a country where the leaders are serious, well then even better. But as you say, it can only work if the other global donors are on board. We are not going to get ourselves into a real political conundrum with these people who view fiscal policy as a debilitating constraint and accountability as anathema to their national cum personal budget.

Monitor that closely and keep us up to date." ordered the DSG with another nod. "Bien sur." replied Etienne.

Etienne was relieved to know that Caramondo no longer had the leeway it thought it did. The circle was closing in. But whether Caramondo would find a way to pierce through remained to be seen in the next 72 hours.

GLOBAL COUNCIL OF DONORS MEETING HONG KONG
DAY 3 – 19:00HRS

It was the 5th day of the conference. Dr. Elizabeth Sheldon had requested the donors pertinent to Caramondo and its continent at large to fly into Hong Kong almost immediately because there wasn't enough time to schedule a separate conference and they were just wrapping up in Hong Kong. She was a brilliant professional and had to see how the blacklisting of the Caramondo government would fit perfectly within the remit of this conference. She decided it would be setting a precedent and clear message to all despotic leaders of beneficiary countries that adherence to their terms and conditions was going to be aggressively pursued and any recipients in violation of the agreements signed to, would be shut out of the global financing community. Some of the new criteria of compliance now included respect for human rights and measurable environmental management. She had earlier requested the secretary of the meeting modify the agenda.

There was a lot to wrap up on the agenda, negotiations to be finalized and deals to be done. This conference was a milestone. The first of its kind, 30 large scale donors and development organizations had coordinated their aid distribution to beneficiary countries. Duplication of aid, manipulation of donors and layers of donor overhead could now be eliminated.

Dr. Sheldon came to agenda point concerning Caramondo. "Ladies and Gentlemen, you all have read your briefs I presume? Can we take a clear decisive position on this to ensure it will send an unmistakable message? I think everyone has on their books, 1 or 2 countries that aptly fit into this category only to find out that they came to you because they were cancelled mid-stream or rejected by another donor." She looked at the Continental Financing Organization focal point to weigh in.

After receiving his brief from Etienne in New York Henri Riseau, Chief Financial Officer, of the Continental Financing Organization weighed in as he looked around at his colleagues, "From our communication circulated to all of you, we are now all aware of the Government of Caramondo and their agreement that they plan to sign to sell off the country's rainforest. I think this is an excellent precedent to set with Caramondo. If they are planning to sign their agreement in the next 3 days we should advise all our offices on the Continent before they try to slip anything through whether as a bi-lateral or multi-lateral financing arrangement."

Sheldon nodded as she noted, "Yes, we all should have done that by the time we leave this conference to allow our regional offices to put their local staff on alert."

"I agree completely." said the Managing Director of the largest funding organization of the Southern Hemisphere.

Henri continued, "Speaking of bi-lateral support, Caramondo has had long-term ties with the government of Coriames on infrastructure development and scattered health or social development projects. I think with them on board the government will begin to feel the screws tighten. The issue is to avoid some of the infrastructure aid being converted into cash for other government expenditures and to survive off that for a while until they're out of the global spotlight.'

The Managing Director smirked, "Yes, we've seen a few of those before when we've told them to start counting what's left in the Central Bank and how much they owe." Sheldon nodded her head, listening carefully as she peered her eyes through the top of her glasses while penning away.

"Too true, I've made a note of it to get in touch with the Coriames government. They do have the policy of damn everyone else and follow their own drum. But let's see what kind of squeeze they can contribute." She removed her glasses, swinging them on her hand. "Ok, I think we all agree then that we will set a milestone precedent to all governments that refuse to comply with the terms and conditions of development aid that blacklisting can work.

For the record, can I have a show of hands of all who agree?"

Every financing organization present at the conference raised their hands. Sheldon closely studied every individual in the room to ensure she did not miss or misinterpret a hand.

"Excellent. Then let it be known for the record that any country that violates the negotiated terms and conditions of development aid will be blacklisted. We shall closely monitor the government of Caramondo and put all funding agency staff on high alert within the next 6 hours. Should they sign their agreement with the corporate conglomerate then they shall be the first to be immediately blacklisted until they are in compliance."

Henri Riseau raised his hand as he added in a last comment, "Let it be known for the record that we the CFO shall work closely with you on this. We fund 22% of their budget and would like to ensure that the message is delivered clearly and concisely should the event arise."

"We thank you Henri. And it is so noted for the record. Next item on the agenda is the program consolidation of the highest beneficiary continent to see how do we get better value for money?"

HON. MAXWELL FISHER'S OFFICE PARLIAMENT, CARAMONDO
DAY 3 – 18:00HRS

The text message Fisher had fired off earlier in Parliament was to Hon. Meshach Manywar requesting a meeting at his office. Fisher knew Manywar's delivery combined with the current political climate would scuttle the Bill. The disillusioned MP said he'd come by but there was nothing they needed to discuss in the office that couldn't be discussed in the Plenary. He too had read the wind and knew he would have won the Plenary vote in the morning. With his colleagues, he would just stay close to their supporters and wait for it to be presented again within the next 48 hours. He told his colleagues about the meeting, they knew Maxwell had lost and told him not to even bother. But Manywar wanted to see Maxwell. The feared Hon. Fisher, on this ever so rare occasion, would have to ask someone for something. Fisher was used to taking, but this evening he would have to ask, and if miracles prevailed he might even beg. But Manywar wasn't going to push his luck that far.

Hon. Manywar knocked once and walked in. The Chief Whip appeared engrossed in 3 separate reports in front of him but they couldn't be further from his mind. "Meshach!" he gaily declared, "so glad you could make it. We don't meet often enough like this. You know, téte-â-téte, getting to know each other better. No interferences of people banging on their benches and all that unpleasant stuff."

Meshach laughed. "But you don't need to get to know people in more intimate surroundings." As he quickly twirled his head around his office, "You just investigate them. I think people are a bit skittish about walking through that door. What can I do for you Maxwell? It would appear you have several reports to get through and probably a few late meetings that await you."

His eyes rummaging through his host's desk, Fishers arm motioned for him to have a seat. Fisher's smile had long left his face and realigned itself into straight-lined lips that could look either like a cold smile or deep seated anger polished by a flat expression.

"So right, there is a pesky little matter that seems to doggedly resurface. In fact I can't remember when another matter was so persistently presented, discussed and negotiated. It is just oh so tiring. I really want it go away.

Don't you?" Fisher wrinkled his face like a frustrated child that was not getting what they wanted.

Manywar's eyes squinted but remained calm. He knew he was in the winning position and this conversation wasn't going to change that. No need to get nervous, he told himself.

"Pesky huh? I didn't know that the survival of 400,000 of us had been reduced to pesky detail. We should really try to avoid inconveniencing you so, that is very inconsiderate of us." Manywar's neck stiffened and his head cocked in a certain direction.

"Alright." laughed Fisher casually. "My vocabulary does constrain me on occasion. Let's get to it. Pointe Trois, that Bill has to pass. This is not my quarrel with you. The President has directed this thing to go through. So we have to make it happen. We'll do everything possible to negotiate a quality of life for your people with the G. Tech group. There will be top quality equipment and expertise from the day they arrive right in your backyard for heaven's sake. Most people would give an arm and a leg for that. Who knows what could become of the relationship of having such a wealthy entity right in your own home. Really, aren't we being a bit harsh on this agreement?" Fisher was starting to sound impatient.

Meshach was disappointed. He thought he was coming to hear a man make a humble appeal. Instead he was listening to his people's intelligence and dignity being even more insulted. "An arm and a leg huh…well we've given much more than that Fisher. I can assure you. Let them move to your area with all these benefits you're tossing around." Manywar was having difficulty controlling his disgust with a glare he struggled to suppress.

"You're the ones with the goodies remember?" he shot back.

Meshach decided to quit the small talk. Without twitching a muscle on his face the words came out hard and fast. "Hon. Fisher from what my reliable contacts at State House tell me about that agreement, my people are required to leave shortly after the signing, the so-called buyer will not be subject to any environmental audits and there will be no revenue sharing of resources extracted from the forest. Of course, we're supposed to have long left by then anyway. Can you believe that? We just pack up and leave. Abandon our homes. No clear destination, no compensation to talk of. The outright extinction of my people, the destruction of our land is contained in this Bill. But don't worry, that issue will never arise. Hon. Fisher I was sent to Parliament to represent my people. How would expect me or anyone else from the Region in their right mind to allow this Bill to go through? I will protect and defend my people to my last breath Maxwell." He looked him up and down for a brief second. "You were in those Chambers earlier this morning. You could see, perhaps even more clearly than I that you were going to lose. That's why you postponed the vote. Don't deny it."

Fisher's calm smile had reshaped into a glare, asking himself who was this character from the woods lecturing to him in his office. Forget the tender mercies and soft talk. He needed to be handled. But Meshach raged on.

"Maxwell, why are you trying to delay the inevitable? This Bill will not go through. I can give you my personal assurance on that." Fisher had had enough of this insolence in his office.

"Alright, alright. Let's not get so uptight about this. Let's approach this from a different angle. One that I call the necessity-survival get ahead angle." Fisher said with an icy soft smile.

"What are you after Maxwell?" Meshach asked with a scowl of suspicion and mistrust all over his face.

He brought out a file buried underneath the reports strewn on his desk. "Aaah haa," As he flicked through each page slowly and thoughtfully.

Partly arising from his humble beginnings Meshach knew he led a simple life. He had no skeletons to destabilize him. "Wow this is impressive, simply admirable." Maxwell pondered as he flicked through the file. He closed it and threw it to Meshach's side of the desk and stared at Meshach. "Have a look for yourself."

Meshach had no idea where this was going. He continued to look at the Chief Whip as he opened the file. All friendliness had long left the room. Meshach flicked through quickly. He saw that they were school transcripts; harmless enough. He looked up quickly at Maxwell whose eyes prompted him back down to the file. Meshach looked more closely. He recognized the names of the school. They were the missionary school in Pointe Trois. He recognized the names on the transcripts. They were his childrens'; twin girls going into their last year of primary school and an elder boy who had just completed secondary school with outstanding grades and distinctions in all his examination results. They had all managed to get scholarships from the Coriamese government reserved for the best and the brightest. The boy was now going to university in Avalon for the first 2 years and then would transfer to a university in Coriames on a full scholarship based on his area of specialization. Shock and fury ran through Hon. Manywar. How could he dare bring his children into this conversation?

Fisher saw the fury and launched his attack. "Now here's the deal. And it is a deal you will take. Your children, God bless their precious souls are all on scholarships. This is just admirable. I've already called the Vice Chancellor of the university, just catching up and all with an old pal you know. And he was sharing with me how they desperately needed more money from government to run the university. I said I'd see what I can do. He was complaining bitterly how they didn't have enough money to cover the students admitted on scholarships. I told him that was just a crying shame. Now it would be a wailing shame if I were to advise him to drop one of the names on the list if he wanted to get the money he needs to run the university. All those years of hard work your son has put in and those wonderful girls of yours; can't go to waste. They'd be the pride of any parents, but what if their primary leaving examination results were somehow exchanged with a couple of students who had bricks of mud for brains. Heavens! I wonder what that would do to their Coriamese scholarships. You see where I'm going with this Hon. Manywar? Are we together on this Bill in the interests of more pressing matters at hand?"

Manywar stared at Fisher for a moment. A long close stare, asking himself how could someone stoop so low for money, moreover when he had more than he could spend in his next three lifetimes.

"Great. I will interpret your silence as a sudden realization and agreement that we all need to do the needful to get ahead. Keep our heads afloat. Once you and your colleagues bow down," he commanded as he lowered his chin, "then the other moderates will bow their capricious selves out." A tight smile came over his face to intonate he was finished dispensing his instructions.

Hon. Manywar stood up picked up the phone handset from its console on the Chief Whip's desk. "Aaah Hon. Fisher, start dialing." Manywar stared at him. Fisher looked stunned. Manywar picked up Fisher's cel. phone on top of the reports. "I said start dialing." He placed the phone back on the desk then picked up the file and threw it back onto Maxwell's side of the desk front and center with a sneer of disgust and started walking towards the door.

"I think you better start preparing your explanation to the President on why you have failed to execute his task. Better make it convincing. I understand he is ruthless with people who fail him on things that he really wants, no matter how near or dear."

Hon. Manywar turned around and headed for the door, "And oh, if anything happens to my children's education or safety, well….let's not go there. I think you know what we Burajon used to do with wild animals in the old days." He threw a look of primal focus and fearlessness like he was facing an animal that needed to be killed. The Chief Whip shrank for a moment not expecting such directness from an MP from the periphery of the country.

He quickly collected himself. "Well that is indeed unfortunate for you and your people. My condolences in advance."

Manywar smiled back. "See you at the Plenary Hon. Fisher." He replied as he walked out. The Chief Whip stared at the door still enraged and then threw the file at it, completely disgusted that some small time MP from the woods would have the nerve to stand up to him. He picked up his cel. phone and dialed. With tension in his voice, he spoke.

"We've got a problem.

"We'll meet tomorrow." replied LaFonte.

CHAPTER 10

THE OUTCOME OF A MEAL

The man was still in a celebratory mood 48 hours later. Over a year of planning had finally paid off. The intelligence had been invaluable. To learn of Montero's movements, track him, trap him and kill him had given him legendary status of fear and respect among the other officers with his similar weak ethical views on life. The problem for the army was that this was a growing crowd.

He was now at his favorite restaurant in his usual private dining room, covered by a bodyguard at the door. General Pitua was enjoying his meal alone while his favorite women were driven to an intimate hotel nearby. He yelled for the waiter. The bodyguard shot an impatient glance at the thickset meek looking man who busied himself wiping glasses at the private bar a couple of feet away. The waiter humbly avoided eye contact. He reached for the remote and turned up the music in the restaurant to maintain the ambience just before he walked into the kitchen. The General had finished his appetizer and was now eager for the entrée and later looking forward to the evening's entertainment. With his sullen shoulders and beaten down gait, the waiter walked out of the kitchen with a large tray that carried an assortment of dishes. He closed the dining room door behind him to maintain the General's privacy.

General Pitua smiled at his food inhaling the aroma as the empty plates were placed aside. The entrée was set in front of him and the empty plates were put onto the tray. The waiter quietly took a step behind the General, removed his QSZ 92 with its suppressor attached and snapped 2 bullets, one into the back of his head and one to bottom of his neck. The man's head fell forward with a thud onto the table narrowly missing his meal. The music covered the thud. The waiter calmly walked out with the tray of empty dishes to the kitchen. Without a sound he dropped them on a side counter. Chef Didier walked up to him. The waiter nodded. Didier nodded back. He handed the waiter a trash bag from a side-rail and instructed him, "Take these left-overs to the rubbish bins outside."

Within 120 seconds the restaurant was on lock-down. All kitchen and serving staff were held at gun point by Gen. Pitua's men, as they called in for reinforcements. Chef Didier looked bored as he put up his long tattooed arms. His brother-in-law was a member of the Military High Council. He respected Didier's history with the militia and was a silent shareholder in the restaurant. By tomorrow evening they'd be open for business again, fully staffed.

PALOMA GARDENS HOTEL
UPSTATE NEW YORK
DAY 3 – 18:00HRS

For security reasons Gen. Piquant did not want to host his son's wedding at a well-known address. Fortunately the bride and groom were also low key people and wanted to have only their loved ones at the wedding. It was a pleasant evening. Not more than 70 people comprised of relatives and friends of the bride, groom and their families. Among the guests were a few Generals and senior officers that had served with Piquant over the years. Rebecca recognized a number of old friends from the scholarship program. She knew she had to tightly manage her time. She'd already missed the Church service due to a pro-longed negotiation of an out of court settlement. As soon as she entered the elegant gardens of the reception Father Raines came from behind, softly grabbed her arm causing her to turn around and gave her an embrace. It was an embrace that Rebecca cherished immensely from a person she could trust; a person that had seen her at her most vulnerable when she was an orphan in the school. He led the direction of the walk.

"On my way here, my network tells me General Paint was scratched off the building. Did you have anything to do with that m'dear?"

"I received confirmation earlier in the afternoon. Given the time difference, the only thing I know is that it happened today. Father, I battle within myself that those days are long gone, but did you really expect me to let that paint continue to breathe all over us like that? My breath feels empty, the hole in my heart does not get any smaller. It just becomes something that I must deal with. The paint had to be scratched off the building. My past momentarily nullifying my present, but without regret. The price of war I must be willing to pay."

They walked into the hotel up to the mezzanine level and found a small meeting room that overlooked the gardens where the reception was held. They sat at the bay window.

"We walk with you Rebecca." Was his soft but solid grip of her hand. He abruptly changed topic. "You know this torturing of people to reveal information and butchering the militia has become par for the course. News coming in says a few villages are already talking about surrender because they simply can't take seeing the onslaught of their families anymore." He said in a hurried hushed tone.

"Now that's where we'd have a problem with intelligence leaks and a defeatist spirit that would put the lives of everyone at risk -whether militia or not. It is just a few more days. Let them hang on. I understand and respect their pain. But let them hang on." She beseeched Father Raines.

Rebecca's anger began to seep through as she asked herself how it could be so good for the bad and so bad for the good as she looked out and saw some of the Generals mingling at the reception.

"Yes I know m'dear, but the real fear, point of fright that I have" he looked at her face closely "is that my network tells me the government has put a hit out on you." The worry in his eyes could not hide itself.

"Yes, tell me about it. I've already received a few body parts as a greeting card." She calmly continued wondering out loud, "But really isn't it a bit obvious to them? They might be able to kill me but they surely will not kill the cause, as normally happens I would become a martyr which would give more fire and anger to the fight. And this would be on an international scale given where I work and my contacts. Wouldn't they figure out by now I'd be sure to leave a very clear trail of bread crumbs so it won't take a minute to reach the murderer comfortably sitting in his chair in Caramondo. Father, you are my guardian angel that is always able to pick up any critical information."

"Rebecca I want you to be extremely careful. Too many people are depending on you. Oh!" He put his hand on his chest remembering, "What I wanted to tell you is my people on the ground tell me that the G. Tech. people are moving out into the forest with increased frequency like they were scowling the forest floor for something and they're remaining tight lipped about it. One of my contacts in the army has seen them haul off the black shiny Chikua soil that I'm told the few medicine men in Pointe Trois revered many centuries ago. That tradition is still there but very rare. Just very odd, don't you think?"

"Oh maybe that's the soil they're looking for in the photos I was looking at as well. But what on earth does that mean?" she asked herself squinting her eyes. Out of the corner of her eye she observed the bride and groom walk into the gardens, both beaming with rice grains from Caramondo showered on them. "Time to give our best wishes!"

They entered the gardens to find guests still congratulating the newlyweds and mingling among themselves. The largest wide brimmed haute couture hat competing with the roses in the gardens gravitated her way,

"Reebecaaah daaahling!" as two air kisses flew to either side of Rebecca's cheek. "Really! You mustn't stay so awaaay like that. Alexander keeps asking after you."

"Oh, for once Jemimah tells the truth about me behind my back." laughed Alexander.

Alexander Bijoubela came from one of the wealthiest families in Caramondo's private sector. Starting out in farming almost 100 years ago they expanded into transportation and subsequently real estate. He attended Harvard Business School and came to know Rebecca through the many Caramondo social events over the holidays.

Everyone admired the latest sport coupe he always seemed to be driving during his University days. Rebecca ignored the material luxuries of Caramondo's privileged.

She was only interested in justice. He was smitten by her, especially when she helped him study Tax Law during a particular winter break. Rebecca remembers how this had made Jemimah and her future mother-in-law extremely jittery through a barrage of friendly visits and phone calls to her. Jemimah was the daughter of an ambitious, officious Brigadier.

"I'll call you later", Raines whispered to Rebecca as he hugged her. Jemimah had floated in the opposite direction to another greeting. Alexander gently took Rebecca by the arm to guide her in their own direction for some privacy.

"Tell me, how is the Pointe Trois case going? It's making some people in Avalon's business community very nervous, like they were counting on that government transaction to go through. The politicians are also getting ugly about it because it could go either way and as you know some of those guys are also banking on getting some of that butter on their fingers. The inside talk in the army is not pretty either. Rebecca everyone is on some kind of extreme tension. I've never read the environment to be like this before. People don't know which way this cookie could crumble and nobody wants to be around during the fall out if it doesn't go the right way for them." He looked at her like he was trying to gauge how tense she was about the whole case. "Tell me what I can do to help? Would you like me to arrange some meetings for you on the local scene, make a contribution, source some information for you?" Alexander had a strange glossed over smile of sympathy, like he was assessing the strength of someone under attack in the friendliest way he could put up at that moment.

She sighed, "Well, you're aware that they plan to sign in 2-3 days. Everyone's whispering that the Head of State is the kingpin behind this, but no one can put a trail to him." They continued their stroll on the outer periphery of the guests nibbling and chatting among each other.

"That's an open secret Becky. And he's not taking any prisoners. Want to hear an unlucky story on how things work out there for people who talk?" as he quickly scanned over his shoulder to make sure no one was too close by.

"What? Tell me?" sounding like she couldn't wait another second.

"Ok. Do not tell this to another soul or it's my neck on the line. In fact, you're the last person I should be telling. But when it comes to you, my heart always bludgeoned my head."

"Now Alexander!" as she dug her nails into his arm as hard as she could.

"Okay! Kill me after." He took her arm in his as they continued their peaceful stroll a safe distance from the guests.

"Well, some of our friends in the private sector had been medium scale operators for many years and all of a sudden became flush with cash about 2-3 years ago and nobody could figure out where from. Turns out they'd been acting as an agent for the President. They had been siphoning out gold, diamonds, cobalt, you name it and selling it on the black market. About 6 months ago, one of the sons of this family had a little too much to drink while at a party of some mutual friends. Well, he starts to rough up the girlfriend of one of the sons of the family hosting the party. They have an all-out brawl in the garden for about two minutes before security shows up to pull them apart. The guests are staring on in utter horror. But within those two minutes, the son defending the honor of his girlfriend insults this boy telling him he comes from a family of thugs and vultures that are void of character or class. The drunken fellow, while re-arranging the young man's more delicate features tells him his family is more powerful than his. That they have been working for the President for the longest time in Pointe Trois as his sole representative. That his family could make a phone call right now and his whole family could be wiped out. You know the type of thing you tell your children to never ever say even if they're being tortured or death might not be such a bad option."

"So the drunken fellow spends the night in jail or what? What happened?" asked Rebecca.

"He wished he had." Alexander chortled. '"One security officer threw him off the premises. A friend drove him home."

"How the hyenas behave among themselves doesn't exactly attract my sympathy." Rebecca angered at how the

Avalon thieves wined and dined at the expense of her people.

"Now this good-guy friend tells me this part himself like a week later. Being a good guy, he helps him through his front door and drops him on the couch in his living room. He heads out. A few feet after shutting the door behind him, he hears this forceful crashing like someone's been thrown against an armoire. He runs back, but the door's already locked. He climbs through some shrubs and desperately peers through the living room bay window. He sees these 3 huge men in complete black outfits with ski masks and all and these huge swords strapped on their backs. They are throwing this big guy around like he's a kilo of meat. After a few rounds of connecting him with his furniture, the guy is out unconscious. They throw him onto the kitchen counter. The guy regains consciousness with his head being forced to make a hole on the granite top. Imagine the feeling of that."

Alexander casually continues his recount as they keep strolling around.

"The poor fellow in a world of pain can barely move. One of them removes his sword from its sheath and chops this guy into bits, legs, arms, hands, feet, torso, head; you name it. Another pulls out a neatly folded trash bag from his inside vest, unfolds it, opens it and puts the body parts in the refuse bag. The buddy said he peed in his pants out of pure fright of what he was seeing through the window. There's blood everywhere. The whole body is now in the refuse bag and one of them neatly ties it brings it back to the living room and calmly places it on the coffee table at the center of the living room."

Rebecca couldn't hide the disgust on her face.

"The third guy brings out a large size sheet of paper, walks back to the kitchen and returns with a steak knife. He pierces the sheet of paper through the knife then pierces the knife through the refuse bag and the flesh in it like they're putting up the beef of the day on the display counter. You know what the piece of paper says? '*Don't talk about things that don't exist.*' The friend sees that they look like they're leaving. He realizes he's still standing in the shrubs at the living room window. He turns around, knocks over one of the plant pots and runs for dear life. He said he even forgot he had his car. He just kept running down the road. He heard a car side mirror shatter behind him. He knew it was a bullet chasing him. He said he just kept running, until he reached a main intersection and got into a cab. Don't ask me what he told the cab driver with all that pee in his pants."

Rebecca didn't know whether to be amused or plain unsympathetic. "Poor bugger. He should choose his friends more carefully."

Alexander continued. "His family advised him never to report this to the Police. Get this, the family of the fellow who was chopped up within a week packed up, sold their assets, left the country and now live in the U.K. I ran into the brother of the deceased during one of my usual trips and he says the father had a meeting with the Head of State the morning after the party and was told to find another home and life within one week or his whole family tree would be dead."

Rebecca looked at Alexander inquisitively. "That would be invaluable testimony to us now."

Alexander's neck leaned into her. "Becky, this is not the time to joke around. These guys I'm sure would slit your throat without batting an eyelash. Yes, the family might be a bit jittery about providing State's evidence."

Alexander's mix of seriousness and sarcasm did not distract Rebecca.

"But these are very people willing to exterminate my own people. And they expect me to back down now? I have to be ready for anything. I'll just keep pressing on."

"Oh what am I going to do with you?" Exasperated he looked at her as he held her hand. His concern was interrupted by the eye contact Rebecca made with Simone as the bride and groom scanned the lawn of people who loved them.

"Time to give hugs. Always good to see you and if anything comes up, promise you'll let me know."

"Of course I will my love. We'll do lunch or something." He gave her a warm bear hug. She pulled away, looked in his eyes and turned to head towards the bride and groom.

Simone and Rebecca shared an extra-long hug. A long line of well-wishers had developed. "After the honeymoon, I'll come by and we'll have a long chat."

Knowing that this would be well after the signing of the agreement, Rebecca could spend as much time as she desired with them. Their history stemming back to the days of the missionary school when Sunday evening supper was the big meal of the week and exam results day was the highlight of the term. She looked forward to heading back to her apartment to put the finishing touches on the case. Her mind kept banging away asking whether the evidence in the file already sent to Ambassador Holstein coupled with the footage being collected from the forest would be sufficient. From the gardens she walked towards the banquet hall that would take her to the reception area nodding to a few guests that were vaguely familiar and waved to others that were professional acquaintances. Out of the corner of her eye Rebecca noticed a dashing gentleman and two others with whom he was chatting.

"Rebecca," she questioningly looked at this stranger who seemed to know her name. "You don't remember me, do you? Raphael Pachara, Elder Pachara's son. I used to pull your ponytails when I sat behind you all throughout primary school."

Rebecca grappled with the memory and embarrassment for not recognizing him. He had evolved from this playful naughty boy that enjoyed teasing and cuddling her every chance he got into this elegant specimen that stood before her.

"Oh my Raphael, should I say you've...changed?" Her eyes widened slightly while trying to reshape her pleasant shock into a smile.

"And you are still as beautiful as ever Rebecca. You never figured out why I kept pulling on your ponytails."

Rebecca blushed for a moment. She knew it was a genuine emotional compliment and did everything possible to change direction of the conversation. Rebecca remembered that Raphael's family were of the Pekweh tribe but were one of the largest land owners on both sides of the border. They later settled on the other side and became citizens of Seremanta the neighboring country. His family could afford to have taken him to school anywhere in the world, but being the eldest son they wanted him to stay as close as possible to home and took him to the missionary school in Pointe Trois for his primary education in order to learn the culture and ways of his people. He took her hand raised it to his lips and gently kissed it before returning it to her side. He then shot a look of distinct dislike across the gardens. Rebecca could not contain her curiosity and casually glanced over to see who was the beneficiary of this sudden change in social graces.

On registering her surprise, he said in a low warning voice, "I see you've been speaking to that evil creature who is one of the key architects of the money stashed away in back accounts of most of the senior army officers desecrating our land. The clique of the key army officers in all of this, each have at least $10million to their names all over the world. It all goes through his Investment Bank that has their offices between London, Coriames and New York. Rebecca, he is a spitting cobra clothed with charm that would disarm even the worst of their kind. I hope you didn't tell him anything of your developments so far? You can believe he will be providing a full update to all concerned, starting with some of the Generals here.' Rebecca's mind became temporarily foggy with shock as she tried to recall what she had just told Alexander.

"Well nothing of substance really. He did most of the talking, telling me about the chap that got chopped up." Raphael interrupted with a tinge of sarcasm. "Oh, did he tell you that it was his family that recommended to the Head of State that the boy's family be exiled and they happened to be conveniently positioned to buy up all the assets of that family at bargain basement prices?" He said stealing another sneering look at Alexander who pretended to be oblivious to Raphael's contempt towards him.

"With those retractable fangs, Rebecca you need to keep a safe distance. He is a central figure outside of Caramondo in charge of laundering their blood money that is killing Pointe Trois."

As she turned around to look at Alexander, she asked herself if this very person who had just given her such a warm bear hug was the same person responsible for putting a civilized, legitimate face to the torture and brutality of her own people.

"Rebecca, I'm sorry we've not stepped forward in such a visible way as you may have liked. But you know my family has been supporting displaced and injured people both here and Pointe Trois in whatever way we can."

"Yes, Raphael. I know they've been doing that for many years and I cannot express to you how appreciative we all are for that. Many people would have died had it not been for your father's and now your intervention. It's funny, maybe sad, that you're a citizen of Seremanta yet you have done so much more than most of the citizens of our capital city."

He grabbed her hand again and looked straight into her eyes. "That's because we the Pekweh and Burajon are one ever since time began and we roamed the lands. These borders are mere recent formalities of paper. Call me if you need anything, anytime, anywhere. Take good care of yourself and stay away from reptiles in tailored suits. Their venom can kill a whole tribe."

"I'll take good care Raphael. I'm glad we met today. Let's stay in close touch over the next couple of days." He assured her and gave her a brief hug and waved goodbye as she walked away.

Rebecca still tried to bring her mind to grips with the level of desperation the most powerful and privileged of Caramondo would go to for Pointe Trois to be sold. She swore to herself she would dig deeper than they and do everything possible to ensure that this sale would not go through. In her heart of hearts she knew she had the confidence and willpower of all of them combined to kill this agreement, get the army out of Caramondo and get their people onto a track of development whether through government or other direct interventions. Her heart screamed enough is enough. Rebecca's head pounded with fury at the humiliation her people experienced for so many years, while others of her same nation just looked on. She felt her heart ache. She felt so loved, yet so lonely in this fight for so many lives. She reminded herself it was not her battle but the battle of her people. Losing was not an option.

REBECCA'S APARTMENT
UPPER EAST SIDE, NEW YORK
DAY 3 – 22:00HRS

The emotional exhaustion was draining her. From the wedding, Rebecca had rushed back to the office to attend 2 late evening meetings with other senior associates that required her input in tackling defendants in the court room. Towards the end of the second meeting she excused herself worried her monster in its cage would take advantage of her weakened state and, without warning, release itself. Throwing her keys on the side table she dropped her satchel on the floor next to the couch and fell straight onto it, not wanting to think about anything or anyone. It was just too painful. Rebecca closed her eyes in the dark and let the tears run down her temples as she hugged a cushion. Ten minutes later her cel. phone rang. She rummaged through her satchel and picked the call.

"Rebecca, it's Ian. I know you need your rest but I just got off the calls and wanted to give you an update."

Rebecca sat up. Still in the dark hugging the cushion she cleared her nose and throat with a quick snivel. "Shoot, I'm listening."

Ian sounded geared up. "Well, we've got 10 of the 15 so far. Let me tell you what the problem is with the other 5."

"Tell me...." Her concentration fully honed in on his voice, glad to be taking cover in the dark to protect her anyway it could from her stress.

"Ok, Wildlife Fund, Plants for Medical Research and People of the Earth must have had lunch together because they all say the exact same thing."

"Oh, what's that?" Knowing that these were the heavy hitters in their respective spheres and everyone else was watching what they would do before they came to their own decisions. Rebecca's heart beat sped up.

"Because these guys have so many activities going on around the globe they're very particular to remain apolitical as they have done so far. Meaning, if this Bill is ratified into Law, then the Legislature has approved the transaction and it would look like they're poking their noses into somebody else's business. It becomes a legal transaction. The willingness of the buyer or seller are all shades of gray. That's the 3."

"Gotcha, and the other 2?"

"Corporate Environmental Group just signed a $2million partnership with all the major corporate offenders and these so-called sponsors of theirs have made it clear they'll choose another battle, another day. This one's too close to home. Today it's G. Tech., tomorrow it could be one of them. You remember the Citizens Environmental Alert, the new NGO trying to break into the environmental advocacy and lobby world?"

"Sure I do. They asked me to serve on their Board. I turned it down because it looked like someone was calling the shots in the background."

"Well, as recently as 2 days ago they received a cheque for $900,000=, from guess who?"

"Who?" as she clutched the cushion even harder.

"No bonus points for you. From G. Tech. And word is, the Chairman of the Board's instructions when receiving the money was to scuttle this consortium if he could do this within the next 48 hours, there would be an extra $100,000= bonus for him personally. I just wanted you to sleep on it and we could exchange notes in the morning. Say, by the way, our researchers say the name Global Investment Banking Services keeps surfacing with anything related to money movements, in particular a certain Alexander Bijoubela. In a nut shell, he makes some dirty money from army officers look laundry sparkling fresh. Oh and the live feeds should start streaming in tomorrow."

"Oh really? Bijoubela huh? That's just great. Ok, let's see how to move forward tomorrow on the organizations. Thanks for the update." Rebecca closed her eyes and fell back on the couch furious at Bijoubela and wondering whether this consortium could ever really come through in time. The couch felt comfortable, too comfortable to fight.

CHAPTER 11

THE INSPECTION

DAY 4

AVALON INTERNATIONAL AIRPORT
08:00HRS

Simmons figured to himself he did not want to be disappointed today. There was too little time for the army to fix a crisis if one existed. During their briefing meeting this morning Kreshnakov kept tight lipped. Said he wanted to see, to smell the situation on the ground first and meet with the army field command before he gave an assessment. Simmons knew, that for the years he'd known Kreshnakov that meant that the client had lost control of the situation. He was hoping Kreshnakov was wrong, which he had never known to be the case.

The sun was already hot. The humidity pumped away pressure cooking anything that could breathe. It was a sleepy capital with the steely hard glass upcoming high-rises trying to drown out the soft unrushed feel of the colonial buildings. They whizzed down the main street in their luxury van of government license plates and tinted windows, priority clearance at all intersections. The mood was quiet and pensive in the vehicle. The pressure was beginning to mount. Whether their capabilities contained in that vehicle could deliver was not the question.

Whether this government overwhelmed by personal greed could pull off a miracle was the ulcerating worry. In 20 minutes the van sped from the hotel through to the airport's first check point.

Chain link fenced gates guarded by 6 soldiers welcomed them with no eye contact or smiles. 3 on the inside and 3 on the outside remained closed until they approached. Kreshnakov studied the 3 on the outside doing their duty.

One rolled around with his under-mirror, the other scanned the interior of the vehicle, and the third read the clearance letter. He could see that their equipment was very good. But their speed, analysis and precision of task were poor; no profiling, sensing or preliminary observation. If the training was poor, the supervision was probably worse. This would be an army not too difficult to take down. The gates were opened. The entrance to this premise was deliberately designed to be at the back of the building. They drove about quarter of a kilometer then made a sharp right to the side of the building and another diagonal right reaching the entrance. The contrast was stunning to the civilian terminals that looked subdued by a lazy pace of the morning's heat. In this military building the pace was frenetic and purposeful. All variety of air transport parked on the runway and the hangars appeared to be storing large amounts of cargo. All of this unclear activity carefully concealed from any traveller that may be straining to look from the civilian terminals.

They drove past the building itself and were driven straight towards one of their aircraft. The flight crew had arrived an hour earlier to prepare.

Reginald laughed to Kreshnakov, "With this beehive of activity do they allow any civilian aircraft to land at all?"

"Only if it's carrying out their cargo when leaving." Kreshnakov dryly responded, pondering his environment. "Someone around here is really trying to stuff their pockets before we move in." Drier dryly commented.

The movement of jeeps carrying army officers, lorries ferrying soldiers and cargo being moved between the air transport and hangars did not leave any doubt about the urgency of their operations. Simmons nodded to Drier and jutted his eyes in the direction of small size tent looking plusher that the others around it. There were four officers trying to look like they were busily engaged in their own discussion but were obviously standing at the doorway trying to size up the people that were soon to be the new owners. Simmons smiled to himself, even with this beehive of activity, their presence was definitely recognized. Hopefully they'd put in some effort to pulling off their miracle of a few days.

Within 10 minutes the jet was taxing on the runway requesting takeoff clearance. As they looked through the windows, most of the staff on the runway had stopped for a moment to observe their takeoff. Drier wondered to himself, why so much attention? What were they flying in to?

Benjamin LaFonte was hurriedly trying to organize his papers in his office. The day carried with it an unusual amount of pressure. Pressure because there was no certainty of the outcome. And an outcome not scripted could unravel an extremely unpleasant result and certain end of the power structures that existed in Caramondo. And he knew he was among the top of that list drawn up a long time ago. Carrion and Pratt had been waiting for Fisher to arrive in LaFonte's vestibule before they announced themselves. Fisher strolled in. Looking tense with a fixed a smile on his face like he was ready to play ball. The other two rose up as soon as he shut the outer door of this private vestibule.

The P.A. picked up her intercom. "They're here sir." She nodded to the 3 gentlemen to open his door.

Completing his search for one last memo, LaFonte barely made eye contact as he muttered, "Good morning gentlemen." Further hinting with his eyes for them to have a seat.

Pratt pulled up the third chair from the conference table nearby. The Speaker spotted his lost sheet at the right corner of his table and slipped it into his large diary already stuffed with the same. Then he leaned forward, his fingers interlocked as his elbows spanned across his baroque oak desk and eyes fully rotating among the gentlemen in front of him.

"It's show time. We have our part to play today. As you know, we have the Bill being presented at Plenary today." He shot Fisher a warning look like he didn't like the look of that scenario. "And as you *very* well know, the G. Tech team flew in last night. They should be arriving in Pointe Trois any moment soon to admire their bride. The legal and military meetings as well as the final round up with the President will be this afternoon into the evening. That's where we need to report that the Bill was passed in the form it was supposed to pass. Also on the agenda will be the paperwork and arrangements for the money transfers, enquiring whether all is in order with the expectation that one is just waiting for the ink to be dry on the agreement before funds start flowing. So! Where are we on the vote count? Let's start with that. There are all sorts of rumors sprinting up and down this corridor about your purported attempt to threaten Hon. Manywar, and him telling you to start dialing the President to inform him about your failure to deliver on this vote. Frankly I don't care whether it's true or not. I only want to know you've got those votes neatly tied up in advance of this afternoon's session. Now if this vote does not go through, I'm sure you can see why it would be perfectly understandable for G. Tech. to pull out. They wouldn't have a legal leg to stand on. No Law. No Agreement. No money flowing. Not to mention, I was summoned to State

House last night and the President was clearly saying he didn't want any surprises today."

His unwavering eye contact to Fisher had turned into an impatient stare. Fisher hated being put on the spot under such intense pressure like this.

He cleared his throat. "True. The truth is not the issue. We've got a problem."

LaFonte interrupted as his head lunged forward, his eyes ablaze. No one had ever seen him like this.

"We? We've got a problem? No Fisher. You. You've got a problem. This is your sandbox. No one else can jump in there and throw a fistful of sand in someone else's eyes. It would cause too much suspicion. Look too irregular. Now find a viper or a scorpion of your choosing underneath one of your pales there and throw it at someone and get that vote passed. Forgive me for thinking you've developed a moral conscience. The legal meeting with the G. Tech. group will be within an hour after the Plenary. And this will be the number one item on the agenda. So there is no room to maneuver. I can't fake any more delays."

Fisher didn't appreciate the lecture. "I'm on it. Benjamin. It'll be handled. Not to worry." Fisher couldn't believe those words just rolled out of his mouth. He knew there were just no guarantees today. No matter what he had lined up for it.

"I hope so." said LaFonte as he shot him back another look. LaFonte knew the two men had developed a solid respect for each other over the years and had even become some manner of friends. But this transaction had put a strain on everyone. Because they knew of the risks required to get this deal through and the implications if they didn't.

LaFonte turned his head to Carrion. "Any word from your external offices and getting the details from G. Tech. in Paris?"

Carrion and Pratt had been tense observers of the exchange between LaFonte and Fisher. They could feel the atmosphere had become thick. Carrion tried to lighten it up. With a slightly cheery tone he updated.

"Sure. Everything is in place. A day or so ago a couple of my people from the London office flew out to Paris. The bank details were given to G. Tech. The money shall be wired in two installments. i) $450million when the agreement has been signed and ii) $450 million upon the first installation of G. Tech. equipment into the rainforest which essentially means they are moving into an undisturbed area, the militia has been neutralized. The money will go to a Swiss Bank Account. From the SBA it'll go to our London account. London is finalizing the paperwork with our people here today. It has all been merged into the construction of the public housing units and extension of the army barracks upcountry arranged between 2 of my companies the Ministry of Housing and the army. But the money goes from London to the Central

Bank and then to the Ministry of Finance. The Ministry of Housing and army approve the paperwork and then Finance wires the money to my companies."

Carrion looked at Edgar Pratt who was completely transfixed by every word of Carrion. Pratt chimed in, "That's okay. But you're people shouldn't even e-mail the details to me. Just give me a call and I'll come pick-up the file myself. We have a team of anti-corruption officers at the Bank now. The political opposition feels that the Central Bank is a primary hot spot for money laundering. I am aware they're tracking some of my colleagues trying to figure out how this transaction is taking place."

LaFonte interrupted, "Ok gentlemen. We all know what we need to do. Let's get on with it. Call me only if it's an absolutely life threatening emergency."

LaFonte gave them a conclusive smile and nod before he stood up to shake hands with each one of them as they stood up and filed out. Pratt was the last to close the door behind him.

Exiting the outer door into a quiet corridor, Carrion joked to Fisher. "Looks like you've got your hands full."

"Lawrence, you don't know the half of it. I have to dig those vipers and scorpions out of the sand in a few hours."

With a small laugh he replied, "I don't envy you right now. Those opposition members are probably waiting for you with a few big clubs today."

Heading in opposite directions at the T-Junction of the hallway Fisher remarked, "This is going to be a day to remember. That's the only certainty in it." He waved back while walking down the immaculately polished wood floor.

AMOUR DIEU AIRPORT, POINTE TROIS
DAY 4 – 09:30HRS

The pilot circled the airport once as he waited for clearance to land. This gave the team a chance to see what all was going on around Pointe Trois. Each person had taken up a window to have a preview of this spot on the planet that was so important to G. Tech. The plane taxied off the runway and was directed to park not too far from their military operations, rather than closer to the 2 passenger propeller aircrafts on the other end. This terminal of Amour Dieu airport was a simple 1 story building. That was the civilian movement. Then there was the rest of the airport. The organized sea of tents and Hercules transporters, utility choppers, attack choppers, armored vehicles and jeeps.

Drier laughed as he wondered out loud, "Are these fellows fighting battalions of thousands of militia out there or just a few hundred extremely competent fellows showing the difference between ammunition and adeptness."

"This is definitely not a good sign, numbers versus know-how." Kreshnakov responded. "When you see a client calculating like this, you know something is very wrong behind the curtain. We're going to have a slight change in plan." He decided.

They filed off the aircraft. The contrast of the temperature controlled cabin and wild humidity outside immediately produced beads of sweat on their foreheads. Quickly moving out to receive them was James Prescott. As Team Leader in Pointe Trois for the past 2 years, he had come to know the inner workings of the government and knew how to work around them to get what he wanted. His predecessor had been shot in the stomach while checking on one of the mines one year into his job. Simmons through his contacts had heard about complaints from the army concerning his rigidity, not playing ball in the system. They said it was a drunken soldier who shot him. Prescott seemed to get on very well with everyone and knew how to manage his team. However the annual HRIR (Human Resource Investigative Report) of staff in high risk areas revealed a villa, some luxury vehicles and bank accounts that could not be explained. Simmons decided to hold the file until the right time. Just watch and wait on the man.

Prescott shook Drier's hand, smiled and nodded to the rest as they briskly walked. "Whatever could not be put in the regular report briefings to you because of the panic it would raise in Paris, now is your chance to see it firsthand."

Just then Major Calizar walked up alongside the head of the Field Command-Pointe Trois. His tight smile and sweaty handshake revealed his nervousness had not abated since last night.

"Gentlemen, I introduce to you Brigadier Arman Velasquez, Field Commander of Pointe Trois Operations. I shall be along, but any questions, issues or concerns can be ably handled by him."

The Brigadier did not appreciate the directness of accountability by an officer below his rank and brusquely interrupted, "Gentlemen, you are most welcome to Pointe Trois. We have several places to see that are on different sides of the rainforest. Shall we get on?" As he beckoned on them on a short walk towards the area where the utility helicopters were lined up and ready for immediate flight.

While they walked, Velasquez provided a briefing, "Pointe Trois has been divided into Quadrants and detailed into Sectors as a universal navigation system. Spread out among these sectors, today we shall see two mines that have the black shiny soil that seems to interest you. The locals call it Chikua soil. Fortunately, or should I say interestingly, they always happen to be next to a diamond mine, like the shiny stuff is an off-shoot of diamond deposits or vice versa. Anyway, that will allow you to also take a look at 2 diamond mines."

Brigadier Velasquez quietly prayed to himself that no one would be astute enough to ask whether these were the largest mines they would be looking at. Because he knew full well those had been blown apart in the last 24 hours and the main task of the flight plan drawn up was to ensure it did not bring into view any large gaping holes of destroyed sites from engagement with the militia.

"Brigadier, our intelligence updates have reported a marked increase in exchange of fire in different quadrants of the jungle, even reports of a couple of mines that have been blown up." Was a bold questioning look from Kreshnakov. Drier and Simmons looked at each other surprised. Their own sources had not been as forthcoming with them.

Kreshnakov continued, "I am sure you will not mind if you arrange a separate chopper for me to move around with one of your people to certain points in the jungle that will provide us with the confidence with which you assure us."

From Kreshnakov's build and look, Velasquez knew he was staring at the security focal point of the team who was just about to blow apart to smithereens a very fragile picture of control and confidence of the army's operations that he and his team had put together. Kreshnakov handed the Brigadier a map that was a detailed satellite photograph layered with extraction points of every type as well as villages in the Region. Velasquez admired the map itself for a moment. Drier had already highlighted in red the places to be visited. Velasquez briefly studied the map then eye-signaled to the Major. They walked back to the Command Center.

"Mines? Which mines have been exploded?" Simmons asked Kreshnakov.

He answered quickly before the officers stepped out of the tent. "Late last night I met my local contact who told me of the very recent activity in the rainforest. As long as the mines with the Chikua soil were untouched, then I was not going to cause un-necessary alarm about a place already torched. The downside is that the largest coltan mine was among those attacked. I wanted to inspect the extent of the damage myself first."

Five minutes later Major Calizar returned with an enthused Lt. Col. Fachante. The choppers were quickly wheeled out to their takeoff points. Brigadier rejoined the group politely instructing everyone to enter their choppers. He gave his apologies, about some skirmishes still going on that he wanted to personally oversee. The birds were powered up and blades started to turn. The mineral specialist and software analyst were analyzing a map of their own. Carthwaite sarcastically waved to Kreshnakov who was still getting in to his chopper. His was an Apache Longbow attack helicopter, given the territory they'd be flying into. Kreshnakov was very comfortable and even excited to be in a Longbow. He had flown it during other assignments and was fully conversant with the finer points of its dashboard. Drier's utility chopper quickly cruised past Amour Dieu airspace. They did not expect to find any heavy militia activity so close to the airport given the scale of response they would encounter. In another 10 minutes, below them was a thick carpet of foliage. The pilot spoke loudly through his headset.

"We shall arrive at the first site in 15 minutes. The first stop will be the shiny black stuff in Quadrant 1."

Drier and Simmons carefully scanned the trees below them. Simmons motioned to the mineral specialist, "See what you can do to figure out the link between the black shiny stuff and the diamond mines. Is this inter-relation a freakish coincidence we shouldn't invest too much into or is one a product of another."

"Got it." replied the mineral specialist leaning forward towards the window straining to get as much as possible an aerial view of the jungle. Simmons also scanned the immensity of the expanse beneath him. He knew that this was arguably the largest acquisition of G. Tech.

The software analyst was stunned at what he saw beneath him, commenting "Ok. This is really different."

In a flash of a second out of the corner of his eye, Carthwaite spotted a missile making a fast rise towards them from the right rear. Just then the target lock alarm on the dashboard went off. The pilot firmly called out, "Hold on." and pulled a sharp left down turn to miss its path. There was a brief spray of belt fed machine gun fire. The rear rotor had taken a small hit. Grondike, the minerals specialist, slipped out of his chair and tumbled across the cold iron cabin floor and hit hard against some metal cases stacked and strapped in on the body of the craft. He quickly came out of his ball and scrambled back to his seat. The machine gun fire continued and hit the engine followed by the chopper's left gun carriage.

"Another RPG at 3 o'clock." yelled Simmons.

"Strap in folks." yelled the pilot again as he pulled a direct lift to the left then a diagonal right drop while he deployed his anti-missile flares. The software analyst, Speewell, vomited on the cabin floor, the fluid trailing out down the aisle. With a stiffened spine he pulled his head back while taking heavy shallow breaths. The pilot quietly let out a sigh of relief to himself. Then a loud cracking sound like pellets in a large tin can prattled against the left side of the chopper. The machine gun carriage had been mangled. It sounded like little stones running through a turbine before being spun out into the air.

"We're hit. Trying to see how much longer we can stay up." The pilot said as he struggled to maintain control of the helicopter. Without notice, it was a brief hissing sound while it materialized shooting up from the left rear. The dashboard gages spun out of control. Barely implementing evasive maneuvers, the RPG's trajectory continued. The majority of his dash board controls had now given out, struggling to maintain altitude.

The chopper had begun to rotate into a tailspin. Drier calmly asked, "How much further to Site 1?"

"Another ten minutes landing. Problem is there is no clearing that could serve as a landing point between here and there. He called into Field Command, 'May day. May day. This is Uniform Hotel 1 Victor 3 Tango. We have been hit, we're going down. Current location is Foxtrot Juliet 12. Do you copy? Over?"

"We copy, over. What is your condition? Can you make it to destination, over?"

"We're losing altitude and going into tailspin." The pilot could overhear orders being yelled out in the background by Brigadier Velasquez.

"UH1V3T, we have deployed 1 Apache and 1 Blackhawk to use as your cover and transportation for the rest of this tour. It seems it's still a bit hot out there, over."

"Copy that, over."

Carthwaite matter of factly quipped as he looked around, "Well, we're all still in one piece except for Speewell who seems to be sharing his guts with us." Carthwaite offered a reassuring sarcastic smile. "We'll set down soon enough and then you can spew your guts over every tree you find, and there look to be a few of them down there."

The pilot then started to rigidly focus between his controls.

"What is it?" Drier asked with hardened attention in his voice.

"Now we're on a wing and a prayer if we make it to our landing site." He turned his neck as he quickly pointed to the back of the craft.

"Guys, load on those parachutes just as a precautionary measure, because if we take another hit we're bailing out."

Simmons moved to the back of the craft, unhooked the parachutes and threw them down the aisle one by one. Moving back to his seat, he sat next to Speewell who did not even bother to catch his chute when it was thrown to him. It instead rolled over onto the floor right into his vomit that oscillated with the movements of the craft.

Simmons couldn't afford such technical expertise to die out on this mission. He was not replaceable over the next 24 hours.

"Ok Speewell, take a deep breath." Simmons encouraged him while picking the knapsack from the floor. His hands were balled into tight fists, his knuckles had gone completely bare white.

Simmons expertly opened the chute.

"Ok, put this over your head and tie the straps around you. We don't have much time. Try to make it fast." A huge clunk sound was heard in the right belly of the copter. An alarm went off with red light flashing.

"Oh great. This is what happens when you buy cheap. It's new, but it's still cheap. We've just lost the engine. Ok people, I need you to hold on."

CHAPTER 12

VISITORS IN THE NEIGHBORHOOD

Still in her pastel green and cream halter neck dress holding onto her cushion so tightly, Rebecca tossed and turned in deep sleep. No particular dream just turmoil, fear and pain. Thrashing about on the couch she realized she had thrown the cushion over the back at the breakfast table. She came to, picked up her cel. phone rubbing her half-closed eyes and walked to her bedroom. Without turning on the light Rebecca unsteadily made it to her bed. Barely pulling back the bed covers and with a simple smile of relief settled into her heavenly pillow and luxurious beddings. Removing her outfit was an interruption to her sleep she was not willing to make. Her cel. phone was nestled underneath her pillow as if also finding its comfortable pocket of rest for the night. Rest overdue, rest welcomed.

There was a soft gentle exploratory climb up her leg, non-threatening, just a climb also searching for its own warmth with a moist tip. But the feel was not natural. It was cold and scaly but felt powerful. In the same instant she felt a heavy movement on top of her covers now stirred into action, also not far from her legs.

"What are these movements?" Her mind shot awake, knowing it was only she in the apartment and had never owned a pet.

Rebecca immediately reached out her hand for her bedside lamp and threw back her bed cover. Upset by the light, all of a sudden there were hissing sounds from 3 different directions. Her eyes met the six foot svelte body of a black mamba now shyly trying to retreat under her dress. In one firm lightning move she threw off the snake that was trying crawling up for the warmth of her thigh that very second. As the snake landed onto the floor, it was a python she saw taking cover under the beddings now heading towards her side.

Rebecca sprang out of the bed in shock and fright but did not scream. She felt something rush over her foot, quickly slithering for cover under her bed. It was the tail end of a coral snake also light averse. She recognized most of the snakes spread throughout the floor of her bedroom, on her chest of drawers, make up desk and study table. They were a variety of rainforest specialties, most of them venomous. There were about 30 snakes of which 10 had now started to hiss in irritation feeling increasingly agitated and threatened by the light.

Closest to her was a gabon viper, in the corner next to the window was a diamond backed rattler and just behind the door she needed to get passed was a king cobra.

Between her and the door on the floor were a mixture of garden snakes some poisonous some not, but Rebecca could tell them apart which she knew would protect her from any fatal errors. She saw that the viper had locked in on her and the king cobra was starting to raise its head.

"I need to get out of here, fast." The words rushed through her mind.

Tip-toeing around the harmless ones and staying as far as possible from the venomous ones Rebecca stretched underneath her pillow for her cel. phone. She took a wide curve to ensure that the door was the barrier between her and the cobra that was sensing for its target-lock.

Unsure of what she might find in the living room, she turned on the light. The floor was clear. She grabbed her satchel and shoes in her hand, still in long tiptoeing steps sprinted for the door. In the safety and bright light of the corridor, Rebecca checked herself for any bite marks while she put slipped on her shoes. She then preferred to walk down 4 flights of stairs to the building lobby.

"Call the Police and a snake specialist. There's a problem in my apartment." "Excuse me madam?" The concierge was sure he had not heard correctly.

"My bedroom specifically, someone broke into my place and threw a variety of snakes all over the room. Now how the hell did that happen?" She glared at the concierge and slammed the keys on the counter.

"Make it happen. You have my number."

Her fright had turned into fury. She hailed a cab. Her office couch was her temporary, but secure, respite before daylight came around. She mumbled the address of PR&S to the cab driver as she crouched in the back-seat relieved to be in this temporary mobile safe zone.

13TH ARONDISSEMENT
PARIS SUBURB
DAY 4 – 10:00HRS

Sergei found the most mundane parts of his work to be the most interesting. Sifting through medical records, phones, laptops, credit card bills among other documentation revealed the most intimate details and sultry secrets about the inner lives and in some instances double lives of people. Just as a cursory check on the power brokers of G. Tech. that could reveal sleepers or hidden agendas in their midst, Sergei was perusing through this digital trail of senior staff and board members of G. Tech. Some webbed lies covering the long weekends with their mistresses and others webbed intricate networks to cover up their sizeable tax evasion schemes; despite the virtuous spotless fronts they all presented. But one board member appeared to lead an unusually boring life for someone of his level. Sergei wondered to himself while humming away on his keyboard.

"Hmmm…this looks interesting." He began to sift through the deleted folder carrying several files on the gentleman's personal laptop. Update reports to a certain address were always encrypted with a very sophisticated program and the reply had a similar encryption program only with a few extra precautions thrown in. They appeared to be regular updates from this Board Member to what appeared to be the silent but majority shareholder. After a few minutes of breaking the encryption code, the reply was anything but mundane.

"Interesting, why would a mundane update draw the ire of a shareholder with assets in the billions and require a fairly high level encryption program?"

3 lines stood out.

"We shall wipe out the infidels using their own tools. We must continue to lie and wait until the right time presents itself. Because when we strike there will not be one infidel standing in that sinful country. No matter how long it will take." Sergei's eyes squinted as this job had just become much more interesting than the usual corporate greed. He decided he wasn't going to let Simmons know what they were actually dealing with until he followed this thread from one point to another.

QUADRANT 1
POINTE TROIS RAINFOREST
DAY 4 – 10:00HRS

The system set up was long-winded, if not convoluted, but it was the best cover. Emily was waiting to receive the feeds and get them to Ian and the group for worldwide media coverage. Rebecca was keen that Holstein at the U.N. also receives the most up to minute live coverage of Pointe Trois. It was agreed that all the key activist offices were under close army watch. So Chenchon was deployed to the missionary school, a 10 minute drive from town, as the undercover receiving point from where he would receive, edit and transmit the footage to Emily in New York. It was only 3 days back Chenchon had walked a beaten up Frapacha out of the Police Station. As Chenchon went to his home to check on him, Frapacha explained that once the trackers reached the sites and took the footage, it would be transmitted to Elder Katan who would then dispatch a fresh set of trackers from different points to get to the school posing as the humble assistants of the plumber, food supplier and stationery shop respectively.

With the intensified government attacks it was impossible for the supply trackers to move without the escort of the heavily armed militia trackers. Elder Katan already had his militia trackers on stand-by waiting for his signal to move to agreed coordinates to receive Frapacha's men.

Within an hour, the first pair was underway. The site to be filmed was about a 7 kilometer run from town. The trackers were crawling up on a cloud of dust created from the high powered drills still trying to cut their way through rock formation. The supply tracker lay on his stomach and took the video coverage as the militia tracker focused on ensuring the army security ring did not spot them and if it did, there was an instant disappearance into the forest. There were teams of Burajon men holding 3 gigantic drills, hammering away from different parts of the site, the women scattered around were designated to breaking down the rocks into small stones using rough hand-made tools that blistered their hands. The younger children were forced to pull trays of stones to the trucks and the older children raised these trays and tipped them on to the trucks. No one had protective or basic clothing or even shoes. Basic waist wraps for the men and chest to knee wraps for the women. Their wounds festered and cooked in the humidity, regularly fried by the sun on a cloudless day.

The liquid run from the mine was absorbed directly into the soil or flowed further into forest cover to find its own end in ground foliage. About 12 minutes had passed. The militia tracker tapped the foot of Frapacha's man. Time to go. He pulled back, sat up and transmitted his footage to Elder Katan. Just as he stood up they heard a cry of alarm from a group of women. The 2 trackers stepped back and watched a boulder roll down a slope. A little girl stood up and turned around but it was too late. It ran over her 4 year old small frame. The mother ran screaming to her child. The supply tracker looked on in frustrated anger. He knew he couldn't fail his mission. The militia tracker pulled him back into the foliage. They had to leave the tragedy behind.

QUADRANT 3
POINTE TROIS RAINFOREST
DAY 4 – 10:15HRS

Already 10 minutes into the flight, Fachante tried to keep the conversation with Kreshnakov to a minimum pretending to busy himself with his control panel. The strategy was to visit the furthest site and work their way back in. It began with the blown up coltan mine. Kreshnakov wanted to talk to the units that had just been involved in these field skirmishes. Did they look overwhelmed and distraught by their defeat from a ragtag group that actually happened to be an extremely capable and disciplined group of young men and women?

The metal shells of vehicles, exploded faces of the mine, cut up disorganized vegetation did not leave much to the imagination as they descended. There definitely had been a major fight over here. Even before Fachante had a moment to put down the helicopter and shut down the systems, Kreshnakov was removing his helmet and seatbelt. A few soldiers guarding the place emerged from the trees surrounding the clearing. They looked at Kreshnakov suspiciously, but relaxed when Fachante jumped out of his bucket seat.

"Officers, this gentleman is one of the team who are scouting the place today before they take over."

Kreshnakov did not have a moment to waste and politely interjected, "What is the position here now? Are you getting any return visitors trying to install themselves?"

"Well that's the interesting thing. The strategy is not necessarily to attack the site and install themselves, but really to destroy the site and move on to the next. Make it useless to the government completely forcing it to abandon operations. Though our trackers can see that the militia is moving past us and they know full-well that we're here. But they don't engage us. Either they don't have enough personnel to install themselves where they have attacked or they simply want to make the place uninhabitable and commercially useless for the government. In this state it would be a huge cost to revamp the mine." replied the most senior among them.

Fachante glared at the soldier warning him not to say too much. The soldier got the cue. "Have a look around if you wish. It's been pretty quiet in the last 24 hours." The other soldiers continued to examine him cautiously. Not sure if this was a different kind of enemy.

Kreshnakov walked straight into the mouth of the mine to survey where it had caved in. He noticed fissures that ran on both sides of the tunnel walls at different points in the mine. The whole structure had become unstable and how deep this went was difficult to say. But one thing was for sure, this place was completely out of bounds until a full technical audit was done.

"No money from this coltan mine for at least the next 6 months." He said out loud to himself. He could see the expression on Bayne's face when he'd read that in the field report. Kreshnakov quickly moved out to the chopper where Fachante appeared to be deep in conversation with the soldiers. As he approached, Fachante hurriedly wrapped up.

The last thing Kreshnakov heard him say was, "These are not the sort of skirmishes we can afford. Better to take preventive measures. I'll send reinforcements to them."

"Reinforcements to where, for what?" Kreshnakov firmly enquired.

"Oh, nothing to be bothered about. We've got it covered." Fachante dismissively replied.

The Lt. Colonel looked miffed as he headed back to the chopper annoyed that Kreshnakov would so firmly demand about details not yet privy to him. They were in their bucket seats. Fachante engaged the controls. Kreshnakov gave the mining site a last look-around and did not have too much confidence in the military. The evidence had clearly presented itself. They were over run and the largest coltan mine was destroyed despite the large army deployment they had in Pointe Trois. The next site was Sector ET68 where a recent fight between the militia and army had taken place. He wanted to see the place and assess what would have been the best strategies and tactics from his thoughts before he listened to the army commanders narrate their versions this afternoon. Kreshnakov knew his sympathy for unfortunate incidents was not very high. Everything was lumped into the category of incompetence. On rare occasions that could be forgiven, but on all occasions never to be repeated. He could tell Fachante was receiving a barrage of communication from headquarters.

"Then send the necessary reinforcements. It is the same information I've just been receiving from the team guarding the attacked coltan mine. That is not too far from the flight plan of the other G. Tech party."

Kreshnakov decided on a diplomatic tact. "Fachante, I have extensive experience on this type of terrain. Let me help you while I'm here, and of course I'll not allow my people to be in any kind of danger."

Fachante did not even wait for the overture to finish. With a slightly irritated tone like he was being interrogated by a subordinate he replied, "Yes, we are aware of your extensive experience and of course we will not allow your people to be in any kind of danger."

Kreshnakov knew he hated amateurs and their pissing contests. "Good, because you'll be the first person to answer if anything does happen to them."

Fachante replied as if completely unaware of the last comment, "ETA 15 minutes to sector ET68-site."

Ten minutes later. "Lt. Colonel Fachante, this is Field Command. Urgently abort flight to ET68. About 7 minutes ahead, our drones reveal the militia is waiting for you with a cocktail of surface to air missiles. Even with the Apache, there is no guarantee that you'll make it through, because it's only one of you. You need to abort immediately sir."

Fachante switched to his intercom to advise Kreshnakov of the same. Kreshnakov could have stared a hole through the back of Fachante's head.

He simply cut back, "Understood." While his mind screamed out loud. *Tell me something new.* Fachante gleeful, tried to distract him from the disappointment, talking about their last skirmishes with the militia.

Looking at his dashboard, Kreshnakov warned Fachante "Incoming!"

It was a distant object in the sky shooting in from the rear left. Its trajectory was straight and fast. Fachante engaged the decoy flare and pivoted a drop diagonal right in evasive maneuvers, but it was a split second too late. The missile had already closed most of the distance. The bright orange ball in the sky was seen far and wide. Their flight plan and the remains of the helicopter would be the forms of identification of Fachante and Kreshnakov in the massive rainforest.

QUADRANT 2
POINTE TROIS RAINFOREST
DAY 4 – 10:30HRS

Ok guests. The best I can do for you right now is to crash land about three kilometers from the mining site. It means we'll land just two kilometers outside the security ring so depending what state we land in, we need to get running pretty fast to trek it into the safe zone.

"Got it folks?" Drier confirmed out to the group in the back. The helicopter was now starting to go into a free tail spin with black smoke spinning out.

"I'm surprised the militia hasn't tried to finish us off." the pilot said while deftly moving his fingers between non-responsive controls. The descent accelerated with the ever more violent movement of the helicopter, the huge trees looked larger by the second like unforgiving obstacles that would break the helicopter body and their more delicate frames. "Ok people. Start lining up at the door." The pilot ordered. Drier crouched as he moved to the back to join the group.

"See you on the ground. I'll jump out as soon as you're all out." Drier nodded and gave him a light pat on the back as he moved to an oscillating windy main cabin where Simmons had already opened the door.

Grondike, the minerals specialist, jumped out first and kept some kind of composed figure. Simmons could see this definitely was not the first time he was parachuting. Carthwaite looking focused on his unexpected task was right behind the minerals specialist. Speewell, the software analyst, clutched the body of the helicopter and refused to let go. Drier pulled him off like he was pulling off a chicken clawed to a fence trying to avoid hell below. His face had turned ashen white, terrified of the fast air and chopper see-sawing that challenged his grip. Drier shook him by the shoulders to force him into eye contact to help him get a grip.

"When you fall out there, wait two seconds then pull this toggle. Do you understand Speewell? Do you understand?" He nodded his head up and down still in a state of shock, with the helicopter getting rockier every passing moment.

"Good!" Drier turned him around and pushed him out. Speewell let out a faint yell as if unable to complete his last cry before his unknown. Drier signaled to Simmons. He executed an expertly defined jump in a second. Drier was immediately behind him with an air of calmness.

Simmons started to look at the foliage in order to negotiate himself an agreeable landing. Fortunately there was a small clearing he spotted. He noticed one parachute stuck in the trees. His feet touched down dry forest floor partly covered with foliage. He immediately collected his parachute and rushed into the cover of the forest to avoid easy detection by any militia.

"Simmons! Simmons!" He heard someone call out. He looked towards his two o'clock. It was Drier motioning to him to come over to his spot where he was looking up above at some branches.

"Looks like someone didn't land on their feet." Drier climbed his way up a few branches about 15 feet up, pulled out a Swiss army knife and cut across the parachute strings. Carthwaite came tumbling down to the ground.

"Great start. Looks like he snapped his neck when he was in between the branches." Drier observed. Simmons clenched his jaw for a minute. He couldn't believe he had lost such a valuable asset with the mission barely started. Grondike quietly walked up behind Drier, eyes wide open expectant for the next steps. He could see Simmons trying to compute why he looked energized rather than petrified and shocked.

"What? I've taken 3 extreme sport holidays. The adrenaline rush of the near death experience is why we sign up."

"Where's Speewell?" Simmons asked while still looking at Grondike.

His tubby shape accentuated by his round head was walking up panting with large yellow stains of vomit on his pink rose polo shirt, he answered "I am here, miraculously alive. I guess this is what we call field work ey? Desk work is good for me. Oh no!" he gasped and wobbled back struggling to regain his balance while looking at Carthwaite's lifeless body.

"Speewell how did you pass the HR psychological endurance test when being interviewed?" Drier asked in the form of a warning.

"Oh that was 15 years ago. The nice young lady who tested me is now my wife and we have 3 wonderful kids. She kept saying something about my puppy eyes that melted her hard heart."

Just then the pilot surfaced from behind some trees.

"I trust you all had a similar rocky landing, but glad to see you are in one piece. Let's get hoppin' shall we? We didn't exactly quietly drop from the skies. I'm sure the militia is making fast tracks this way." He looked at Carthwaite's body with sympathy.

"I'll carry him as we move." Drier answered the question in his mind.

Without waiting to see whether the others would follow, the pilot broke into a light trot through the jungle. In instant reflex, Drier picked up immediately behind him with Carthwaite's body over his shoulder. Simmons had decided he'd take up the rear to ensure he kept all his remaining expertise intact during this mission. A pumped up Grondike followed behind Drier. Speewell heaving, was positioned in front of Simmons.

It was a trot for about 20 minutes before 3 soldiers surfaced right in front of the pilot. "We saw you come down. C'mon, let's get going. We expect the militia also enjoyed the sky show and are making fast feet this way."

"Yes, we figured." The pilot replied.

The lead soldier turned and continued with the trot. Another relieved Drier of Carthwaite's body and the third took up rear cover. Everyone was at different levels of breathing hard. They finally reached a clearing about 600 meters across with dark clay soil on the ground. Simmons thought to himself that the only reason they did not spot it is that they were focused on their chaotic descent.

Grondike was thrilled. "Look at this! We need to find out how deep this mine goes." Without thinking, while in the helicopter, he had strapped his knapsack of his kit and tools when Simmons had gone to the rear of the helicopter to get the parachutes. He turned around to the others still surveying their surroundings of torched vehicles, remainders of tent frames, charred desks, chairs and iron bed frames that landed anywhere during the multiple explosions.

Grondike called out to the soldier, "I need to get in there!"

"This mine is not stable." The soldier replied with a look of concern.

Grondike shot back, "Yeah…that's why I'm taking you. We shouldn't be too long."

The soldier looked a bit surprised but impressed by his determination. "Let's go." said the officer. "I'll come with you." Drier replied.

He looked at the software analyst as if asking him what he was doing just standing there. "Right behind you." Speewell called out.

The pilot interrupted Simmons looking for remainders of records not completely burnt up, "You may also want to take a look at the diamond mine. That's about 500 meters that way. We don't have much time. As soon as the reinforcements arrive we will need to fly out of here. It's that way."

The pilot signaled to the soldiers to let the other 3 know where they'd gone. Simmons and the pilot ran across the clearing and had to struggle up a short steep hill, holding on to tree trunks to help them get past. The ground leveled and they made it a fast run west for about 400 meters. They came to another extensive clearing. But surprisingly the diamond mine was almost untouched. Maybe it's some cultural belief of theirs, he thought to himself. The vehicles, tents, mining infrastructure, all remained undamaged there. It looked like personnel had only abandoned the site. Another soldier appeared out of the brushes behind.

"What is the meaning of this? How come it's untouched while the others are torched?" Simmons asked.

"For some reason they don't touch the diamond mines. We can't figure that out. These guys are a weird bunch." The soldier looked bewildered.

"Why do you think they do that?" Simmons looking genuinely puzzled, asking the soldier again.

"I have no idea. It's all over the jungle. They destroy the coltan, the gold, the cobalt, but the diamond mines remain undisturbed." The soldier replied as his arms rested on his AD 101/107 holstered on his neck.

Simmons shifted his attention to the task at hand and started scaling his way down a steep descent of a mine. The pilot followed behind him. Simmons opened his small knap sack and opened a tray that contained small self-contained boxes. He dug a little deep and scooped a sample of the kimberlite from one of the pulleys that had been moving up the mine to the surface. The pilot watched him remove his cel. phone to take some footage and shots for the technical teams in Hong Kong and Paris to be able to gauge the quality of the veins, the type of rock and soil around to be able to assess its viability. Was it a profitable catch for the multi-national or could it be leased out to another conglomerate at a handsome price? Precious minerals were only important to G. Tech. if they had a contribution to their technology development and the company had already appropriated several other diamond mines throughout the world. Simmons scaled the mine wall for more samples.

A soldier yelled down the tunnel. "Folks, time to go. Your transport's here."

Simmons put his kit back in his bag. The pilot had already turned around and was heading back up the tunnel in a crouched run. Back on the surface of the mine they made a light jog across the clearing, sliding down through the trees. As they negotiated around the large trunks and unpredictable forest floor, the low purring sound of the helicopter engine could now be heard. Simmons could see one UH-60 preparing to land and what appeared to be a Tiger chopper standing guard about 1,000 feet above. He broke out into a light run to catch up with the pilot. In a few minutes they were back at the border of the first clearing as they watched the chopper almost touch ground. They also observed Drier, Speewell and Grondike at the mouth of the other mine waiting for the chopper to settle. The blades continued to rotate. The pilot in the chopper gave the thumbs up to the other pilot moving with Simmons.

It was evident that the pilot had no intention of settling on the ground. He was going to pick his passengers while barely touching down. The soldier with Carthwaite's body was already fearlessly running across the clearing, placed the body inside, jumped in, lay him securely in the back, jumped out and ran back across the clearing into the forest. Simmons gave a last fast scan at the tree line, removing his Glock-17 tucked in his back at the same time. It was a flicker he barely noticed. But it was the sound that was too familiar. Before his mind could process it, the corner of his eye was instantly drawn to the sky watching an explosion erupting into a ball of fire. The attack helicopter above was now in charred pieces on the ground a short distance away.

"Hurry!" The pilot yelled to them. The other 3 had started to sprint to the chopper. Drier in one nimble move was in the chopper. The minerals specialist athletically leapt into the body of the chopper. Speewell clawed and knee balled his way clinging on to the legs of the seat that were bolted onto the floor.

The pilot started to very slowly lift off as he could see the other pilot and Simmons racing towards the chopper. Simmons's eye focused in on the pilot to make sure he wouldn't get too scared and high tail it out of there. Instead the pilot's body jolted as a bullet pierced through his left chest leaving a neat red hole. The chopper gave a heavy thud down. The ground pilot running in front came to a sudden halt and put his hands up. Simmons frantically tried to figure out what could be happening to his colleagues in the main cabin of the chopper. Had anyone been hit if the bullet pierced through?

At the same time they both noticed that they were surrounded. Within seconds a group of over 30 militia encircled them. About half had an assortment of sophisticated RPGs, detonation gear and hand-grenades, strapped to their backs and holstered on their arms. The other half carried a mixture of assault rifles, belt fed guns and bullets. One signaled to Simmons to throw his weapon on the ground, another ran up to grab it not releasing eye contact.

Like a synchronized dance, 5 militia ran up to the chopper. One parted from the group and ran to the pilot's door, opened it and pulled back the pilot's body away from the controls. He turned off the engine and stood back on guard as the other 4 split into 2 groups; 2 each taking a side of the helicopter. Simmons watched this group that was so invisible moments ago take full control of the surroundings and total control of their cosmopolitan fate. Drier was pulled from one side, the other 2 were pulled from the other side. Simmons shot a look at Drier, a quick check to see if he was thinking to try something and he should be ready to handle his side. He could see Drier was still trying to figure out an exit. But in 30 seconds they were all corralled into a corner of the clearing about 40 feet away from the chopper and signaled to sit on the ground by one of the larger militia who looked like a mobile ammunitions depot. Simmons quickly looked at the Grondike and Speewell to see how they were coping up. The G. Tech. training for high risk areas could never substitute for the fear that screams through you during a real ambush. But they looked deeply curious, rather than scared. Yes, it was clear to Simmons too. The militia looked fearsome, but not harmful. There wasn't a streak of rage, uncontrolled anger or destruction that ran across their faces, but more so of determination and focus.

Speewell whispered to Grondike without removing his eye from the big militia that stood before them, "Where do they get this stuff from?"

"At your local department store I guess. It seems we missed the specials." replied the minerals specialist.

As if he'd been observing the whole operation, the man that looked like the Commandant of the group calmly but purposefully walked towards them.

"Ah so, this is the Global Tech. group." He said as he approached. There was no swagger in his voice, just a plain practical identification.

Deep inside Drier could not deny he respected the group for their competence and control they had displayed.

He knew he would have loved to have worked with them in another time. It had been a while since he had been with such quality. But this was an entirely different set-up of events. This group was now an intractable inconvenience to his conglomerate's current project, a thorn in his side that had also ably punctured a lung of a national army. Simmons found himself presented with two unacceptable possibilities. They could either be dead or presented to the world media as intruding hostages colluding with an army trying to kill off a population that was forced to defend itself while trying to grab a rainforest under the table.

QUADRANT 1
POINTE TROIS RAINFOREST
DAY 4 – 11:00HRS

In a somewhat deep valley of the forest floor, what may have been a dip of sorts between mountains was an expanse of not less than 2 kilometers in length and width, a graveyard of felled trees. Even Frapacha's tracker thought this must have been the largest logging excavation site he'd seen in all his movements. The excruciating buzzing sound could be heard up to a kilometer away like someone cutting away at a live organism fighting for its life.

The supply tracker settled the video cam. in for the best vantage point ensuring it was not obstructed by the leaves and cross-checked the microphone was working. The militia tracker kept a look out while his partner focused on the task at hand. Any viewer could see each tree was not less than 100 years old. This was primary forest of an untouched eco-system being erased by the mega chain saws using two lean but strong physiques per machine brutally sawing across each tree trunk. There were no less than twenty five pairs of men cutting down these trees with these jumbo tools.

A sea of tree stumps mixed with large branches created their own carpet floor of destruction. Thin Burajon men that once looked to be well-built had log chains strapped diagonally across their chest like vests of valor. The haulers were reversed in at the end of the site ready to join the wide enough road the government had carved out to allow them to get through the worst terrain and probably to a makeshift airstrip. The militia tracker could see a detailed sweep was heading their way. He tapped Frapacha's tracker on the shoulder. He had already filmed 15 minutes of footage of this extensive logging operation and transmitted to Elder Katan. They quietly withdrew and blended their way deep into the forest.

CHAPTER 13

FOOTING THE NEIGHBORHOOD

Fisch, now the leader of the militia, spoke without emotion. The shrapnel cuts and wounds from years of battle were reduced to a variation of moon craters throughout his face. It was a statement of an unending fearless war to the last man standing.

"Gentlemen, I know this is among the biggest transactions for Global Tech., but this is not your war. You must walk away from this transaction." A chilling expression of revulsion shot through his face as he looked at the mine. "We see what you are collecting. Why are you interested in this black soil anyway? None of the other thieving black marketeers are at all? Your employers would be making a serious mistake committing a horrible crime for which we would make them pay if they insist on pursuing our homeland."

A few lines on his face surfaced as he spoke. The warning continued, "We are determined to the death. Your company is only a recent event in this struggle. Your so-called agreement would mean the certain extinction of our people and death of our land which I'm sure you'll agree we could not allow. Take that back to your shareholders. You shall leave immediately and no further harm shall come to you. Alright, we look forward to not seeing you again in this neighborhood. Oh sorry about your man. He was moving with the wrong man that we'd been targeting for some time now. He had commanded several field operations, razed our villages, him and his fellow animals raped our women and maimed our men. Don't take it personally, collateral damage. Run along now."

The militia escorted them back to the chopper. Drier and the mineral specialist moved the pilot's dead body from the cockpit to the main cabin. Simmons moved it to the back next to Carthwaite's body. The pilot strapped himself in and blades started to rotate. The militia group moved back a distance as they watched the chopper take off. They were airborne now. The pilot set a flight plan back to Amour Dieu.

Drier in a bothered low tone muttered to Simmons as he pointed his head down to the forest floor, "Well that went well. It seems we now understand each other. They told us to get out and we have our HQ orders to move in. Let's see how this plays out."

Simmons sounded pensive. "Yes, let's. Hey..." as he looked over to the pilot. "What did he mean by Kreshnakov? Please radio in and find out."

The pilot put field command on the general intercom. "They were on their way to Sector ET68, were told to abort flight due to anticipated enemy fire further down the line.

But it turns out the militia were ready for them much earlier. A Surface to Air Missile went straight for them. There was a period of silence in the chopper. Drier couldn't believe that an intelligence failure by this army had resulted in him losing one of his best operatives in the field. 5 minutes later the pilot broke silence.

"ETA to Amour Dieu is 10 minutes."

Drier asked the pilot, "How good are you with this bird?" The pilot knew what he was thinking.

"The other guy wasn't a pilot. We were all shocked when Velasquez proposed he take one of our most expensive machines to move around with, yet he had very little experience with those Apaches birds. There were experienced pilots seated right there. That man was a bit of a reckless show-gun and insisted on taking on the assignment."

"Amateurs." Drier muttered to himself. "Simmons, what d'ya say we go and take a look at another mine of our interest?"

"I was thinkin' the same thing." replied Simmons as he continued to scan.

Drier looked over to the pilot and asked, "How far away is the closest mine similar to the one where we were just dis-invited?" "15 minutes away. We may encounter some traffic, we may not."

"Well what are you waiting for? Let's put a foot on it." said Drier.

The software analyst pursed his lips. "Not again."

The mineral specialist simply checked his kit to make sure everything was still in-tact.

AVA MARIA MISSIONARY SCHOOL POINTE TROIS RAINFOREST
DAY 4 – 11:30HRS

Chenchon was now seated at his desk in one of the guest houses of the school with his laptop and a bunch of fake paperwork around him waiting to receive the memory cards of film footage from Frapacha's 3 trackers. It was Kamara's job, as Father Raines assistant, to have put the word out to military intelligence agents that normally came around to the school to say hello; that Chenchon had been called to completely re-do the foreign student and visa application paperwork of a number of the school's students already in the U.S. They were about to lose the opportunity of acceptance to Universities because someone had bungled the students' names, bio-data, universities applied to and visa type required; a total mess. He was called in to straighten it out on the cheap and would require a couple of days to do so.

The trackers would all look technology averse in their respective covers. Chenchon was surfing the net when there was a gentle tap at the door. He anxiously answered it.

"Yes sir I'm told the hot water heater is not working here too. Frankly I think it's that hopeless solar panel on the roof, but Mr. Kamara thinks I should take a look at the pipes inside. Mind if I come in?" His chewing gum doing summersaults in his mouth, tired looking bandana tied on his head, greasy overalls and oversized tool-belt on his small physique stepped into the guesthouse. Chenchon shut the door. The young man moved extremely fast as he went straight to Chenchon's large cloth bag hanging on the side of the chair, removed the memory card from the inside pocket of his overalls and placed it in Chenchon's bag.

"Mining." he whispered.

Chenchon opened the door. The tracker walked out and loudly concluded, "Well if the problem has solved itself, that's just fine. But I'm tellin' yah, it's that damned solar panel sunbathing on the roof. You can't guarantee the quality of some of these donations."

"Okay, thank you." Chenchon waved and closed the door. He immediately removed the memory card from the bag and set about the task of editing for on-send to Emily in New York within the next 15 minutes. She had already prepped a global network that was waiting for the actual footage.

CORIAMESE EMBASSY, CARAMONDO
DAY 4 – 12:00HRS

The Coriamese Ambassador had been receiving his regular intelligence briefings and was aware of the recent acceleration of government activity and certain visitors to the rainforest.

Funding the only hospital and major social development activities had provided excellent cover to establish a thorough intelligence network in Pointe Trois. For many years, some MPs had kept the Embassy briefed on the activities of Parliament. The Ambassador was now on the phone to his Vice President updating him they had just completed an air tour of a 500 kilometer road network their country had built. The formal launch would be in a month; a first class road network for a horrendous amount of money that the Caramondo government would never have been willing to put in itself for the excellent workmanship. The Coriamese government had known about G. Tech.'s interest in Pointe Trois, but this sudden signing within a few days and preliminary visit before take over before caught them off guard and had them extremely unsettled.

The Coriamese Vice President had groused bitterly to his Caramondo Ambassador on the phone, "And they think all this investment was for nothing. Are we a charity? Now some company shows up and they're overwhelmed by the whiff of their cheque book? What we've put in their road infrastructure and social development projects comes up to tens of billions of dollars in the past 15 years. Now they think we're just going to give that up and walk away? Problem is that G.Tech. has Pointe Trois in its mouth like a baby attacking its candy. We better hope that this ongoing Parliament debate scares them away. Perhaps G. Tech. would be interested in taking up further infrastructural investment and social development activities in Caramondo?" Something he knew was impossible.

"They would do straight business with the incompetents, but would never move in with them." Were the Ambassador's words to his Vice President.

STATE HOUSE, CARAMONDO
DAY 4 – 12:15HRS.

As President Gebajara reviewed the summary report of the same road network of his Minister of Works, Belinda walked in with a file not more than 3 pages in it. "He says it's urgent sir." She said with a tense tone.

"Oh?" he immediately opened it with a mildly frowned brow. The letterhead revealed that it was from the Chief of the Joint Intelligence Council.

"Alright, thank you." He murmured swinging around in his chair to face the sun rays streaming in through the French windows.

It was titled '*Extra-Ordinary Update Briefing: G. Tech. Pointe Trois Visit and Other.*' "What now?" he asked.

His eyes anxiously tore through the pages. He read, '*Heighted activity in Pointe Trois within the past few hours....*' 2 sentences jumped out at him, '*Lawyer killed in emergency parachute jump when chopper was fired on. Second chopper (Apache – soldier no experience with the copter) carrying G. Tech military expert hit by militia, no survivors. Guests held hostage but released when visiting the mines.'*

The rest of the report provided updates on skirmishes ongoing and coordination meetings by militaries on both sides of the border.

On the second page it read: '*Main female in New York receives threat of body parts at office and snakes in bedroom respectively.'* But he knew the purpose of the report was to let him know that his guests were not doing so well under the custody of his men. "I need to fix this fast." He muttered as his mind scrambled.

G.TECH HQ, PARIS
DAY 4 – 09:15HRS

At the same moment in time, Baynes head of legal burst through his Chairman's door grabbed his remote control from the coffee table and switched on the TV. Baynes was already in his own world of shock on receiving the news from his field staff about the others in Amour Dieu. The legal chief stood there with his hands on his waist like he was spoiling for a fight with events on the screen. Edward DesChampes was narrating along the footage of the mining sites Emily had received from Chenchon and forwarded to the network. "*We the human rights and environmental community, see these atrocities every day because we must mobilize funds for their medical needs, find new homes for them when the government sees them as a 'threat to the State'. This conglomerate, Global Technologies, and the government of Caramondo are hell-bent on the extinction of the Pointe Trois rainforest and its inhabitants. And these are the corporate cannibals you give your hard earned dollars to, buying their products? There is nothing fair or sustainable about the business of this so-called extraction, absolutely nothing.*" The head of legal turned off the screen and looked at Baynes whose eyes had a glaze of fury, his jaws clenched. They understood each other. The head of legal walked out. Baynes picked up his phone.

STATE HOUSE, CARAMONDO
DAY 4 – 12:25HRS

Back in Caramondo, rarely did Belinda bolt through his door without knocking. The protocol was always to knock once, wait for a second and then enter. "William Baynes sir. He says it's urgent."

Strangely, Belinda watched the President wildly waving one arm, with the report in his other hand, vehemently shaking his head rejecting the phone call. She whispered even more forcefully this time.

"He says it's priority urgent, concerning his people in Pointe Trois."

He rolled his eyeballs as he slowly reluctantly picked up the receiver. His mind swirled at lightning speed to come up with an excuse for the death of two of his guests under his watch within hours of their arrival.

"William!" he called into the receiver with a sense of outraged concern. Baynes did not have time for chit chat.

"I'm sure you're aware two of my people have been killed while moving up and down under the protection of your soldiers. How could that happen? How did you let that happen?" Baynes launched in, slightly losing control of the formality of this conversation.

"Careful there now." The President hated that he was caught in a moment of unpreparedness with this arrogant corporate dictator of a different address that was willing to buy up a pound of flesh of anyone else without so much as raising an eyebrow.

"I totally understand your anger and desperate concern for the safety of your staff; an arrogant inexperienced soldier with a very sophisticated machine. I can assure you this was an isolated incident."

Baynes interrupted, "So, this also includes the rest of my people being shot down and kidnapped by your militia but luckily released. Not to mention losing my legal expert."

The President was seething with anger. This visit was just not going as planned. Listening to this arrogant CEO rant and rave was an insult he thought to himself. Someone in Field Command was going to pay for this incompetence and severely embarrassing situation. Then the words he was least expecting.

"Mr. President, I'm afraid we're going to have to pull out. From what we're experiencing on the ground in just the few hours we've been there; it looks like your people don't know what they're doing. This looks too high risk a transaction for us. Do you even see the global press we're getting, calling us corporate cannibals? There are still a couple of rainforests out there we could explore without the stress, that seems to be your own unique kettle of fish. I'll contact my people in Pointe Trois and tell them to fly home immediately."

In his mind President Gebajara was scrambling for a panic button. "William, tell you what. I'll triple the security on them. Let them complete their tour and I'll meet with them this evening to see what needs to be fixed where and I'll give it my personal priority attention. I couldn't agree more. This incompetence is completely outrageous."

Baynes was not interested to hear the politician speaking. He snapped in, "Let's see how the remaining hours in the day go by. If one more person dies, we pull out immediately. Deal's off. We also need to look at the extent of the damage to the rainforest. Those militia apparently have been a lot busier than you've been updating us. At the very least, this significantly factors into your price. We'll be in touch."

"I'm sure we'll have mutually fruitful negotiations with your people here. Very well." Closed the President with a hint of sarcasm in this voice.

Baynes stared at the phone for a second, he couldn't believe the level of incompetence he was dealing with. "Just keep the man panting. Keep him apologizing. We'll get a fair deal, a real fair deal." He said softly.

Baynes decided he could get this rainforest at basement prices. He would make sure the President never found out that they had no intention of backing out of this deal. That what they had in Pointe Trois was a priceless unique resource that could change the fate of global security and economic positioning.

"Belinda!" he called out.

When he called her like that, she knew he was badly rattled, slipping into a mild panic. In a flash she stepped through the door. The rage embodied in his look conveyed a very clear demand. "Bugazon! Here! Now!"

There was no time to go through the protocol of aides and assistants. She dialed Bugazon's mobile number immediately.

"Yes Belinda, what is it?" answered the General sounding slightly perturbed. "The President would like to see you in an instant without a second to delay."

QUADRANT 2
POINTE TROIS RAINFOREST
DAY 4 – 12:30HRS

"Ok folks. Thank your lucky stars we've arrived here without incident, now that we've alerted our friends we're in the neighborhood. I can't guarantee the same on our return. Touch-down in 3 minutes."

Drier leaned forward to keenly scan the neatly cut hole that was more than half a kilometer wide. He felt encouraged by what he saw. Like they were on the same wave length, Simmons called out to the minerals specialist.

"What do you make of it so far?" as he also peered through the window while the pilot negotiated the landing.

"Difficult to say from afar, but the quality of the mineral itself looks good. It's the volume I want to get a handle on." He continued while he delicately moved his gadgets around prepared to collect as much information as he could. He handed over a few plastic containers to Simmons while whispering instructions to him. Tasks had to be shared in the time they had. The wheels touched the ground. He zipped up his backpack again with initial equipment in hand.

"What I's figuring is to simply level that mine face and set up another opening about ½ a kilometer or so away. Just a pity we didn't have more time here."

Drier opened his front cabin door and sprang out scanning for any hostiles as the blades were slowing down. The pilot shut down his controls, leaned over and pulled out a tool box tucked underneath the co-pilot seat. The clearing was dry with the soil typical of many rainforests.

"Hey Drier!" he called out. "This might come in handy." stretching over a SIG-P250 to him.

Drier checked the handgun's clip, the safety and inserted the pistol back into the back of his khaki slacks covered by his safari jacket. With one leg out of the chopper Simmons felt his Glock 17 underneath his khaki shirt just confirming it was there. His back-up was a Mark 23 on its ankle holster. Carrying anything more would have slowed him down for the cramped quarters he knew he'd be visiting and he didn't want anyone raising questions beyond the task at hand.

Assisting Grondike was his priority in the next few minutes. Grondike and Speewell were already on the ground catching up fast with Drier. The pilot removed his AK-5 assault rifle strapped to the top of his cabin. He whistled to Simmons who turned around and signaled to him that he'd keep an eye on the area while they were gone. Simmons gave the thumbs up.

Drier barked out the order as he worked his way through the narrow tunnel. "Ok guys, 10 minutes tops. So do what you need to do now."

The minerals specialist had directed Simmons and the software analyst around the mouth of the mine to dig and collect samples from a couple of feet deep. Dashing past Drier, Grondike charged down the mine to what he spotted as a narrow deep tunnel not more than 3 feet wide with a tiny iron ladder. He climbed down about 20 feet stopping intermittently to take more samples of the varied layers of mineral and soil compact. He reached another tunnel, not more than 3 feet in height. This spot was serving as a junction point.

"Wow!" He exclaimed as he looked ahead and behind. "We hit pay dirt." He excitedly called back to his colleagues at the top. "We've hit a vein that is exactly what we're looking for and goodness knows how far it runs." He hurriedly unzipped his back-pack; now putting samples in some prepared solutions in jars and other larger quantities in bags.

The pilot took a hiding position on the left nose of the helicopter, the same side of the mine.

While Simmons and the software analyst took their samples from the outside, the pilot noticed a flock of birds fly off in agitation. A bush hog scurried out into the clearing and run right across into the other side of the thick foliage. He whistled to Simmons and Speewell who turned around. The pilot vigorously signaled to them. Speewell ran back to some shrubbery next to the mouth of the mines trying to advance to the chopper. Simmons sprinted back into the mines and yelled out to Drier. "We have to clear out now!"

Drier called out to the minerals specialist, "Grondike! Haul ass up here now! We've got company!"

"Coming!" The minerals specialist couldn't hold back his fear and excitement as he threw the small jars, bags and retractable dip stick back into his backpack in one calamitous mess and crawled back to the ladder at breakneck speed as he scraped his knees. His muscles burned as he scampered up the ladder. He congratulated himself for maintaining his fitness after running the marathon last month. Sweating and soil ridden, he reached the top, Simmons started to run ahead to provide front cover.

Drier met him in the tunnel yanked the back-pack off Grondike, "Now bolt!"

Grondike broke out into a mad dash, occasionally rubbing his shoulders against the tunnel walls. He made it to the mouth of the mine. Simmons signaled to him to stand back a second as he quickly scanned before he did his final sprint into the clearing.

The pilot whispered out, "C'mon! Get in, now!" Vehemently beckoning him to run over.

The pilot ran around the nose to his cabin door expecting Drier and Simmons to maintain cover. Simmons nodded to Grondike giving him the all clear. He broke out into his last sprint to the chopper. He made it. Speewell was still stuck in the bush, panicked and paralyzed, staring at the clearing then at the chopper then back at the clearing. Petrified he could be hit while making it through that clearing. Simmons leaned his head out and saw Speewell with his eyes wide open and hands shaking. He used the mine wall and some dusty shrubbery as cover to get to where Speewell could see him. He pointed to him commanding him to run to the chopper.

Speewell broke into a run with his eyes half-closed. Grondike rallied him to come on. The 70 yard dash felt like 10 kilometres of time. Then *schwk!* Speewell went down.

"Oh m'God! Help me! I'm dead!" He yelled out. Drier and Simmons had already taken off but with their own training knew to run in a zigzag lines crossing each other at least 3 times. The pilot was punching away at his controls. The blades slowly started to rotate.

Like an orchestrated dance, they picked up Speewell by his armpits. Simmons grabbed him by the back of his belt, lifted and threw him onto the cabin floor like a piece of meat that needed to be loaded. Grondike pulled him further in. Drier folded Speewell's legs at his knees which caused him to let out a suppressed cry of pain. He knew he couldn't have been in better hands and didn't want to appear the problematic flake. The chopper started to lift. Simmons pushed Speewell's feet in, hopped in and slid the door behind him.

Drier had already opened his front and sprang inside. "Let's get outta here!" He ordered as he scanned with his gun in hand looking for targets that may have already locked in on them. The pilot navigated full throttle up.

"I'm not up for a second lecture after we were ordered to leave. Can't tell how that might turn out." Drier still continued to scan the ground as if cross-checking there were no direct hits to maneuver around immediately.

"Well what d'ya know? Is someone having a good go on us?" The pilot asked.

Simmons and Drier hastily shifted from their own surveillance and saw two militia men give them a comical sarcastic child's wave. One held his M110 sniper rifle then slung it back, folded his arms with an amused smile and waved. The other militia watched. Their rifles were firmly strapped to their backs as if they had been watching them all along. They slowly walked back into the forest.

Grondike helped Speewell onto one of two stretchers strapped onto the back of the chopper without disturbing Carthwaite's and the other pilot's body and started tending to the wound with a first aid box.

Drier felt he had just been served by the militia with the utter lack of seriousness or regard for the army transport or the guests that it carried. He looked over to the pilot who was now intently looking at the skyline and tree cover for any missiles zoned in on them in multitudes.

He sarcastically queried, "Alright, these guys know they can knock us out anytime, anywhere, but they're just not doing it? Like they want to see what we're up to first before they do it. This doesn't smell good. Telling us who's in charge."

"I agree." responded Simmons with squinted eyes. "I have never viewed myself to be of entertainment value."

"Next destination?" the pilot asked.

Drier warily responded, "Let's get back to the airport, I think we've got a fair enough picture on things and don't need yet another casualty." Speewell smiled at Grondike in heavy relief. Grondike looked mildly disappointed at the chance of another adrenaline rush being quashed.

AVA MARIA MISSIONARY SCHOOL POINTE TROIS
DAY 4 – 13:00HRS

The beaten up lorry of the school's wholesale supplier pulled up at the gate with sacks of flour, rice, baskets of fresh fruits and vegetables. He drove straight to the large kitchen doors. The chief cook came out and gave a quick look-over the truck as he signed the delivery note.

Frapacha's tracker, with pencil tucked on top of his ear underneath his navy blue cap, was wearing an oversized Hawaiian shirt, baggy blue trousers and black tennis shoes. Holding his clip board he casually hummed his way to Kamara's office. The tracker knocked at the door, entered and closed it behind him. He cheerily announced, "A delivery being made sir?"

The tracker handed over the clip board to be co-signed while he reached for the memory card that was comfortably snuggled in a handkerchief in his pocket. He handed over the memory card as Kamara gave him back the clip board.

"Logging operations." he whispered.

"You know you guys gotta do better with your prices. We haven't raised our school fees in 10 years." Kamara loudly complained.

"Yeah well our suppliers keep raising prices every year. Thank you sir. Have a great day." He turned around, closing the door behind him.

From the guest house once Chenchon saw the truck drive off, he grabbed a pile of paperwork and walked to Kamara's office pretending not to even notice the vehicle drive out. He entered the office and announced, "The visa applications of Susan, James, Judith and Mirabelle are all sorted out. They shouldn't have any problem. Still waiting for word on the other 6 though."

As he spoke, Kamara handed him the memory card and Chenchon placed in his pocket. "Alrighty, we'll continue to wait. Catcha later."

He casually walked out of Kamara's office, down the steps and back to the guest house. He had already sent the first feed off. He started to work on the second one to dispatch to Emily within minutes possible.

HON. MAXWELL FISHER'S OFFICE PARLIAMENT
DAY 4 – 13:00HRS

Fisher sounded frantic and demanding, "Did you get the man? Put the file in front of him?"

"Yes, he didn't like that it was a bribe, but seemed ecstatic by the idea of his debt being completely paid off and still plenty remaining to pay off his colleagues for a vote change. Said there were no guarantees, but he'd see what he could do. Complaining he'd have to reach out to some unlikely ones and this has been too hot an issue for too long."

"I'm sure you have all his numbers as well as his wife's. Call them every hour to remind them of the downside if he doesn't pull these votes through. Something about providing bank deposit slips to ensure previous votes went through on other controversial matters that the Press and law enforcement agencies might find to be interesting information."

"Will do."

The conversation left Fisher's heart pounding. He hadn't felt such stress, felt so uncertain; in years.

CHAPTER 14

THE BOILING POINT

STATE HOUSE, CARAMONDO
DAY 4 – 13:00HRS

"Bazilio!" He never called Bugazon by his first name unless he was exasperated, disappointed and fueled by anger at whatever failure threatened to overpower him at that moment.

In a daze of 20 minutes after being summoned by Belinda, Bugazon found himself saluting in front of a President intensely shaking the 3 page report at him. "I think you already know what's in these pages that I would prefer to call dribble but unfortunately is the confirmed truth from two other sources I prayed would tell me otherwise. Our buyer's security person killed within two hours of being in Pointe Trois while we have a whole army there? Their lawyer dead, emergency jumping out of our copter being shot out of the sky like some hot-air balloon tour?" his mouth agape, eyes widened in questioning shock as he slammed the pages on his desk. His fixed stare was now clearly a warning he had seen only once before in his life, when the coup d'état they executed 20 years ago almost came apart mid-stream.

"And what about this girl?" His lethal gaze had downgraded itself to anger. "I read you're sending her lessons in anatomy and house calls to the local reptile zoo? Bazilio, do you forget who you're dealing with? This is a child of war who, by the way, spent her childhood in the rainforest with the very same snakes you're sending to her home? Trying to make her nostalgic?" the threat in his eyes returned. "Her lungs were working overtime and you just gave them a whole new lease on life with this wave of sympathy she'll ride to become an even bigger nuisance to us now. Her people will now really rally around her. This screw up in Pointe Trois and that woman are giving me a very expensive headache."

He ranted on, "I mean, this one-woman-show is beginning to make us look like moody, greedy kindergarteners. Since when were you Mr. Velvet-Gloves, Feel-Good-Fairy? Now what I despise most is that they're expecting us to try again. Patiently waiting, and the wisest thing we can do is nothing at all. Stand down. We get our agreement signed and then send her an invitation with lots of incompetent escorts to visit her brother's grave. If anyone wants to knock her off as a souvenir, I couldn't care less. We can't swat every fly in the room the way we'd like. We stick to the paper route for now. Just get *thaaat* agreement signed." He said with his head slumped sideways, leaning forward in his chair. His expression of disbelief had usurped even the slightest trace of professional respect for his long-time commander.

"Yes sir."

The President gave a dismissive stare. Bugazon exited himself in shock at the dress-down he had just received. Back at his desk in absolute rage Bugazon dialed away.

"Hold off on the disinfectant for now."

"As you wish sir, wishing you a germ-free day." was the flat unemotional reply.

QUADRANT 1
POINTE TROIS RAINFOREST
DAY 4 – 13:15HRS

Frapacha's third tracker was met by a militia tracker not more than 100 meters from the filming site. Frapacha's tracker was well familiar with the spot. There was no trail, no tended gardens. The foliage had become thick and thorny. The militia tracker let out 3 gentle bird calls in short sequence. Very quickly a thorny make shift door of 3 feet opened back. A wiry tall man met the tracker with a flame torch in his hand. Clearly this had been a formidable warrior some time ago. Probably still was.

"Come in." Spoke his soft deep voice.

Frapacha's tracker put back in place this camouflaged entrance and then secured it with the help of the warrior by placing two logs diagonally across each other. It was not possible to imagine the interior from outside. They climbed down a few feet onto a narrow ledge and then took a narrow path about twenty feet below to a large central water point, lit by torches along the wall that gave way to five foot entrances to other pathways. This central water source appeared to be the meeting point from a nexus of caves but it was difficult to say how far they went or where they led to. They quickly moved with the warrior down some narrow steps carved out of the wall. Women and children came out of some of the pathways. One of the elders of this place had been briefed of this filming to take place and spoke into the camera.

"No one has ever entered our home before. Welcome to our underground village. This place has been here since the time of our ancestors. Youth in the village used to play among the honeycombs of caves until the war really heightened about 15 years ago and the militia began to use it as an underground bunker and major weapons hiding place. But with the wipeout and torture of the villages that were caught in the middle of the ever changing firing lines, they told us to relocate here. We're 40 families, about 250 of us."

The tracker spanned the lens around.

"It is a maze of caves, some with smaller water points. The whole complex runs almost 2 kilometers. There are several exits but we've sealed off most of them. Only a selected few of our men go out to find food for the community. It is the lack of antibiotics for wounds for the adults and damp conditions producing pneumonia for the children and elderly that are a constant threat to us. At times when the army has camped in our area for weeks, we cannot go out for food. It is too unsafe. So we try to stock up."

The militia tracker also followed close behind as the elder continued. Frapacha's tracker zoomed in on the wounded men with broken legs and gun-shot wounds. He zeroed in on two women, one with a burn scar running across her face from her right temple to the black of her left jaw, the other had her eye gouged out and the skin sealed up its surface. The 2 were among a group preparing food around a small fire. Others were combing their children's hair in groups of three or four as they quietly talked among themselves. There was a certain sense of safety that floated through the rays of soft amber light of the torches around. A piece of safety from the ambushes and terror meted out on them.

Frapacha's tracker turned to the men, "So what kind of wildlife are you able to trap from around here?"

One of the group inquisitively asked, "What wildlife? They've been killed off out of spite and the remaining few fled beyond the borders, just too stressful. We only catch the occasional warthog or large size rodent."

Frapacha's man moved in and out of some of the smaller tunnels to capture the tiny off-shoot honey combs that could barely fit two people for sleeping space. It was cramped and damp. A health hazard waiting to happen, an elderly man was heard spitting a gut wrenching cough to clear his lungs. The militia tracker pressed his hand on his ear to hone in on his communication. He gave the signal it was time to go. Frapacha's tracker stopped filming.

"Let's move." he whispered.

The village guide started out in a crouched run with the torch. They turned with a short curve then came the narrow brief climb up a rugged ladder made from branches. Without knowing it, it had earlier been a gentle decline of which they now had to climb back up. The tracker raised his hand to stop. He signaled a sound into the microphone wired into his shirt. At the ceiling he made another bird sound into his microphone. After about five seconds, the circular lid was lifted by another militia standing guard. Frapacha's tracker and his militia escort lifted themselves out. The village guide nodded and closed the entrance. Frapacha's tracker took 3 dangerous seconds to get a signal and transmit the footage to Elder Katan. The two started off in an uneven run imitating a pair of wild boars running through the forest. The large canopy of trees high above had swallowed up most of the sunlight.

AMOUR DIEU AIRPORT, POINTE TROIS
DAY 4 – 13:30HRS

The helicopter landed on the edge of the runway and was wheeled to its parking next to three other helicopters. Velasquez rushed out of the hangar with a grave look on his face. Guests had been killed and shot-up on his watch during a mission that he was instructed to impress and give an air of conclusive competence and wrap-up of the situation.

Drier had already started to close the distance to the hangar. Simmons motioned to the medics to hurry.

"Disinfect the wound and contain the bleeding. The surgeon at your military hospital in Avalon is on standby to treat it."

Speewell winced as Grondike along with the medics pulled his stretcher off the chopper. 4 officers followed with 2 body bags to remove Carthwaite and the pilot's bodies.

"Velasquez, now I see why you excused yourself from this tour. You prefer to stay alive." Drier gave Velasquez a cynical dismissive look. Simmons caught up with the 2.

"Mr. Drier, my apologies and condolences cannot begin to even express…"

"Cut the crap Velasquez. You're in way over your head. You know it. I know it. I don't think you even have a way out of this intractable mess." Drier continued with his fast walk across the runway to the Command Center tent as they awaited Speewell's temporary wound dressing.

"I can understand your sentiment given what you've just gone through."

Velasquez re-directed their walk to a small office inside the hangar converted into a basic meeting room. He firmly shut the door behind them. Simmons observed the beads of sweat roll off Velasquez's temple as he reached to pull the string of the ceiling fan above them.

Drier decided to drive the point home. "Just to summarize for you Brigadier." as he emphasized the title for further sarcasm, "in the past 4 hours during your tour" another emphasis on the word tour, "we've been shot down twice, two of our senior staff killed, held at gun point and lectured to like we're children by your militia, shot at as we're running from the mines and toured a number of mines that have been blasted to bits but not a thing looted as if they're talking to you about your competence and conscience. So where do we start Velasquez?"

Velasquez's training had kicked in. A calm look took over his face. His eyes squinted slightly, his brow barely frowned but the tension showing in the hunch of his shoulders. But the stubborn sweat from the day's heat was letting him down. Velasquez calculated in his mind, anything he said at this moment would be the words and binding commitment of his Commander-in-Chief. From unfolding events thus far he did not want to receive a phone call directly from the President raging at him that he could not stand by the promises he'd just given, which would lead to an even further derailment of his career.

Softly and carefully he started, "Gentlemen, I can understand your anger. We will be having a complete change in key positions of our planning personnel." At least this he was sure of, most likely starting with him. Velasquez continued.

"As we speak we are deploying more boots on the ground along with more airpower to flush them out of large expanses of jungle that we know are their hide-outs. We're driving them out into certain small clusters to set a down pour of air ammunition, then surrounded by a ring of fire.

This shall happen in three areas over the next 72 hours. Our intelligence has dramatically improved with the torture techniques we employ." Even Simmons was surprised by the brutality of the campaign. Just then Drier's phone rang.

"Yes, we're back from our tour."

Baynes sounded almost frantic. "I've been trying to get in touch with you but the line doesn't go through at all, total silence."

"Yes, the militia probably knows how to jam the satellite comm. in this area."

Baynes interrupted, "Look, another live feed from the rainforest has just come in of some massive logging site. It looked like slave labor Drier. We are 3 hours behind you, so we get fed activities for our full day on this end. This is not helping us. The first was of an atrocious mining site and calling us corporate cannibals. The share price is taking a nose dive. That's why I've been trying to reach you. To make sure none of you guys are caught on tape in that neighborhood or that'll be the end of everything. We don't want to be seen in Pointe Trois or Avalon now or later. Have those meetings and get out of there fast."

Drier realized that Baynes had even forgotten to ask how the tour went. He knew he was panicking on that end. "Yes Brigadier. There seem to be continued live feeds coming in from the rainforest highlighting your up to the minute government work to the rest of the world. Thought you said you had this jungle secured?"

Simmons immediately walked to a corner of the room and made a phone call, his hand covering his mouth. Velasquez did not even bother to utter an apology. He knew it would be useless, senseless; only confirming the obvious in the room.

Simmons spoke to Drier in a low tone. "The flight crew will be here in 15 minutes."

Drier stared at the Brigadier, a combination of curiosity and camouflaged contempt. "As our crew arrives, perhaps you can show us the deployments you've placed throughout this territory? You seem to be in a bit of a quandary at the moment."

The very words Velasquez knew he dreaded. The show during the fly around was the most he was willing to share. This surely would be his undoing. The coordination issues in the jungle were making it difficult to have coherent progress and they couldn't keep up with the constant changes instructed by Avalon.

"Of course Mr. Drier, I'd be delighted. A man of your military repute would always have something to contribute."

As they walked into the Command Center tent that had a 4 X 4 feet table and spread out was a map of the Pointe Trois rainforest that covered the whole table with drawing pins of different colored heads so it was easy to read. The militia in red, the army in green, the villages in yellow and the respective mines in gold and grey. The left wall of the tent was rimmed with tel. comm. consoles with officers taking down the coordinates and feeding the information to the center table to track changes in movements and skirmishes taking place. The jungle was divided into four quadrants. The Commanding Officer of each Quadrant reported directly to Velasquez on both military and minerals and timber extraction activity. His former Deputy had already been recalled to Avalon when they needed a scape goat to pin recent humiliating defeats on the ground. The communication coming in from Quadrant III was particularly intense.

"We've caught a group of militia. We're running them down towards the ravine. We're about half a kilometer behind them." said a breathless voice you could hear cutting and running past bush and thicket. They're about 10 of them, carrying a combination of RPGs and in particular the Surface to Air Missiles that have been hell on our copters. There are 20 of us, so we should definitely get 'em!" The communication went out.

"Show me where this is on the map?" Drier asked Velasquez.

Both Simmons and Drier studied the map carefully as they listened to the strategists and ground tacticians throw recommendations at each other in fervor. It was immediately clear to Drier that the army had major gaps in between the Quadrant boundaries on which the militia had capitalized. As the militia had picked up on this they had developed pockets of corridors for ambushes as well as certain key supply points. More boots were not going to solve their problems. This poor planning was now also undermining their positioning at other strategic points such as the mines due to the constant attacks. It was obvious to Simmons and Drier that this war could be dragged out by the militia as long as they wanted. A field operations strategist could turn the tables around and finally make this a battle of two equals. Placement of the drawing pins on the table and the people around it were not encouraging.

Simmons noticed the hotel shuttle drive up and position itself in between the two jets. The pilots had been briefed about Grondike's condition in their earlier conversation. One of the crew was walking quickly towards the Medic tent and another was walking to the tent serving as a morgue that kept Carthwaite's body. Drier caught Simmons distracted observation.

"Ok folks. Our crew is here, time for us to meet with your people in Avalon." Drier announced as he gave a worrisome look to Velasquez.

Speewell had a satisfied smile on his face feeling snug in his seatbelt, leg stretched in a make shift caste. One step closer to home he thought to himself. He looked out of the egg shaped window with a perplexed frown on his brow. "I can't believe what's happened to us in the past 48 hours. This place is so vicious, so unforgiving."

"Yeah, welcome to the world beyond your desk." Drier mumbled in passing.

In his mind, Simmons neatly filed the tour of the jungle behind him. He had already communicated to Graciella the arrangements to be made for Kreshnakov and Carthwaite. G. Tech. was known for ensuring families of the deceased were fully catered for during the burial and financially organized thereafter. Their childrens' education was always taken care of. Graciella once told him that a VP's wife bitterly complained to him that her husband be sent on a trip and never come back, in order for her family to finally find peace and stability.

Drier came back from the momentary nostalgia on his several operations he'd drifted into. Sentiments for any losses were suppressed. Execution towards the goal was the primary objective; the only objective.

He searched into Simmons eyes as he spoke. "Let's strike while the iron is hot. We'll start with the military meeting instead while the unqualified embarrassment is still fresh on their faces and use that apologetic defense to burn right through them in the legal meeting."

Simmons made the call to Pican the State House Legal Officer. Drier knew he had the Caramondo government right where he wanted them, apologetic and insecure, but they could already taste the money and probably had already started to spend some of it. Simmons could read Drier's focus closing in for the kill.

Simmons also knew from studying the President's file and the two previous meetings he'd had with the man, that he was a shrewd calculating operator. He could be down but he was never out. There were virtually no obstacles to get this deal through at an amount friendly to him. Nothing was to be taken for granted in the next 48 hours.

PARLIAMENT, CARAMONDO
DAY 4 – 14:15HRS

This was unusual. But nobody could tell what it meant. Almost all of the MPs had arrived on time to the Plenary. Not milling around chatting among themselves but were in their benches looking expectantly at the Speaker's chair. LaFonte opened his door and stepped out into the Chambers to take his seat. He had reasoned they thought this was probably too big a show to pass up. For once the MPs had gotten their act together and were not going to be bulldozed.

"Everybody rise." Commanded the Sergeant at Arms. Everybody stood up.

LaFonte spoke. "MPs, the Bill on government sale of land and the Ministry of Works supplementary budget pertaining to the Frelwegon expressway connecting the north region to the national highway system are the only two items on the agenda this afternoon. And they are both up for a vote. If we don't kick up a fuss about these items, we may close early for the day." came out a quick darting smile that disappeared as fast as it appeared.

He quietly prayed to himself that the first item on the agenda would speedily sail through. He had deliberately scheduled it to be the first item just in case things got off track he could force them back to closure on the premise of moving onto the second item on the agenda.

It was up to Fisher to have done his part. And from the look of the turnout and unabashed gleeful expression on Manywar's face this was turning out to be a difficult day and subsequent near-impossible meeting with their guests thereafter followed by an unthinkable closure to the day with the President. In a no nonsense tone he grinded through, "Without further delay honorable members, we have heard the presentation from both sides highlighting the pros and cons of this Bill. Whether government can acquire or lease out the land without consent of the people pending adequate compensation. Shall we proceed straight to the vote?"

LaFonte did not want to manage any mood swings this afternoon. Whichever way the dice was going to roll, that was it. The simple structures of four voting booths were paired on either side of the floor where 212 MPs were going to register their votes. Fisher was highly regretful of this primitive booth system. A show of hands was much more efficient to intimidate someone with a stare and take stock of who needed to be reminded to vote wisely next time. The MPs quickly filed down the line. Fisher was at the end of one of the queues. He casually glanced over to the Speaker who glared a hole through him and turned away scanning the order in the room. The ballots would be collected and there would be a transparent paper count in front of everyone. The last to vote on his queue, Fisher picked up his ballot paper and closed the curtain behind him then came out and dropped it in the box.

Twenty minutes later at the front of the Chambers, the vote counting started. He couldn't stand it and stepped out to cool off for a minute. He swore to himself that he would punish Manywar for making him sweat so much. He didn't want to go back in and face the result. He walked back in. Without expression, LaFonte read out the results. Those in favor of the Bill 110, those opposed 102. Fisher closed his eyes for a long moment in deep silent relief, opened them again and looked straight at LaFonte. LaFonte gave him a stern look. Fisher understood exactly what pressure was packed in that glance. The deal breaker that he didn't want on his plate. His health could barely withstand it.

This was too close a call for a deal that the Head of State had been nurturing. A deal that he knew the he wanted nothing to have to do with. He now partook of the blood on his hands. The sooner this was over, he just wanted to forget about it. But his conscience would never allow it. He struggled. "Next vote count people. Let's keep a move on, the Frelwegon expressway connection."

AVA MARIA MISSIONARY SCHOOL POINTE TROIS
DAY 4 – 14:30HRS

Elder Katan forwarded the footage of the village-cave to the owner of the town's stationery shop, who was from Pointe Trois and a central part of the militia's information system. The owner handed the memory card to the tracker busy loading boxes in the shop's store room. In 3 minutes he was loading a stock of text books, reams of paper and other teaching materials onto their beat-up pick-up and 15 minutes later entering the school gates.

The humble young man pointed to one of the sealed boxes. "The village." He whispered while handing over his clip board for signature. Kamara signed and handed the clipboard back to him.

"Thank you very much. You're one of our best customers. Good day sir."

"Wish a discount would come attached to that title." The tracker waved as he shut the door behind him.

Kamara opened the box. Threw some files on top of it and proceeded to Chenchon's guest house. "Here are some files on the student's bio-data you'd requested." Chenchon opened the box and removed the memory card. "Oh no thanks, it turns out the information isn't a requirement."

"Alright then, back with the box." Kamara picked up the box and walked out again. Within 30 minutes, the feed had been sent to Emily in New York ready to relay the third feed to the global networks.

CHAPTER 15

SHOWDOWN

President Gebajara had scheduled all meetings to take place within his security circle at home, so to speak. He could not afford any eavesdropping or Press leaks as had happened during a previous visit. Besides, it would be much easier to personally summons and grill someone if things went terribly wrong and required his personal intervention. At the airport, a sleek black sedan was waiting to pick them up at the runway. The fewer people that saw them, got their passport details or even faces, the better. An unmarked ambulance picked up Speewell to take him to the military hospital. Grondike accompanied him.

Reaching the North Wing entrance of State House, Pican was at the bottom of the steps waiting to receive them. With a charming but efficient smile he shook hands as they walked up the stairs. "Gentlemen, my apologies and condolences for the difficulties experienced during your trip. The team from the army is already waiting for you in the conference room. This way please." It was obvious to both men Pican was trying to keep the conversation as short as possible as he kept the pace brisk and a couple of strides ahead.

With grandeur, he opened the 2 tall slender wooden doors. Four military personnel engaged in their own conversation stood up in unison. Bugazon at the head of the table had already made strides to them. Bugazon had a wide very fixed grin across his face.

"Gentlemen! Please."

Simmons standing slightly ahead of Drier responded to the extended handshake followed by a hearty pat on his arm. "Simmons! At last we meet again. I have been so looking forward. And this must be the one and only Mr. Drier whose reputation precedes him." Bugazon motioned to both of them to be seated at both ends of the table. This was all part of the psychology of posture, commanding and managing the mental landscape of the meeting.

Simmons removed his file and notepad from his briefcase. Drier pushed his seat slightly back to accommodate his long thighs crossed as he sat at an angle to the table, able to face all the officers. Present were Brigadier Kazolo now in charge of the elimination of the militia and Major Calizar called in to support General Piquant. Piquant was still in New York after his son's wedding and Pitua was lying in the barrack's morgue. Drier could even categorize the tension on their faces ranging from managing the guilt of their deeds to embarrassment of their strategic gaffes and technical blunders, but nevertheless desire and ambition to see this meeting through. Drier finally settled his gaze on Bugazon who took this as a prompt to start the meeting.

Drier had interlocked his fingers comfortably beneath his navel.

"Obviously gentlemen, our profound apologies and shock would not suffice for the loss you have encountered."

Drier and Bugazon were locked in eye contact. "To give such an inexperienced pilot our most expensive recently procured helicopter and place him with your most senior staff was an order I would have never allowed had I known it." Even Drier was stunned at the arrogance of the man. "Let me come to the remedial measures we've put in place. We cannot undo the last 24 hours."

Drier did not want to be lectured to until he had made their position known. Command of the conversation he was not willing to relinquish. "General Bugazon, your reputation precedes you too."

The General beamed, genuinely surprised by the compliment. But his subordinates immediately read the frozen smile and lack of warmth Drier offered and knew that this was not a compliment.

"If I may highlight during our tour that our staff have been killed, wounded and run out of destroyed mines we came to see. The mines we have toured have been blown up which has significantly eroded the value of the land we were considering procuring or at least the investment costs just shot up. You are still putting out too many skirmishes on all corners of this rainforest, with no hint of anything being contained. We stood at your command table for 3 minutes and could clearly see your deployments did not show any semblance of a strategy. Your Commanding Officer says he's still working out the battle plan as the fighting appears to overwhelm your team. So, really General," Drier concluded, "I don't see how you're going to pull off a miracle in the next 3 days. This means that we could not risk putting our staff on the ground if you don't have control of the situation. Essentially we don't have the confidence or at least are convinced that you have the upper hand in this battle. We need you to change that opinion during the course of this afternoon or we're out of this deal. These are the facts, the experiences we've gone through in the last 18 hours we've been with you."

Bugazon's eye contact remained fixed on Drier throughout this statement determined he would not be the first one to blink. He stared blank, without expression. He was stunned. Not expecting such as sharp rebuke of facts on the ground. No one among his people had dared to advise him of such. The room was stunned into silence. Nobody made a move. It was only the officers. Their eyeballs moving between the 2 gentlemen.

"Mr. Drier I can understand how this situation appears chaotic and without conclusion." He looked away for a brief moment at his notes and past glanced at his officers who were all transfixed on him. Major Calizar relished the moment to see his barbarian caged even for a few minutes. He took sanctity. No one could arrest him from there, in the privacy of his thoughts. Bugazon had recomposed himself ready to fire back. He knew Pointe Trois was fast slipping in between his fingers, but as far as he saw it was not yet out of his grip. This was the transaction of a lifetime, if it meant telling this military expert what to do.

He continued, "Just imagine, in the next 3 days everything will be over. The reports we'd received from the ground painted a completely different picture. We did not get the correct figures on the casualties experienced and the actual number of mines being blown up. People were trying to cover up their failures and losses."

Brig. Kazolo was less than amused by Bugazon's bravado. He had personally fed him the updates every morning before 07:00hrs because they knew these losses would have to be explained to a larger audience and Bugazon had a fixation on the percentage of everything he could take.

"As you know, every war is constrained by the bickering of the budget while our men on the ground are dying. Very recently we received clearance from our Commander-in-Chief to implement more robust plans, the effects of which you'll be seeing very shortly. Probably by this evening, the scorch earth policy will begin."

The meeting was tense. From discussion and mutterings among themselves in the past couple of days, planners in the *Pointe Trois Project* had developed a slow uneasy feeling that this was getting out of hand, that they as the army could not contain constant mine ambushes and fight a war at the same time. Without moving his head, Calizar looked down pretending to study his notes.

Simmons read the breakdown in belief of the boss's response.

Bugazon dug in with his narrative. "In order to maximize the time that we have, myself and the team that you see here shall be flying out to Pointe Trois first thing in the morning in order to avoid miscommunication of reports." He flippantly raised his hands.

"We will manage the battle scene directly from the field. It'll be radical, but effective, surgery."

The officers at the table knew this meant that he was willing to rip up the rainforest, burn it to the ground and gut out the population to be able to get rid of the militia, the inhabitants of which he had lumped to be part of the militia. As long as he got rid of the enemy, he did his part. The condition of the forest was not his worry. He had gained from it. It just needed to look undisturbed by guns.

He forged ahead, "But I can assure you, within 24 hours you shall have a rainforest to your absolute freedom. No menacing militia meandering around that place." Bugazon seemed pleased with himself. He had given assurances. But he knew he had no real desire to be on ground because he knew he could put enough unpleasant pressure on Field Commanders from the comfort of his office.

Drier's eyes softened for a moment. "Forgive me General if I seem convinced otherwise. With the current level of crisis, we will expect to see you shift from chaos to a clear upper hand for a decisive clean up in the remaining 72 hours. Failure to see turnaround at the mid-point, we're out of the deal. I think you can agree that we are extending ourselves beyond reasonable risk going solely by the words you have just uttered to us."

The softness had turned to a silent stare. Bugazon tried to dismiss the command Drier had taken of the meeting. "Mr. Drier I can assure you, we shall be having an entirely different conversation on phone in 36 hours."

Bugazon firmly snapped his dossier closed. He'd decided the grilling was over. He'd been given a lifeline to conclude as he saw fit. Drier stood up. Bugazon, followed by everyone else arose. Bugazon walked over to Drier to offer a handshake. Simmons shook hands with everyone.

Bugazon gently motioned his arm with the same broad grin that welcomed the group as he walked to the door. "Calizar shall walk you to the legal team. They've been waiting."

Drier walked out glad that the ball was squarely in the army's court but at the same time astounded at the difficulties they found and the glaring lack of competence to address them. This was one of the operations where he didn't like the ending that was persistently presenting itself to him. But one thing was guaranteed, it was going to be messy.

Bugazon closed the door behind him. His subordinates watched as he rolled his eyeballs in an odd mixture of relief and despair.

Pican met them in the second corridor, into which they had just turned. He read the look in Drier's eyes loud and clear. He had the upper hand and was now looking to close in on the kill. Pican charmingly maintained his game face, a gentle sharp smile. He turned to direct the walk as he waved to Calizar with a casual elegance.

"Gentlemen, I trust you had a fruitful meeting? Here we are." He made an immediate left to tall rectangular mahogany wood doors.

From one set of uniforms to another. The collection of navy blue and black custom tailored suits from the finest addresses the globe could offer clothed their well-fed physiques. This line of uniforms was the expensive facilitators with their high brand arrows of ink waiting in battle line across the conference table. Then there was one more economical outfit. Simmons knew each one of the faces from previous visits and video conferences.

The private sector of Caramondo could not support the retainer fees and sheer scope of wherewithal these lawyers in front of them had acquired. They earned their living specifically through State and commercial contracts between government and international service providers, not to mention the nameless faces of high ranking officials that needed to process their undocumented natural resources in a legitimate manner out of the country. State

House Counsel in his economical suit moved forward and gave a brief handshake and passing eye contact. Drier knew his suit was only a disguise for his mass of wealth no different than his colleagues around the table.

Handshakes were brief around the table. Drier and Simmons were motioned to sit on one side of the table as the 6 lawyers sat on the other side, similar to an inquisition. Simmons charged ahead, politely ignoring State Counsel's tight smile and positioning to open the meeting and welcome his guests.

"Gentlemen, it seems we have this meeting with you under circumstances that have proven disastrous for us in the past 12 hours. As we sit here, it is not about finalizing the details of this transaction but whether we have a transaction at all. It is not about mitigating measures, but instead about miracles required to turn around what appears to be a transaction we'd rather walk away from as both the short and long term risks seem to have spiraled out of control right before us. Let us explain in the context of the basic tenets of the agreement.

One: This is a sales agreement. It becomes private land. Our sources tell us that the Bill has passed, but you have MPs threatening to make this a Referendum. An outcome of which is beyond our control, but consequences potentially fatal to this transaction. We are even flexible enough to provide a 6 month window for inhabitants to relocate themselves out of the forest, upon signing. If the militia is any representation of the sentiment of the population, they don't seem to be grabbing their bags. Our intelligence tells us it is only the extremely ill that they are ferrying across the border; something about the support of the family that is among the largest land owners in the forest. Word is, residents say they'll fight to the death.

Two: The Government would be fully responsible for eliminating any elements resistant to G. Tech procuring the forest. A resistance of which must have been decisively dealt with within 1 month of signing the agreement. Well, 2 of our staff have been killed under your army watch, we've been captured and lectured to by the militia like we're not sure what we're getting into. Dealing with the militia to any extent seems realistically improbable.

Three: G. Tech would mine and/or extract any resource from this land as they wish upon signing the agreement. However, every mine we've visited has been pretty much destroyed and I would hazard a guess you were showing us the good ones.

Four: G. Tech. would not be subject to any environmental or other technical audits pertaining to the rainforest. I'm sure you have also sensed that the environmentalists in New York are picking up steam. And normally the next sentence out of their mouths in these situations is their demand for a library of environmental audits.

Five: Once the wire transfers are done upon signing, that's it. The transaction is done, no further commercial exchange with any representation from your good country.

Gentlemen, we are now very far from the confidential transaction this should have been. It would be safe to say that what has been happening in the rainforest is worldwide information and that is even while we were in the forest. Seems there is up to the minute coverage by the activists from the forest within past hours alone. As I said, this has proven to be something of a PR disaster for us and we haven't even filled one truck with minerals. I mean, the value of our stock is plummeting even before we have earned one dollar which has made this very difficult to justify to our shareholders at this juncture.

Bottom line is, Counsel," Simmons sprayed a look at all of them, "based on this visit of what we have seen on the ground, the stock as well as PR battering we're taking worldwide; we have just expressed our re-consideration of this transaction to your military colleagues due to the overwhelming risk in Pointe Trois. We shall take our opinion back to our Principals and review this project in context of all the others on the ground. The 7 day timeline looks very difficult for your colleagues in camouflage let alone the 3 day turnaround promised. We are certain that this is no longer a transaction at the value of $900 million, difficult to say where we might actually land. At present, Pointe Trois is not secured so we can't even talk about securing this agreement."

Simmons concluded with a sigh, "But say in the event miracles in multitudes manifest themselves, $700million is the very best we can offer."

Counsel cocked his head to a tilt, with a stiffened sarcastic smile as if to enquire in an un-amused tone, whether he was finished. "Mr. Simmons, really." His smile now widened and relaxed a bit, "I would urge you not to panic over what may appear to be a difficult situation, but nonetheless very manageable."

The senior private Counsel nodding continuously at his colleague's oration locked in a stare at Drier. Drier was unimpressed by the men in front of him that had not stepped near Pointe Trois and the practical difficulties that lay in front of all of them.

State House Counsel continued, "We have a raft of technical difficulties and points of personal persuasion to ensure that a Referendum never sees light of day. Pointe Trois is arguably the second or third largest rainforest in the world. The mineral and plant life are still barely documented. The mines you've visited are but only the surface scratched, literally speaking. You will have the upper hand in industries in which you're not even in yet with the procurement of Pointe Trois. At the risk of sounding insensitive, the remedial work required in Pointe Trois is short term cosmetic surgery. You will not receive any menacing neighbors floating up to your neck of the woods to check on you, see what you're digging up. Pointe Trois is not exactly exit 42 off Highway A1. Our colleagues in camouflage would have shared that this airspace could be easily managed. What environmental audits? We have teams of lawyers just waiting to melt away such requests." His stare was firm but calm.

He continued. "The world will have moved on to its next crisis by the end of next week. Yours is the topical outrage for now. If your PR spin doctors know what they're doing, you'll take a bruising for now but should start to look peachy again in a month. Like I said, the world forgets fast."

State House Counsel was quiet for a moment. Private Counsel took his intrusive stare off Drier and transferred it to Simmons as if giving him clearance to now respond. Drier all along had been calculating the level of planning required to wash the militia out of the Region, the so-called cosmetic surgery required, but he also knew the benefits of procuring Pointe Trois. The lawyer wasn't entirely wrong, but he surely was not going to give him the credit of letting him know.

Simmons took a casual deep sigh with an expression of gentle forlorn. He closed his notebook shut to suggest there was not much more he was willing to say. "Gentlemen, we live on a global stage. Our stock price is not what it used to be in the past 48 hours. Your dismissive description does not address the costs we've incurred as a corporation and most surely would still have to incur. Our staff met with your representatives on the wire transfer details but we don't even have a transaction to discuss. Be prepared for an outcome that neither of us was expecting."

State House Counsel stood up, "Mr. Simmons, I can assure you, there is a transaction. No worries there. It is only on the surface that things look a bit difficult. Let us not over blow the recent difficulties you've experienced and what appears to be a time crunch of sorts."

Drier and Simmons had swiveled around their chairs to stand up as Counsel closed his sentence. Drier sounding unimpressed and conclusive, "Well, we don't know that now do we? It all depends on what happens on the ground in the next 36 hours."

State House Counsel had slowly started to move towards the door. Pican had already started to move in from the other side, as he picked up a brief phone call that did not require any words from him.

"Mr. Drier and Mr. Simmons, it has been a pleasure to have spent these all too brief moments with you. We look forward to enjoying a meal together as we dine with Your Excellency this evening."

"Our pleasure indeed." replied Simmons with a distant smile in his voice as he exited the door.

Pican walked them back to the steps where their vehicle awaited them. As soon as he waved goodbye to them, he reached for his phone and started dialing.

"How's it going down there?" was the question asked. There was no time for pleasantries.

"Rebecca, G-Tech. is putting on a tough face. Their visit to Pointe Trois didn't go too well as far as presentations are concerned. They didn't seem too impressed with the army in Pointe Trois and with the summary meetings that just took place. But the clear message that has been communicated from the military and legal teams here is that the agreement is going through at all costs, no matter what. The fact that G.Tech. did not fly out directly from Pointe Trois abandoning any further communication with the government and if they're still willing to hear what the Head of State has to say, means they're not yet willing to walk away from the table just yet. Once they fly out of here, there will be a phone call in 36 hours to say whether they are in or out.

"Thanks for the update. Let me see how I can further squeeze this time frame."

"By the way, the broadcast feeds from Pointe Trois certainly had an impact at our meetings."

"Richard, thanks for staying true to your values and being a good friend."

The 2 did not even utter a word until reaching Drier's hotel room. Each was calculating their own thoughts, strategizing best possible maneuvers over the next 24 hours.

Breaking the silence, Drier's phone rang. Baynes sounded anxious. "This is getting too hot for us. We need to pull out. This is spiraling out of control and this stock dive is breaking records. Shareholders will have my head on a silver platter. Let's cut our losses and recover on a couple of other projects before the financial year is over." Baynes knew he was fast becoming the Chairman that allowed the company to get involved in such scandalous behavior and reckless activity.

"Hold on Baynes. It ain't over. If there's one thing I've learned, what looks like the end is only the preamble to a whole new beginning. Hang tight. I'll get back to you." Drier was now in the heat of the wrestle with his kill. His heart beat faster, closing in for the slice with the blade. He figured the government was deeply wounded but still giving a good fight. He had just under 45 minutes to discuss the scenario with Simmons and chew it around some more before dinner with the Head of State.

G. TECH. BRANCH OFFICE, NYC
DAY 4 – 12:30HRS

The sleek looking corporate building housed many global names, both known and unknown. Billions earned in profits in these corporate suites. This address was no different than the several other buildings lined up and down the avenue. The only difference between the Globe Tech. address and its fellow glass-door, porcelain floor neighbors further along the block today, was the disruption Police seemed to be gingerly battling unsure whether they could politely keep the protestors distant of the building's entrance but allow them to exercise their rights.

The picketers neatly marched in opposite directions of each other, in unison chanting, "G. Tech. kills little children, pollutes their environments, tortures innocent people. Buy G. Tech products tomorrow or today? I don't think so! No way!"

It was planned just around lunchtime to maximize the attention drawn, particularly in the event of any engagement with the Police. Their placards were images from the live feeds, maimed women cooking in the underground cave, emaciated men dragging huge logs, children with open wounds dragging large trolleys at a mining site. The protestors were wearing black t-shirts and pants. They had done their research and were giving out flyers that listed products powered by G. Tech. software or hardware while they moved up and down in a neat two-way march. The lead protestor yelled to his troops. "We need a U.N. inquiry to reign in such abuse of power and account for these murderous activities." "Yeah, U.N. inquiry, global boycott!!!" chanted back the group.

The sixty or so continued in four rows back and forth a few feet from the building entrance. Just then the burly 6'4" head of G. Tech. security in a navy blue blazer with an earphone plugged in came charging through the door. In 2 giant steps he moved to the lead Police Officer and cradled his shoulder as if talking to an old friend.

"The boss has called from Paris. He wants them shut down immediately. He doesn't want any of this turning up on the evening news.

"Got it." replied the Officer.

What the protestors were not privy to, was the $100,000= contribution that had been made to various political and security offices within the municipality in the past 48 hours. G. Tech.'s nose was beginning to look a little runny and these were the handkerchiefs used to wipe up untidy inconvenient events.

"Ok folks, you've had your say. What d'yah say, we call it a day, huh?"

The protestors quickly locked arms, moved to the entrance of the grand doors, took position in the middle of the pavement and knelt down, then slowly sat down on the pavement. The chant now increased significantly in volume. "G. Tech. baby killers, torturers of an innocent population, forest destroyer!"

The Police Officer looked on with a deep sigh as if dealing with rebellious juveniles. "Okay, round 'em up?"

What the Police didn't know was two protestors were filming the whole event from the coffee shop across the street. About a hundred police officers encircled the group. A struggle ensued. Pairs of legs grabbed, arms flailing in protest with their body parts. Placards thrown aside, the orchestrated protest had deteriorated into a chaotic circus, the perfect material for an attention getting protest.

STATE HOUSE, CARAMONDO
DAY 4 – 18:30HRS

Despite the long dining room table that accommodated 14 guests, the setting and ambience were intimate, soft and thoughtfully elegant. The State House team of lawyers made small talk about global politics which was prompted by events televised on a large flat screen in a corner of the room. State House Counsel had enlightened Drier and Simmons about His Excellency's desire to remain up to date on continental and global developments that may have an impact on their fragile economy such as price changes on the global mineral markets. Everybody stood up as the Head of State entered the banquet room, heavy but brief handshakes were given to the guests. The tension was already beginning to pulsate. Salutes and nods were exchanged with the Caramondo team as he motioned everyone to sit down. Meeting Drier for the first time, President Gebajara did not lose eye contact with the man over whom he wanted to assert control.

Drier smiled to himself in his mind. He had seen the audaciousness of too many Heads of State over the years. The man was both predictable and puzzling. Shame and dishonor from across the globe simply did not register with him. He had amassed enough private wealth for generations at the expense of the people and forest of Pointe Trois. What more could he want?

With a crisp tone of shock and a veneer of sympathy, "First may I extend my heartfelt condolences and apologies at the tragic loss of your colleagues, just tragic." Then an immediate silence fell.

Simmons shot a quick look to Drier. Drier acknowledged with the slightest hint of a smile. It was obvious this was all the man was willing to say, as far as he cared for any losses that were interfering with the complicated conclusion of his transaction. The President's eye trailed to the TV screen as if he was observing something vaguely familiar with distanced annoyance and concern. It seems the feed had been running a few times. The anchor narrated with momentum yet sympathy, *"Global Technologies has vigorously denied any wrong doing or collusion with the government in violation of human rights of this innocent population. Viewers, the upcoming feed is as recent as a few hours ago from an underground cave deep that seems to be a village within Pointe Trois rainforest."*

With an awkward silence around the table, they preferred to focus on the feed rather than dispute the evidence before them with their guests. Drier observed the stone faced expression of the army representatives. The lawyers looked on calmly, yet mildly dismissive and almost fascinated by the extensive coverage of the underground village. State House Counsel stole a look to the President who had already begun to purse his lips and squint his eyes. The inopportune moment of this broadcast was going to cost him.

Simmons shot a look at the man and could see he was scheming his response. The President waved his hand to cut the broadcast. Without missing a beat of concern he reasoned, "As you can see, in these emotional images I think you'll understand this puts a different level of pressure on me."

Drier's phone rang. The only phone call he would allow, "Yes, we saw it. Mmm...hmm." As he hung up he threw a sharp look to the President.

Pretending not to notice the look Drier had attempted to deliver, the President continued. "With this unwanted global attention, my tourism foreign exchange will fall through the floor, not to mention other large scale private sector investment or contributions to our budget. You know how you investors can be oh so fickle. I need to cover the difference of this fall out with the proceeds from this sale." His concerned expression transformed into a glare for a second. He was looking to reclaim Drier's possession of the conversation.

Drier did not relent. "But you probably don't have an agreement with us Mr. President. The militia is still giving you a thorough pounding. We can't put any of our permanent staff in the rainforest in that condition and we can probably get a much better deal elsewhere. Lower cost without the risk of being blown out of the sky and world hate on our doorstep."

President Gebajara thought he had to derail this final drive. He could already taste the money and had already spent some of it. "Let's be calm about this. The military, I will personally supervise." As he flashed a severe look to the uniforms further down the table. "Tell me about the agreement? We're all sorted out on the details I expect?" He turned his head with a cold expression in his eyes to the lawyers. Before he made eye contact with State House Counsel in particular, the lawyer had already launched into a quickly narrated brief.

"The Bill went through this afternoon so the transaction is airtight legal. The raft of legal technicalities and intricacies we're putting in place shall make a referendum an extremely distant and unpalatable option. Once the agreement is signed, they shall be free to work upon their forest." as his head turned slightly to the uniforms and back without losing eye contact with the President. "Residents will move on, especially if relocation incentive packages are put in place."

Simmons gave a hint of a smile at the man who thought everything was up for sale. Counsel gave a hint of a smile back. He concluded his point.

"The world has a short attention span. There will be three new crises by the end of next week."

Counsel shot a final confident look at Drier, "And we have discussed at the length with Mr. Drier the merits of investing in Pointe Trois, the strategic value and long-term competitive advantage G-Tech would have in industries in which it doesn't even exist at the moment. There is nothing ordinary or unremarkable about this transaction. Let's not beat around the bush or play hard to get. The gains from Pointe Trois would put you in a league of your own."

Drier impatiently cut in, "Counsel you seem to persistently dismiss the practicalities on the ground at present." Drier held a cool stare. "Or the present impact on our company's reputation and profitability. Our shareholders are not quite as flexible as you are. Politics and profits are different family trees, albeit in the same forest, if I may say so. Our discussions do not change the facts on the ground. You have three days to show a change in tide or we're out. The present cost does not justify our future jewels. Companies with huge investments and shareholder accountability don't have the flexibility to think that way."

"Enough already." The President snapped as he waved his hands. He could see this was not adding value to his position. "I think we understand each other. Too much talk is ruining my delicate appetite. Shall we?" He gestured to everyone to enjoy the banquet being served.

CHAPTER 16

YOU NEVER KNOW

Balancing the case load and fast building crescendo of the most important thing in her life was beginning to weigh on Rebecca. The emotional toll in her sense of responsibility and duty to her people would not let go of her. Her eyes welled up for a moment. She scolded herself that everything would disappear in a slow and torturous way if she didn't do something about it. A tear dropped onto her notepad. Rebecca almost flipped. She forgot she was supposed to have followed up on the five organizations that were having difficulty staying put in the consortium.

"Marc, let those piano playing fingers of yours do the walking. Dial up Frederick Chiles, Chairman of the Environmental Activists Association."

"On it." He yelled back.

Line 1 flashed on her console, "Rebecca, you know I'm with you. I hear things are grinding down on the last leg." There had been a thorny relationship between Chiles and Rebecca since she left her environmental non-profit work and joined the corporate guzzlers. Some of the clients

Rebecca had to defend at PRS had been among the most abusive environmental polluters but she had always found a just settlement to substitute client jail time and substantial PR damage. However Chiles had found some of these settlements making clients pay deep, to violate the core principals and spirit of the Law. A percentage of the settlement fines were put into a fund that had enabled significant clean-up, hiring of young attorneys to embarrass offenders into compliance and begin several other pro-active environmental projects. It was a quid-pro-quo he had come to live with.

"Frederick, I need your help. Some of these guys you've worked with more closely than I have." "Yes, I've been keeping abreast on matters mmmmm…" prompting her to continue.

"The Bill has passed into Law, so the three heavy weights hesitant to sign onto our consortium are now really skittish."

He interrupted, "I'll talk to them. I know what carrots to bring out of my drawer."

"Thank you Frederick. Then I've got Corporate Environmental Group that has their instructions."

"Yes, I heard. Their sponsors are a bit uncomfortable due to their own similarities with G. Tech." He said with a bit of a chuckle, amused by the irony that many of these sponsors Rebecca had been defending. But to approach

them on this matter would put her at odds with her
employers.

She continued, "Sweetz of his newly formed Citizens
Environmental Alert is my real worry. If he's taken a
$100,000= cheque from Globe Tech. and won't be part of
the group that's one thing, but with instructions to scuttle
this consortium now that's an entirely different land fill
particularly at this moment. I was going to give them a call
myself, but it would carry more weight if it came from
you?"

"I'll get replacements for these other 2. Not to worry.
I'll have a little chat with Sweetz later. I'll remind him that
he may have some seedling of a budget, but it can be very
difficult to get environmental partners when everybody
knows that you were the sell-out or the dedicated saboteur
on such a big project like this. The exit is his choice. But
attempting to break this alliance would be suicidal in this
community. No worries. I'll give him a call."

"Thanks Fredrick. We may have our differences but I'm
so grateful you've been a major power broker behind the
scenes with Ian bringing folks together."

Chiles had a philosophical tone in his voice, "Let's just
say if we lost this, it would be global scale stink for all of
us. We wouldn't be able to explain ourselves."

"Tell me about it." She chuckled finding humor in the
gravity of the situation.

AVALON INTERNATIONAL AIRPORT CARAMONDO
DAY 4 – 20:00HRS

Grondike sheepishly observed Speewell groggily recline in his jet seat, figuring he was overplaying his discomfort just to get more attention from the graceful stewardess that checked on him every minute. Grondike turned to look out of the window. Simmons and Drier were deep in conversation standing in between the two jets. It was a calm but tense conversation. The fuel nozzle was removed from the jet flying to Paris. Simmons took this as his cue to wrap up. They shook hands. Simmons climbed in and situated himself. He briefly watched the cockpit doing their final check.

Drier hunched as he stepped in and headed for his seat, facing the rear of the aircraft. He eyed the two metallic cases that carried the samples in the more delicate jars, packets and test-tubes.

"Systems check complete. We're ready for take-off sir."

"Let's takeoff." Drier ordered despite his very unsettled feeling of leaving an incomplete 48 hours behind him. The co-pilot tipped the cockpit door closed while the Captain communicated off taxing out details to Control Tower. Drier watched the second jet also begin to taxi following them behind. He muttered to Speewell while he cast his eyes over the cases and back to Speewell. "Let's go and see what value for money we really have. Are the future gains worth the past losses?" He watched their sharp incline into the night sky mournfully thinking about Carthwaite in a body bag and Kreshnakov's remains in the middle of the rainforest.

AMB. HOLSTEIN'S OFFICE
UNITED NATIONS, NY
DAY 4 – 15:30HRS

Holstein seemed pleased with himself as he dictated several memos into his tape recorder for Annabelle to type out. He was still the old fashioned type.

Phone calls from various member states streamed in. He read through several background files. He realized he should just briefly check in with Rebecca.

"Rebecca m'dear, there's progress. The Secretary of State had a good conversation with the Chair of the Security Council. An extra-ordinary meeting will be called to discuss Pointe Trois to raise concern about the stability of security in the region due to the movement of distressed populations and build-up of armies at border lines. I had a lengthy conference call with Roman, our point person at UNHCR, to get an official visit on humanitarian grounds. He will then coordinate with the Chair of the Security Council for the Chair to call President Gebajara and express concern and suggest the U.N. Secretary General come out and make a courtesy visit after the humanitarian inspection. Governments tend to shy away from that sort of thing, drying up their donor contributions and killing investor confidence. It's not the investigations or U.N. troop deployment that I'm banking on but the idea of such an inconvenience and a pro-longed spotlight that would pressure him into troop withdrawal from the rainforest. On the matter of preventing the agreement from being signed, the U.N. is too bureaucratic. You'd need to make sure your group seals that end. And I can assure you, this fella would seriously consider eating his own before he walks away from this deal. I've seen enough of them before Rebecca."

"Yes, we're working on it to make sure we bring it together in time." she replied with a long sigh hoping for no last minute changes to the front line.

"Point is, if there's any additional maneuvering you'd want to do, now is the time to do it."

Rebecca quickly interjected, "Oh no. We're in for the kill now, down to the wire. Honestly, I can't say what's going to happen in the next 72 hours but I'm doing everything possible to save Pointe Trois. I just want to save my home and I know the impact of this transaction. I just want to save my home."

Holstein heard the crack in her voice. "I hear yah darlin'. We're with you down to the last second."

On hanging up, Rebecca could feel the weight on her shoulders. She wasn't sure whether it was the grieving process prying for space or the increasing number of things that needed to be handled within this shrinking window. The pain was pounding but she was not willing to let go.

DISCREET LUXURY HOTEL
NEW YORK CITY
DAY 4 – 20:00HRS

Marc hired a bodyguard to escort Rebecca to the hotel and stand outside her door throughout the night. While she looked at the twinkling city below she turned to look at the pile of files that lay on the study table. Flipping through the channels as she sat on the edge of the bed but got up quickly, just to confirm nothing was crawling around. Like a weight on her chest, the worry would not relent. Her finger stopped on one channel upon noticing a familiar face on the news of a global network.

It was Ian talking about Pointe Trois being among the quiet lungs of the earth.

"Without the Pointe Trois rainforest we will not be able to process up to 10% of our greenhouse emissions. Because of its size, it is arguably among the least explored of these eco-systems on the planet so the contribution to medicine from the plant life is unknown and would be a great loss with our finite resources. It is a scientific fact that very rare minerals are sourced from rainforests that we use in our everyday technology from our cel. phones to our video cam.s. All this also will be lost to a few government officials of a country who will sell Pointe Trois to one corporate conglomerate. Consumers, both you and I, need to decide whether we support this kind of activity."

The anchor interrupted, "Mr. Thornton, let me cut in for a moment there, because there are some consumers that are very vocal about their choices, let's take a look for a moment." Ian's face was immediately replaced by the footage of the activists cross-marching with their placards and handing out flyers. Immediately stepping out the door was the G. Tech. security chief followed by the arrest of the protestors. Ian's face came back on screen.

The anchor continued, "This took place in mid-town New York earlier today. We have also been informed that there was an attempt to hold a demonstration at the U.N. building, but that was foiled by the building security and the N.Y. police worried of the security of some of their VIPs and the possible traffic disruption, says a statement from the metropolitan police chief's office. But Mr. Thornton, what will a few protestors do to stop an agreement between a government that has its military entrenched in the rainforest and a global corporation that allegedly has its cheque book on the table for this resource rich land?"

"Well Jules, that's where you come in. It's about 60 protestors using the media to tell the world what's going on in meetings that allegedly never took place or cheques that were supposedly never written. Just because it's not a vacation destination; we don't get to see the wipe out of a population and mow down of a rainforest. Consumers and donors need to shape up and clamp down on this murder they support indirectly with their wallets and budgets. You can buy products from their competition, sanction government officials and re-direct government support to other countries. It's very simple, no one should allow this kind of activity to go on. Make your views known with your money. Shareholder value drop and dwindled government support could turn around this conversation within a matter of days."

The network concluding music rolled in.

"Mr. Thornton, I'm afraid that's all we have time for. Thank you very much for being with us today." The anchor turned her chair back to her desk, "As we can see significant developments unfolding in the Pointe Trois rainforest of the Republic of Caramondo that has global environmental implications with a conglomerate allegedly caught up right in the middle of it. We'll keep you up to date. Don't go away." The network music blended into advertisements.

"Yes!" Rebecca exclaimed to herself. She walked to the console next to the flat screen on the wall to prepare herself a cup of coffee. Leaning against the wall she listened to the water boil. The anchor's voice brought her back to the present.

"Viewers, as a related development to our previous interview", the anchor's eyes referred to the screen behind her that had the major movers on the stock market. "We can see a dramatic drop in the share price of G. Tech. Analysts say in the last 24 hours it has dropped by 43%. As promised we'll keep you informed of developments. Moving on to other news, our reporter Cindy Schill gives us the regular update on the American political scene. Take it away Cindy…"

Rebecca's hope was resuscitated but existed in the shadow of her fear. Was there enough time? The machinery they were up against had lost too much now to walk away from it. She could feel how badly they wanted to cash in and get back to damage control. There was a knock on the door.

"I didn't order room service?" she whispered to herself. Anyway, assassins didn't announce themselves she thought. She looked through the peep hole and saw the back of a head scanning the corridor. "How did he find me?" Her pulse shot for a moment. What did he do with her bodyguard? It was his job to know such things.

Rebecca opened the door. He stepped in and flipped it closed without taking his eyes off her. He stepped forward, she stepped back. The air was already electric. Before she knew it there was no space between them. "I'm sorry you can't be at your apartment. But maybe that's good thing for tonight." as his eyes quickly scanned the room.

His teeth gently bit into her neck as his lips massaged her with kisses. Rebecca almost buckled, immersed in his powerful but subtle cologne seeping from the pores of his 6'3" strong frame. He picked her up and carried her straight to the bedroom laying her down gently on the bed. He unbuttoned her blouse and slowly raised her skirt as his hand ran softly up her thigh.

"You know I have to kill you considering what was running up my leg this morning. It will be the only gratification I can get, at least for now."

"Just don't do it while I make love to you. You're the only woman I can be with, the only person with whom I can let my guard down. He removed his jacket, his Sig-Sauer P250 rested in its holster as he placed them on a chair nearby. He straddled her. "Rebecca forget about everything, this whole mess." They fought each other's clothes off. He buried his head in her breasts as her legs interlocked with his.

"I swear I will kill all of you —well, maybe except you." as he firmly raised her hips towards his. He penetrated her long and hard. Her body writhed in ecstasy. The hours passed, their sweat soaking the bed sheets. Her turbulence unleashed out in a storm of its own madness of poetry. The digital clock on her bedside read 3:30am. She stroked his inner thigh. He groaned awake then suddenly curled down nuzzling her navel. Her giggle had pierced through her pain, even if it was just for one night. At 04:30hrs her eyes were sleepily awaken to the deep kisses on her cheek and neck.

"You know I will never leave you. You're the only woman I love." was his declarative tone. He had already showered and dressed, on his way out. "I'll arrange another bodyguard I trust for you. These ones are too easily distracted."

"Get out before I kill you with your own gun."

"We have the same heart beat." He calmly replied as he walked out. Rebecca threw the alarm clock at him, only to splatter against the back of the door. She furiously pulled the bed cover over her head. Fuming at herself, wondering how did she allow her steel walls to melt away with him of all people on earth?

The affair between Rebecca and General Piquant began about a year ago during one of his presentations regarding security assurances on multiple border conflict to certain powerful offices at the U.N. He met Rebecca with a number of activists at a meeting dubbed 'Peace Talks' where they were trying to talk the militia out of the war. As she went to the ladies room infuriated at his appeal, he followed her trying to convince her one on one. She saw the genuine appeal in his eyes. He gently grabbed her elbow in frustration. She slapped him. He kissed her. She thought she was going to explode. She had never felt so alive, yet so conflicted. She had only agreed to meet him because he was Theodore's father. All along Rebecca knew, anyone —and most of all Montero- could never forgive her for such an act of betrayal. The last two times she saw him, she swore were the last on each occasion. She vowed she would never allow herself to be alone in the same space with that man, even if it was a Church.

CHAPTER 17

TEST TUBES AND TORMENT

DAY 5

G. TECH. LABORATORIES
HONG KONG
09:00HRS

It had been a long but very comfortable flight with a 45 minute re-fuel in between. Landing at a private airport on the outskirts of Hong Kong made processing of particular details so much easier, from the fragile cases of samples to Grondike's hampered mobility. It was another one hour drive to the laboratory. The sprawling suite of mini-labs was brightly lit, precise and spotless. Staff swarmed around in their cocoons, a couple covered in their head to toe protective gear. A speckle of dust on a counter top would have looked sorely out of place.

Dr. Ping's office was on the mezzanine level opposite the enclosed set-up of sophisticated machinery and equipment known as the *Super-Lab*. Many hi-tech. companies in Asia sub-contracted their work to G. Tech. because of this room. From his office he had the vantage point to see the goings-on of the key labs of this branch office. Dr. Ping projected little warmth as he moved from his desk to welcome the trio that was ushered into his office. His demeanor of discipline and precision arguably superseded Driers. His slight, but meticulous, frame was not dissimilar to the specialist officers in the Coriamese Army deployed into non-combatant environs. Drier knew he had to be careful with Dr. Ping, a man of a level of particular know-how and unsettling calm about him. Drier was fully aware of the network of his contacts, professionally and personally. The scope of influence Dr. Ping carried in Hong Kong's business, political and security circles did not match the obscurity and focus required of his work. Unearthing the man required an equally formidable network.

Throughout the flight Grondike and Speewell had been in touch with Ping and his team to organize in advance the list of tests to be done to ensure Drier would be able to return with preliminary but definitive results of the potency of the minerals that was so puzzling yet so powerful. As soon as they were in Ping's office his senior lab. scientists came in and assertively took control of the cases while they heartily greeted each other.

Ping humorously declared with a wooden smile, "Well gentlemen, the moment of truth has come. We have set up the necessary tests of which the outcome will be known in a mere 30 minutes. Without further a due, shall we?" he beckoned Speewell and Grondike to follow his 2 scientists. Speewell kept up as he limped along.

Dr. Ping then beckoned Drier. "May I take you on a tour of our humble outfit here Mr. Drier? I believe this is your first time to visit us?"

"You would satisfy my curiosity in doing so." Drier was fully aware of the technological strides made from this address and the competitive edge maintained by G. Tech. in industries ranging from tel. comm. smart boards of every size to components of national defense systems; but never had the time or technical interest to see exactly how these technological breakthroughs came about.

Ping was confident yet focused in tour, maintaining just enough momentum not to allow too much space for questions. The investment G. Tech. had made was substantial in both hardware and top caliber of talent stealthfully poached or recruited right upon completion of their PhD studies. The mixture of nationalities whispered among each other and moved quickly from one task to the next.

Just as Ping was describing the super conductor mineral composite sensor, one of the scientists walked up to them, "The results are ready sir."

Ping's eyes widened in a look of excited surprise at Drier for a split second before his composure re-surfaced. "Shall we Mr. Drier?"

Drier felt his heart beat increase. If the actual test results were not favorable, the immediate flat line on all activity would be a huge investment loss. One of the largest losses incurred due to the PR and financial beating the conglomerate had taken as a whole. It would be at least one year for stock price levels to recover and that was being optimistic. It would be doubtful that Baynes contract would be renewed during his next performance review and he knew other Board members were already asking why the conglomerate was being caught so flat footed when he, as one of the Directors, was in the field on this transaction. Their pace quickened slightly keeping up with the scientist on her march back to the laboratory where the others waited.

Adjacent to the super-lab where the final stage of tests had taken place, there was a small softly lit conference room. It was separated by a glass wall to the laboratory with a short connecting door. Grondike, Speewell and two of the scientists were in deep discussion on 2 sheets of paper on the small round conference table. There were perturbed expressions on their faces. As Drier and Ping entered the conference room from the main corridor, they broke off.

"Well people, let's have it. No drum roll am afraid." said Dr. Ping.

The lead scientist did not hesitate, "We've tested the samples of the black soil from the different locations in the rainforest." he pushed forward on the table one of the sheets of paper that had 2 graphs full of peaks and troughs closely matched but not identical.

"The good news is that there is consistency in the content levels of the minerals in the soil despite the different locations of collection. The even better news is that upon extrapolating the mineral it is actually much more potent than we envisaged. It requires smaller quantities than we'd calculated for production to work with the software programming in order to produce an effective download."

Dr. Ping's eyes lit up. "In essence this finding puts G. Tech. in an incomparable position to become its own super power."

"However there is one concern we were discussing when you came in. We do notice our formula is neutralized when another un-named material appears. But where this mineral surfaces from or how it deactivates our composite is scientifically difficult to pin point because we haven't completed assessing its composition or veins of travel which may require some more data collection from the rainforest. This, we must be mindful of. In the meantime the best one can do is dig up our soil very carefully from locations we shall communicate to you."

"Understood. You have one week to get to the bottom of that. We have skeleton technical staff in the rainforest still searching for more of the soil. Correspond with them as much as you need to. They also know how to move the mineral from there to here quite efficiently." Drier ordered.

Their experiment neutralized was one detail Drier did not want to deal with at that material time. He could also see that this meeting was becoming too sensitive too fast. The implications of these findings would be tempting to even the most pure of human beings. In his mind, Drier concluded that confidentiality of both the people and the process of this secret needed to be maintained. Drier looked around the room and without expression or a threatening tone he said, "I don't care about the contracts of confidentiality you've signed. If any of this gets outside of this room, each one of you will be a dead man walking. Call it collective responsibility. That's my personal guarantee to you because *that* will become my personal pet project for you."

Drier turned around to Dr. Ping "We'll have to return to Paris together to refine the stability of the mineral during circuit board production of the laser system. Please bring all your notes and files with you as a precautionary measure." This was as diplomatic as Drier was willing to be to advise the Doctor he was now going to be under 24 hour watch on his territory.

Ping feigned an expression of understanding. "Of course, such a delicate process."

"Flight take-off will be 2 hours from now. We will rendezvous in one hour at the hotel lobby taking the company limousine back to the airport."

Grondike and Speewell maximized the time with the scientists to further develop their own research linkages with their offices in New York. Drier used the time to make sure ears and eyes were put on each of the local staff that had ever had anything to do with the project. He wrapped up with calls to New York arranging the same for Speewell and Grondike.

G. TECH. HQ, PARIS
DAY 5 – 07:00HRS

Baynes tortured himself as he barreled from the elevator into the executive lobby then swinging an immediate right down short hallway to his private reception area. He barely lifted his head to respond to greetings from his receptionist and personal assistant. Dropping his briefcase on his semi-circle glass table and slapping his jacket onto its coat hanger, the barrage of thoughts would not concede.

Running down the militia by a government that was out-matched was about to cost them this deal. The shot in the kneecap their stock price was receiving from this persistent media attention was making it extremely difficult for them to do their usual gloss over of events and maintain control of all factors concerning the transaction. This transaction had all but exploded and a damage control plan had not even been effected Baynes realized to himself.

Crisis management and mitigating measures were his primary interests in the two days he had remaining. He quickly perused his e-mail for any urgent issues.

A slew of meetings had been arranged with various European research organizations that had suddenly found reasons to re-think their partnership with G. Tech. Many of these organizations took the moral high ground in their investments. The footage from the broadcasts was more ground than they were willing to give. Time to re-think business vulnerability of guilt by association and find partners that were not willing to plunder in such a violent way to get the raw material for the research they could just as well find in another forest through other partnerships.

The day was dedicated to fire containment. Everything hung in the balance. He could not remember a 48 hours like this before. One e-mail caught his attention. A rare communication but from the address he had to give it his immediate attention. It was from the majority shareholder of G. Tech., *SaHraa Saif*. His eyes immediately scrolled down to see who exactly from this mysterious group had sent it? As usual, it was unsigned. They were very supportive on how G. Tech. ran its business and wired supporting investment capital with little bureaucracy.

The note today carried a completely different tone. It read: *"We have been monitoring developments of the last few days closely. Movement of personnel and technology from Hong Kong to Paris or New York is not allowed. You shall instead transfer the same to an address in the Middle East. Details shall follow in the next 12 hours. Instructions on travel shall be forwarded. Be on stand-by."* Baynes read the e-mail 3 times looking for the prank or any details revealing the mistake in this communication.

He sat back in his chair and exhaled deeply for a moment. This was not the type of departure or difficulty he was expecting. Not now. He racked his brain. Nobody was going to snatch this deal from him to become the next most powerful Board Chairman in the world overnight. A deep frown had surfaced on his brow.

"How do I handle this?" He whispered to himself as he nervously tapped his desk. He snapped his fingers in relief at his new found solution. He rushed for his jacket pocket that carried his cel. phone with its scrambler that he'd used to call Drier exclusively. It was a new number, even his P.A. had not seen it lying anywhere on his desk. He dialed another Board Member with whom he'd been childhood friends since the days of his private boarding schools and they had also spent a number of family dinners together.

Tristan Coldwell had become a high powered lawyer in Washington DC working with several advocacy and lobby groups, winding laws to get certain interests and positions endorsed by the House and Senate thereby opening doors of substantial transactions for his clients. He was well connected politically. Baynes had recommended his invitation to serve on the Board.

"Tristan."

"Hey big man!" responded an enthused voice of a 6 foot 4inch man. "Getting a lot of action I can see on your end."

"Yes, and you'd be surprised which end it's coming from." Baynes anxiety slipped through in his voice.

"Oh, do tell. What's the real story? I hope things can be contained?" he asked with more curiosity than concern. "Well, that's where you come in dear friend."

Coldwell had now detected the hint of fear in Baynes voice. It was his work as a lawyer for so many conflicting stakeholders to read people with skill.

"I'm just looking at an e-mail from the *SaHraa Saif* and it's not with their usual flowery endorsement or paternal recommendation on matters presented. Obviously they've been keeping track on developments of the past few days. The email issues strict instructions that any findings, equipment and personnel related to the Pointe Trois transaction be sent to the Middle East; final address to follow. Either way you look at it, this doesn't sound good. I don't know who we've been dealing with all this time that is now revealing their true colors." The anxiety in Bayne's voice was now unmistakable.

"You mean being screwed by the devil in a blue dress all this time we were so damned happy we couldn't see straight. People were virtually envious of us, now the pillow talk doesn't seem so pretty?"

"Yes, in a manner of speaking." replied Baynes.

Coldwell continued in a matter of fact tone, "Ok buddy, let me make some calls on my end and appraise the folks in D.C. of this sudden heightened interest in normal technical research and development. We're starting to look like little fish with mama piranha licking her lips looking at her own. Am in London until the end of the day, I'll get back to you if there's anything to be done on your end."

"Thanks Trist. I'll wait to hear from you in case of anything."

Baynes was slightly relieved. His bigger problem of the transaction was not solved, but a smaller much more dangerous one had been contained. He knew he could not tell Coldwell about the technological breakthrough made from the minerals in this transaction, not only because the fewer people that knew the better; but also because of the massive conflict of interest for his friend whose sharkish instinct would never allow him to walk away from such information. Coldwell did not waste a minute. In the plush suite of his London branch office he immediately dialed.

"Hello Tristan. Early enough hours and every time I hear from you I know some whale is going to land on my doorstep any minute and my room to maneuver around it is going to be slightly limited. What can I do for you friend?" asked Senator Hill with an intrigued smile.

Tristan provided a synopsis of the phone call he'd just received.

"Interestingly, that particular problem has been brought to our attention. We have our network looking into to it. Once we know, we'll see what to do."

"Alrighty if mama piranha is in your radar, that's a starting point. If this fish swims beyond our corporate pond, it's in your ocean of national defense. This could be a real doozy for us because they are our majority shareholder. We'd need external forces to change this reality. We'll do lunch on some of those other files that are sitting on your desk."

"Deal. You're paying." replied Senator Hill with a chortle.

It was only 07:20hrs in Paris. The day had not even started, but unscheduled difficulties were already demanding his immediate attention. Baynes called Drier and told him to tell Simmons to acquire an anonymous line. He'd call them back in 10 minutes on a conference call. Drier was in-flight with the group, flying over Italian airspace. Simmons had landed in Paris 4 hours ago but had not yet shown up at the office. In 8 minutes Baynes was on the conference call updating them of the e-mail and deciding on the next best move to protect this finding from the new unknown enemy that was their parent. Drier's voice was firm, calm and instructive.

"The next best thing to do now is protect our assets, which we're already working on. Ping is with me."

"I'll handle Fruthers. We're running out of time." said Simmons.

"I agree. To move quickly is paramount or they may take the initiative and swoop in." Drier responded.

Simmons replied, "Send Ping to the neighborhood deli. with your personal security. I'll take it from there, not to worry."

Drier knew the neighborhood deli. meant an anonymous gymnasium clear across town from G. Tech. that they'd used before. The manager was a reliable drop point for Simmons in both personnel and cargo. The gymnasium had several exits. Both Baynes and Drier were acutely aware of Simmons ability to get things done behind the curtain. How he did it was not their interest. His portfolio of skills was essential to the company he diligently served.

As soon as Simmons hung up he called Sergei.

"Oh welcome back darling. I so missed you, lots to share."

Simmons heard the mild clang of cutlery on plates and voices in the background.

"I need you to go to the local deli. this afternoon to ensure two of our guests enjoy our hospitality like you did a year ago with our Russian friends."

"I shall do just that darling. I missed you too, kisses."

Sergei hung up and apologized to his guests for the restlessness of his female friend.

STATE HOUSE, CARAMONDO
DAY 5 – 09:30HRS

Belinda had not seen President Gebajara so tense so early in the day without having received a phone call to spark it off. Staff at the residential wing would have tipped her off if there was a domestic problem that would deliver him to the official wing in a bad mood. This had not been the case. She had been briefed on the difficulties arising out of yesterday's meetings and dinner when receiving the meeting minutes from the P.A.s to State House Counsel and General Bugazon.

President Gebajara did not bother to use his intercom. "Belinda! Put finance on the line." He barked out.

Within a second, line 1 flashed on his phone console. "Breege, you need to come up with budget alternatives. I received an interesting phone call from the Finance Minister of Coriames. Something about re-distribution of support to the various countries they give aid to throughout the world; based on their President's observations of how he sees their country's interests being treated. He continued in consternation, "I mean, can you believe, if your mere counterpart is calling me at 3:00am in the morning on my cel. phone, which I gave only to their President by the way, that our own budget lines are not entirely secure with these people's money? Such a veiled threat delivered with such loutishness. You know better than I, if we quantify their infrastructural development, health, education and soon to be energy; it's easily almost 20% of our budget. Breege you need to find some other money, like now."

"Well that's just it Mr. President. There is no alternative money! These people seem to be talking to each other these days. Like a coordinated front, the majority we've spoken to have become very unresponsive when we approach them for emergency or bridge financing." said the be-speckled stout Minister with distress in his voice.

"Keep working that bridge Breege. I don't want to hear about broke coffers." The President ordered back.

"Your Excellency…"

"I need \$3 billion to fill that hole if they pull out. Their pulling out of the budget, my pulling out of this transaction are neither options on the table." President Gebajara banged the phone back down, boiling and frightened at this uncertainty.

G. TECH. RESEARCH WING
AN ORDINARY SUBURB, PARIS
DAY 5 – 10:00HRS

The research wing in Paris was housed in a non-descript building with a small entrance that completely hid the sprawling complex of its two level basement facility in this very mundane looking middle income suburb. Being cleared through the lobby area, the un-announced visit of the CEO marching through the facility without a word to anyone caused some frowns of concern. Out of the elevator, the second floor down, he quickly cleared a maze of large cubicles and laboratories to reach a corner office. Passing the Personal Assistant, Simmons entered Fruthers office without a knock.

Fruthers was taking readings from some test tubes and petrie dishes on a small side counter. He then took a brief glance under a microscope before lifting his head up with a boyish smile. The abundance of large curls in his dark brown hair and large spectacles was a portrait of a man coming of age at 39 as his hormones and social graces wrestled inside.

"Aaah Mr. Simmons, word shot around you were in the building. Had we known in advance we would have prepared the very thing you had come looking for…"

Simmons cut him off, "Fruthers, the technological breakthrough is outstanding. The results look very promising and due to the security implications of such a breakthrough and your personal vulnerabilities we have to put you out of sight for a little while where the bad guys can't get to you. Let's just say you are currently exposed."

Fruthers squinted his eyes, cocked his head sideways, looking cross and confused all at once.

"Would you care to clarify on the personal vulnerabilities? I haven't the foggiest to what you're referring."

Simmons became slightly impatient. "Fruthers, let's skip the handholding. The monthly blackmail you're paying to the investigator to make sure you're case never comes together is now a company problem. We wouldn't want the bad buys to get a hold of you telling you they'll knock off the case-detective so your case can be presented in Court within the same week unless you start divulging formulas on this recent breakthrough. Or better yet, present you with an irresistible package of free escort services and take some compromising photos of you, lest you open up and share your corporate secret…mmm? That would put us all in a very unseemly position don't you think?"

Fruthers took this revelation as a very personal affront and humiliating exposure of the monthly chore that had clawed him for years. This was now more than he was willing to take. He knew that with the buy-off from QSD he had enough to live a very comfortable life. G. Tech. was surely not his lifetime home. Only their additional perks they kept adding had kept him here. He decided he wasn't going to be bullied.

"Mr. Simmons, with all due respect, I'm not going to be blackmailed by some over-zealous executive." His eyes squinted even further, "If anything happens to me, I've already arranged that an envelope of those secret formulas you refer to will be sent to some people who could be very interested in the findings."

Simmons was amused at the gallant effort put up, but more un-amused at the time he was losing with the youngish character in front of him. In two long fast steps Simmons had moved around to the back of Fruthers who stood at his small cocktail conference table and casually but very powerfully gripped him in a neck and shoulder brace causing Fruthers to muffle a shriek he let out just in case his P.A. come rushing in to this embarrassing situation.

"Dr. Fruthers, we do not have much time. In the next 60 seconds I would like you to go to your safe, remove all your files, notes, research, you name it, concerning this breakthrough; and clear out a couple of critical test tubes and fill them with something else to ensure you derail anyone trying to retrace your steps."

Tears welling up in his eyes, Fruthers gathered his notes, cleared a few test-tubes as he stole glances at Simmons who nodded him on. He walked out with Simmons walking closely beside him. His P.A. was not at her desk to note his departure. They drove away in silence. The driver was given the address. Twenty minutes later Simmons assisted Fruthers out of the vehicle with some of his files. After the lift and a short flight of stairs leading to a narrow corridor, Simmons hit a button on a door on the right and they were buzzed in to an open floor of the most expensive looking gym equipment but no clients, just a mixture of skimpily dressed slender and bountiful ladies chatting around the equipment. The address was a front for the most unsavory transactions. Fruthers followed in silence still in shock from the violence of his CEO. The large muscular manager in a sleek black t-shirt tucked in expensive black slacks rose from his bar stool behind the front desk. It was strictly a nod exchanged between Simmons and the man.

"The other one shall be along during the day." "Understood." replied a deep Siberian accent.

DISCREET LUXURY HOTEL
NEW YORK CITY
DAY 5 – 04:30HRS

Shortly after dozing off, Rebecca's arm searched for her cel. phone she heard buzzing away on the bedside table. "Rebecca, this is Parsien. I must be brief. We have much to do here. We suspect the Chief has been poisoned.

The hospital Director in Pointe Trois tells us he is comatose. We don't know if he will pull through. Butawan is standing in for him until the Council agrees on the replacement through the customary protocols."

Rebecca was too exhausted to express the emotion she was feeling. "Alright, let me get right on it from this end and see what specialist we can get out there as soon as possible." Almost immediately upon hanging up, her cel. rang again.

"Hi Rebecca. It's Raphael. Your line was just busy so I guess you've heard. I want you to know we're on it. Our family physician is being flown in from Seremanta and we have a poison specialist from New York on the way to a private jet we have waiting. Don't worry, we'll do everything possible to save the Chief. You just focus on the agreement."

"Thanks Raphael." Now alert again, she knew the very next move was to get the agreement in the Chief's hand. There was no telling what would happen to the man in the next 24 hours or less.

UNKNOWN LOCATION
ARMOUR DIEU, POINTE TROIS
DAY 5 – 11:00HRS

It was one phone call, one sentence, to a contact in the Caramondo Army. "It is done. I saw him take the solution with my own eyes." The caller hung up.

CHAPTER 18

WRESTLING WRAP-UP

"Hey Rebecca. How are you're holding up?" As my pop used to say, time to hunker down and settle in for the kill. It's the moments leading up to the kill that are the sweetest."

"Hey Julian, it's dicey but we're putting all the pieces in place to lock it up. The donors and the U.N. seem to be coming together. However the village chief has been poisoned and we need his signature for the agreement to be valid. The bright spot thus far is the PR damage inflicted on Globe Tech.s pristine reputation and subsequently their stock price. I saw Ian's interview on the network last night, brilliant. The footage of the demonstrations was just the right flavor to bring it closer to home. The recurring footage from Pointe Trois is irrefutable. Great work."

Julia laughed as she spoke. "Yeah, I hope someone at Globe Tech. had their nerves go through the shredder. The brief opinion pieces and editorials with the major dailies on the East and West coast should be out today. Issue is the world gets bored fast. We might not get so much attention beyond today unless something dramatic happens in Caramondo."

Rebecca thought out loud for a moment, "You don't know how comforting the idea of a coup d'état sounds to me right now."

Julia let out a bear laugh. "I can cook up a storm but that one's beyond my menu. I'll keep you posted in the event of anything."

Rebecca removed the files from her satchel to her in-tray. Five minutes later Marc popped his head through the door and urgently whispered, "Holstein on line 2."

Rebecca picked up immediately. "Morning Ambassador."

"Morning Becca. Just called to let you know that the meeting is in 45 minutes. Pray that the vote goes through."

LUXURY HOTEL, LONDON
DAY 5 – 13:30HRS

"Oh my dear friend, it seems things have been getting a bit busy in Caramondo. If I must share with you, I'm actually in London trying to wrap up on some opportunities. And from what my eyes and ears repeatedly tell me, some people may have to make a hasty exit and I may find my cover dissolved. So I need to wrap up on whatever stock I still hold or ongoing transactions and perhaps start a new life somewhere unknown." Lannier clearly hinted at Simmons and their ongoing transaction. This was the last thing Simmons was looking for.

His tone was unsympathetic and abrupt. "I've been busy. Check your account this evening."

PR&S, NEW YORK CITY
DAY 5 – 17:30HRS

The day had been perilous and treacherous at one or two junctures with clients that did not want to pay for the sins they had committed near and far. To Rebecca's relief, there was little they could do as the Court would read the sentence without a care in the world of the client's reaction. She walked through the lobby of her office pre-occupied. Her cel. phone rang. She stopped in her tracks as she heard Holstein's voice.

"Rebecca, the vote went through. The Security Council has voted to issue a statement of condemnation to the Government of Caramondo and invoke sanctions on the President, government officials and army officers indicated in the file you forwarded. If there is no indication of substantive withdrawal in the next 48 hours, they will explore sending troops to the borders of the neighboring countries in the interests of regional security. But you know they can't set one boot on the Caramondo side itself unless they're invited."

"Yes, I'm aware."

"The idea is to create enough uncomfortable pressure and attention that they're forced to ask themselves, is it worth it? But I think the collective pressure will get to them. Even some of these shameless ones have their limits when they know their personal ill-gotten fortunes are threatened."

Rebecca smiled as she listened, knowing that smile could be short-lived. Securing the agreement of the environmental consortium was one outstanding challenge. Getting this agreement to the Chief in time, who could die any minute was another deadline she couldn't guarantee she could make. Globe Tech. and the government of Caramondo signing their agreement was another factor beyond her control. Every minute of the next 48 hours, every development, would be major. There was no room for miscalculations, delays or unforeseen derailments. The tension remounted in her. She felt her pulse race even faster.

STATE HOUSE, CARAMONDO
DAY 5 – 23:00HRS

The roaring laugh as he greeted could not cover the tension in his voice. "Mr. Baynes. With our doing such good business together, if I haven't spoken to you after a few days it feels like a lifetime."

"Oh really now?" Baynes mind was racing. If the man was calling, something must have really come apart. Baynes didn't want to think any further. He might as well just be told. He prompted the man.

"To what do I owe this call from such a busy man with such vast resources?"

"Busy yes, natural resources yes, immense pressure, yes. Look Comrade," Baynes was now partially amused. What could have caused an outpouring of such sentiment?

"I was thinking, our people have met, we seem to be on the same page concerning this agreement. All this legal punctuation can be such an inconvenience. You can't deny the vast resources you'd be buying. This is a minor brouhaha. In the next 5 minutes or so you'll be down to mining all the coltan your heart desires. Yes, let's be honest with each other. We know the coltan found is in such large quantities, only a couple of other spots in the world have comparable deposits and your competitors are pretty far along in locking up those agreements."

Baynes tried to sound pressured with this erroneous conclusion. It was extremely useful to let the man think that he was way ahead of them. He was easier to manage that way. "Well now you know what I'm going through."

"Comrade, if the agreement has met its key legal criteria then send it down to me with one of your people and I'll sign it. We've both played hard to get with each other and we're now getting some unwanted attention from other loud quarters."

Baynes was relieved that the man was more desperate than him. "I'll get back to you Mr. President."

"Fair enough." Gebajara replied.

Baynes knew he'd love to do that, but everything was too hot at this moment. His instinct told him this was not the right time.

<hr>

PR&S, NEW YORK CITY
DAY 5 – 20:00HRS

<hr>

Rebecca was using every minute available to her. Marc was organizing the legal briefs for the next two days. He could sense the tension and it was clear nobody owned their schedule over this short but crucial spell of time, let alone his opportunity to keep an eye on Rebecca. She was busily cross-checking names in the environmental community. She abandoned the search after 20 minutes noticing the files on her in-tray staring at her.

She refused to let the PR&S partners think for one moment that she couldn't sustain her full workload while battling a state army and conglomerate. Her cel. phone rang, "Yes Ian. Who's getting cold feet or being bribed now?"

He sounded exuberant, "Well, just wanted to let you know that we have it in our hands. The agreement for the rainforest consortium signed by the fifteen conservation and environmental organizations committing to a 98 year renewable lease to provide technical, material and financial support to the Pointe Trois rainforest and its people. An important clause is that any company or organization that wishes to access the rainforest for research must pay a non-refundable fee of $200,000=. Any commercial activity is approved by the Council of Elders and surrounding villages with a percentage commission to a rainforest fund. And any activity by any organization that has resulted in environmental pollution shall attract a fine of $500,000= plus the estimated damage cost to the environment and its population. The monies shall be put into a consolidated fund towards the development of the people of Pointe Trois. It goes on and on. But you know this agreement better than we do."

There was a momentary pause, a silence. Marc had silently walked into the room to place some paperwork onto her desk as both of them listened in. Marc came onto the line. "Hi Ian, it's Marc. Forgive the silence, Rebecca is crying."

Marc gently rubbed her back to let her know it would all be okay, all soon be over. Rebecca had covered her eyes with her hands. She managed to silence her heavy sobbing as her chest and shoulders heaved up and down. She struggled to compose herself for a moment and came on line.

"Ian, I can't thank you and the wonderful team enough for the organization and lobbying it took to maneuver this agreement together in the time that you did. I am filled with gratitude."

From the background Chiles came on line. "Rebecca, your home is indeed a special place on this earth. You are a special person for taking on some rather large hyenas that have their jaws into it. You should know that we all stand with you. You and Montero are very special people for the sacrifices you have taken on behalf of your people. I'm sorry your brother is not here to enjoy this special moment with you. It has been a difficult long road for the families of Pointe Trois, but we intend to see this to the end with you."

Rebecca couldn't hold her sobbing. The support, the stress all seemed to be suddenly erupting through her. "Thank you again guys. Let me call you again when I've composed myself."

"A philanthropist for Institute for Plant Research, increasingly irked by the broadcast feeds, availed their jet. Emily will be in-flight in the next two hours to get the Chief's signature on the agreement." Ian said.

In her heart, she heard Montero say, *'Mom and Dad are so proud.'*

Rebecca called Raphael and asked him to please coordinate with Ian and Emily getting the agreement to the chief once she was in-flight.

"It is done. Say no more, my love."

SIMMONS PENTHOUSE, PARIS
DAY 5 – 23:30HRS

After dropping off Fruthers at the gymnasium Simmons was at the office also doing damage control with institutional partners in meetings. He continued throughout the night working steadily through his files that had piled on his desk while he was in Caramondo.

Upon reaching his penthouse before unwinding, he went straight to his private study, studied his account and could see Mr. Avi Goldman had done the wire transfer from his account Commodity Traders International to his account North-South Trade International in the amount of $16.75million.

Simmons then executed a transfer of $14,237,500=million to Lannier's account, Products International, retaining his 15% commission of $2,512,500=. Simmons had to pay for people such as Sergei Bladovich. The North-South Trade account that came in very handy to facilitate his desired objectives when action required was beyond the company's risk analysis assessment or budget.

CHAPTER 19

A SWEATY BROW

DAY 6

GLOBAL INVESTMENT BANKING SERVICES, LONDON HEAD OFFICE   08:00HRS

It was a fast but devastating phone call.

"I'm closing down shop on all your activities for now. My network is picking up all sorts of alarms about Parliamentary, U.N. and international activist enquiries, all going off at the same time. Can you believe it? A contact in the U.N. even alerted me my firm's name is on a list of name and shame. I had to shed out lots of dough to get it erased off that one, but Lord knows where else it may have sprouted up already. And hot off the grapevine is that the conservationists have signed their agreement among themselves."

Alexander heard a cup bang on a saucer. The listener choked and struggled to contain his cough of his morning beverage.

"Hello! General! Everything okay?" Bugazon's P.A. rushed in to see her boss struggling to wipe off the deep brown coffee stain that had already found a home in his camouflage jacket. He angrily waved her out as if he didn't want this clumsy moment to be witnessed.

"You said what?" Bugazon barked over the line.

"Hey don't shoot the messenger. It's confirmed. What their next step is, I'm not sure." Alexander spiritedly continued with his concerns, "So look, we're going to wrap up with these last transactions, credit everyone's accounts and call it a day. We've all benefited handsomely from this forest but now time to put on our virgin white suits and look legitimate and pure. I'm on my way back to New York and close shop there. I'll be in touch General."

Bugazon could not control the anger that ran through him. Some tree huggers had shut down his main pipeline of income and there wasn't a thing he could do about it. His mind raged to itself.

G. TECH. HQ, PARIS
DAY 6 – 09:00HRS

Baynes decided that the damage control in the string of meetings arranged was the most immediate priority on his desk. If the research partners lined up in today's meetings pulled out, G. Tech would find it difficult to remain among the top four in technological breakthroughs in several of their industries. The thought that if they pulled out and quietly leaked out some of these findings to their competition was not just stressful, it was downright unpalatable. Reclaiming their leadership position would be at least another 5 years. Baynes just could not allow this for the corporation or for himself. The pounding the G. Tech. stock price continued to take was like a pounding on his head directly.

The silence of the Board members was another ache throbbing on his temples. Their silence was much more dangerous than hourly phone calls politely, but firmly, expecting a turnaround straightaway. He knew they were meeting behind his back. It was a sickening feeling in the pit of his stomach. He felt his age had accelerated in the past few days. He gave a shallow breath of relief. At least he knew Ping and Fruthers were secured away. Where exactly he didn't even want to know, before he started second guessing their safety. That was a detail being handled by people much more qualified than he to execute such an operation.

Monique, his P.A., walked in without making eye contact. She directed her walk and eyes to the signed paperwork on his desk. As she quickly perused through to ensure all the required pages were signed and initialed, she quickly flipped her eyes up at him with a short pleasant smile.

"You have a guest sir."

"Oh who? Meetings with the research organizations aren't due to start for another 10 minutes?"

Baynes wasn't used to surprise guests. Meetings with him had to be well within a scope of identified mutual interest via appointment. Surprises were only at the

Country Club or exclusive cocktails. Baynes struggled to remove his eyes from his reports for the upcoming meetings and shifted to Monique's large brown eyes and copper bronze lipstick that matched her thick brown curls coiffed up into a graceful high bun.

"Wouldn't give his name but says something about being your escort to Caramondo to sign the agreement?"

Monique had maintained eye contact awaiting his response but had already turned her sophisticated designer heels towards the door. Baynes became enraged as he ran his fingers through his silver gray crew cut. Too many people were hoping he'd split under the pressure and position themselves as the perfect candidate for his replacement. He fought to keep calm.

"What the devil are these people about? To be so arrogant…tell *him*," while forcefully pointing to the door, "I don't take orders and I'm sending my own person at the right time. I won't be so polite with my response next time."

"Yes sir message will be conveyed verbatim." Monique had not changed her calm morning pleasant smile. She had seen her boss in a worse state before in the last few days.

"The Research International meeting is in 5 minutes, top floor boardroom."

STATE HOUSE, CARAMONDO
DAY 6 – 10:00HRS

Belinda swung her body in the door, but remained standing there. Without any voice her lips very clearly communicated, "Minister of Foreign Affairs-Coriames, line 2."

President Gebajara swung his head sideways in dismay recalling the rude awakening he'd received over 24 hours ago from his finance counter-part. Gebajara had never been a man to be bullied. This situation felt so strange and humiliating. He had been the one to bulldoze through whatever he set his sights on. This morning he felt one more phone call from the Coriames government would grind into creation another kidney stone. Belinda had long securely shut the door. He leaned his head back in his leather chair, elbow pointed up in the air as he held the receiver.

"Hon. Minister, as always such a delight to hear from you. I'm certain foreign relations between our two countries have never been better, always happy to receive your phone call re-emphasizing this fact."

The gentle but authoritative tone caused Gebajara to grind his teeth. He listened, not sure what to expect.

"Mr. President, the pleasure is similarly mine. The President of Coriames has become extremely concerned. So much so, I have tried to assuage his misgivings, but to no avail. As you are aware, we are a permanent member of the Security Council where our input matters. This group or what-have-you of environmentalists has some heavy hitters swinging around for them. The donor community has even reached out to us about you. Anyway, any moment from now you shall receive a communiqué and in a few hours the global press should be on it; something to the effect of a statement of condemnation and targeted sanctions. You shall receive the details in good time."

President Gebajara now leaned forward. His elbows on his desk he was now looking down as his forehead found rest his left palm. He continued to shake his head in despair.

"I'm afraid it is within this framework that the President has asked me to ring you. You are aware he has expressed strong interest in exploratory rights of Pointe Trois rainforest."

Gebajara knew exactly what that meant.

"He has assessed that the Republic of Coriames has invested so much in your country's infrastructure as well as social development in this geographically remote area of your nation. We had even begun discussions about the energy sector with your good-selves. To date Coriames has not benefited one iota from this investment."

Gebajara became impatient at the less than subtle diplomatic hammering. "What exactly are we implying here Hon. Minister?"

The Minister's tone was light, but direct. "My good man, let us get to the nitty gritty of this. We know the price at which you are selling the rainforest and given the number of you lined up in that transaction, the population of Caramondo shall never see that money. We have been quietly tracking every inch of your activity and how you've structured this transaction. We have enough dirt to leak out on your group that would bury you in every domestic, regional and international court that ever existed. Need I be more direct good sir? Those exploratory rights are not a request."

The President could stand it no more. "Look here Mr. Minister, nobody will tell me what to do in my own country. I don't care who you are or what you've done for us. Don't you understand the character of mutual respect?"

The Minister cut in with a burst of laughter in a tone of sarcasm and ridicule. "Mutual respect? I dare say the people in the slums of Avalon and pit mines of Pointe Trois would love to hear you expound. Won't be told what to do? I'm afraid this is increasingly your new reality my dear man. I shall let you reflect on this over the next day or so as you try to weave us in and carve others out. As always best wishes from my government to yours."

As the President hung up the phone he didn't realize he was still grinding his teeth, only faster and more furiously than moments before.

G. TECH. HQ, PARIS
DAY 6 – 11:00HRS

Baynes got back to his office from his second meeting of damage control feeling hot and sweaty despite the sensitive air-condition system in place. Was it the stress or was he really coming down with something his mind questioned his body? He can't remember ever in his career having to eat so much humble pie and dish out so many apologies.

At the first meeting, Research International left with a sharp warning. Any more significant bad PR and they were pulling out. They had no intention of being beneficiaries of secondary boycotts due to their affiliation. In the second meeting, the partner said the jury is still out. Their Board would revert in the next 24 hours. They simply needed to meet with G. Tech now to get the update position. He slumped down in his chair closed his eyes for a moment of quiet away from the crisis to settle his nerves. Just as he started to find an inner calm, his cel. phone buzzed, a message streaming in. One of the Board members of Citizens Environmental Alert communicated.

"My sources inform me the conservationists have signed their pact. Seems like end-game. Hope you're way ahead of them."

Baynes did not even spare a second to reply. He speed dialed Simmons. "Look, we're running out of rope here. Drop what you're doing, put your last spears in those clauses and get that Agreement to me in the next 30 minutes. Let me look over it then be on the fastest jet we have to Caramondo. He signs first. I want you standing in front of Gebajara by sunset. I'd prefer he sign it with his blood, but I'll settle for a pen and then get back in the instant. I don't want anyone there to know you were anywhere in the neighborhood. We sign, no one knows about it. We can't afford a final hell and damnation judgment from the public, our share price simply won't sustain it."

Simmons tried to sound calm and re-assuring. "Not to worry. I'm on it. Expect the paperwork within 30minutes."

STATE HOUSE, CARAMONDO
DAY 6 – 11:30HRS

His main document of interest was his security brief. He couldn't understand how the Coriamese had been tracking him so well, yet none of the intelligence agencies had picked up on this or put counter resources in place. He didn't know whether it was his dismay or disgust towards his security heads that heightened, but heads were going to roll. People were going to pay. The intercom rang.

"Yes. What is it Belinda?" while perusing through the pages.

"The Minister of Health is here sir. It's un-announced but says he'll be brief."

The Minister walked in, a portly spectacled gentleman who espoused the picture of excess of comfort rather than good health.

"What good news do you have to announce to me Dr. Panat, because I could certainly use some just about now?"

The good Doctor remained standing, deciding not to get too close. He could see the President looked a bit unsettled.

"I had come by to recommend a crisis meeting with Finance, chaired by you Mr. President. They are insisting that they don't have any reserve funds. This is unheard of. I'm here because you urgently need to know our funding has just been pulled on the next tranche of all our key projects phased out over the three months like some kind of coordinated dance. They're oddly all saying the same thing: pending monthly review of government's adherence to donor support criteria. We won't have any immunization vaccines, malaria, TB, ARV medication or condoms.

With these sicknesses and lifestyles not seeming to change, our health costs will spiral out of control very quickly. We will have a full blown health crisis in our poorest areas before we can contain anything. What is so frustrating is that the cost of containment and treatment is three times the cost of prevention. We are already staring at a large hole in our budget and would surely not be able to sustain the cost of such interventions." The Doctor's eyes had widened. Perspiration had set in his forehead and his arms had started to gesture mildly, struggling to retain respect for the office he was in.

Gebajara decided he was not going to be further stressed by some detail of a national health crisis, while he had world agencies name calling him and hurling threats at his government while he watched his most treasured deal slip through his fingers under this mounting pressure. He concluded to himself that the man standing in front of him was a distraction from his task at hand, how to rescue his agreement. He calmly lifted his eyes from his security brief.

"So Doctor, what do you want me to do about it under these circumstances? Please. Come to me with solutions, not problems and I'll see what I can do." The fixed glare continued. The Doctor could see he was not going to make any further progress.

"Of course Mr. President, but your intervention with the Ministry of Finance would save this nation from a health crisis never before seen on this Continent."

"Figure out something with Finance, Penant. I'm the President, not the Cabinet baby-sitter." said his rising voice.

"Mr. President, I'll communicate my concerns to you and Finance in writing for your further consideration."

"Very well, will that be all?" His glare was fast losing its semblance of patience. The Minister suppressed the anger in his posture as he turned to walk out of the office.

"Yes Belinda?" Gebajara was now looking through the budget to see where he could grab money from to avoid impending problems from becoming crises front and center on his desk. Who could he bully to sacrifice a chunk of their budget that would all but shut their Ministry down?

"The Minister of Works is here, says he urgently needs to meet with you." "Marvelous, show him in."

The tall chunk of a man was an engineer who was used to standing in the sweltering heat to ensure the layers of road were constructed correctly in the most remote parts of Caramondo. A known perfectionist in his work, from a humble background, other Ministry officials found him to be a significant obstacle that needed to be dealt with. Only problem was, the Coriames government had strongly recommended his appointment as Minister and made sure he stayed there due to his integrity and noted dedication over the years.

Engineer Ponsiano started to talk as he walked in. "Your Excellency, I shall only be a moment. The Coriames government has not released the wire transfer we were expecting today. It has been religiously punctual for the past 5 years and our contacts we would call on such matters are mysteriously unavailable. My counterpart finally calls me with a very official tone saying the Coriames government is still in negotiations with you, that I should check in with you?" He said with a question in his voice.

Gebajara put on brave face and derisively chuckled. "In negotiation with me, huh? More like handling me." Ponsiano looked puzzled.

"Let's see what happens in the next 48 hours. People won't come apart without the roads now, will they? Anything else, Hon. Minister?"

"No Mr. President. I just felt it urgent to bring to your attention and coordinate with you on this matter."

"Noted. Now please go and see how you can re-work your budget without the contribution of the Coriames." The Minister of Works knew that this was not even remotely an option and could see the President was in a real problem of sorts. This was not the time to press further. Sensible, logical exchange was not forthcoming.

PR&S, NEW YORK CITY
DAY 6 – 09:00HRS

This childhood trauma had become too much torture. Keeping it bottled up inside had neatly infected every part of her life in a way that she could manage. She lied to herself all this time that she was in control. The pain had become a crushing feeling. But with the agreement signed, Rebecca was beginning to feel a ray of hope fighting through.

Marc called out, "Julia Dames on line 1."

"Hey, good morning to yah. Good news travels fast. Bad news travels even faster. I couldn't be more thrilled that the Rainforest Consortium signed the agreement. That's why I called. Things are coming together. The bad news, that's for G.Tech. anyway, is I've had a sneak peak at the poll results that'll be out in tomorrow's dailies bi-coastal. And trust me, this has got to be as bad as it gets for any corporation, whether you're selling Grandma's mashed potatoes recipe or titanium dioxide for toxic disposal. Right now they're hovering between a 12% - 15% approval rating when asked whether the company should go ahead with the procurement of the rainforest. It gets better. Over 75% of people surveyed would like to know who they work with to boycott any company that does business with Globe Tech. and 62% think that they should be taken to some international court if they think of even stepping foot in Pointe Trois. All this is looking pretty costly for the company. Being able to recover from this social condemnation is no short order. Not sure what it'll do their stock price that's barely staying afloat at present."

Rebecca had listened quietly. "This is indeed brilliant news."

"I'll keep you abreast of any developments."

"Thanks Julia." Rebecca hung up, now feeling an urge to charge ahead. It was a constant battle between her adrenaline and fear of failure. A few moments later Marc walked in with some paperwork.

"Hey boss, we have a very interesting finding. Remember those photos you were flipping through of the G. Tech. people looking at the soil but we have no idea why? Well I had one of my research —okay, geek- friends who works at some lobbying think tank and their job is to know who's fingers are into which pies that may impact their interests. Kinda like a databank of the nitty-gritty of powerful things and people."

His left hand animatedly gesturing as his right hand waved the papers he was holding in the air like a wand. "Well anyway, we're starting to get a clue."

He finally placed the sheets of paper in front of her on her desk. Rebecca's eyes honed in with such deep interest, taking in the details of the large portrait shots among the information while she read the stellar CVs of these 9 recurrent faces from previous photos from Pointe Trois brought by Father Raines. They were all no less than Ph.D.s from the most prestigious universities, Cal. Tech., MIT, Stanford and now worked in fields of cutting edge software, engineering, military and defense and the environment. These were arguably among the best minds in the world out for hire to the highest bidder. As if in slow motion Rebecca wondered out loud, "The type of work that they do very quietly and they make sure you don't find out what they're working on. It's not an immediate priority, but we need to plant ourselves on the same workshop circuit as these guys. Put an irresistible spy on it will yah?"

"Okay boss."

CHAPTER 20

CIRCLE OF CONSENSUS

The President had put out word to his Cabinet that no one should come to see him without a solution attached to whatever crisis befell them. This shortened the list of impromptu visitors significantly. The afternoon breezed by with foreign delegations pre-scheduled months ago from the introduction of agricultural projects that sought the President's blessing for swift execution to certain trade delegations anxious to benefit from an unstructured political economy. Finally he grabbed a moment to asses if there had been any change in the situation. Baynes had not gotten back to him. Bugazon seemed unusually silent, whom he was not willing to pursue at this moment. These activists still seemed to have the world on their side. All he needed was a signed agreement within the next 12 hours and the money credited into his personal account. What happened thereafter is a bridge that he would cross when he got to it. He just needed to be sure he was sorted out personally before he begun to navigate through the public persecution. Presidential immunity was a blanket he was trying to see how it would best fit his need.

Not commonly done, Belinda marched straight into her boss's office with a sticky yellow note and placed it right square in front of him to emphasize who was on line 1 without saying a word. She knew the nature of this relationship. Shocked for a moment, he pushed his chair back from his desk wondering why the U.S. Ambassador would be calling him. They had taken a position to be highly selective in financial support to the country. It was strictly through project support in areas such as agriculture, health and education; not direct government budget support. The corruption in Caramondo simply broke their scale of flexibility. But they seemed to have a very sophisticated security unit in their Embassy.

President Gebajara had made it known in the most subtle of ways that he was not so keen or cared so much for a country that contributed virtually nil to his direct budget support, yet had such a healthy cheque book for project support in areas he did not deem a priority. The Ambassador also ensured it was understood that he offered no endorsement, open or subtle, of the unfortunate activities of his host. His Deputy was the main face at official functions. A diplomatic slight, Gebajara contemptuously tolerated.

"Oh Ambassador, it has been months since we last spoke. I don't know who is responsible for this, my staff or your officers?" He mustered a jovial laugh as he spoke while his brain racked on what could be the purpose of this call.

"Your Excellency, let us both charge ourselves guilty and make all manner of efforts to change. But let us skip these pleasantries for a moment shall we? Your time, I recognize, is far too valuable in view of recent developments."

Gebajara felt a large nerve pinch in his gut. There surely was no room for another bull in this kraal that had become chaotic.

"You seem to be getting pressure from all sides; the donors, your activists, neighboring military machineries, international broadcast networks, other superpowers and for goodness sake the U.N. This is what I call a full plate. Frankly, it makes us uneasy. We're strong believers in stability in the region. And a word to the wise, the company with whom you are getting into a lifetime partnership, wel...oh my...that's downright discomforting. I won't talk about who will be wearing the pants in that relationship. Bottom line is, these people's activities are a threat to our interests. Your partnering with them makes you an indirect threat to us. I won't bore you with the details of what they're up to because that is the not near your scope of national interest. You know, it's always a pleasure to speak with you and I just wanted to call and share with you what you mean to us and that we're keeping a long eye on your developments, Your Excellency."

"Ambassador now really? We? A threat to you? This could not be possible even if we wished it so?" Gebajara thought that was too delicious a consideration to even dream about. "Such a long eye would be a waste of your resources. Let us keep in touch Ambassador."

Gebajara despised the lecture being drilled through him. But what caught his attention, playing further on his spent nerves, was that this man had never called him directly. He felt his mind race in angst but a feeling of angst that he could not control or contain as he addressed the crisis in front of him. He had to discuss this. He wasn't going to sit and stew on this alone. He needed his trusted group to consult on this whole situation.

Everything was just getting too hot. He yelled out to Belinda one sentence of instructions while he busied himself on the documents and reports that required his signature.

In 45 minutes Bugazon, LaFonte, Fisher, Carrion and Pratt were marched into his office by Belinda's fixed eye to warn them of the type of terrain they were walking into. Each wore their own look of great discomfort and strain of personalized stripes but all from the same source. By now the President had rolled up his sleeves, unloosened his tie and was on his third sip of chilled soda water.

"People!" he announced. "We need to discuss this. This is getting hot for us, real hot. Even the one man I enjoy not hearing from, picks up the phone to call me. Going on and on saying he's concerned about our so-called business partners and how we would be *screwed* in that relationship." as the President emphasized the word. "Then something about keeping a long eye on us as if we're some misguided characters to be managed indirectly from a distance. And the worst part is, the man threatened me. He used the word 'threat' in a sentence to me. He actually dared to threaten me like he was talking to some fellow Ambassador." Gebajara angrily pointed at his own chest as the 5 men had now safely positioned themselves far away enough from him between the couches and armchairs.

"I don't know which is more humiliating, the source of the phone call or the contents of it. Bottom line is we have a situation no longer playing to our net advantage. We need to see how to navigate through this. Issues on the table are; one: I can't tell what G. Tech is thinking anymore from this debacle of a visit." He flashed a look at Bugazon. "And their share price dive is all the man can think about not taking into consideration the domestic political and global battering I'm taking. Two: All of a sudden the Coriames have become the chief complainer donors virtually telling me, not proposing or asking, that they have exploratory rights in Pointe Trois. Their Ministers continuously call me telling me their President has instructed them to communicate to me their concerns and demands. Can you believe it?" He rolled his eyes in consternation as he paced up and down.

The eyes of everyone in the room warily followed behind his back and remained askance when he turned facing their direction.

"That they have invested so much with nothing in return. They see the lobbying damage the environmentalists are doing in New York. One of these characters said he could leak out the details on this transaction. The thing about them is that if they choose to pull out of funding the roads and social development projects, we don't have that kind of money to substitute from our economy." Gebajara stopped pacing for a moment, then threw a fast turnaround followed by a warning stare to make sure he had the continued undivided attention of everyone. "Three: Then these bloody tree huggers have their agreement stitched up." He ranted with a wicked snarl. "We just need to make sure that it isn't signed when it gets here." He threw another look at Bugazon who breathed a heavy sigh of strain.

"Folks let's discuss before I make a decision and we move forward. Share the guilt and share the gain. Because if we sign with G. Tech and take the money with the massive donor pull-outs we'd have in the budget and specific project support, there would be no money to run the economy. Within a month -and that's long- we'd have several health epidemics knowing the habits of the population. This would soon be followed with civil protests, unrest and arrests, which are all rather taxing thoughts right now. He came around back to his arm chair reserved exclusively for the President.

Speaker LaFonte could not hide the strain in his face. He was thinking about his undisturbed retirement and his pancreatic cancer. The distinct orders from his Doctors were to avoid stress and further aggravation to avoid rapid multiplication of the malignant cells. He was regretting he got involved in this whole fiasco but remembered he wasn't given much of a choice.

He spoke up first, "With these people, I say we abandon. The deal can't be sold to the population in any form, because they know they'll never see the money. They will hunt us down with one inquisition or another. It will never end. Let's just get to the next election and hand over to whoever wins. You have all benefited from Pointe Trois. What more could you want? This deal won't take you from rags to riches."

"You talk like that massive commercial farm in your home town materialized from nowhere and your children's education at all these elite universities in the U.S., U.K. and Europe came from your humble salary." interjected Gebajara with a straight look.

Fisher wasn't interested in the digression. He knew his suitcase could not even compare in size with the President's. He wanted his viewpoint to be known as the guiding benchmark. He leaned forward from the couch. "It's a chance to finish off the militia in Pointe Trois. Tell G. Tech. 6 months. We wipe the place rabid clean, stock enough money to keep the economy afloat until the end of the term. We all retire after that. Whoever wants to remain in the country thereafter is free to do so." Fisher knew full well a gentle retirement in Caramondo would be impossible if this deal went through.

Pratt kept his back up stiff and straight as he sat on the other end of the couch. He knew he was there merely to provide technical advice and guidance. He had amassed wealth but only enough not to cause any attention among the watch dog groups. He was well below the radar of many of his colleagues in the system that had personalized the term 'service delivery' to the people. His hands were on his knee caps with his note pad deep in his lap. He cleared his throat before he spoke. "I have to agree with LaFonte. With the taps running dry on us we wouldn't be able to borrow from somewhere else or at least enough to piece together a balanced budget. I've run some numbers with trusted colleagues at Finance and the economy would come down like a pile of cards. Better to back down now rather than have an economic meltdown later."

Carrion didn't like the sound of that. He sat in grateful pose on one end of another couch. His strain had reduced itself to a calm concern with a slight frown on his brow. Letting out a sigh before he spoke, "Well if the public sector isn't working, the private sector will soon follow suit. Government is the biggest client of the private sector so there will be a distinct ripple effect. This short term profit would definitely uproot the long-term of many of us."

The President prompted Bugazon with eye contact. Bugazon had been vaguely keeping track of the conversation taking place. His position had only intensified in the last few days. He wanted to annihilate anything that could draw breath in Pointe Trois and leave him to his precious minerals. "I agree with Fisher. They've been a thorn in our side, the painful recurrent knot in my passing thoughts. Let's see this through and ease ourselves into economic retirement."

Pratt looked at Bugazon, shocked for a moment. He couldn't believe the reckless assessment Bugazon had just spat out without hesitation or concern. Bugazon caught the look and cocked his head at the man with a cold stare prompting him to say something.

The President had closed his eyes in a moment of deep thought then flashed them open, slapped his hands on his knees and snapped up from the chair. He walked back to his desk but remained standing as he announced his position. "I don't like being told what to do in my own country, being made to yield and cow tow to the interests of some superpowers. We need to dig that place up before we hand it over. I find it unacceptable being forced to quit during my term due to ungovernable circumstances or external forces engineering coup d'etats or my pull-out of something so major due to shredded popularity. Sounds like for 3 for 3. Let me sleep on it."

They all exchanged a flash of uncertainty at each other as if thinking the same thing. All wishing he would make a conclusive decision once and for all to bring this nightmare to an end. But still, some thinking he was just going to dig his heels in and this nightmare was getting started.

"Alright Mr. President, we'll wait to hear from you." The Speaker replied. They all got up in unison and walked out of his office. The President sized each one of them as they marched out. He could see this was working up a temperature for each of them but didn't know what the point of the meltdown was for each man. He needed to think about something else other than the crisis he was creating for his country.

Belinda walked in and informed him that the Minister of Trade had arrived. They were expected to drive out to a fruit juice factory being opened by an investor that appreciated the business model of cheap labor of the capital city and even cheaper raw material from fertile land nearby the city. An aide swiftly marched in and put his speech in his hand as he put on his jacket at the same time.

GENERAL DUEGARO'S BOARDROOM ARMY HQ
DAY 6 –18:00HRS

Gen. Duegaro called an emergency meeting of the Military High Council. Everyone was present except Gen. Bugazon, deliberately not informed.

Duegaro briefed the Council, "This afternoon the Minister of Finance called a meeting with the Inspector General of Police expressing concern about the almost guaranteed civil unrest due to government staff not being paid, inflation spiraling out of control, hospitals running out of drugs, an inflamed idol youth being used by the opposition, among other concerns in coming months. Finance needed to be sure there wouldn't be any fall-out into an internal civil war with security forces being called in to wipe out their own folks in the event of any peaceful demonstration. IGP took along the Minister of Defense to ensure they'd be on the same hymn sheet knowing how the President would react at the sight of one protest, let alone multiple voices of discord. We've all seen how H.E. has a military reaction to protests instead of calling Police. During their meeting, Defense called me for a game plan. I rushed over. Within 30 minutes we all agreed on what we have previously discussed around this table and had started the preliminary groundwork." Nobody had moved so much as a finger as Duegaro spoke.

"Among us here we have the Heads of the Land, Sea and Air Forces respectively, the Head of Finance & Administration and the Head of Integrated Operations Command. You all already know who you need to put under house arrest or some form of lock-down until we've started our internal investigations. You should also know I received an interesting phone call from an old friend in the Netherlands. It seems the environmental network has been talking to their friends far and wide. The Hague is trying to figure out what is the Army's official role in all of this. I told him we take no part in this filth of decades and we can no longer let this go on further. His point of inquiry is that they've got Gebajara in their sights from a file they received from the environmental and human rights activists but there are a few other names indicated and were inquiring to know how these were being handled domestically, especially since these were Army officials. He wanted to check in with me first. Did we wish them to be taken up by The Hague as well? I told him yes, but we would handle them locally first. In the interim we'd send the file we'd put together from the army's perspective and told him we were also busy digging up all the rot out of our system that has been using this project as their platform."

"How about this chief co-conspirator Bugazon? Remember, he's also a member of the Council." asked F&A.

"Yes, his file is ready. My office is quietly processing his papers. You will receive them shortly to conclude the administrative processing and ensure not one comma is missing in all his activity. The man sometimes has an instinct to sniff something's amiss a mile away."

F&A inquired further, "And the others? I don't want these chaps shuffled around just waiting to give me a different brand of headache in a different shade of uniform?"

"Everyone who was part of that clique is having their paperwork processed. I am aware that this was not entirely a coalition of the willing. We've collected the background information we have the fingerprints so to speak. But the investigations will take place and then they shall be presented with minimum fuss. This shall not only relate to the corruption of Pointe Trois. Their conduct and career with the institution shall also weigh in on the investigations."

"Fair enough, let the paperwork flow." replied F&A.

GEN. BUGAZON'S OFFICE, 2 FLOORS DOWN

Rocking back and forth, Bugazon almost fell out of his chair as the read the *Procurement Update*. The delivery of his four KA52 Alligator Helicopters had been delayed indefinitely, reason unknown. This was after 100% payment cash in advance. He dialed F&A's cel. number. It was off. He yelled out, "Genine, find me F&A."

Within a minute, she dashed through the door. "He's in a meeting at Gen. Duegaro's boardroom with other members of the High Council. It started about 30 minutes ago."

"What?"

Genine had a hint of worry in her eyes. She didn't like the fury in her boss's eyes as he charged out his lobby door.

Gen. Bugazon did not knock and barged straight into General Duegaro's meeting. This was an obvious and deliberate sign of disrespect. Six men were distributed along the polished oak conference table, Duegaro seated at the head. Everyone turned to the door in shock at who could dare make such a move. Duegaro already facing the door in his large build, cold stared Bugazon.

"What is the meaning of this? How come I was not informed about this meeting as a member of the High Council?" Bugazon demanded.

Moving his eyes from Duegaro to the other 5 men around the table, the fury could be so clearly felt. Duegaro had not left eye contact to tame down the upstart that had just disrespected every code of conduct of the institution. His soft tone carried a streak of contempt that did not require interpretation. "Just some changes. You will be advised in due course."

Bugazon smelt he was walking into a sharp corner. "I will not stand for this. You will hear from the Commander-in-Chief." He spun on his heel and stormed out leaving the door wide open. Returning back to his office breathing heavily, he called his wife.

"Yes darling?" Was her no nonsense greeting.

"Start arranging for all our prize possessions to be sent to our favorite residence abroad."

His wife knew what this meant in previously agreed code. The residence that no one knew existed but ensured an anonymous, luxurious lifestyle. Be ready to move at any minute. She immediately walked to the Safe in the study, removed the $2 million worth of diamonds saved for a rainy day and stuffed them in her blouse. She'd be damned if anyone walked through that door at any moment and she needed to take the secret passageway out. Inventory of high value items for swift exit began within minutes.

CHAPTER 21

PIECES FINDING THEIR PLACE

Raphael and Ian had made superb arrangements. Emily's wardrobe matched the phony identification and CV of a missionary English teacher on an 'open journey' to spread the Gospel in the most desperate places on earth and bring a bit of connectivity with the outer world to their lives, starting with the English language. The philanthropist's jet flew from New York to Petremah, the regional town closest to Pointe Trois in the Seremanta. Seremanta was the neighboring country to Caramondo sharing the border of the rainforest.

It was a humid night as the jet landed into the small airport. The pilot taxied to the extreme end of the runway. An old, but well maintained, vehicle parked at the side of the passenger terminal rolled up to the aircraft. Chenchon gave a signal with his arm. The stewardess let down the door. Emily took 5 steps to the vehicle. She entered they shook hands. Few words exchanged beyond the welcome greeting. Chenchon received her passport and threw a few stamps of different dates in it.

They drove into Petremah town straight into an alley way. Emily immediately removed one layer of clothing and handed them to Chenchon. Chenchon handed the clothes and the immigration stamps to the driver. He had his specific instructions as one of the security operatives of the militia. There was no talking but the tension carried more noise than the loudest conversation. They shook hands, the vehicle reversed back with no lights until it rejoined the main street.

Chenchon and Emily continued to walk off in the opposite direction of the putrid alley. She removed her folded wide-brimmed straw hat from her bag and put it on. It attempted to hide some of her softer up-town features and long wavy brown hair. They immediately joined the hustle and bustle of market day. They took a right turn and leisurely walked about 100 meters, crossed a narrow cobbled street, continued just another 50 meters before Chenchon gently guided her arm in a romantic gesture to another alleyway. A battered old cab was already parked facing the other direction of this alleyway. They casually jumped in and the disheveled looking driver, also militia intelligence, slowly drove into the street and straight to the airport.

The immigration officer looked at Emily's passport, looked at her, then looked at it again. It was no longer than a 15 minute wait before they were in the propeller Cessena. Twenty minutes later they landed in Pointe Trois.

They both coolly stayed in the middle of the line of passengers disembarking, filled in their immigration cards and were again back in the line looking tired and generally unremarkable.

Chenchon, ever so slightly, nodded to Emily to look to her left into the room titled, *Police*; where army officials swarmed in and out with paperwork and a mid-level officer questioning a lady similar to Emily's build except the woman was a brunette and Emily had sandy brown hair. The lady pretended to look flustered and outraged because she was pulled off the queue answering endless questions for over an hour since her flight had landed.

Ian had coordinated with Raphael to send a decoy. Raphael had subsequently communicated to a Colonel Zenota, the head of Military Intelligence of Seremanta and childhood friend of his, for him to communicate this mis-information to his counterpart in Caramondo. The army in Pointe Trois had been keenly waiting for this decoy to arrive. A decoy that was also a trained mercenary and knew how to answer their questions in an anxious enough manner, that would release just enough information to keep them asking for more while Emily slipped in, met with the Chief, and slipped back out again. The diversion was essential and she had to play her role for the extent of time required. In 15 minutes Emily and Chenchon were in a battered cab pre-arranged that drove them straight to the Chief's residence.

GENERAL DUEGARO'S OFFICE
ARMY HQ
DAY 6 – 19:00HRS

"Gentlemen, we have had a few discussions among ourselves as the Military High Council about this." Duegaro sounded calm and completely un-phased about the matter at hand. Michael Anderson, the Deputy Minister of Defense and Victor Mekash, the Head of the Sub-Committee on Defense in Parliament nodded their heads as they listened attentively.

This discussion point was at the end of a meeting on a number of perfunctory issues that required substantial exchange between the head of the army, the legislature responsible for military matters and Ministerial representative. Justification of recent significant procurements, participation in regional operations, the state of accommodation for lower level officers in addition to streamlining the hiring and salary structure of cadet officers were issues on which they had just concluded discussion. The 3 gentlemen each had a distinguished military background even though Mekash and Anderson had retired out at different times due to a changing culture. They had all taken major steps towards professionalizing the army and making the Ministry of Defense more transparent. Activity in Pointe Trois was also unraveling and eating away at the morale of officers.

"The files are ready. These are your copies."

The General brought forth 4 files from underneath a pile of files on his desk. Anderson and Mekash were to serve as the messengers to the Legislature and Judiciary, as well as retain their own copies. It was just a stroke of luck that the Chief Justice had locked horns with the President on several cases ranging from Point Trois clans filing lawsuits against government to the safety of the Judges being threatened by certain army officers to rule a certain way when sentencing of their subordinates was due. About a year ago, the Chief Justice and Head of the High Court called a meeting with the President and Duegaro. Told them they would not tolerate one more threat, they were happy to resign en-masse explaining to the Caramondo population and international community what exactly had been going on. Saying they had seen too many careers ruined because Judges ruled according to the Law and not the whims of a chosen few. Duegaro made it clear the army had nothing to do with this. President Gebajara told them not to get their wigs in a knot.

The evidence was damning in the files he had just presented. It had been collected systematically over a year. Duegaro had watched the trail of money, precious minerals and other natural resources that been left along the way of their plunderous, criminal activity. The crumbs had been neatly picked up by the eyes watching them. Bank account traces, documentation showing the lines of ownership of prime real estate in various cities around the world, Alexander's investment bank at the center of the movements, transcripts of meetings by army officials had all been documented and carefully filed. This was coupled with photos upon photos of the movement of minerals from the aircrafts to the trucks at both the capital city and Pointe Trois airports and the falsified paperwork on taxation provided, courtesy of CAA staff.

The point was to show army supervision and implementation using its transportation system of such activities where they had no mandate to be there as well as the paper trail of the President's and Bugazon's signatures masterminding the operation and using the army's resources at will. Duegaro had made an unusual inquiry for information about 9 months ago. When this officer came forward, information came flooding through from the different offices. What Bugazon never picked up on was that someone among their clique had turned into a spy.

This officer came forward shortly after the inquiry when he saw the human rights atrocities and decided he could no longer continue to be a part of this so he approached Duegaro directly. Duegaro agreed not to court martial him in exchange for his systematic gathering of every scintilla of information he could dig up. He would have the whistleblower demoted by 2 ranks and be part of the team that would clean up the environmental poisons in Pointe Trois.

STATE HOUSE, CARAMONDO
DAY 6 – 20:00HRS

Simmons jetted into a quiet spot of the airport. He was a man on a mission. Not a moment to waste. Prescott was in a vehicle waiting for him the runway. With a handsome bribe, the immigration officer stamped his passport at the exit gate of the airport. Within 30 minutes they reached the gates of State House. Simmons and Prescott waited patiently as the security officer called the head of security who in turn called the chief of protocol who in turn called Belinda.

President Gebajara was in the midst of a State banquet with a large investor now keen to set up a tyre factory to become the major supplier on the Continent. The rubber, of which, he was planning to source from Pointe Trois. The investor had felt the wind getting warm and wanted to secure the rights to this supply point now with the man he knew was corrupt enough to sign off with personal incentives. He was among a short list that had access to His Excellency and was going to do the needful before the wind got too hot. The merrymaking was lively.

Belinda marched in with a post-it note slip written, *"Richard Simmons here at gate to see you. Receive clearance?"* Gebajara felt his heart come to a stop. His temperature shot through his skull as he felt his palms sweat up. Belinda and his chief guest noticed his face redden slightly.

"Everything okay Mr. President?" The guest inquired.

"Of course, everything is fine." He flashed a smile at the gentleman.

"Yes, send him through. Tell State House Counsel to come by immediately." Belinda marched out. Gebajara forced himself to realize they wouldn't have come all this way to say no. As they drove up the driveway Simmons started out of the car before it came to a full stop. The security officer efficiently greeted him as soon as he got out of the vehicle.

"Good evening sir." With a fast pace he was escorted through the maze of corridors. Simmons wondered to himself. He couldn't tell whether the man could have changed his mind in the past twelve hours due to global and local pressure. The deal was no longer so attractive if the world viewed him as a criminal and he could not travel freely or at least in his accustomed luxury because of the sanctions tagged on him. If he had changed his mind, it was his task to change it right back to where it was when they left him two days ago. The officer opened the door to a large lonely conference room. With his portfolio leather brief in hand, Simmons could not bring himself to sit down.

Prescott burst through the door a few minutes later. "Just wanted to be sure I hadn't missed the action." as his eyes jokingly scanned the room. The tension in Simmons cracked slightly.

"No, you still get to witness the marriage." Simmons replied.

2 minutes later, State House Counsel opened the door with a smile. "Now I know you didn't come all this way to say no. Planned surprises are always packages of sunshine, not sorrow."

Simmons ignored the bright talk from the man who had been so dismissive of their concerns less than 48 hours ago.

"Counsel." He gruffly responded, that intended to serve as the greeting as well. Simmons had already begun to open his dossier that held an expensive, delicate ivory envelope. He brought out 2 sets of the agreement and slid one across the conference table to the man who quickly began to review it as he stood behind one of the chairs.

"I trust you'll find the slight modifications to be agreeable and as far a compromise we're willing to make."

Simmons gave a stern eye to Counsel as the man continued to peruse through without comment. His sleeves were rolled up. He hadn't left his office for the day. He flipped the pages up as he continued to peruse and finally got to the end of the document and flipped the pages back down. Counsel looked up at Simmons with zero expression as if in a battle of who would blink first then in a tone of a man very wary about what he had just read, said

"I'll be back shortly gentlemen."

It was a long 10 minute wait. Then suddenly Counsel burst through the room. President Gebajara was immediately behind him. "Gentlemen!" the President exclaimed. "It appears we have an agreement. I was always confident of your coming around, but just wasn't expecting it to be this soon. I agree with the treatment of confidentiality. I will ensure no one will know you were ever in country from my end." President Gebajara talked as he signed and initialed both copies of the agreement and Counsel witnessed. Simmons observed closely. Simmons and the President shook hands.

Prescott and Counsel looked at each other with polite, tense smiles and a gentle nod. "Then I shall take that as my cue to leave."

Simmons had started to walk towards the door. There was a small but profound detail they understood without having to discuss because it was so obvious. They left the date open. No one would ever know when this agreement had been signed. The most convenient date was to their making. In 30 minutes sharp Simmons was climbing the steps of the jet. The pilot had already received his runway clearance as they started to taxi within minutes of the stewardess closing the door.

CHIEF DEZANGA'S RESIDENCE
ARMOUR DIEU, POINTE TROIS
DAY 6 – 20:00HRS

The mood was somber. Uncertain of the life of their leader that lay listless on his bed slipping in and out of consciousness, Council members were in deep discussion among themselves in an area of the living room. The poison specialist had arrived from New York only 2 hours before. It was agreed he could not travel with Emily to avert the risk of drawing attention to her. He flew directly into Pointe Trois town. The heavy weight activists from the capital city were patiently waiting for the Doctor in the arrivals area of Pointe Trois airport, ready to step in at the slightest interference of his immigration processing. One of them whispered to Velasquez that they were quite happy to state in the global and local press that the army had killed the Chief. Velasquez did not want to further contribute to his current career crisis.

There were only 3 people allowed into the bedroom; Elder Butawan, the acting head of Pointe Trois during the Chief's incapacitation, the Chief's personal aide and the Doctor. From the driveway Chenchon and Emily were hurriedly ushered into the vestibule. Elder Katan immediately broke away from the Council and welcomed them with a warm handshake. He did not bother to hide the urgency and worry in his eyes. This was no different from the other Council members that regally but quickly walked to greet them and walked away. Family members in another corner of the living room were engrossed in their own somber discussion.

"It may be only moments remaining. Come, let me take you." Said Elder Katan.

He walked them down the corridor. Approaching the door that was guarded by 2 huge men, the Chief's aide immediately ran out with tears welled up in his eyes trying to suppress his sobs. They entered. Softening the pale complexion of this face that perspired, the gentle yellow lighting brought an aura of peace and holiness around the Chief. The Doctor sat on one side of the bed taking his pulse, Butawan sat on the other side taking notes on anything he may utter. They acknowledged Emily and Chenchon with a nod as they tip toed their way in.

Emily moved towards the Doctor. "How is he?"

"The poison worked through his nervous system very quickly and he's already experiencing critical organ failure. Even though we're expecting the results of the blood tests from the hospital any minute now, I'm not sure there will be enough time for an antidote to work."

Looking at the Chief's state of semi-consciousness, she looked at Butawan and Chenchon. "Please, help me."

Emily brought her dossier out of her satchel that had a plain brown envelope. Her hand shuffled inside the bag for a moment looking for a pen, but never losing eye contact with the man in his last moments. Using his armpits, the two men tried to lift the Chief's back upwards only slightly. She had taken the agreement out of the envelope handing over the pen to Butawan to help the Chief clasp it in between his fingers and thumb. Due to the movement of his body, he had fleetingly opened his eyes. A smile seeped through.

"It's so peaceful here…Serinda is here telling me to come with her." Butawan looked at Emily. "Serinda is his late wife. She died 5 years ago."

Emily motioned to Butawan to help him write his signature. "Chief I need you to try."

The muscles of the Chief's hand flinched. An expression of effort came over his face. Emily's face also gave an expression of pushing out the strength to complete this one action so key to the life of his people. The pen touched the paper. He knew what he was signing. Ever so slowly, he signed the agreement. He let out a long breath and then leaned back into the arms of those who held him. His mouth remained open. The agreement had already been dated for that very day. Butawan and Chenchon signed as witnesses. Emily spoke with calm and respect in her voice.

"I'm so sorry, but I must go now to get this back to New York and complete the process of formalizing it." Butawan raised his hand as tears already streamed down his cheeks.

"Please, our future is in that agreement, God's speed." He replied.

Chenchon guided Emily out and they were driven straight to the airport. As they drove out, 3 bells immediately chimed. The wailing and grief rang throughout the house. They sat and waited another 20 minutes before boarding the flight to Seremanta and without incident to the jet rushing her back to New York.

PR&S, NEW YORK
DAY 6 – 14:00HRS

Rebecca called out, "Marc, get me Lieutenant McPherson on the line. But first find out whether Bijoubela is still in town and the details of the latest sports car he's driving." Rebecca knew she could call in a few markers on the Lieutenant after she forced a client to pay the medical costs of a group of school children who were collecting flowers in a forest that the company had quietly littered with toxic chemicals over the years. The Lieutenant's daughter was among the children. The expensive intricate treatment was life-saving.

"Rebecca, it's been a while. My daughter is constantly nagging me to bring her to your office to understand how you saved her life. I tell her you're busy. Tell me, what's on your mind?"

"She can name the date and I'll make the time. Say, I need you to pick up someone for me, while I get my ducks in a row on the real reason he should be enjoying your hospitality. The right international security or judiciary agency should then follow-up, hopefully within the next 24 hours. I was thinking any historical parking tickets or even a minor crack on their tail light."

"I get the picture. I'm sure we can figure out a way to hold on to him, just long enough." Rebecca asked Marc to give the Lieutenant the details of the vehicle.

CHAPTER 22

DIVERGENCE AND DISCOVERY

DAY 7

TOWN CENTER, ARMOUR DIEU
06:00HRS

News of the Chief's sudden illness spread fast through the verbal network between villages, news of his death was instant through the radio announcements. Emotions were aflame and increasingly difficult to contain.

By break of dawn, men and women of all ages had run out into the streets. They knew which shops and businesses were owned by army officials. As a spurt of calculated anger, some people had inscribed an ancient Burajon symbol in red paint on each of these store fronts. For the few among the elders of the rainforest they knew it said *'revenge is ours'.* Up and down Main Street along and the smaller trading centers in simultaneous chorus, large objects and stones were thrown through the front windows and doors of each establishment. Not an item was stolen from these stores. Velasquez received the call from one of the army officers whose wife narrowly missed a brick when opening up for the day. He deployed soldiers throughout the town and trading centers but only to stand and observe, not to engage. He had to place the call to

Bugazon immediately. A call he desperately did not want to make.

"General, I cannot avoid this early morning interruption but we have a crisis flaring."

"What is it this time Velasquez?" Bugazon sounded disinterested and out of breath as he insisted on continuing on his running machine.

"The people of Pointe Trois sir, they have erupted. They seem to be taking the news of the death of their Chief not too well, chanting we will kill you today or tomorrow. They have already targeted businesses owned by army officials, putting some funny symbol on the door. Radio Pointe Trois says the man died under unclear circumstances while being treated by an eminent poison specialist." Velasquez was careful not to complete the sentence stating that the specialist was from New York lest he make his own situation even worse, allowing such a security breach to happen.

Bugazon interrupted, "Alright, alright. Keep your knee caps on Velasquez. Let me think for a moment. I'll get back to you."

Bugazon slid off the running machine. He thought he couldn't let this fire burn out of control. There were too many other factors that could spark this off making Pointe Trois impossible to manage and forcing the deal to come to a screeching halt.

"Ah! Yes, yes." He dialed as he walked out of his elaborate exercise room walking from one wing of the house back to his master suite.

"Velasquez this is what you do…"

MILITARY PRISON
ARMOUR DIEU, POINTE TROIS
DAY 7 – 06:30HRS

Even before the day began it was the stench of rotting flesh in diluted disinfectant that greeted the morning of this cramped complex of small tents. Manning the entrance at his simple beach chair and table, the Sergeant with the keys to the prison navigated his way through his breakfast tray of eggs, bacon, a bun and baked beans like he was working his way through a battle plan. He sipped his coffee while he chewed on the bun and settled into the paper.

The early edition of the newspaper headline was intriguing enough. The Sergeant's curiosity for the unsolved threw him into the story. The front page headline read: *Mystery: Central Bank Official Found Murdered.* The story read on, *'Criminal investigators are still trying to establish how Edgar Pratt, Senior Manager, Institutional and Corporate Accounts was found shot with a clean bullet to his head while seated in his office.*

Scene investigators suspect the murder took place between 7pm and 12midnight. His lap top and desktop along with its CPU were taken. It would appear he was forced to open his safe before he was shot. Files appeared tampered with, but bank officials would not divulge what had gone missing. A source that preferred to remain anonymous for fear of reprisal indicates that parts of the Central Bank server has been hacked into and bits of its memory wiped out while the large majority of it remained intact. Mr. Pratt was known to be a mild mannered, principled and disciplined man by his colleagues. He had worked with the Central Bank for 22 years. He leaves behind a wife and 3 kids. Leads are still being developed. More on this story as it unfolds'.

"Now who would go and do a thing like that?" The Sergeant muttered to himself.

Just as he turned the page, he scrambled to pick up his cel. phone on its first ring. Promotability was the priority. "Prisons Wing." The Sergeant listened to the instructions being darted off the phone in rapid fire. "Yes Brigadier. Yes sir. Yes sir." During the conversation, someone walked up to him and put a list of names in his hand. "The list has just been brought to me sir. Shall execute as ordered sir."

Velasquez had just instructed 250 of the 2800 sickest, maimed prisoners to be released. Bugazon figured it would save them the little stress of those captives dying under their watch.

The Sergeant called out, "Gentlemen, I have good news! 250 of you are being released for good behavior. Don't some of you wish you were better behaved?"

ARMY BARRACKS, POINTE TROIS
DAY 7 – 08:00HRS

Meanwhile across town in the Pointe Trois barracks a group of 15 men of varied ranks of the Caramondo Army pretended to be in a casual breakfast but only with the gravest of expressions. Barely a word was uttered as they chewed slowly. Only sadness and anger were their bond.

Finally the most senior spoke, "First Montero and now the Chief? We cannot let these two incidents go without a local statement."

There were nods all around, staring at each other.

"Remember the Mayor's untimely death? Shot on the runway" one of them asked. They nodded again at each other in affirmation.

PARLIAMENT, CARAMONDO
DAY 7 – 09:00HRS

LaFonte had stuck strictly to his secure line in the last three days. His wife had argued with him about this increased jitteriness that he would not talk about that was going to exacerbate his cancer. Whatever it was, it was undoing all the good they'd achieved so far in remission. He had thought about this phone call long and hard all night. He didn't want to think about it anymore. Sick of it. Sick of everything. He started to dial.

"Carrion, look, I just wanted you to know that I'm resigning as Speaker of the House. I've got a bad feeling about this. I'm not seeing a tidy end to this whole mess, at least not one where anybody in Caramondo is in control. When people from all corners start digging it won't be long before someone's knocking on my door with a shovel. And I'm just not up for all of that, especially defending my name in the title of that office."

La Fonte's voice had started to trail off into a reflective tone. Carrion sounded a little hurried. There was some wind on the line.

"Benjamin, I think that's a good idea. If I were you I wouldn't stand on ceremony. Just handle the letter, the paperwork and let the Deputy take over. Actually I'm already on the way to the airport with my family for an extended holiday. I will carry out business from elsewhere for a little while. Sometimes it's wiser to lay low. Being visible, or in the vicinity, just makes you vulnerable and forcefully available. Make sure all your files are in order. Have one of our usual killer law firms to run lethal defense for you just in case they even sniff your name coming up. Try to make a habit of flying out for treatment discreetly, but regularly. Be on very good terms with your Doctors abroad in case their medical opinion is the only opinion that'll save you from an inquisition hearing. Alrighty, am here at the airport now. Gotta run –literally. Stay in touch." Carrion's voice trailed off.

"Sure, stay in touch." replied LaFonte sounding despondent that one of his partners in the storm was deserting the unstable landscape.

With Pratt already dead, he did not consider Bugazon to be a partner. They didn't share the same moral compass. It was just he and Fisher remaining. Fisher had the means and malice to complicate or neutralize anything coming his way with his Private Investigative Firm. LaFonte felt a heavy regret, a horrible remorse come over him. There was no guarantee that the President would run cover for him despite the several occasions he had done just that for the man.

NEW YORK POLICE DEPARTMENT
DAY 7 – 08:30HRS

Alexander had been impatiently pacing up and down his cell, furious at his lawyer's advice to be calm and not kick up too much of a stink, despite the unbelievable overnight delay. His lawyer was clear. He really needed all the friends he could get given the way things were unraveling around them. Coincidence or conspiracy, the point was, this was not the time to threaten. The cops knew the Law. No need to draw attention to what was going on around him. Lieutenant McPherson walked up to his cell with two men in standard issue suits. But they had different identities tagged to their breast pockets.

"Good morning Mr. Bijoubela. These two men came to my desk asking to meet with you. This is Mr. George Gilmont from the Securities and Exchange Commission

Financial Crimes Desk and this is Mr. Charles Renoir from Interpol's New York office's money laundering and financial fraud desk. He'll explain his link to Scotland Yard's request to your headquarter office in London, I believe. It seems they have been meeting among themselves but I'll let them share with you. Your office advised them of your whereabouts. I took the liberty to call your lawyer, told him of the gentlemen at my desk. Says he'll be right over in about 15 minutes."

Alexander remained speechless. He knew what this meant. "Lieutenant, I'll wait in my cell until my lawyer arrives."

"As you wish. Gentlemen…" The Lieutenant motioned to the two. "I'll show you to a meeting room where you can wait."

Alexander's hands were sweating as he gripped the cell bars, watching the three men walk down the corridor.

G. TECH. BRANCH OFFICE, NYC
DAY 7 – 10:00HRS

The Board of Directors was losing its patience with Baynes. The conglomerate's reputation was being shredded. Overnight he was on the corporate jet to New York. At 10:30am he was in the Boardroom. Even he had to admit to himself he was feeling particularly anxious. Twelve men representing the most powerful companies in military equipment, software development of different sectors and everyday electronic equipment sat around the table in a background panoramic view of Manhattan.

"Gentlemen, I know what it looks like. It's not as bad as it seems. Trust me."

The largest shareholder among them let out a laugh. "Yes, you're right Baynes. It's surely not as bad. It's worse, much worse. Around this table we've lost over $3 billion in shareholder value. Pity you missed the welcoming party the tree-huggers staged for you right outside this front door a couple of days ago. Well, made it all over the evening news. What I call, shareholder priceless material." It was an intimidating glare he shot straight at Baynes. Baynes felt his digestion curdle and start to run north.

Another shareholder jumped in with a warning eye. "Remember, G. Tech. is large alright but it's not irreplaceable. We've put in place our exit strategies if we don't see a sudden turn of events. And I mean sudden. No second chances."

"Speak for yourself Douglas. This is just a courtesy call. We're here to say we need to put our remaining $300million elsewhere that was $500million a week ago. Our own shareholders don't have that kind of stomach."

The other shareholders gave unsympathetic, unwavering stares to Baynes. One company, a little less unsympathetic that had seen their profit margin quadruple from G. Tech.'s breakthroughs broke the silence.

"Okay, we didn't come all this way to slice and dice you only. Let's hear what you have to say first before we make our final decisions."

"Thanks James." Baynes brought out a one page dossier that he had personally crafted on his flight down. The number of analysts at HQ he'd woken up to verify every fact, left whole departments with their mobile phones in their hands in case of a call from the Chairman. He distributed the synopsis of new products and services that would make G. Tech. a very attractive partner within a few months. He was relieved for their lukewarm reception given current circumstances. After his meeting at his reserved office space, he enjoyed a few moments of peace. He looked at his cel. phone vibrating on his desk.

"Hey big guy, let's set aside mama piranha for a moment. There's another growing fish turning into a mammal that can bring down anything -or anyone for that matter. My contacts in New York and Paris are feeding me nails for lunch. Brace yourself." Tristan barreled on. "Word is, the activists in Caramondo and the Global Association of Human Rights Organizations and some global environmental consortium have a string of lawsuits with cute little pink hearts drawn all over ready to hit my desk – via yours- within the next twelve hours."

Baynes instantly broke out into a fever, but tried to sound cool and composed. "These folks don't have anything better to do with their time?"

"Am afraid not. First there are two lawsuits for environmental damage and human rights violations respectively in Caramondo by the local activists. Then they've coordinated with these international outfits on three separate lawsuits; one in conservation damage of flora and fauna in the world, the second in attempted eradication of endangered animal species and the third in illegal extraction, transportation and procurement of precious minerals across continents. These are bitter, angry people because they're naming each Board Member individually and severally, as well as the conglomerate. Interestingly, I'm told they've been very generous with your name all over the charges, but no mention of the CEO. They're even trying to work in a clause that you'd be personally responsible even if you left the company. They seem to have ambitions with you. How do you figure that big guy?"

Baynes felt himself shrink in his chair. Tristan continued.

"Now we both know that any member of the Board won't stand for this kind of static for less than a second. Let's not even talk about all our institutional partners out there. I'm just giving you the heads up to start thinkin' of a graceful way out of this situation, before the Board gives my instructions. And by the way, I haven't heard anything about mama-Piranha from my sources. Will let you know if anything new comes through."

"I catch your drift Tristan. Thanks for the warning. Let me see how to organize my way out of things." Baynes sat completely still in his chair for a couple of moments, dazed, unsure of his next move. All he knew is he wouldn't be left holding the bag on his one. Someone else would be the lamb at the altar, not him. He needed some external Counsel to guide his key moves and keep his reputation intact.

AN APARTMENT – BROOKLYN, NY
DAY 7 – 10:00HRS

"You know Insurance Agents don't wear such expensive suits now days?" quipped Sergei.

"I'll announce I'm your personal jeweler next time. I'm glad you were able to make it to New York at such short notice. I received your message when I was in-flight, came over as soon as I could. Is there a problem with our 2 guests?" replied Simmons.

Sergei smiled. "They're not exactly the type to pass time with the most recent video games but most surprisingly they didn't object to my offer of the platinum treatment at the Fortunesque Spa which had all sorts of goodies attached to it at your expense and with your guaranteed confidentiality. Some mumblings about getting stir crazy in a sinister gymnasium. Fruthers was insistent in his justification. That it was not he who just packed and left. It was the company who packed him up and threw him into a business brothel, why not take advantage of more pleasant surroundings offered. Ping made a curious statement though, as he coolly placed his bags on the floor when he arrived. Mutterings about his people that would follow-up at the right time and would not be so forgiving. But when a leggy Asian goddess walked up to take off his jacket, he had a sudden change of attitude. I was surprised by him. Weirdly lamenting that he might as well enjoy the offer while he was kidnapped by his own employer. I'm still unpacking the man. He's not your typical sophisticated mole."

Thinking this is not what he came for, Simmons interrupted. "So if they're ok, what am I doing here? I think you of all people can appreciate every minute of the next twelve hours counts."

"Alrighty, no bonding today. Lots to share. Information you can just keep in the back of your mind. But you need to bear one thing in mind though; I could not help but follow your movements during your trip. A caveat has been placed on the diamond mines. The owner also owns a fair bit of land that surrounds them which includes the mines that you visited. He bought this land many years ago, something about protecting his investment."

Simmons knew the precise implications of this statement. This individual could be a major spoke in their wheel that would send their barely signed transaction into a rather ungraceful roll into the ditch. Simmons thought all of this could boil down to one individual denying them access to their mineral combination that had cost them so much in the past week. Sergei noticed Simmons mind trail off. He nodded for him to continue.

"They are owned by a certain Mr. Lannier who carries a variety of identities; apparently an accomplished chameleon."

Simmons couldn't believe that Lannier actually had the upper hand on a transaction, much less something so central to him at the moment. Sergei casually flicked through about twenty identities of Lannier's on his screen as Simmons looked on indifferently.

"Wait!"

One face caught his eye. He moved the office chair up to the screen with such speed. Sergei couldn't remember the last time he saw Simmons look so surprised.

"I'll be damned." He softly exclaimed to himself. "I have that face in our country background file. That is the damned Headmaster of the Missionary School, Father Peter Raines. Just how the......"

Simmons looked at Sergei in shock.

"Yes, I thought you'd put the pieces together." Sergei replied with a calm incisive smile like he was leading a friend to a discovery. "It's a bonus that you've met the man, dealt with him on several occasions maybe in a different guise. But he appears to be the negotiable type, who is a very interesting man –or at least with a very interesting background should we say."

Simmons now looked deeply disturbed. He needed to know exactly who he was dealing with. He still wondered how this detail had previously escaped him.

"Should I bore you further?" Simmons stared at the screen and nodded. "Well, our good man comes from a lineage that engaged in military and general trade, 'anything goes' kind of thing between the Colonialists and Muchanta tribe that were based on the East coast of Caramondo."

Simmons started to look surprised in a sarcastic sort of way as he prompted Sergei.

"Yes, he comes from one of the pre-eminent Muchanta families, at least at that time. The young man Lannier, or should we call him Raines, was being groomed to take over the reins of his family. Lannier was to be enlisted in the army at 18 years old. The colonialists also had political ambitions for him and a select few of the Muchanta moneyed had become aware of this. These families found it too much of a threat to have a President with a military background who was also backed by the colonialists. So they banded together and had Lannier-Raines family killed off. They say the quick thinking maid grabbed the boy and rushed him to another maid in the neighborhood. That they hunted for the child within a few houses to make sure he was dead. Said they wouldn't give up, would regroup and find him later. She was of the Burajon tribe so she decided to send him to missionaries she knew in the city. The maid was informed that he was still a target. She told Lannier-Raines he had to forget his past if he wanted to stay alive. Then she took him to Pointe Trois with a new identity to be raised by the missionaries there. These other family heads killed each other off over time. I myself have to wonder what he plans to do with this quietly amassed wealth from his multitude of deals as Lannier – which includes a rather impressive real estate portfolio all over the world? Well anyway, as I said, he's negotiable." Am told he lives rather humbly in Pointe Trois in the identity, as you say, of the school Headmaster and Priest.

Simmons walked out of the apartment in shock now knowing who was standing in between him and those mineral deposits. He continued to berate himself, how could he have not picked up on the identity camouflage. Everybody's photos of who's who in Pointe Trois were in that file he'd looked through several times. He didn't know if he felt a certain sympathy for a man who festered the same secret wound he did of his whole family killed off and walking away from his own identity.

CHAPTER 23

REVELATIONS & THEIR ROOTS

Baynes nervously swiveled in his chair unable to concentrate. All he wanted was the confirmed signed agreement in his hand for him to sign and the nightmare was finally over. His morning had been pure hell, feeling beaten and battered with threats from his institutional partners and shareholders. He was turning around scenarios with Drier when Simmons walked in.

Right behind Simmons walked in one of the engineer analysts with straight clear confidence handing Drier a crisp white slender envelope. "This showed up in my in-tray yesterday with a note to give it to you in coming days." The young man strangely walked out right away not waiting for any questions to be asked.

Drier opened the envelope equally not interested in the messenger. Baynes and Simmons looked on as Drier pulled out a small round locket that was a photo of Kreshnakov and a boy about 5 years old who was a replica of him. A note enclosed said, *"This belonged to your man. Take care of the boy."* The smiles on their faces looked like any everyday close father-son relationship. He handed the note to Simmons without saying a word who read it.

Simmons smirked out a laugh. "They found this in their rainforest and bothered to send it to you? Are you supposed to take this as kick in the groin or an act of respect and honor?" Drier smirked back thinking these were indeed a group that he couldn't help but respect no matter what their intention may have been.

"Our assets are in safe custody?" Even though the question was for Simmons, Drier's eye contact was on Baynes who had shifted his attention and was frowning at a report earlier placed on his desk.

"Yes they are, like a little vacation." replied Simmons.

Baynes interrupted un-amused by the lighthearted response. "The agreement, the man signed? It's airtight? I don't have a thing to worry about? I can take that off my to-do list? It's a done deal? I don't have to discuss it or run after it anymore?" Baynes line of questioning was rushed. His gaze at Simmons was anything but friendly.

"Hold on just a bit longer. It's being authenticated by legal, usual preliminary copies made and will be with you shortly for signing."

There had never been such tension in the room among the three men. "Now I've got these mysterious shareholders of ours toasting my balls over a fire on what should be a crown jewel moment for the corporation in its history." Baynes lamented. He was rubbing his forehead deeply with the palm of his right hand like he was after the headache at the center of his head.

"It's enough to deal with G. Tech. super-power status slipping through our fingers with all this negative attention. I called on you 2 because I want you to both be aware that now mama piranha shareholder is searching for our findings for some possible sinister world agenda? I have no idea. It just gets better and better with each passing moment."

There was a moment of silence in the office. Drier and Simmons could see Baynes was approaching a meltdown of sorts. They hoped he would recompose himself. Simmons spoke softly. "Well just to brighten your day even further, I've learned of another small wrinkle in our plan." Baynes glared at him. "Someone already owns the land attached to the mines that have the particular mineral deposits we're looking at. They're not interested in the soil. It's the diamonds mines that they are protecting."

Baynes raised his hand up as if he couldn't stand to hear another word. He cut him off. "Just buy them off. I don't care about the cost right now."

"Will meet the man. I have a couple of loose ends to handle." Knowing Baynes wasn't settled enough to strategize on any developments he started to walk out of the office. Immediately leaving the executive office reception area, Simmons sent a message to Lannier. "Let's meet in Washington DC in 2 hours." There was another key stakeholder meeting he was to have in Washington

D.C. He then sent another message to Sergei, *"I need you to clean up my study."* Sergei knew exactly what that meant in case any of his immediate supervisors or shareholders tried to breakthrough thinking they could find answers to critical questions to this transaction.

Drier's phone rang as he looked out at the Manhattan view from this office. He took the call as he nodded to Baynes while heading out. Baynes was already back frowning at the report on his desk and briefly nodded back.

"Excuse me Mr. Drier I'm glad I finally reached you. Pardon the urgent intrusion, but there were 2 men at the lab again this morning from the Ministry of Defense and Ministry of Internal Affairs respectively very politely commanding us that Dr. Ping needs to materialize within the next 72 hours and it is only Dr. Ping that they deal with. I've tried him on all his numbers but to no success. His family is off limits to G. Tech. Because you were the most senior member of the executive last seen with him, I have to call you to tell me what to do with these gentlemen?"

The British trained accent continued, "Further yet, our security have noticed some plain clothes army officers monitoring our building. I mean the ones from our main land Coriames, not the Hong Kong offices."

"Okay Lilly, I'm glad you called. The next time they check in with you, let them know Dr. Ping will have everything ready for them when he's done on this end. He'll give them the time." Drier decided to park that anomaly while he concluded the present crisis. Simmons was handling conclusion of the agreement. His main concern was ensuring the next phase of G. Tech. was underway in securing the minerals required, the talent doing their work and identifying the first few target satellites.

Meanwhile across the floor in another executive office, the person opened their e-mail. *'The 2 scientists have been taken into hiding. It is your task to find and deliver them to details that shall be provided.'* The reader closed the e-mail immediately knowing G. Tech had the best technology. Just when you thought you were in the privacy of your office is when every detail of action was on camera. This had been the fate of 2 others at the pinnacle of the conglomerate's hierarchy. Professional relationships he had to gently forsake lest they discover the real problem that was nestled within their team.

STATE HOUSE, CARAMONDO
DAY 7 – 16:00HRS

President Gebajara thought he had been able to fend off his counter-part across the border. With the death of the Chief, the labored act of peace and stability had just run out. "Yes, Your Excellency. I can understand your concern. But so far there has been no engagement and no violence between the army and the young lads of Pointe Trois." Gebajara was however thinking to himself how he'd love to eliminate human beings of the male anatomy in the rainforest with all this untold difficulty and humiliation they had visited on him. He leaned forward on his desk feeling less than Presidential. "How can I get this man to stop calling me twice a week? We'd hardly talk twice a year before." He murmured to himself.

His office door opened. Belinda decisively walked in with a pile of files for his input and signature. She carefully placed them on his in-tray, removed the little yellow sticky note that was on top and placed right in front of him. It read, '*Coriames, Minister of Foreign Affairs on line 2*.' She nodded at him with a smile. Gebajara had not even noticed the flashing phone console. The voice on the other end was instructive.

"Your Excellency, I'm sure you're holding up well in spite of the circumstances. Our Head of State has met extensively with our technocrats on this matter. He has asked me to call you to inform you we are pulling out of your national budget, in terms of direct government budget support and infrastructural development countrywide. We'll be focusing on infrastructure and social development activities specifically in the Pointe Trois region."

Gebajara's lips hunched up to their top right corner in a contemptuous smirk as he listened. He reached for a toothpick and started chewing, shaking his head sideways. This was incredible he thought to himself.

The Minister fired on. "This will look like you're asking your donors to invest in the right places. The positive PR wouldn't hurt right now wouldn't you say?"

Gebajara continued shaking his head, threw out the toothpick in disgust as he couldn't chew anymore of this humiliation.

"That continued investment which we've costed at an approximate $3-4 billion per year would be in exchange for exclusive exploratory rights in the rainforest. We see this to be such a bargain as we quietly go about our business. Really, this is such a good deal."

Gebajara didn't want to hear anymore, departing from the polite protocol he interrupted, "Hon. Min. we shall get back to you. Your offer sounds very interesting at best, regards to the Head of State."

"I shall convey." They both hung up.

Gebajara rolled up his eye balls complaining to himself, "For heaven's sake. Where is this going to end?"

ARMOUR DIEU, POINTE TROIS
DAY 7 – 17:00HRS

The village elders had agreed they were not going to be sucked into a blood bath. When news of the death of Montero had broken out, Elder Katan was the appointed Council member to coordinate with the respective village elders to ensure that all the non-militia men were indeed accounted for and no independent violent rebellions were springing up. Many men had signed up with the militia since the day of Montero's killing but it was the militia that sent them back telling them they needed strong people to stay and protect their most vulnerable in the villages. The death of the Chief had simply released a steaming valve of revenge. It was difficult to control the rage of the young to middle aged men in the community feeling helpless to defend the honor of their homes. The women were to make sure the younger children were home safe and not easy targets of kidnapping.

Velasquez and his senior officers were perplexed and uncomfortable at the quiet throughout the town. One of his officers suggested that he may be able to retrieve valuable information from a popular watering hole Velasquez patronized. The main customers were a combination of army officials and wealthy Pointe Trois business people. The fittings, ambience and prices kept everyone else locked out. He figured he could get some tit-bits of information from Avalon based contractors that passed their evenings in weak and strong beverages, especially those that owed their contracts to him. He drove his open top jeep straight into the parking space reserved for his vehicle. He removed his pistol from the glove compartment and placed it in his waist holster as he normally did. A phone call came in.

"Yes Lieutenant. What is it?"

Velasquez zoomed his concentration in on the call. The officer knew exactly how long to keep him on the line, based on the line of sight from which he observed. From a different location, the sniper zoomed in on the back of his neck through his scope. It would be a straight clean shot to his to the base of his neck.

"Schwcck!" Velasquez lunged forward at the force of the bullet shattering the link between his head and his shoulders. Miraculously he did not land on the horn.

The sniper quickly put his HK PSG1 into its ragtag looking bag, grabbed his cane and sprinted down the five flights of stairs then switched to his old man's shuffle that matched the rest of his disguise of white hair, beard and disheveled clothes.

MINISTRY OF DEFENSE, CARAMONDO
DAY 7 – 18:30HRS

Anderson dialed on his secure line that had a voice converter. "Hon. Manywar, if you're still determined to undo that joke of a Bill that passed in Parliament days ago, I have something that may be of interest to you and change the direction of the dialogue. All the major players involved in the desecration of Pointe Trois are mentioned. I'll leave the file with Chef Didier of the restaurant that you know in town. Only you personally can pick it up."

"I don't know who you are. I don't know whether to cry. But all I can offer you is my humble thanks from me and on behalf of the people of Pointe Trois."

PARLIAMENT, CARAMONDO
DAY 7 – 18:30HRS

Mekash privately invited the Chief Justice to his office on the pretext of general legal insight on procurement issues to avoid so many cases winding up in Court and how to address the lot already piled up in the Judiciary. The file exchanged hands as they spoke on a completely different subject.

Mekash soberly slipped in the words, "For your urgent attention." and returned to the unrelated subject of discussion.

RESIDENCE OF THE LATE CHIEF
POINTE TROIS RAINFOREST
DAY 7 – 18:30HRS

The Council meeting was held in the guest wing. Elder Katan had called the meeting. He tried to be brief. Elders knew that the intelligence briefs were particularly important at this time. "Members, our late Chief tasked me to investigate who had leaked the information of Montero's coordinates at Negras Ledge –rest his Soul in peace. Something only we in this room knew. He played a recording of a phone conversation. Someone was talking to Brigadier Kazolo giving the planned route of Montero and the squad crossing at Negras Ledge. He played another conversation.

"It is done. I have seen him with my own eyes swallow the solution in his drink." The voice was unmistakable.

Not a word was uttered in the room. It was a silence of graven shock, disbelief. There was no expression on the face of the elders. Faces were ashen. That voice was in the room. The realization that betrayal existed among them choked their intimate space. Their bond was shattered, the collective responsibility to their people no longer sacrosanct to each Elder. They looked at each other then looked at him again in continued silence. They knew it was him to clarify. The evidence had spoken for itself. There was no need to interrogate and accuse. Speechless they all looked up at Elder Punakata, the head of Social Welfare. Not sure what to say.

Punakata wailed out as he buried his face in his hands. In between sobs he told his story.

"After a vicious attack on the village they threatened to come back, mass rape and dismember the old women and young girls in our village if I didn't give them some information within 24 hours. It was a choice. Either the men who I thought could at least defend themselves, meaning the militia, or the targeted females in our village who were utterly defenseless. Most of our able bodied men were already part of the militia." He continued as his chest heaved. "When they came back in another 12 hours to see what we'd come up with, they raped and killed 2 grandmothers and 2 young girls then dismembered them in front of the whole village and said I better talk now or all of them would follow."

No one moved forward to hold him as his sobs were deep and fast with tears and mucous running down his face. He excused himself to the bathroom adjacent to get some tissue. He shut the door and was heard forcefully blowing his nose. Everybody was looking down in their own worlds of thought. Two minutes later they heard a gunshot muted by a silencer but the sound was unmistakable and all too familiar in their experiences. The QSZ-92 pistol had been easily hidden in his traditional attire. Katan and Dhaka were closest to the bathroom door. Butawan joined them as they used an iron lamp stamp to break the door handle and push down the heavy wooden door. They rushed in and found him on the bathroom floor. A pool of blood flowed from his temple. On the sink counter was a note. *"Forgive me. I knew you would find out soon. I just couldn't live with the truth."*

"Dear God." Katan murmured. The other Elders rushed to the bathroom.

"We shall handle this quietly. We shall find the right time to announce his death. It surely shall not be over the next few days and there shall not be one syllable of betrayal attached to his death. The choice he was given was unimaginable, unforgivable." Butawan spoke in a commanding tone.

All the elders nodded and responded. "It is agreed." "Leave the wording to me." Parsien said.

Katan looked at Dhaka. "We shall handle matters here. His body shall be preserved in confidence at the morgue. Nobody shall know."

PRIVATE SUITE – HOTEL
WASHINGTON D.C.
DAY 7 – 13:00HRS

"So, it seems you have something we're interested in." Simmons made every effort to sound casual and even slightly amused.

"So I've heard. This land around my diamond mines. Call it coincidence, sheer luck or perhaps good fortune."

Simmons could not believe the misfortune and major inconvenience that had just beset his employer. There was still some measure of disappointment in himself he had not tracked or somehow caught the dual identity of the man. This mere tool of a trader was actually a carefully crafted multiplicity of characters. Simmons prodded further.

"Please, clarify. So is it Philippe Lannier or Father Peter Raines or whoever else? I'm not sure how your darling devastated Rebecca would be able to handle this piece of news? Or how they would handle your double dealing thieving of minerals off their land for years on end? Would love to know how you finagled acquisition of those mines over the years without anyone noticing it was you? I'm impressed. But your background and how you seamlessly fitted into the environment is equally impressive. We share a common wound of losing any trace of our families at a young age." The aim of the prodding was to let down his guard and assert some control over him, get a clutch on the man. But the calm smile on Raines face made it clear there was no effect.

"You're interested in those particular mines. I'd be curious to know why. Is it worth further investigation?"

"Let's pick this up later. I only needed to see you face to face. I'm sure we'll come to an understanding."

THE PENTAGON, WASHINGTON D.C.
DAY 7 – 14:00HRS

Senator Gregory Hill had been receiving 12 hour updates on events as they unfolded and was now meeting with other intelligence heads that formed the National Security Council. They reasoned that now was the appropriate time to bring things into order before an imminent change of events by certain obscure but powerful parties caused a dangerous shift in the power centers of the world.

Senator Hill amiably chatted on a of variety topics with six other security heads in the room. It was to be a brief meeting. He picked up an intercom call.

"Alright, show him in."

In full military attire he walked in and saluted the military brass in the room. An envelope was tucked under his right arm. Julian Richard Farah Simmons Fitzgerald walked up to Senator Hill and took two steps back to the center of the room.

"Fruthers and Ping are in safe custody and can be arranged to be handed over to the contact point within the next twelve hours."

Hill perused the document with a rueful smile. In the envelope were the location of Fruthers and Ping as well as the case details of the Pointe Trois transaction. Simmons gave a salute, spun around on his heel and marched straight to the door. Simmons could not reveal to anyone, including his parents, that while in the Armed Forces he was identified and recruited into a particular branch of the Special Forces. Officers deployed for their exceptional professional skills. According to their talents they were deployed all over the globe, mainly in the private sector and diplomatic service to be able to have access to cutting edge developments and have an impact on geo-political tectonic shifts. Developments taking place throughout the world had to be beneficial to U.S. interests or it was their national duty to ensure such movements would never materialize.

"Good work son. As much as we didn't want to do it, these findings and preservation of world order were worth pulling you out. Hope your affairs are neatly tied up to make for a tidy agreeable exit to all -if not most.

Report back to HQ for debriefing, some R&R and your next assignment. Now I'm in a position to make a couple of phone calls."

As he completed his turn Simmons was struck by the impeccably smooth hands he knew he'd seen from somewhere before. He couldn't believe it. These were the hands of the jeweler, Mr. Avi Goldman. The gentleman saluted him giving a comforting, yet authoritative, smile.

"You know we have to check in on our operatives from time to time through certain avenues that give us a picture on what they are really up to, see how they're doing in the field. That is the only identity I haven't given up, reminds me of the old days. Our tourist following you when receiving initial contact on the diamonds was a bit sloppy though."

Simmons had a smirk of genuine surprise. He had been too busy to notice who had been checking in on him. Simmons saluted the crisp, gracefully aging face to whom those impeccable hands belonged.

CAPITOL HILL, WASHINGTON D.C.
DAY 7 – 15:00HRS

The next 30 minutes were going to be comprised of phone calls only. The only common denominator was the attitude of the callers on line. Senator Hill had informed Eden, his P.A., that he did not want to be disturbed under any circumstances.

He knew his two main objectives. The first was that agents or the American companies themselves were to have free access to the minerals required for their communications, electronic and defense equipment. The U.S. was not going to find itself held ransom with dried up supply and at the whim of the owner of this territory. The second being any technological breakthrough that was going to have an impact on the current balance of superpowers would not be allowed. The potential scenarios arising out of this were simply too indelicate to think about. Times had changed. This was no longer a period of mutual respect and disdain coated in one bitter pill slowly chewed by both superpowers. It was now a period of rage ablaze, meticulously fed to the most vulnerable through a recipe of warped ideals that multiplied in the gut of those who needed to swallow something today, at the expense of tomorrow.

PHONE CALL # 1 – 15:05HRS:

Senator Hill dialed the personal cel. phone of the receiver. "Hello there." was Hill's leisurely but somewhat hard tone.

"Who is this?" was the force of words.

It was 9pm in Caramondo and Gebajara was exhausted reading security briefings, turning scenarios around in his mind. Holding out in hope for something to change and see a wire transfer come through in the next few hours.

"We have something that you think is with somebody else and you now think is going to wire you a cool $900 million in the coming hours. You see, there's a little problem here."

Gebajara listened, not sure what this new development was, but knew something was terribly wrong.

"It's called a file, a file that some of your people have put together and we have accessed. It has tracked the numerous transactions of wire transfers to your accounts and astounding unexplained real estate ownership in your people's names of all age ranges we can see here. Now, we were thinking of sending this fascinating information to any local or international authority along with the global TV networks that might be interested in such evidence."

Gebajara lost his cool. "Whoever this is, I don't know how you got this number but you'll be dead within hours and I will have you killed very slowly." Gebajara felt he was watching his world melt.

"Now, now." Came a rolling laugh from Hill. "Let's calm down and think clearly for a moment. It's only your life on the line. Let me get to the point. Chit-chat doesn't seem to be your thing."

Gebajara wondered who could threaten him with such confidence. Who was this person? The anger and fear raced through him.

"Your transaction as you know it, no longer exists and I think you have bigger worries on your desk at the moment. Besides, our ground intelligence seems to indicate you have more important things to think about. Our single strong recommendation is that you do not try to resuscitate this evaporated transaction in any shape or form."

"I'm talking to a dead man." Was the only brave reflex Gebajara could muster. He hung up knowing that this had gone too far. Everybody had some kind of lethal cocktail of recommendations or threats hanging over his head. This had to change. Something had to be done to regain control of the situation.

Hill took a cup of his distilled water and organic lemon mix. Particular about his health, he always found time to be on one cleansing program or another. He couldn't atone for the sins of his own government but he wondered to himself how such toxic men were allowed to stay in power by their own populations. He took another sip and dialed away.

PHONE CALL #2 – 15:10HRS:

"Hello." Was the stressed hurried greeting on the other end. "I believe we have something of yours." said Hill.

"Is this you crazy people again?"

"Oh no. We're not those bad guys. We're the guys who manufacture happiness in a way that we can understand it."

Baynes squinted his eyes and settled in with a deep frown on his brow. He desperately wanted to simply hang up and let that friendly ominous voice carry through its threats to a dead phone line. But his instincts told him to stay on the line. It was wiser to know what new problem was growing roots and how to dig them out, rather than be blindsided with an emergency particularly because of the extreme stress it just shot through him.

The relaxed tone continued, "Tell you what, you know that discounted $700million you were about to wire to someone?"

Baynes tried to collect himself. "I have no idea what you are talking about, no idea who you are and have no intention of pursuing this conversation any further."

Senator Hill's tone became a little sharper. "Hanging up would be far from wise now."

Baynes instinct to stay on the line pushed a little harder. His hunch folded in even more as his elbows on the table took on more weight. He suddenly leaned back rubbing his eyes in physical discomfort.

"Because you and I are so pleased you have chosen not to pursue that agreement, $350 million of that will go into a conservation and social infrastructure fund for Pointe Trois. I think that sounds like a grand idea for your Corporate Social Responsibility projects. What d'you say sport? Really set the record for generosity among your peers and give you serious back-tracking mileage of positive PR, possibly even shareholder value. I won't charge you for that advice. You've benefited handsomely from this rainforest over the past years. Time for a little payback."

"As I said, I don't know who you are, but threatening a multi-national conglomerate will leave you dead before the day is over."

Hill chuckled in mild amusement, "Do you know that's the second death threat I've receive today? Consult if you must. Huffin' and puffin' won't make you feel better. Just find your Financial Controller. Someone will call six hours from now to confirm establishment of the fund with the money actually in the account. Great day now."

Baynes threw his fountain pen across the room, as he watched it splatter an assortment of visible ink spots on the cream-white leather couch. How far is this going to go? Where or when is this going to end? How the hell did this man know anything about the agreement or money attached to it that would have ended his misery in an instant? Simmons! He had a hell of a lot of explaining to do.

Baynes fired a message to Drier. He was too enraged to talk. *"Find Simmons! He's our problem!"*

Hill didn't want to take up too much more time on these calls. It was infringing on his time at the early fundraising dinner of his favorite charity. He knew Baynes so desperately wanted the agreement that he could actually taste it. He knew he'd budge in some way. In what way though, he wasn't sure. He started to dial the third number.

PHONE CALL #3 – 15:15HRS:

"Yes?" was the low key impatient tone of the receiver.

Whether it was his tailor, banker or business partner; to the receiver, all of these characters were just the same: infidels.

"My, my, you've certainly been busy, engineering hell wherever you can. Well, we've put a crimp in those plans for now. We've put your 2 experts on indefinite leave for now, given that we wouldn't want you changing the current state of security in the world. We seem to like it just the way it is at the moment."

The voice had remained silent on the other end. But Hill continued knowing that they had been watching developments closely and knew that they were looking for their talent and their notes. There was only a momentary pause as if the phone call did not register an impact. The receiver was calm but scornful.

"Please do not insult us with your trivial dribble. You think we don't know. We are everywhere already; in your cities, in your small towns, your schools, your farms, your laboratories. This is no longer about momentary satisfaction of military might. This, is economic terrorism and bio-chemical warfare. We will eat away at the core of your social fabric and control every corner of your consumer culture devoid of any values. One hundred years is but a moment in time for us. We shall own you."

Hill added more levity to his tone to communicate his dismissal of this threat. "Do I detect a hint of hate with a trace of misguided emotion? In the meantime, we'll hold on to our new assets and find something more positive for them to do in the interests of us all. Maybe you could do the same with your resources? I won't hold out for a Christmas card."

Hill stared at the phone for a second. He wondered where such anger and hate came from and could only feel pity. He reversed out of his chair and walked to his door.

Leaning out of his doorway with the sweetest smile, he asked "Eden could you please schedule meetings with the Secretary of State and Homeland Security for tomorrow?

"Will do sir." Her land line rang. "Senator Hill's office."

She covered her mouthpiece and whispered out to Senator Hill, "It's Ambassador Holstein."

CHAPTER 24

THE SOIL SETTLING

Baynes could not remember much of what had happened at the meeting right after lunch. The phone call he'd just received was just as absurd as the day itself unraveling. He wanted to be seated in the privacy of his personal lawyer's office where he could let the worry show all over his face while he got the advice he needed. The driver had brought over his MLK-500 he used when in New York. He negotiated the curves of the multi-level parking finding it strangely peaceful. He heard an engine rev up. Then came around this beat up pick-up with a pumped up suspension putting it two feet higher than its normal height in addition to its twenty inch wheel rims. What Baynes had not seen was the long plain sedan that trailed him a couple of levels higher that had now caught up and parked itself diagonally across the ramp so no one could drive around it. The pick-up without warning switched lanes on to Baynes side. Baynes panicked looking into his rear mirror as he engaged his reverse gear to try and drive around only to find this long sedan blocking his way.

"What now?" he asked himself as he gripped the steering wheel.

He watched three men jump out of the pick-up. One had a monstrous looking shot gun. Another had a knife with a long wide blade that could have passed for a little sword. The other had a pistol with its suppressor attached. Two men got out of the rear doors of the tinted window sedan behind. Baynes looked on in shock and fear. These were large men in trench coats and long leather jackets with hands that could punch a hole through a brick wall. One of them knocked on his passenger window. In a trance, Baynes complied.

One got in the passenger seat the shot gun menacingly rubbed around Bayne's chin and cheek taunting his nose. Baynes pushed it away in disgust. The man now let the barrel squeeze him right underneath his chin. His two colleagues settled into the back-seat and the other two from the sedan kept a look out as they chewed their toothpicks with assault rifles swinging alongside.

"Now ain't that nice of you to open up for us. Most people wouldn't, seeing we don't look that pretty and all."

With the shot gun underneath his jaw Baynes could barely move his head. The one with the large knife leaned forward and with the tip of his blade, pressed around Baynes groin area like he was looking for just the right point to make his way through. Then he jabbed through opening up a shallow flesh wound. Baynes shrieked as he tried to jerk back but was constrained with his limited head movement.

"What do you want? My wallet is in the jacket pocket."

"You really think everything has a price, don't you now? Tell me, does your life have a price?" He tapped Baynes cheek and nostril with the barrel of the gun again. "It seems our people in the rainforest are very unhappy with you. As Branch Office Relations, we like to call ourselves; they say we should pay you a visit. And here we are."

"What do you want from me you bastards?" as he grabbed some tissue from the pocket between the two front seats to dab his bleeding wound that had started to soak into his trousers.

The man turned around to the other two with a perplexed look. "Dear colleagues, do you hear the man using such…such…unpresentable language on us? Client Relationship Manager please, press around again and perhaps you should aim a little higher. We may, after all, require proof of our visit."

The man with the knife leaned forward, "Of course boss, receipt books are so easily forged these days. Let's see what we can extract…"

"Ok, ok, I'm sorry." Baynes winced with the perspiration soaking his forehead.

"Let's get to business. The tel. comm. department informs us you're jittery about taking up the onslaught of charges coming up against you. Well, our colleagues in the rainforest seem to think otherwise. Their strict instructions are that you track right back to that office and face every charge coming up. Is that clear?"

The colleague leaned forward and pressed the blade against his eye. "Feel that cool metal against your eye. Do you know what it feels like when the metal is burning hot?"

"Alright, I think the man sees your point." Said their lead man.

"I can't face those charges. G. Tech will just dump me and let me sink with those lawsuits. Are you crazy?"

The man in the front seat gave an apologetic smile to the man in the back seat. "I'm sorry. I don't think the man sees your point." In a second, the man in the back lunged forward, jerked Baynes back by the shoulder, slit the inner top eye lid, sliced his cheek and cut a long vertical opening down his neck.

"Oh dear God, please don't kill me. I can't face those charges." Baynes cried out.

"As the Branch Relations Manager, I must advise you that you will die if you don't go back this instant. And if you try to escape at any point we shall find you and kill every family member of yours, slowly, in front of you. This is the price you will pay. Now get out and walk back. I can't stand that you'll ruin this nice upholstery."

Baynes clumsily stumbled out the car, half crawling up the ramp as he tried to hold his eye and neck. He heard the cars reverse and screech off. He clamored back to his, drove down to the next level and called his driver to come rescue him in tears of terror and rage.

STATE HOUSE, CARAMONDO
DAY 7 – 21:30HRS.

Upon hanging up from that anonymous threatening phone call, Gebajara dialed Baynes. Baynes was recovering under his physician's orders. Lying on his living room couch, he saw his cel. phone vibrate on the coffee table. He took a deep breath upon seeing Gebajara's number.

"Aaah Baynes, did I miss an attaching memo to the agreement that says upon my signing this document it now becomes subject to whims of the U.S. government rendering this transaction null and void?"

"Look, I have more questions than answers. I'm even more confused. Am still trying to trace our so-called CEO I sent to you."

"Uh…huh…well this ship just sank." Was the response of the stunned man on the other end of the line.

He closed his eyes and inhaled deeply and exhaled with an air of resentment. He couldn't believe he had to make this phone call. Gebajara thought to himself he profoundly hated and despised anyone that brought him to this moment.

He dialed directly from his cel. phone at that moment. He felt just too humiliated, disgusted and confused to call out to anyone to dial a number.

The President thought about his impending national health crisis.

"Hon. Minister, let us fast forward on the pleasantries for now. This is the deal that I'm giving you. Take it or leave it. You can explore quietly in a way that nobody knows that you're there. There will be no official agreement between you and the government and in fact it is part of your social development activities and infrastructure development as far as we the government are aware. Any agreement you put in place is strictly between you and the local population of Pointe Trois. But what you will do is send $500,000= per month to an anonymous bank account of mine. The details of which shall be forwarded to you.

You don't like it, too bad. Then leave Pointe Trois altogether, everybody else gets to enjoy the place while you watch from the outside. And with that access we expect your continued government budget support. That is the deal." Gebajara snapped with a tone of finality.

"Good. I'm glad we've come to some arrangement Mr. President. I shall advise our President accordingly. Our first deployment shall be in the forest within a week."

Gebajara turned on the screen to distract his mind with the banality of commodity mineral reports on the international broadcasts. There was a breaking news flash as the anchor changed subject mid-stream.

"Ladies and Gentlemen we are currently watching the press conference on the milestone signing of the conservation consortium agreement to protect the Pointe Trois rainforest. Take it away Matthew..." The broadcast switched to Rebecca about to begin her speech. The Dames communication team was giving out fact sheets and press releases to journalists anxiously requesting them.

Gebajara's nerves roared in too much pain to talk.

DAMES COMMUNICATIONS, NEW YORK
DAY 7 – 16:30HRS

Rebecca placed the cloth that had kept their home-made knives in the cave over 30 years ago, on top of her speech on the podium so she could see it. It was their journey together. Her symbol of Montero and the people of Pointe Trois who had not died in vain and the living that could now start to heal from this horrible nightmare. Rebecca felt some pain lift from her heart, a new beginning a place of hope. The team in Avalon had put out word to everyone who had helped them telling them to be glued to their screens. This was their moment. Elder Parsien ensured every soul in Pointe Trois was watching a TV screen or listening to a radio.

Rebecca cleared her throat. "Ladies and gentlemen thank you very much for coming. This agreement has been a long time in coming, accelerated by events of the last week. In this agreement is the protection and conservation of a very unique place on this planet that plays its role among others in operating as the lungs of the earth. This place also still has the gifts of medicines and technology to give to us from its plants and minerals. It is also home to a wildlife that is rare to find on this planet let alone being home to a community of 400,000 people of the Burajon tribe that have lived in peace with mother nature of which I am a proud Burajon." She squeezed the bloodied stained cloth in front of her. "This agreement is a symbol that we are all from the same home. When my home is raped and pillaged, it is also your same home that will suffer tomorrow from pollution and poisoning with no way out. Because it is only one home, the same home and we get no second chances for ourselves or our children's great grandchildren."

Rebecca felt like the floodgates were opening up a torrent of emotions trying to set her free. "The people you see here beside me, represent a consortium of human rights, environmental and conservation organizations that came together to commit to protect and preserve Pointe Trois rainforest. The ones in Avalon and Pointe Trois that you don't see standing here were the backbone that made this agreement possible. This agreement..." Rebecca fought back the tears, "...is for all of the people that died protecting our home. Those that were murdered or maimed as innocent people because a government, using the army, along with a ruthless conglomerate wanted them erased. I take a moment to remember my brother, mother and father that gave me the strength to put one foot in front of the other as I remember running from our home to a cave as a little girl chased by soldiers in the middle of the night. This agreement is to say to the government of Caramondo, 'Never again. Never again shall we allow one more killing or further desecration of our homeland. The Law awaits you. And it to say to my fellow Burajon and all the sister tribes that received so many sick and dying across borders; we stand with you, we stand in front of you, we stand beside you, we stand behind you. To the Rainforest Consortium, we walk with you into a path of peace and development; a new day, a new beginning for the Pointe Trois rainforest." Rebecca closed her speech.

"This is the agreement that is the truth to be known and this is the agreement that we shall all use to protect our home, our planet. Thank you." Rebecca stepped back off the podium.

Ian stepped up, "Yes, the question in the back…"

She had stepped back to be among the group that had stood with her, fought with her throughout this journey. Raphael wrapped his arm around her as a brief hug. He whispered, "Nothing could make me more proud than this moment my love."

G. TECH. NY BRANCH OFFICE
DAY 7 – 17:30HRS

Baynes struggled to get himself back to his office with his slight limp and bandages dressing him all over his head. In his mental state he didn't even notice the stifled looks worry and shock. He needed to show his new friends that he was still in the picture of things and he confessed to himself that he was petrified of one phone call from them. Baynes could not stand another threat to materialize out of thin air. The pain killers were not strong enough as he strained to put his files in order for these law suits. He also sent a communiqué to other Board members that as per Executive Order of the Chairman he had instructed a $200 million contribution to conservation activities in Pointe Trois. Finance and Public Relations were handling the details. He knew he had never been a combination of so miserable and so scared in his life.

A text message streamed in from his source at Citizens Environmental Alert, *'Turn on your screen. Better you know, than you don't.'* Baynes got an instant migraine at the replay of the Press Conference on the international broadcasts, which was now global acknowledgment of the agreement. He rushed to his private bathroom to vomit out the stress that had just exceeded its limit in him. This was more than he could digest. The lawsuits, court room theatre, possible arrest and maybe even imprisonment that had graduated from a possibility to a probability, left him thinking about his pistol he kept in his bottom desk drawer.

AMB. HOLSTEIN'S OFFICE
UNITED NATIONS
DAY 7 – 17:00HRS

Ambassador Daniel Holstein dialed Senator Gregory Hill. "Afternoon Gregory. Any finding that could be helpful to us in protecting our interests?"

Holstein sounded calm but concerned. He didn't know how far the situation had gone and more importantly who exactly was behind it to know how to treat it on his institutional world stage.

"Always good to hear your voice Daniel. Yes, a couple of findings. The situation has been temporarily cooled but we need to keep our eye on the ball. It's no longer a military threat only. This also involves socio-economic and bio-hazard risks all rolled into one. It's in the arena of systematically neutralizing and removing every threat that has been planted in the most innocent flower or the darkest corner of our homeland. But we have our people working on it."

"I hear yah. If I may recommend Gregory, that you have a conversation with Secretary Billington. She was meeting some folks from a region of the world very concerned about unknown financial support to vulnerable marginalized youth radicalized to kill off other youth that looked to be espousing western lifestyles. We may have 2 different holes coming from the same bucket. One hole dealing with a rainforest that has minerals we need and the other dealing with sleepers planted all over our nation ready to strike at a moment's notice."

"She is already on my schedule along with the Secretary of Homeland Security. But there will be a joint meeting through the National Security Council as well."

"Alrighty Gregory, keep me posted in case the ball lands in my court." "Will do Daniel."

Hill thought he'd make one courtesy call. "Tristan, why must you always send a whale to my doorstep? Why can't I get a cute little gold fish in its even cuter little bowl from you? Yes, this shareholder doesn't have maternal instincts. This problem is bigger than your corporate pond and is definitely swimming in our ocean of national defense. Let it go. Further inquiries or action could be a problem for anyone."

"Gotcha loud and clear Gregory. Call yah when I'm next in town."

GEN. BUGAZON'S RESIDENCE, CARAMONDO
DAY 7 – 20:30HRS

Bugazon's security took a second longer than usual to open the gate. As his driver pulled up the driveway Bugazon's eyes closely scanned the meticulous front lawn given the murder of Pitua and events of the past two days. His mind prattled away letting his paranoia work on him.

The butler opened the front door as the General got out of the vehicle.

"Good evening sir." Bugazon noticed the lack of eye contact and the living room lights that were never off. He went into red alert and stretched for his HS2000 Pistol tucked under his arm. In a second four military officers stepped forward from the dark room moved to his rear, respectfully but firmly handcuffed his hands behind while one of them disarmed him. Bugazon elbowed one in the ribs as they did so.

"General, we mean you no harm. Please stay calm."

The living room lights were turned on. Seated on one of the sofas were the Head of F&A and Head of Land Forces. The Chief Legal Officer was in the high back arm chair with his dossier.

Counsel stood up. "General Bazilio Bugazon, by order of the Chair of the Military High Council and powers vested in me as Legal Counsel of the Armed Forces of Caramondo, you are hereby placed under arrest to be presented before the Military Court Martial facing charges of abuse of office, mismanagement and fraudulent use of institutional resources and grievous persistent human rights violations causing financial loss, loss of property and life to the institution and citizens of the Republic of Caramondo. You will be entitled to Counsel of your choice to represent you. Without further delay you are hereby remanded to the cells in the army barracks."

"You pen pushing idiot do you know I can have you shot any time I choose?"

"Sir may I advise you that anything you say may be held against you during your proceedings and threatening a lawyer may result in a lawsuit that will strip you down and tie you up into time immemorial in a court room."

The Head of F&A gestured to the luxurious surroundings and sarcastically remarked, "The last I checked we were all in the same pay grade that didn't stretch too much." He rubbed the fabric he was sitting on as he smiled at it. "This couch would set me back a few pay cheques and no food for the family for the year. Sacrifices we make, I guess." He looked at the General with incredulity. "You can afford a butler?" Bugazon sneered at him. "Anyway, we have tracked your wife apparently on the way to the airport with a rather large truck towing behind. Not to worry, she is completely unaware of your situation. Upon her arrival at the military check point she shall be subjected to a thorough search and will be expected to have the complete customs paperwork clearing all goods with her for travel. Without which, she shall be detained until we can sort that out."

The Chief of Land Forces matter of factly pointed out, "I have taken charge of your office. Operations shall continue smoothly. Any irregular activity shall be the subject of investigations and suspected illegal activity shall be turned over to Counsel."

As the Chief of Land Forces spoke, Legal Counsel received a phone call. He saw it was Duegaro's number.

"Ok, we shall prepare accordingly." Was Counsel's reply. Counsel whispered to F&A, "Apparently the Hague has perused the file Duegaro sent to them and they think Bugazon is worth their attention."

"Shall we, gentlemen?" As F&A stood up. motioning everyone to the beautiful front door.

RESIDENTIAL WING, STATE HOUSE
CARAMONDO
DAY 7 – 22:15HRS

Unable to concentrate any further on the paperwork in front of him or the international broadcasts, President Gebajara picked up his jacket and walked out of his office to the Residential Wing. Feeling drained and exhausted Gebajara walked through the doors opened for him.

"In here, darling." Was his wife's warning request beckoning him to the living room. President Gebajara walked in to find 4 military officers standing at different parts of this tastefully decorated space. Immediately after another 6 officers showed up from different corridors of the residential wing.

"What is the meaning of this?"

Seated on the couch Mrs. Gebajara calmly stared on, legs leisurely crossed and one arm resting along the back of the couch as a full glass of whisky rested on her knee with her other hand. She coolly looked on as if she knew this day would come.

A Brigadier stepped forth and saluted. "Sir by the order of the Military High Council, as of this moment you are under house arrest. This is in effect a peaceful, bloodless, coup d'etat with snap elections to be held immediately after. The Judiciary and Legislature will be made fully aware by first light. By this order of house arrest you no longer have Presidential Immunity as a sitting Head of State. The Military High Council hereby also informs you of other cases being filed against you from other entities which include, abuse of office of the armed forces that resulted in the destruction of Pointe Trois, environmental desecration by the a network of environmentalists, gross violations of human rights by the international human rights activists, a series of corruption cases over the past 15 years by the national anti-corruption coalition and fraudulent use of resources of the Caramondo army resulting in loss of life and massive environmental damage to the nation of Caramondo. These are the charges we are aware of to date."

"This is ridiculous. As the Commander-in-Chief I shall personally arrest the full Council myself, starting with Duegaro." He fumbled for his cel. phone. The Brigadier stepped forward and politely took the phone from his hand. "I am to relieve you of all communication property sir. No one in this government shall be harmed in any form whatsoever. Anyone who has broken the Law shall face the Law.

"May I, sir?" As the Brigadier pointed to the President's foot. The President rolled his eyeballs in approval. "Kicking you in the teeth wouldn't change my situation right now I suppose?" The Brigadier removed the FNP-45 saddled in his holster that was wrapped around his ankle.

"Right now sir I think you have bigger things to worry about than the dental work of a Brigadier. You have been limited to this floor only until you are remanded without delay."

DAMES COMMUNICATIONS
NEW YORK CITY
DAY 7 – 17:00HRS

As Rebecca stood among the group; joy, relief and grief worked their way through her system. She quietly excused herself to the closest restroom. Marc, never letting her slip from his eye, discreetly followed her. He stood around the reception area for all of 5 minutes then knocked on the door before he entered.

"Rebecca...Rebecca...!" as he rushed to her on the restroom floor he pulled out his phone frantically dialing. "I need an ambulance here now!" Marc rattled off his location and hung up. The tap was still running. From the trail he could see Rebecca had been vomiting violently from the toilet and fell unconscious as she tried to pat her face dry. "Stay with me Rebecca."

Marc dialed another number. "Yes Marc what is it?"

Describing where he was, "It's Rebecca, she's unconscious, barely breathing. I know you're the only one she trusts. You're her next of kin. She needs you now. Please pray for us Father Raines."

"I'm not in town but I'll leave right now. Will call you when I've landed."

Marc hung up fighting back the tears as he talked to Rebecca in his arms, "This is not your end. It cannot end, like this."

End

Hello,

I hope you enjoyed reading this, please leave a review on Amazon. I read every review and they help new readers discover my books.

If you would like to know when the next book is coming out, please drop us an e-mail at:

akblock2022@gmail.com

Thank you!